Save the Dragons!

Save the Dragons!

Martin Berman-Gorvine

WILDSIDE PRESS

For Jackie, now and always.

And with thanks to Laurie Christianson and Dave Argentar, who helped Ashley fly and breathe fire.

Published by Wildside Press LLC.
www.wildsidebooks.com

Part I

When Worlds Collide

1

This must be the most ridiculous thing I've ever done—writing this letter on the blank pages of your diary and leaving it here for you to find. After all, I've never met you! All I have is your forgotten diary. Please forgive me for reading it... but now I know we must meet.

I paused with my pen over the page. *Dope, what's the point boring a stranger with my babbling?* My hand cramped; I was too used to tapping away at my cell phone or computer to write with a pen for very long.

I sat in the new treasure chest I'd discovered, hidden away on a back street of South Philadelphia. I've never been in this street before, even though I grew up here. Finding "Gloria's Gateway Books and Records" was like winning the lottery, especially after the extra-yucky day I had at school.

* * * *

I shivered and pulled my coat tighter around me as I walked through the blue-gray dusk. I was lost. It usually takes me fifteen minutes to walk home, and I take the same route along Snyder Avenue every day, turning right on 9th Street and then left on Wolf Street, where I live with my mom.

But here I was hurrying nervously along an unfamiliar cracked sidewalk, past low anonymous buildings. Must not have been paying attention. A lone orange streetlight flickered feebly to life overhead, and a cat yowled somewhere. No one was around, so I couldn't even ask for directions. All the houses had peeling paint, the potholes were even bigger than usual for Philly, street signs were missing. Even the cars parked in the street looked more beaten-up than you usually see in my neighborhood, and it's not like folks where I come from drive the latest model of anything. But these...they looked like cars out of some old movie, or in those pictures you see from Cuba where they're still driving Studebakers from the 1950's. The moon was only a foggy bright patch behind gray clouds, but I had a feeling that if it did come out, it too would look like a crumpled up scrap of paper.

Just where *was* I, anyway? I should come out on Moyamensing Avenue, but everything looked totally unfamiliar. I couldn't read the shop signs in the darkness, and anyhow, they looked dark and deserted. Locked door followed locked door. There weren't even cars driving on the street. Nothing moved but my twin shadows, the one in front of me looming longer and longer as I walked away from the streetlight behind me, the one behind me shrinking as I approached the next streetlight.

So the warm yellow light spilling from the building on my left came as a shock. A rainbow-shaped arch of chipped gilt lettering on a dusty plate-glass window said GLORIA'S GATEWAY BOOKS, with AND RECORDS written in a smaller arch inside it. On the blue paint-peeling door a little red sign said "HOURS" in white letters but was otherwise blank. What drew me in, besides the hope of warming up, were the heaps of books stacked right up against the window, books of all shapes, sizes, and colors. It was just like a bigger, better version of my bedroom, which was crammed full of books—some older, some newer, but fewer and fewer from recent years as everything migrates online. As if books were birds, flying to a warmer climate than dusty old shelves could offer them. Don't get me wrong! I love my cell phone as much as anyone else, but I don't want to read books on that tiny gray screen, with every author's words looking exactly like every other author's.

Speaking of cell phones, I had a special one—an especially annoying one, since my mom got some kind of advanced model from a friend of hers who works for one of the big carriers. It seemed to have a rudimentary intelligence, sort of like Mom herself. Now it wanted to talk to me—its screen flashed red to blue and back again—like a police car's light. I shoved it in my pocket, not wanting to listen to it—of course Mom had programmed it with her voice. "Teresa, you're an hour late for dinner! Teresa, Mom called three times in the past ten minutes, and she sent you five texts, why don't you answer? Teresa D'Angelo, are you listening to me? All you have to do to get home is—"

Anyway I was so cold and tired I barged through that hourless door. On top of the heap of books in the window, just visible in the space between the two rows of lettering, an orange tabby cat dozed. A cowbell clanked overhead as the door swung shut behind me. Now awake, the cat leaped off the book heap and landed purring at my feet. I stroked her, scratching behind her ears like I used to do with my old calico Fuzz when I was growing up. My parents didn't even tell me that Fuzz died when I was away at camp that awful summer before I turned thirteen, because they knew I'd be a wreck. They were right, too; they told me when I got back home, and I couldn't go back to school until the middle of September, I was such a mess.

This cat had a little heart-shaped tag attached to her collar that looked as if it had been inscribed by hand. *Tiferet.* What a strange name. She rubbed against my legs, purring, and I immediately felt warmer. Then she looked up at me with her amber eyes, and, to my astonishment, she slowly shut her right eye, then opened it again.

"Did you just wink at me?" Well, of course she didn't answer; with a sniff she darted around a row of shelves and disappeared. I followed.

Was that the rustle of a dress? Where's it coming from? As I searched, I bumped into an old wooden countertop. On top of it sat an antique gilt cash register, and next to it sat a large, steaming mug of.... I sniffed. Hot cocoa! The marshmallows floating in it were starting to melt, just the way I liked it. I picked up the mug and underneath sat a note written in scarlet ink on plain lined paper. *"For you,"* it said in a curvy, feminine handwriting. *"Please be careful not to drip on the books. When you find what you need, you will know what it is worth and what you must leave in exchange. Your humble servant, Gloria."*

I scratched my head. None of the books I'd peeked into so far had prices on them—no stickers, no penciled-in scrawl on the endpaper, and the publishers' prices stamped on the dust covers had been blotted out with heavy, black ink. I walked around the counter and examined the cash register. A miniature silver-framed mirror sat where the keys should have been. I frowned at my reflection. Pudgy, pale, with acne scars on my cheeks. Mousy brown hair falling over my ears. And glasses. Nobody wears glasses these days, especially not old wire-rims, but I like them, so there.

A loud bang made me jump so high I almost dropped the mug. A hiss followed—an old steam radiator, like the one in Nana's old house on Juniper Street, near the Methodist Hospital? But I couldn't see one here. Another mystery.

I shook my head and finished the cocoa, putting the mug down carefully on Gloria's note so it wouldn't leave a ring on the counter. Then I started peering around in the gloom, until I spotted a passage-way between the bookshelves and book-heaps. An irregular wedge of light danced with bright dust motes, like a tiny spotlight. The light shone through a gap between the top of a row of books that stood at about eye level (well, level with my eyes anyway, barely five feet above the floor) and the shelf above them. *There must be a room back behind there.* Was that where Gloria was? But nobody answered when I called. Still, there was something back there.

I removed the books blocking the light, stacking them carefully on the floor beside me, and glanced at a series of oversize volumes with marbled covers, which were stamped in strangely shaped gilt letters:

New Almanack Of Khazaria, Tartary, Turkestan And The Lands Of The Caucasus. Where was Khazaria? I'd never heard of it, and I get A's in geography.

A cool breeze wafted through the gap the atlas had left behind, smelling of ozone and salt water. But the space behind had no windows or doors and was lit by a bare light bulb with a chain. How could that wind come from the city outside? To find out, I had to empty three more shelves full of books, then lift out the shelves themselves and put them on top of the books. That made a gap so narrow I had to turn sideways and duck my head to get through. But it was worth it. I was in the secret room!

As well as books, there were shelves of antique vinyl records in their silly oversize cardboard jackets. I picked up a thick boxed set. On the front was an overhead shot of a huge crowd filling an enormous green space between skyscrapers. At the corners were circular photos of four middle-aged men. I giggled at their funny hairstyles. Printed across the top of the box was *The Reunion. Central Park. September 6, 1983.* The cover opened out, like a book, but the liner notes weren't much help. "Greatest event in the history of rock and roll. The Fab Four come together again!" Yeah, right. Must be someone's idea of a joke. Even I knew that the Beatles never played together after they broke up in 1970. And by 1983, John Lennon was dead.

Nana always used to talk about how hard she'd cried the day he was killed by a crazy fan. "I was twelve years old, Teresa, the same age you are now, when I first saw them on the Ed Sullivan Show" she'd said, ruffling my hair. Then she taught me the words to "Eleanor Rigby." *All the lonely people, where do they all come from? All the lonely people, where do they all belong?* I wiped away a tear. That was five years ago, when Nana was still alive, before my whole world blew up.

Even if this was a joke, now that I held the box in my hands, I couldn't bear to put it down. So I clutched it under my arm as I browsed through the shelves of books. There was something thrilling about these books, as old as they were and despite the fact that many were in foreign languages I couldn't read or even identify. Most of the ones in English were by writers I'd never heard of. I dawdled, trying to decide what to read first, until I spotted a bundle of papers on the floor and knelt down to pick them up, expecting to see Gloria's handwriting again.

The paper had a heavy, old-fashioned texture, and the ink was like the stuff used to blot out the prices on all the books. Had the writer used an actual fountain pen? Or maybe a quill? The bundle was a section that had fallen out of a book—a lined journal from the looks of it. Excitement bubbled up. Was I holding part of a centuries-old diary? But then I turned to the first page. The date was just last week.

14 November

What luck to have stumbled upon this unknown bookstore. Or maybe it is a Dewey Lending Library, since there are no prices on any-thing. What shop owner does not want his shillings? None that I have ever met. I should say her shillings, since this place is called Gloria's Gateway Books and Records. Touring King's College last summer—Dad so hopes I will go to his old school, and I so much want to go farther away!—I already learnt that I am not nearly as well read as I thought I was, but this place! So many books I have never even heard of! The history sec-tion is especially confusing; it seems to be filled mostly with fantastic fiction about histories that never were, written as if they were straight fact. Imagine, America and England two separate countries! Napoléon defeated at some place called Waterloo! And most amazing of all, drag-ons as myths!

I wish I could find the owner or the librarian or somebody so I should feel right in taking a book home with me. Yes, there was a note on the counter beside the cash register and a nice hot cup of tea that said, "Please be careful not to drip on the books. When you find what you need, you will know what it is worth and what you must leave in exchange." But I have nothing with me that could possibly be worth the book I have chosen—an elaborate fantasy about a teenage girl and her genius little brother, who have to rescue their father from a distant planet where he is being held captive...

Wait a second. That's *A Wrinkle in Time*, one of my all-time favorite books! I read it my first year in middle school, with my all-time favorite teacher, Miss Keylor. Maybe I could find some clue about where this guy lived, or at least his name. But there were only a few more lines. Some-thing about how he (I *knew* it was a guy, from his odd, neat handwriting) was worried about finding his way home, or actually, back to his boarding school, "for I was quite lost when I arrived here, in a blizzard that seems to have sprung out of nowhere. I'm afraid the staff will tell my parents I have run away after so many miserable weeks at St. George's Academy, with that horrible Jeremy Adams lying in wait for me every day. Not that running away would not be a good idea. But I must be going!"

I closed my eyes when I reached the last line, the secret room tipping slowly around me, as if I was an astronaut in free fall. If I'd *tried* to imagine a guy right for me, I couldn't have come up with anyone more perfect. And yet—dragons? Napoleon? Was this another joke, like the impossible Beatles reunion album? It wouldn't be the first time that had happened to me. My face burned.

Last year I found a note in my locker from Kevin McCabe, the captain of the football team.

> Teresa, I know this is stupid. I'm the big dumb jock who copies off you in chemistry class and you're the brainiac nerd. But there's no one I can talk to on the team, and Kylie's pretty and all but she isn't sweet and understanding like you. Those big brown eyes behind your glasses! Can you meet me after practice today?

Could I? I waited shivering under a December sky as cold and gray as a dead computer monitor, watching the boys slam into each other. As Kevin puffed off the field, I reached out and touched his sleeve. He frowned, then curled his lip, as if he'd found a rotten apple on his lunch tray.

"Who the hell *are* you?" he said, as laughter came from the girls' locker room. They stood watching me, Kylie and all her crowd.

But could they think of a prank *this* elaborate? No way they're smart enough, or hard-working enough. Besides, how could they create a whole mysterious bookstore and lure me into it?

Still, I stood. "Kylie? Heather? You can start laughing now. I fell for it!" Silence.

Tiferet appeared and rubbed against my legs, purring. My fat lumpy legs. How could I have the nerve to talk to any boy? Especially one I didn't even know. Well, *because* I didn't even know his name. And I wouldn't be *talking* to him, I'd just be writing to him. If I never found the bookstore again, or if he never answered, what would it matter? Before I could talk myself out of it, I fumbled around in my bookbag, found a pen (a smeary cheap pink pen, but that was all I had) and began after his note stopped. Taking a deep breath, I ignored my racing heart and wrote—

> I'll be back Sunday afternoon at 3. Did you know Madeline L'Engle wrote four sequels to *A Wrinkle in Time*? I'll bring all the ones I have in case Gloria doesn't have them. See you then! Teresa.

I put the pages back on the floor and wormed my way out of the secret room. I must've moved too fast, though, and I brought down an avalanche of books that covered the opening. What a mess! Clumsy Teresa! I picked up a few books and reshelved them, but even more came tumbling down, and I backed away, biting my lip. Then my glasses slipped off and landed on the floor, and when I bent down, I caught a glimpse of the bookstore window. The black sky was full of swiftly falling snowflakes. Oh, no! How could it have gotten so late? Time to turn the phone back on and find out where the hell I was and how to get home. But when I powered it up, my phone was ominously silent. NO NETWORK blinked in large, unfriendly red letters on the gray screen.

"How can you be out of range?"

It just kept flashing NO NETWORK. My eyes filled and tears rolled down my cheeks. How was I ever going to find my way home? I paced back and forth, trying to find a magic spot where NO NETWORK would vanish, but the whole bookstore seemed to be a dead zone. I wiped my eyes. Maybe there was a street map behind the counter. I searched the counter and tried to lift the cash register. Maybe a street map was hidden under it. It was heavy, too heavy to lift, but I caught sight of a narrow slot under the mirror.

> When you find what you need, you will know what it is worth and what you must leave in exchange.

Did I have what I needed? What I really needed right now was a map, but all I had was that impossible Beatles reunion album. And my useless phone. I shoved my phone into the slot.

Wait! What had I done? I tried to shove my fingers through the slot and retrieve my phone. Hopeless. I wiped away more tears. Mom was going to kill me. I slouched out of the bookstore. Guess I'd have to find my own way home.

The streets had turned bright orange with the light reflected off a new blanket of snow. Where had all this snow come from? It was already half an inch deep on the sidewalks. Flakes as big as my thumbnail were drifting down thick and fast. I stuck my hands in my jacket pockets, the album cradled under my left arm, and began walking as quickly as I could. Although my socks instantly got soaked, somehow the air seemed warmer than before.

I soon found myself on familiar streets, walking past saggy rowhouses with their weed-grown front yards. *Be grateful you have a place to live*, that's what Mom always says, and I *am* grateful. Even though home is half of a century-old duplex, and you reach it through a shrieking gate in a chain-link fence, and the Peruzzos' dogs start howling every time you walk by. Mom stood at the door, wearing the ratty old sweatsuit she uses for pajamas. She grabbed my shoulders and shook me so hard my braces almost came loose.

"Where were you? Do you know how late it is? I was so worried, and then it started to snow…"

On and on as we went inside, ending with "You lost your cell phone? *Again?*" And the usual tearful hug in the dark little kitchen with its hot plate and its dorm-size refrigerator the size of normal people's TV sets, the TV set the size of normal people's toasters, the table set with two chipped bowls covered with chipped salad plates to keep the macaroni and cheese warm. Because of course Mom couldn't choke down her food when I was late, could she? What a mess. But at least I kept my head enough to toss the record album into the corner by my bedroom, putting my backpack down on top before Mom noticed it.

At last she calmed down, brushed graying hair out of her eyes and sat down to eat. I gulped my own food and headed to my room, scooping up my backpack and the album. My unmade bed was barely visible beneath piles of books, sort-of clean clothes, and electronic junk. I nudged aside an old computer monitor and flopped onto the gritty sheets. Despite my exhaustion I lay wide awake listening to Mom moving around the house, talking to herself, the words too low to make out. Eventually she went upstairs to her bedroom and the house grew still.

I waited what seemed like forever to make sure she was really asleep before tiptoeing out of my room. The coat closet by the front door was full of all kinds of old junk. A heap of old clothes, a blue raincoat and pink rubbers I had worn when I was in second grade, old cell phones, bits of plastic, a vacuum cleaner missing its hose... Finally! I lifted the bulky greenish-blue case and dragged it back to my room. Nana's old record player. I opened it up, plugged it in, and blew the dust off the turntable and needle arm. Then I carefully removed a shiny black disk from the Beatles reunion album, and put it on the turntable.

A pop and crackle. The needle arm nodded slightly. A hiss. Then music. Some of the songs were the old ones Nana had taught me, sometimes in different versions; "I Wanna Hold Your Hand" and "Octopus's Garden" were as bouncy and cheerful as ever, but "Eleanor Rigby" sounded more haunting than in the original version, with unfamiliar little guitar riffs running through it.

> *All the lonely people*
> *Where do they all belong?*

Between and around and under each song was a faint crackling like static and a much louder drumming. Like rain with a hint of something harder in it, maybe sleet or hail? No. The sound of a huge mass of people applauding.

"Thank you, thank you," said a nasal voice in that Liverpool accent. A wise voice with undertones of sad laughter. I shivered.

John Lennon.

"Now we'd like to play a new song, something Paul and I wrote specially for this concert. It's dedicated to my little daughter, Rosie—she's two—" Another cheer. "It's called 'Courage.'" Applause rose, then died back to a near whisper.

Courage, girl
You'll need courage for the road ahead
For the road full of dread
I'd give you more, girl
For this cold old world,
But all I can give you, girl,
Is your heart that's oaken
Even when it's broken
You'll have your courage…

When the song was done and the applause had swelled and faded, the needle arm slid out of the grooves and bounced gently. I carefully lifted it and replaced it on the armrest. A single tear rolled off my cheek and fell on the label, staining it a darker orange. I lay down on my bed and looked at the ceiling. I'd just heard the impossible. There was another of Nana's favorite Beatles songs, one of their early tunes, "I've Just Seen a Face," a fun little song about a guy who's just met a girl and is falling in love with her. There's a line in it: "Had it been another day, I might have looked the other way, and I'd have never been aware, but as it is, I'll dream of her tonight…" What if both things could be true? That the guy *did* glance her way and fall in love at first sight, but in some other place just as real, he *did not* glance her way and fell in love with someone else instead?

This idea made my head hurt. It was more incredible than magic, which I didn't believe in. Magic was something that only happened in books, to fairy-tale people. But what else could explain my finding a bookstore that I'd never seen before in my own neighborhood, one that had a Beatles reunion album in it and the lost diary of a guy too perfect to be real? *I know, I'm a fairy changeling, and my mean old mom isn't really my mom! But now my fairy people have found me, and they're going to take me away from here, so I never have to take a math test or look at Kylie's sneering face again!*

Little did I know that my first idea, the head-hurting one about "parallel worlds," would turn out to be right.

2

I hurried through the darkening streets of a wintry Philadelphia afternoon, annoyed at first at my inability to find Gloria's Gateway Books and Records, and then increasingly alarmed as I realized I was lost.

I had soon discovered there were pages missing from my diary. In fact, I realized it as soon as I returned to my room. I clutched at my throat, trying not to vomit. If Adams and his clique found my "sensitive" musings, they would torment me forever. Or blackmail me, and I have no funds, since I am a scholarship student from the sticks who's only in St. George's in the first place thanks to my so-called brilliance.

I took a deep breath and scanned the pages again. It was not that bad. I had only misplaced what I had written while actually in the bookstore, as well as a number of blank pages. There was not much they could do with that even if they did find it. Anyway, I certainly lacked the time to go out again and look for the missing pages. As it was, I had barely returned before curfew, which was lucky since I suspected my roommate Curtis would have been more than happy to peach on me. If I tried to peach on him in return, I would not be believed, and I would only be hated the more by Curtis and the others.

I do not understand why the rotter has it in for me. Unlike most of the other upperclassmen, I get no kick out of lording it over underclassmen, even snobbish rich ones like Curtis. I do not even require him to make my bed and shine my shoes for morning inspection. Mother raised me to take care of myself, and I do not see why turning seventeen should mean I do not have to do it anymore.

After lights out that night I broke out my electric torch and stayed up for hours reading *A Wrinkle in Time*. As usual, I ignored the scufflings and giggles coming from Curtis's side of the room after he sneaked his girlfriend Martha in. Martha is a junior at Cleodolinda Preparatory, St. George's sister school. The few times I have seen her in full daylight I have been confronted with that ancient puzzle of just what *she* sees in *him*. It cannot be Curtis's money, or the fire-red Churchill he drives. Her bright blue eyes are too intelligent, her air too fine, for me to believe she is that shallow.

"It's the moves, Purnell," Curtis said to me once. He had seen me eyeing Martha and her friends.

"What?"

"The moves. You don't have them." Curtis always spoke to me in that condescending tone. It served him in place of friendliness.

"No, I suppose I do lack them."

"Yep. You *certainly do* lack them," Curtis said cheerfully. "What girl would look at an egghead like you?"

"None at all." Brutal, but true. And I had learned long ago that putting myself down would ensure that the other chaps would leave me alone. Curtis laughed and clapped me on the shoulder—he is three inches taller than me, despite being two years younger.

* * * *

Darkness intensified around me. Streetlamps flickered on, barely cutting through the gloom. What a great way to spend a Saturday night, when everyone else was out playing football, kicking that round black-and-white ball back and forth on the field, or walking out with their girlfriends. Curtis must be slobbering all over Martha's delicate white neck right now. And who was truly intelligent, him or me? After all, I was the one wandering deserted streets looking for a run-down bookstore.

I do not know what drew me back. Maybe it was that peculiar cat, Tiferet. What a strange name! After chapel, I had asked Reverend Marks if he knew what the word meant.

"Why, yes, Tom my boy." Reverend Marks raised a single brow on his round, clean-shaven face. "I studied Hebrew in seminary, as do all in the teaching order. 'Tiferet' means 'glory.' But where did you run across the word? Do not tell me you're so bored studying French along with Latin that you have decided to take up another language." He chuckled.

St. George's is very progressive in some ways, or at least Mr Kirkwood is. He introduced modern languages alongside classical Greek and Latin when he became headmaster four years ago, much to the annoyance of the more conservative faculty and graduates. They were even more scandalized when he brought in a French master, one from Europe itself. *French*, for heaven's sake! So unpatriotic! Of course Madame Dantès claimed to be a defector, but someone so old and ugly and shifty-looking just had to be a spy, or that is what most of the chaps think. Her class is very unpopular—some days, I have her practically to myself. Well, that was everyone else's loss.

"Bored with Madame? I don't think so!" I told Reverend Marks the strange story of how I had found Tiferet in Gloria's Gateway Books and Records.

"Really? It sounds wonderful! Where is this bookstore? You must take me there!" Reverend Marks cried, clapping his hands together.

Ah. I had to admit to not knowing where the store was or how to find it again. The Reverend and I looked in the voicegram directory, and when we did not find it there he asked the school's babbage, but even that fine old machine, with its brass fittings lovingly polished by the underclassmen, had never heard of a bookstore by that name anywhere in Philadelphia, or anywhere as far south as Baltimore or as far north as Manahatta. Finally the Reverend had to abandon the search, but he made me promise I would take him there if I could ever find it again myself.

Which was looking increasingly unlikely. And I had thought I had left myself all the time in the world, leaving campus as soon flag raising was over Saturday morning—how I had fidgeted, standing at attention with all the other chaps while the good old Union Bars-and-Stars was un-furled. Now I had been walking for hours, and dusk was fast approach-ing, and I did not know where on earth I was. I could not even glimpse the tops of the gold domes of the Houses of Parliament where they rise a few miles to the south, near where the Schuylkill River empties into the Delaware River. I shivered and pulled at the zip on my well-worn but still comfortable goosedown jacket, making sure it was all the way up. A cat yowled somewhere, and the churning clouds overhead faded to a featureless grey.

There it was! I hurried to the door, now painted a bright turquoise. The store hours were still blank, however, and my heart sank when I looked through the window and saw darkness. But the door handle turned, and a welcome blast of warm air met me as I walked inside. Something brushed against my legs, startling me. Tiferet.

"How are you, girl?" I squatted and scratched under her chin. She purred, but then turned up her nose and leapt onto the counter. Oh, no. I had been so panicked about getting back before curfew I had forgotten to pay for *A Wrinkle in Time*. I fished about in my pockets for something, anything, of worth. All I had was a comb, my billfold (empty except for two five-shilling notes), and four halfpennies, with Sir Ben Franklin's three-quarters profile gazing shrewdly at me. I suspected that none of these were what Gloria had in mind when she wrote her note.

I walked around the counter, found a slot in the cash register, and tried to slip in the five-shilling notes. But the slot narrowed before my eyes, like a mouth closing, and the bills would not fit in, even when I folded them.

"How can that be?"

On the countertop, Tiferet gazed at me with her amber eyes, then winked before jumping down and darting away.

"Well." I had another look through my wallet. But I had no other money, except for the halfpence, too thick to fit in the slot. I gazed in the mirror. My too-long, thick, sandy hair was in its usual untidy state. I pulled out my comb and ran it through my hair. Granny had given me the comb—she died when I was eight, but I still thought about her every day. This comb was made of fine mother-of-pearl, with gleaming ivory teeth.

I glanced from it to the waiting slot, and without quite meaning to I slipped the comb in. It disappeared without a sound. Immediately I regretted its loss, but I knew I had done the right thing. I sighed, rubbed my eyes and began searching for history books that might interest Reverend Marks. There were many, but all were very fantastical, and I did not know if he had a taste for fantasy. Really, imagining a Europe that's not a French-speaking empire? Ridiculous. Many would think it an impossible dream, especially the idea of the Home Islands being free of Parisian rule. Yet aspects of these imaginary worlds seemed nightmarish—this fantasy-Europe had seen two horrible wars in the twentieth century, under tyrants who made Napoléon I seem as benign as a Connecticut country curate.

Maybe I could find something that Reverend Marks would enjoy in that weird hidden room. I started to make my way back there when a noise from the counter startled me. I turned around—a mug of steaming tea waited for me.

"Gloria?"

There was no answer, but a note waited for me under the mug, in the same hand as last time. My skin prickled the way it does when I walk out of the showers on a freezing cold day.

> What you gave is of much value—too much for what you took last time, my dear. Consider that you have paid in advance for this time.

"Right-o."

I wanted to find a gift for Reverend Marks, whose wife Belinda was a retired opera singer. They loved music and had a wonderful stereo system in their home in Chestnut Hill—I'd been invited there for Sunday dinner many times. I liked their company, which I suppose made me an odd duck. I suspected that I was a substitute son for them—they did not talk about it, but their only son had been killed in the Florida War thirty years ago. But when I was with them I forgot how homesick I was for Nanticoke Colony, where Mum and Dad and my little sister Jodie lived in our little wooden house on Gingo Teag Island, by the sea. Jo was something of a violin prodigy at age twelve, and when she came to Philadelphia I knew she would love the Marks' stereo, which is connected to the British Library's master babbage in Brandywine, down near the Nanticoke line.

"That's what we spend all our money on." Mrs Marks had gestured apologetically at the modest helping of fried oysters on my plate, the last time I went to their house.

"I am very grateful. You know this is a genuine taste of home for me," I had said.

Now I headed to the back room. I had to find a gift to pay back her kindness. I stopped short. Someone had dismantled enough of the shelving to make a doorway, stacking the books that had been on the shelves in messy piles. I proceeded to tidy them before walking into what I thought of as the secret chamber. This time the room smelled resiny, like the little stand of loblolly pines in back of our house on Gingo Teag. And my journal pages lay on the floor, right where I must have dropped them.

3

Dear Teresa,

I would love to meet you here! But I am afraid I promised to help my friend Dennis revise tomorrow afternoon. He hasn't a prayer of passing his natural philosophy midterms if I do not help him. You are so brilliant I am certain you do not have any trouble with that subject. Anyone who loves a good used bookstore as much as you do probably does not have any difficulty in school. Except for the kind that other students cause... you know what I mean, I expect. Are you in boarding school, like me, and must put up with them twenty-four hours a day?

You know, though, this bookstore is the strangest place. Have you met Gloria yet? I have not, though she keeps leaving me notes and mugs of tea. I do like the new colour she painted the door, though. Blue is my favourite. What is yours?

I probably will not be able to get here next weekend at all, since my parents are traveling from Gingo Teag, down south in Nanticoke Colony. They have the entire journey all planned out so my little sister Jodie can see everything in the capital. Would you meet me in Parliament Plaza, under the statue of Sir Andrew Jackson, at five o'clock Tuesday evening, and we could go to the kinetoscope? You should be able to recognise me without any difficulty—I am a tall, skinny bloke and will wear a navy blue down topcoat.

Your humble servant,
Tom Purnell

P.S. What is a cell phone?

I sighed as I put down Tom's letter and began absently stroking Tiferet's ears—the cat was curled up in my lap. Parliament Plaza, huh? Not Independence Square. And I noticed all the British spellings and expressions, like "bloke" instead of "guy." Well, if this was for real, it confirmed what I'd suspected since I first stumbled on Gloria's Gateway Books—that what I had here was a gateway to parallel worlds.

I knew all about parallel worlds from last year's AP Physics class with Miss Chen. She's very popular at my high school; the boys of course drool over her since she's hot, but everyone loves her for her exciting class lectures. In May, when most people's thoughts were already on summer vacation, she managed to keep our attention for the quantum mechanics unit by telling us that everything we thought we knew about atoms was wrong.

"You learned something like this, right?" she said, patting a little kid's mobile of the solar system that dangled from a stand on her desk. A bright orange Jupiter promptly broke off and rolled away and immediately became the object of a game of catch. "That actually helps illustrate my point," she said cheerfully. "Not knowing what you guys have done with that particle is a good illustration of the Heisenberg uncertainty principle. You see, what you've learned in school until now, this mini-solar system idea, is called the Bohr model of the atom, after the Danish physicist Niels Bohr. But quantum mechanics tells us that subatomic particles are not in fact like little balls," she added, casually knocking the model over with a swipe of her hand.

"Instead, these particles are sort of miniature dice. You can't know everything about them at any given time, no matter how good the tools you have to measure them. If you know an electron's momentum, you can't know its exact position, only probabilities of where it might be. If you know its position, the momentum is a matter of chance. And so on. Now, my man Al Einstein—he *hated* this idea. 'God does not play dice with the universe,' he said. But for once in his life, he was wrong. God positively *loves* these things," she said, producing a large pair of fluorescent green fuzzy dice and tossing them at Tony Bertelli, who started awake. Everyone laughed.

"He built the entire universe with them," Miss Chen continued, as Tony sheepishly tossed the dice back to her. "Maybe more than one universe. See, there's this crazy out-there idea that most physicists don't like, but that nobody has ever been able to disprove, that every time we have this quantum uncertainty about a subatomic particle, *all the possibilities come true*—only in different universes. The electron may be *here*, or it may be *there*," she said, as Jupiter bounced out from under the front row of desks and rolled to a stop at her feet, "or we may have one universe where it ends up *here*, and another where it ends up *there*."

"But then trillions of new universes would be created every second," I objected.

"That's right," Miss Chen agreed, picking up Jupiter and peeling it with her hot pink fingernails. The giant planet was really a navel orange. "Every possibility you can imagine, and more, is real *somewhere*. There's a universe where this is an apple I'm eating. There's a universe where dinosaurs still walk the Earth. Most incredible of all, there's a universe where Tony was not out with Gina O'Donnell all night, and has actually not had to sleep through this entire class," she said, beaning him awake again with a large juicy section of orange.

Then she got into the mathematics. My head still hurts at the memory. At least she made it up to us by having a fun class where we got to make paper from scratch, after we took the AP test, which of course I bombed.

Well, Miss Chen. I may suck at the math, but I've got something better than that. Actual proof that the many-worlds theory is true!

So I understood what was going on, sort of, but how was I going to explain it to Tom? Well, I decided to give it a try. I took a piece of notebook paper out of my bookbag, along with an actual fountain pen that was part of a calligraphy set that Nana had given me for Confirmation. I'd never used it before.

I tried to explain what Miss Chen had said, though I knew my explanation wasn't anywhere near as good as hers. I sounded clumsy and ridiculous. Besides—it occurred to me after I'd already written about Bohr, Einstein, and Werner Heisenberg—what if all these famous scientists aren't known in Tom's world? Even the word "physics" might not be used in a world where science was still called "natural philosophy," as it used to be called two hundred years ago. Part of me wanted to crumple up everything I had written so far and start over from scratch, but my second attempt would probably be even worse than the first, and so I just kept writing—

> See, so that's why I can't meet you in Parliament Plaza. In *my* Philadelphia, there *is* no Parliament Plaza! My city isn't even the capital of my country, which is the United States of America, not Great Britain or whatever you call your union of America and England. It seems like the only place we *can* meet is here, in Gloria's Gateway Books and Records. Here our worlds touch, for some reason. And maybe more than just our two worlds, judging by all the weird books on the shelves.
>
> Next weekend I can't come because it's Thanksgiving—if you have that holiday in your world. Well, here it's a big national holiday that starts on Thursday the 23rd. And I have to go out of town to stay with my father all through the holiday weekend. I won't get home till Sunday the 26th. (My parents are divorced, and my dad lives outside Washington, DC. Ha, you probably don't have that city in your world at all!)
>
> So can you please, *please* come here next Monday evening the 27th at 5:00, after your family goes home? Your midterms should be all over by then, right?
>
> Yours truly,
> Teresa

Well, "yours truly" was pretty lame-o compared to "your humble servant," but it was the best I could do. Though maybe there were one too many "pleases" in that letter. I added a P.S.: *Where is Gingo Teag? I never heard of it.* Then I folded the letter in half and put it exactly where I had found Tom's letter, in the same spot on the floor where I had found the loose pages from his journal. I weighed it down with my battered old copies of Madeline L'Engle's *A Wind in the Door* and *A Swiftly Tilting Planet*—the only sequels to *A Wrinkle in Time* that I'd been able to find in the disaster area of my room, but those are the best ones anyway. As I stood up I knocked a couple of books off the shelves and had to bend over again to pick them up. The books were *The Mystery of Edwin Drood*, by Charles Dickens, and *Josef in the Promised Land*, by Franz Kafka. (Doesn't Gloria use alphabetical order? Maybe they have a different alphabet where she comes from.)

I stood up and put Tom's letter in my bookbag, yelping as the cramps in my thighs turned into pins-and-needles. Maybe I'd been crouching down reading too long. Then I started going through the piles of books I'd moved last time to make the doorway. I silently promised Gloria I'd only take one home this time—Mom would kill me if I lost my replacement phone, and the only other thing of value I'd been able to find that morning was the framed certificate from when I won the spelling bee in third grade. But who cares about spelling? Most kids my age sure don't, not when their computers can spell anything for them. Still, I must admit I'm a little proud of having spelled "porphyry" right when I was only eight. *Maybe the certificate will be okay as payment after all.*

So after rubbing my legs until the pins-and-needles disappeared, I squatted down once more. There was a 950-page history of the twentieth century by someone named Janusz Spiegelman, which seemed to have been all different after 1916—the Allies had won World War I two years ahead of schedule, and nobody had ever heard of Hitler or Stalin—and it looked like it was very *important*, but not a lot of fun.

But there were two other books I liked so much I had a hard time choosing between them. *Race To Mars* was "the authoritative account" of how four American astronauts beat the Russians to the Red Planet during the Bicentennial in 1976, at the end of President Robert F. Kennedy's second term. It had a fold-out poster with a detailed blueprint of the ship, the *Joseph P. Kennedy, Jr.*, nicknamed "Joe-Kay." *NASA would love that, but why would they listen to me?*

The other book was *The Ultimate Aubergine Cookbook*, which had more ways to cook an eggplant than even Nana knew about. It was published by something called the Brook Farm Collective in Massachusetts. "To celebrate our Sesquicentennial—150 years as a model for these Co-operative States of America!—this humble cookbook is offered to our friends in all the phalansteries and cooperatives from Nova Scotia to Key

West." (CSA? Phalansteries? Even Wikipedia probably never heard of some of this stuff.) Maybe I could use that book to get Mom interested in cooking again, instead of microwaving Ramen noodles all the time. As it is, I have to do the cooking if I want anything fancier, but I only know the hearty Italian basics Nana taught me. Don't get me wrong, I love them, but it would be great to try something different for a change—and to get Mom to help out.

I took my time, because I loved the cozy safe feeling of being in the bookstore with Tiferet around somewhere, and also I was afraid of walking home through the cold, strange streets. Once I got home, of course, Mom would want to know where I'd been. Italian mothers are the worst!

"You said you were only going out to South Street for an hour," she'd say, "it's been dark for hours, where were you?"

What normal 17-year-old girl has a sunset curfew, I wanted to ask her? But I wouldn't because I hated seeing her get all frustrated and then crying. Still, better thinking about that than the fear in my guts, growling softly.

Suddenly there was a scrabbling and a thump. I looked up, startled, as Tiferet padded into the secret room.

"Where have you been, puss?" I asked, stroking the cat, which mewed and darted away. "Okay, I'll come see what you want," I said, following her out.

I stopped short when she came to the counter where the cash register sat, because there was a handwritten note there, just like last time.

> What you have brought is enough for both of the books you want, dear. And don't worry so much about walking home now, or finding your way back next time. Don't try so hard. Relax and enjoy the walk. Your feet will take you where you need to go.

"That's ridiculous," I grumbled aloud. Wait. How did Gloria know what I had brought with me and what I was thinking? Chilly bugs walked up and down my spine. How had Gloria even known I was interested in two books? I wasn't carrying them—oh yes, I was, they were tucked right under my arm. *All right, then.*

I walked around the counter, glanced at myself gloomily in the mirror, and slipped the spelling bee certificate out of its frame. Tucked behind it was a picture of Nana tickling me when I was a baby. Oh, Nana. Tears trickled down my cheeks, and I quickly put it in my pocket. *No way is Gloria getting that!*

The certificate, however, fit easily in the slot. What should I do with the empty frame? Sneaking it out of the house had been hard enough, and I didn't want to risk bringing it back and having Mom spot it and ask a lot of questions. There wasn't a trash can, so I just left it on the counter. Now I had to face the night walk home. I took a deep breath and pushed my way out through the door into the cold and damp.

4

It was not at all difficult for my parents and Jodie to note that something was bothering me all Union Day week-end. I had been taciturn ever since Tuesday evening, when I had stood and waited under the statue of Sir Andrew, the mighty conqueror of West Florida, for an hour and a half as the cold bit deeper and deeper at my fingers and the tips of my nose and ears.

Mum would have shouted at me for half an hour at least had she known that I had braved the cold without the mittens she had knitted me. She still wanted to protect her poor baby against the Arctic cold of a Philadelphia winter. Well, that may have been how she saw it, but what seventeen-year-old bloke is going to go out wearing handmade baby blue mittens, with little brown harry bears on them, yet? Nor could I explain that to her and hurt her feelings.

So instead I practically got frostbite waiting for this imaginary Teresa to show up, which of course she failed to do. The time passed slowly as I clapped my hands together and watched the M.P.s in their frock coats or long skirts and the Lords in their periwigs and ruffled shirts strut past, along with businessmen, tourists, and students like myself.

As a diversion I eavesdropped on a honeymooning couple from Louisiana. I am a good student in Madame Dantès' class, but it is not her fault that she teaches Parisian, not the dialect they speak out West, which she calls with a sniff "Créole jargon."

Some parts of their conversation I could understand fairly easily, while other times I could only make out maybe one word in three. Jean-Pierre could not find their passports, it seemed, and Anna-Louise berated him.

"We came all the way from Nouvelle Orleans to be arrested in Philadelphia?"

"Don't be silly, girl, the British don't arrest you for not carrying your papers. It is not the Imperium here. You know what they are like." And he started talking through his nose, doing such a good impression of a Continental accent like Madame Dantès's that he soon had Anna-Louise giggling. "Your papers, if you please, monsieur. Where do you think you are, among the red savages of the Grand Massif? This is a civilised country here, and you must carry your papers!"

But Jean-Pierre soon found the passports in his inside jacket pocket, and the two of them walked off happily arm in arm.

When Big Benjamin struck six-thirty, I gave up and made my way back to St. George's. The streetcar was late and by the time I returned I was tired and hungry and ten minutes late for curfew, which is at seven o'clock on weeknights in winter. Worse luck, Hartles was on duty that night.

From half a block away I could see him skulking around the gate, just waiting to catch any unfortunate tardy soul, so I sneaked around to the back. Luckily for me, Curtis was there snogging Martha, and they helped me through a well-known gap in the stone wall, where the ivy grows thick and the streetlight has been out for months, if not years. Every time it is fixed somebody puts it out of commission again.

I was grateful, but before I could thank him Curtis sneered, "Out with a girl?"

"Actually, yes. I was out to meet a girl."

"Oh, that's wonderful!" Martha cried, patting my arm. "What's her name?"

"Teresa," I said.

Curtis stared at me in open disbelief. "Indeed? What did you two do?"

"I met her in Parliament Plaza and we went to see 'Florida Homecoming,'" I improvised. Which was the kinetoflick I had planned to see with Teresa, if she had kept our appointment.

Curtis would not leave me alone. "A war 'flick on a first date?" he said.

"Well, Teresa is no ordinary girl. Not that you are," I quickly added for the sake of Martha, who proceeded to question me about what Teresa looked like, where she lived, where she went to school, and heaven knows what else. I cannot even remember all the lies I told. So when Thursday finally came and the family carriage pulled up at the gate of St. George's, like a liberating armored chariot in the Latin Wars of Independence, I was not as happy as I should been. My little sister was first out.

"Hi big brother!" she cried, bounding right up, her dirty blond hair flying all around, as she threw her right arm around my neck. She didn't have to reach up very far to do it, either. She had grown in the three months since I had last seen her, and now the top of her head was level with my nose.

"Hi Jodie," I said and hugged her back.

"It's Jo now," she said, pulling away and planting her hands on her hips.

Mum rolled her eyes as she walked up and planted a kiss on my cheek. "That is all we have been hearing since the beginning of school term," she said. "But even her friends forget sometimes. She was so angry at Marcia for calling her Jodie that the poor girl went home practically in tears."

"Mum, you're exaggerating. I just want to be treated like a grown-up."

"Contractions, dear. What have I warned you about them?" Mum said. As a refugee from the Home Islands, where they speak an even worse Creole than the Louisianans, Mum is death on contractions and anything else she regards as not being the King's English.

"Just because you're getting so tall doesn't automatically mean you're an adult, pet," Dad rumbled.

Mum winced at the contractions as he ambled up to shake my hand. He is a head taller than her, and three or four inches taller than me, and his grip is as firm and unyielding as the moving part on the school's babbage I once caught my hand in.

Still, I was glad to see him. I was glad to see them all and hear that familiar soft Nanticoke twang, and I was only a little bit embarrassed. So what if Curtis or one of my fellow upperclassmen was lurking somewhere nearby, watching everything so they could make me pay for it later? It did not matter! For one whole weekend, I was going to stay with my family in the Franklin Inn, the fanciest hotel in town, founded by Sir Benjamin himself, and forget all about school.

But first we were going out to eat in a superb Siamese restaurant in Rittenhouse Square; Dad was really splurging. Over the Pad Siam, with its crushed peanuts and Gulf of Louisiana shrimp, I had to endure a much more thorough interrogation than Curtis and Martha had subjected me to on Tuesday night, though thankfully, more about my marks than about my nonexistent social life.

It is Dad's dearest wish that I attend King's College, Oxford University next year (the one in Nanticoke, of course, not the one in the Home Islands, which is officially called Université Louis-Napoléon) and then follow him to work at the Directorate Royal for Research in Aerospace and Ground Odysseys National at Wallops Island, an easy half-hour ferry ride from our home in Gingo Teag.

I do not know what career I want to pursue, but I am certain it is not that. While I am proud of Dad for all his work on heavier-than-air craft, a young fellow must have his own dreams, even if he is not quite sure what they are.

So I tried to muster as much enthusiasm as I could when Dad asked if I had my university recommendations lined up. "Well, the pastor will write me a nice letter of recommendation, of course," I said, shifting in my seat.

"Yes, Geoffrey Marks is a good bloke," Dad allowed. "But what about your natural philosophy master, what's his name."

"Mr Goldberg. Yes, he is pleased with my progress."

"'Pleased with your progress?'" Jo mimicked. "That doesn't sound very good to me."

I gave her a dirty look.

"Jo is correct, dear," Mum put in. "and Michael, please set a good example for the children. Tom, you must ensure he is more than simply pleased. You need to have him write you a glowing recommendation so you can be admitted into Oxford's technical program, the way your father was."

Jodie made matters worse by prattling on about her latest achievements, such as the Rachmaninoff violin solo she had played for an audience in Baltimore, with the Duke and Duchess of Maryland in the audience.

"And did they bow and curtsey to you?" I snapped.

"No, but the duchess did tell me afterwards that she was moved to tears," Jo said, immune as always to sarcasm.

Mum tactfully changed the subject to her community work. She is chair of the Gingo Teag Tourism Advisory Council, which may not pay much of anything but is a very important job in a town that has basically two industries, the DRRAGON base and the dragon herself, Assa Teag Ashley, in her lair across the channel on Assa Teag Island. Mum also serves on the Island Beautification Committee and is a longstanding member of the school board.

My mum can bake a carrot cake and brew cardamom-spiced coffee for a dozen people in our spotless living room in less than an hour, and she knows how to sweet-talk the mayor or a key school board member into giving her what she wants, which is always something good for the town. If she possessed any ambition at all she could be mayor herself, or the M.P. from Nanticoke's Sinepuxent Riding, but she prefers to stay out of the limelight.

"I am grateful to Gingo Teag for taking me in, and Gingo Teag is quite big enough for me," she always says in her salty Liverpool accent. And, she has recently been able to add, "Besides, Franklin University Press is going to publish my book on the birds of the Chesapeake Bay, and that takes up the rest of my time. When I am not picking up your dirty socks after you."

Then too, perhaps she thinks it as well not to stir up ignorant suspicions, being a refugee from the Home Islands. Anyone who is not a native-born "from-here" from Gingo Teag itself, like Dad, is a "come-here" in some people's eyes. Like rotten Johnny Dorsey, who taunted me in third grade about being the son of a "French whore" until I bloodied his nose for him.

All the villagers knew about Mum was that Dad had brought her here suddenly, at the age of twenty-two, in the middle of what was supposed to be his graduate year abroad at the *other* Oxford. Not that Jodie, excuse me, Jo and I knew much more than that.

"Oh, I rescued your mother all right," Dad would drawl whenever we asked what had really happened. He would look her straight in the eyes, and they would both burst out laughing. We could no more pry any details out of them than you can pry a live clam open with your bare fingers.

So I was relieved to let her go on about the Council, which was already busy preparing for the pony swim next July, when the Dragonfire Club rounds up the wild horses that live on Assa Teag and herds them across the channel to Gingo Teag. It is a great tourist event that draws almost as many people as come to town in the spring, when Ashley goes hunting in the marshes.

For *that* event, the Council is ready years in advance, not that that kept Mum from grumbling about the Nanticoke House of Burgesses' failure to pay for a bridge across the marshes from the mainland, which has been in the planning stages for the best part of a century.

"If we had the bridge," she complained, "we could accomodate twice as many tourists as we do now to watch Ashley catch her springtime breakfast."

"Yes Mum, but where would we put them all?" Jodie—all right then, Jo, I *will* get used to it—pointed out. "We barely have enough hotel rooms as it is to house all those who do come over on the ferry. And all that carriage traffic might disturb her, and we haven't got near enough recharging stations for all their batteries."

"Look who's an expert in dragon biology *and* carriage engineering," Dad said, smiling as he ruffled her hair, cutting short whatever remark Mum was about to make.

But Jo is really not such a spoiled little brat—at least, not most of the time. After Mum and Dad checked in at the hotel she told them she wanted to show me the ornamental fountain in the lobby—which really was very impressive, with jets of water playing over a flock of brass swans that looked ready to take flight.

"So what's troubling you, big brother?" she asked as soon we were out of earshot.

"I am not much bigger than you anymore," I sighed, tossing a ha'penny into the sparkling water. "And who says something is bothering me?"

"You can't fool me, Tommy boy," she said, flicking my earlobe with her fingernail.

"Ow! All right, I'll tell you," I said, and proceeded to lay out the whole story from my first sight of Gloria's Gateway Books, to its strange, impossible books and phonograph records, to Teresa's failure to appear in Parliament Plaza Tuesday afternoon. She looked skeptical at first, then interested, and finally amused.

"What is so funny?" I demanded.

She giggled, covering her mouth with her right hand. "Oh, Tommy. Don't you see what happened?"

"Yeah, your dumb big brother cannot get the girl. Again."

"No, no, that's not it at all! You said that bookstore is called 'Gateway Books.' Think about it. That name must be significant."

Jodie—*Jo*—likes using both big words and bad grammar. It can be very confusing! I squinted at her. "What do you mean?"

"You said the books in the store have strange, made-up histories in them, like something out of scientification—only not written like a scientification book," she said as I wrinkled my nose in disgust, "but like a genuine, boring, academic history book. Right?"

"Yes?"

"Well then," she said, folding her arms and smirking.

"Well what? So what?"

"So, why would a scientification author go to all the trouble of writing one of those silly books full of things like heavier-than-air travel to other planets but in such a boring way?"

"Why indeed?"

"And if someone *was* dumb enough to write an imaginary book that way, no-one would publish it! Unless it wasn't fiction in the first place!"

"I do not follow you." Not for the first time.

"It isn't fiction, big brother, *in some other world!*"

My mouth fell open. "You mean that Gateway Books is a doorway to other planets?"

"More amazing even than that, big brother! Think of that letter Teresa wrote you. What's a 'cell phone?'"

"I asked her that myself, in my letter back to her."

"You see? She's from *somewhere else*," Jo said in as dramatic a voice as possible. "Maybe she's a ghost of some kind. A ghost from another version of Earth, an impossible one!"

"Ghosts cannot write letters," I pointed out.

"Sure they can. I read a story by E.A. Poe once, 'The Spectral Letter,' which was about that exactly."

"Well I am certain that E.A. Poe, whoever he is, is a great expert on ghosts."

"Was. He was a great expert. He lived in the nineteenth century. You're supposed to be the literature person."

I sniffed. "Some trashy Gothic writer? I never heard of him. Anyway, I do *not* believe in spooks."

"Listen to you. 'I do *not* believe in spooks.' You sound like the Fraidy Lion in 'Dorothy, The Witch of Oz.'"

"Oo! I *do* believe in spooks, I do I do I do I do I do," I imitated, making her giggle. We both love that kinetoflick.

I met Judy Garland once, when I was little, before Jo was born, and Mum and Dad took me on a trip to Hollywood. She was an old lady by then of course, living in a huge old mansion outside town on Lake Michigan, and we ran into her going for a walk on the promenade. But I remember how she smiled down at me when I asked if she had lived happily ever after with Auntie Em on that farm in Indiana.

"Well, regardless, I think the only way you're going to meet this Teresa of yours is back in that old haunted bookstore," Jo insisted.

"You may be right," I sighed, more to shut her up than for any other reason.

"So let's go there together tomorrow."

"What?"

"You heard me. Any girl mad enough to want to go out with my big brother *that* bad, or at all, I just have to meet!"

That was too much. I grabbed for her but she skipped out of the way, and I was the one who went headfirst into the fountain.

* * * *

"It's Jodie's fault!" I spluttered as my mother stood with her arms folded and shook her head slowly back and forth. "She provoked me!"

"Are you five years old?" Dad snapped, grabbing me by the arm. "Do I have to put you over my knee and spank you?"

Little sister, of course, was laughing so hard her eyes were streaming and she could only make little squeaky noises. And of course I was the one who was confined to the room, with nothing but the kinetoscope for company, and I had already seen all the flip-pictures the hotel had, while that rotter Jodie went out for gelato and a walk along Boathouse Row with Mum and Dad.

And yet the next morning, while Mum and Dad were still sleeping, she woke me up in typical charming fashion by flicking my earlobes and putting her hand over my mouth so I could not protest.

"Shh! We have to go to Gloria's Gateway Books so we can find your girlfriend, remember?"

"She is *not* my girlfriend. I have never even met her! She may not even be real!" I said in a furious whisper. "And you have a lot of nerve, after what you did yesterday!"

"Quiet, you'll wake Mum and Dad," she said. "I already wrote them a note that you're taking me to the Franklin Institute to see Sir Ben's inventions. You know, bifocals, the glass harmonica, the carriage battery—"

"The little sister strangulation device," I said. "All right, fine. But dress warmly. It is a long walk from here."

I was not about to admit to her that I did not actually remember where the bookstore was located. She figured it out soon enough anyway. We headed south and east, in the general direction of Parliament Plaza. Soon we were lost in an unfamiliar, deserted part of town. There were neither moving carriages nor street signs. But after two visits to the bookstore one would expect a familiar sight. I looked around with increasing nervousness for some kind of landmark.

"You don't know where we are, do you, Tom?" Jo asked. She pressed herself against me.

I put my arm around her. "It's all right, Sis, we shall find it," I said, trying to sound more certain than I was. Although the sun had been shining when we left, the sky was now covered with a seamless layer of blank grey clouds the shade of the suit my father had worn to Granny's funeral.

I shivered as the wind got under my coat collar, and, though most of my classmates would have mocked me for it, I tried to remember the prayers the pastor had taught us for times of trouble. But nothing came to me, and I found myself whispering a lullaby Mum used to sing. The lyrics were written by the father of a friend of hers back in Liverpool—Paul something. McCurry, maybe?

> *Courage, lad*
> *You'll need courage for the road ahead*
> *For the road full of dread...*

"There it is!" Jo exclaimed, pointing.

I rubbed my eyes. The friendly, dusty plate-glass window was patrolled once again by Tiferet, who meowed as we opened the door and walked in.

"I am sorry, Tiferet," I said, reaching down and ruffling the short soft fur on top of her head, "I came as soon as I could."

She trotted away toward the back.

"That is where I found the notes from Teresa," I said, pointing where the cat had run towards the secret back room, "but first we should check the countertop."

"Check for what?" Jo asked, adding in a squeal, "Peppermint tea! My favourite!" And there was my favourite Ceylon tea, in a mug right beside it. I picked up the note that the two mugs had weighed down. Jo peered over my shoulder.

"Do you mind? It is for me!" I said, snatching it away.

"Not just you. See, it says 'Welcome Jo' right there."

And so it did.

Welcome, Jo. Tom, it's good to have you back. I think this time, you need not take anything with you, except of course for the note from Teresa. Jo, when you find what you need, you will know what it is worth and what you must leave in exchange.

I hurried off toward the back room, while Jo, her eyes gleaming, began browsing the music section. I found Teresa's letter and the books she had promised, and I only vaguely heard Jo's exclamations, absorbed as I was in Teresa's explanation, most of which I did not really understand. But, meet her here Monday afternoon? I would need the pastor's permission to skip out on advanced Bible studies. Perhaps he would allow me a break, just this once.

There was a clatter and thump of books falling down in the next room, and then Jo burst in.

"Look at this! Just look!" She was panting, and there was a wild look in her eyes.

"Jo, what is it? What did you knock over?"

"Never mind that. Look what I found!" And she thrust an oversize book into my hands.

I glanced at the elderly periwigged gentleman on the cover and shrugged. "Yes? 'Wolfgang Amadeus Mozart, The Later Symphonies and Sonatas.' So what?"

"So what?" I have rarely seen Jo at loss for words, but she was positively spluttering. "Mozart died at age thirty-five, in 1791! There were no 'later symphonies and sonatas.' The man in the picture has to be what, at least as old as Granny when she died?"

I winced. Our grandmother had passed away the day after her eightieth birthday after complaining of a bad stomachache. She ate too many oysters at her birthday party, Dad had said. Mum had fried them for her, and she had done as good a job as any from-here. Better, even.

"Did it matter?" Mum had retorted. "She died happy, did she not?"

"So he looks old in this picture," I said, annoyed at Jo for bringing up the unpleasant memory.

"So here are two complete symphonies that Mozart never lived to compose? This book has complete scores for Number 67, 'London,' and Number 82, 'Undiscovered Worlds.' In real life, Mozart's last symphony was Number 41, 'Jupiter.' Plus there are four violin sonatas in this book, which I could play myself!"

"I suppose you could, but how would you explain where you found them? Who would believe unknown works by Mozart exist?"

She lifted her chin. "I could say I wrote them myself." But she withered at the look I gave her. "No, I suppose I couldn't. But shouldn't I bring this music into the world somehow? And what about this book here, the one that talks about colonies on the moons of Jupiter! Don't you think that could help get people excited about what Dad and everybody are doing at the DRRAGON base?"

I did not know how to answer so I changed the subject, showing her Teresa's latest letter. Her face lit up as she read.

"See, I was right! She's from a different world. *Ooh*, and look at this... Monday afternoon, huh? Tom and Teresa, sitting by the sea, K-I-S-S-I-N-G. First comes love, then comes marriage, then they ride off in their 'lectric carriage... Ow!"

"Do Mum and Dad know you sing such naughty songs?"

"The main point is, I was right. She *is* from another world. You're in love with an alien!"

"I am not in love with anybody. I have yet to meet this girl. She may not even exist."

"Oh, she exists all right. Though her handwriting is pretty messy for a girl's." A mischievous look came into Jo's eyes. "What do you suppose she looks like?"

"She is a tall redhead with jade-green eyes and long legs... No! I did not mean to say that!"

"That's your 'type,' huh? Oh, I remember! That's what Ginny Jones looks like."

Ginny was in my class at Gingo Teag High School, before my parents sent me off to St. George's. She was Miss Junior Nanticoke two years ago. As to her awareness of my existence, we might as well have lived in different universes rather than the same island village.

"It's all right, big brother," Jo said, giving me a hug. Clever—I could not hit her while she was hugging me. "I'm sure she's beautiful, whatever she looks like. Hey, do you think I could convince Mum and Dad to let me stay here through Monday? No? Well then, you're just going to have to send me a voice-gram as soon as you return from walking out with Teresa!"

"And what makes you think I would do that?" I said, pushing the annoying little pest away.

"Because if you don't, I'll tell Mum and Dad everything!" She squealed as I grabbed for her, ducking under my arms and scuttling off to the front of the store. By the time I caught up with her she was behind the counter, frowning thoughtfully at her reflection in the mirror. "What am I supposed to put in here that's worth six unknown works by the greatest musical genius who ever lived?"

"I do not know," I growled. "I do not think you own anything worth a farthing!"

"Now Tom, that's just mean. You have to try for witty, big brother. Like, 'I do not think you own anything that is worth as much as my life once Dad discovers that I do not want to become a DRRAGON engineer!'"

This time I actually tried to punch her in the nose, but I could not reach her over the counter. However, she ducked and, with a thump, hit her head on the corner of the counter.

"That's it! I'm telling!" she howled.

"Go right ahead," I said nastily. "And you can tell them where it happened, too, which is not where you said we were going in your note!"

We had both forgotten about Tiferet, who suddenly leapt on the counter between us and hissed, with her tail fluffed up and her teeth showing. We both started back. But instead of being afraid, we were both ashamed. Or at least I was, and Jo blushed. We both straightened up, Jo rubbing her head where she'd hit it.

"You're not developing a lump, are you?" I asked uneasily. *Mum would kill me if she heard me contracting my words! If she doesn't kill me for what just happened to Jo!*

"I don't think so," she muttered, avoiding my eyes. "Let me see what I have to leave."

She spilt out the contents of her pockets on the counter. Some loose change, a miniature harry bear—one I had not seen before, so it must have been new, with its hopeful smile and little bow tie—and a tiny cobalt-blue whelk shell, worn smooth and bright from years of being carried around.

She had found it on a trip to Assa Teag. Only six or seven at the time, Jo was so proud when she found it out on Dragon's Cove Hook, a long flat streamer of grey sand at the southern tip of the island. What she never knew was that I saw it first, rolling around almost invisibly in the swirling muddy water of the cove, and I picked it up and put it carefully down beside her when her back was turned so she would think she had found it. Now she looked at the shell, and raised her head, tears in her eyes.

"Shelly? I have to give up Shelly?" she whispered.

I shook my head slowly, not to say no, but because I did not know what to say.

"Can't I give up new harry bear instead?" she pleaded.

I looked away so she would not see that my eyes were damp too. A moment later I heard a clatter from the register. Then she took my arm.

"Come on, Tommy, let us go find Mum and Dad now," she said. She took Teresa's letter out of my hand as we walked out the door into the grey cold. "Remember, big brother, not to worry about anything. As Gloria said, just relax and enjoy the walk." Then she paused with a frown. "Who's this 'Einstein'?"

5

Mom drove me to 30th Street Station the day before Thanksgiving, grumbling all the way about how unfair it was that Dad got me for the holiday "when we've always gone to Aunt Maria's house for Thanksgiving."

That had been our family tradition only since Nana died, but all I said was, "It's all right, Mom. I want to go."

This didn't improve her mood any, and besides, she was still unhappy about me taking the train on my own. As if I was ten! But she looked so miserable I hugged her extra hard.

"Save some of Aunt Maria's cranberry sauce for me. Make sure it has lots of orange peel in it," I said.

She nodded, her eyes welling up. Sheesh, you'd think I was going off to college. I was so glad they don't allow non-passengers down onto the platform anymore. I didn't want Mom to make a scene and embarrass both of us.

The train was super crowded, of course. I sat next to an old lady who reminded me of Nana. She was so nice I had to bite my tongue so I didn't start crying.

No wonder the other girls always make fun of me, being such a sap. I pressed my forehead against the cold window. What was Tom doing? I hoped he had some kind of holiday weekend. Would he get to see his family? If he was in a boarding school in Philadelphia, they must live far away. And if he'd never heard of cell phones, who knows, maybe they were still using horses and buggies and he wouldn't get to see them at all for, like, *months*. Could he be even lonelier than me? It didn't seem possible.

Outside, darkness was falling on the bare trees and empty fields south of Wilmington. A silvery gleam shimmered off the water as the train crossed a bridge high over the Susquehanna River, just north of where it broadens into Chesapeake Bay.

Tom's family probably came from somewhere down the bay. I'd looked up Gingo Teag on the Internet and came up empty, but the Nanticokes were an Indian tribe who used to live in Delaware and on the

Eastern Shore of Maryland. Maybe his family were crab catchers. What did they call them? Watermen.

We took a trip there once when I was little, when Dad was still working for that big architecture firm downtown. We used to joke that he was Mr. Brady from the Brady Bunch, and I had to be all six Brady kids by myself. It seemed like forever ago, watching the wild horses of Assateague Island, the "Chincoteague ponies," who were potbellied from their marsh grass diet. I thought they were pretty anyway...

Chincoteague. Gingo Teag.

"Why are you giggling, dear?" the old lady asked. Then she peered closer. "Why are you crying?"

None of your business. But I'm a good girl, or a goody two-shoes, more like. "I'm all right."

I didn't want to answer any more questions, so I sneaked off to the café car and spent the rest of the trip gloomily staring out the window. I exaggerated a bit when I told Tom that Dad lives in Washington. Actually, he lives with his girlfriend in Frederick, Maryland, which is at least an hour away.

Was I trying to impress Tom when I told him my dad lived in the capital? Well, he wouldn't have been so impressed if I'd told him that my father not only lived in that Hicksville—the old-timers there actually call themselves Fred-necks—but that he had found himself a young, pretty girlfriend. I mean, way to be original, Dad!

Heather is twenty-eight, but she looks a lot younger. People who see us together always say we could be sisters. Yeah, if I had a big sister who was as gorgeous and skinny as I'm fat and ugly.

* * * *

My stomach tightened as I stepped off the escalator from the platform and Dad reached for my suitcase.

Heather said hello—no, sorry, she said, "Hiiiiiii!" with that big shiny grin of hers—and I glared back.

She's so dumb she probably didn't even notice. She reached over and touched my greasy hair—her own short black hair was perfect, of course—and said, "Your father and I have a surprise for you. We're getting married!"

I was about to tell her to get her hands off me, but then what she said sank in and I tripped over my bookbag and landed flat on my face.

"Heather, dammit, I thought we agreed I was going to break the news to her when we got home!" Dad said, helping me to my feet. "Your nose isn't broken, is it, sweetheart?" he said, handing me a tissue.

I dabbed at the trickle of blood running down my lip.

"I dow'd thing doe," I said, shooting Heather a look that should have turned her into a steaming puddle. She blinked and twisted her face up, trying to look sorry. *God, I hate her!*

"We want you to be the flower girl," she said.

I said nothing, just picked up my bookbag and let Dad lead us out to his car. He has a used green '96 Honda Civic that is still better than the old red Pontiac Grand Am Mom and I are stuck with. The Grand Mal, we call it, after its habit of stalling in busy intersections.

But Dad's Honda wasn't our family car. It didn't have the tear in the back-seat upholstery where I used to hide coins and pebbles, or the familiar stains on the floor mats that looked like a map of Alaska, or at least I thought it did.

I held it in till Dad had shut the doors because I didn't want to make a scene in public. See, I can control myself! Then I yelled, "You're getting *married?*"

"Yes, Heather and I are getting married."

"So *soon?*"

"Honey, it's been two years since—"

"Since you walked out on us, yes, I know." Mom says they're still married in the eyes of the Church and God and everything, so Dad and Heather are living in sin—and even in the eyes of the law, they were dating before the divorce was done. Ugh, couldn't that woman have kept her paws off him at least till then?

She had to put her two cents' worth in. "Teresa, that's not exactly what your father—"

"Shut *up*, Heather. This is none of your business! You are not my mom!"

"I never said I was," she said in a small voice.

Not good enough! "You are not part of this family!" I snapped.

"Teresa, that's enough. I'm marrying her, and she *is* going to be part of *my* family."

"Well, she's not going to be part of mine!" The weekend sort of went downhill from there.

* * * *

Dad made a big deal of cooking Thanksgiving dinner himself, and Mom was right: I missed Aunt Maria's cooking.

If Heather hadn't been there I wouldn't have minded so much that the turkey was dried out and the homemade cranberry sauce had so much sugar in it that it made me gag (and I prefer the jellied stuff out of a can anyway), and as for the roast sweet potatoes, the less said the better.

Honestly the only edible thing was the salad, but since Heather had made it I didn't want to eat that either.

Also we ate in a freezing silence, which I suppose was mostly my fault.

"So how's school been?" Dad asked.

I grunted.

"What's that?"

"What the hell do you care?"

"Teresa, that's not very nice," Heather said.

"Wasn't very nice of him not to be around at all for tenth and eleventh grade."

Dad put his fork down and looked at his plate.

"So, I thought we could hit the stores early tomorrow for Black Friday!" Heather said cheerily. "I need some new boots for winter, for sure! Frederick's got a great 'Golden Mile' along Patrick Street. Wanna come?"

"I need some new boots for winter, ferrrr sherrrr," I mimicked. "Seeing that you're such a fashion charity case, Teresa, why don't you come too? That way I get more brownie points with your Dad!"

"Teresa, that's quite enough," Dad said, as Heather shriveled in her seat.

"Quite enough? I haven't even gotten started yet!"

"Well, you can go to your room if that's how you're going to be," Dad said.

That was all the permission I needed to put down my fork and stalk off to the overgrown closet Dad had said was my room. But the walls were bare and there was none of my clutter anywhere, so how could it be my room? Even the bed felt strange, with its crisp new sheets and light green blanket like a motel bed. Heather must've made it, Dad is such a slob. I threw myself on it and rumpled the covers as much as I could. There was nothing for me to do! So I reread my old battered copy of *A Wrinkle in Time* and felt sorry for myself for not having parents as cool as the Murrys.

Tom has to be having more fun than me. His parents must be just perfect. And his little sister too—I bet she's wonderful. Their world sounds so cute and charming! It wouldn't be so bad to have a king, and not to have any idea what a cell phone was.

The TV went on in the living room, tuned to Dad's stupid bowl games, of course. Heather was cheering right along with him, where Mom always used to nag him to turn it off or at least way down. God, how I wished I was back in Gloria's Gateway Books. What did Tom look like? Blond hair, kind brown eyes, and a soft smile, for sure. But

I couldn't quite picture his face.Eventually I got so bored I dozed off, though Heather's stupid cheering and high-fiving Dad woke me up every now and then.

When I woke up in the morning Heather wasn't there. Dad fed me lumpy oatmeal and we ate in silence. I didn't want to wait around for his cheerleader girlfriend to show up and try to get me to go shopping with her, so I threw my coat on and ignored Dad when he asked where I was going. I headed straight for the "Golden Mile," since I really did need some clothes, especially if I was going to be meeting Tom on Monday. I mean, I didn't want his first sight of me to be a grungy girl in torn jeans. But I had only two twenty-dollar bills for spending money. Luckily I found a Goodwill, where I picked out a sort of patchwork skirt, a sequin-spangled lavender blouse and moccasin boots. Maybe I would seem like a mysterious gypsy to Tom. He'd have to fall in love with me at first sight! But first, he'd have to show up.

I spent the rest of the weekend mooching around the stores, trying to ignore the guilt gnawing at my guts over the way I'd treated Dad. But I didn't know how to make it up to him, and I was still mad at him anyway, so I avoided him and especially Heather, that snake in the grass. If not for her I would still have been mad at Dad for running out on Mom and me, but we could have talked about it. Maybe. And the weird thing was it was true what I had told Mom: I really had wanted to be with him for Thanksgiving. But now that I was here I couldn't wait to get away, although as soon as I got back home I would want to get away from Mom too. Would all of this get less confusing when I met Tom? I sure hoped so.

* * * *

On Sunday morning I was wandering through a park with a duck pond, aimlessly throwing potato chip crumbs to a flock of Canada geese that were paddling around in the grimy water, when a voice called my name. I stiffened.

"There you are," said Heather, less cheerfully than before.

Good, she's afraid of me. She was dressed in a fake white fur of some kind, with little black gloves that didn't look very warm. She was shivering, hunching into her coat against the bitter wind.

I was none too warm myself, but I stood there with my chin thrust out and asked her what she wanted.

"You know your father's very upset we've hardly seen you all weekend," she began.

I said nothing.

"Listen, nothing says you have to like me, but Frank, well, he's your father."

"Not that it's any of your business, but he hasn't been much of a father to me for the past two years."

"Now about that—he doesn't like to talk about it much, not even to me, but you know he was terribly ashamed when he lost his job."

I shut my eyes but that only made my memories of that terrible day burn brighter behind my eyelids.

"Things were already bad with Celine—"

"Leave my mom out of this!"

"—and he was too ashamed to face you, when he couldn't even bring home a paycheck anymore. So he moved out so he could find a job and start sending your mom money. And the only job he could find at first was down here, driving a truck to construction sites. That's how he met me—I'm the office manager at Sardinian Brothers, and I got him the job there. But he was sending your mom money all along, and writing you all those letters you never answered."

I froze. "What letters?"

"Every week a letter. Don't tell me you never got them!"

I opened my mouth but nothing came out but little squeaky noises. Dumb Heather didn't even seem to notice, just kept babbling about how Dad didn't even try to see me at first because he figured *I* didn't want to see *him*, and that she, Heather, was some kind of big hero for making him go to court so that Mom would have to let me see him.

"I have to go now," I finally said. "I have to pack."

"Oh! Well, I'm parked right over there," she said.

"No! No thank you. I'll walk," I said.

And I did walk all the way back, my head spinning.

Luckily my train was coming soon, so I didn't have to talk to my dad much. I did give him a quick hug goodbye before going down to the platform.

* * * *

All the way back home I sat and stared out the window into the darkness. My eyes kept tearing up although I tried to think of Tom. When Mom picked me up and started questioning me, I stuck to yes and no as much as possible.

"Did Dad do something to upset you?" she asked finally, as the Grand Mal pulled up in front of our rowhouse. "Or *that woman*?"

"No, Mom. I just don't feel well. I might have to stay home from school tomorrow."

She leaned over and put the back of her hand on my forehead, like she used to do when I was little. Her skin was cold and I could feel her bones. She had just come off the late shift at the Hilton, where she works at the front desk, on her feet eight hours a day, before she even goes to her waitressing job.

"You don't have a temperature," she said. "Let's see how you are in the morning."

* * * *

When morning came I said I still didn't feel well—stomach cramps and nausea, which was even sort of true.

I waited till Mom headed off to her other job, waiting tables at Dino's Diner, then I slipped out of bed and went up to her bedroom. It was a mess, as usual. Mom hadn't even made the bed, so I pushed aside the rumpled sheets and blankets to find what I wanted—some banker's boxes of papers she keeps lined up under the bed, with the dust bunnies.

At first I just found a bunch of legal papers. *Maybe Heather was lying. She was just trying to make Mom look bad! And checks, from Dad? He never sent money till the judge made him, Mom told me so a thousand times!*

Still I kept searching, and then I found them, all those letters Dad wrote me, mixed in with old unpaid bills and threats to cut off our electricity and repossess our car. Those stopped when Mom got the hotel job—I had offered to get a babysitting job to bring in some extra money, but Mom always said no, I had to concentrate on school. But the letters from Dad had kept coming all along! A bunch of them were held together with a thick red rubber band, the kind that holds together broccoli stalks at the supermarket.

None of them had been opened. Did I want to read them now? I stared at Dad's handwriting on the envelopes. No. I grabbed the ones I could find and took them to my room, where I hid them under my pillow.

Then I got together my gypsy-lady outfit from Frederick and took a shower.

You'll be meeting Tom in just a few hours. In fact, why not head off to Gloria's Gateway Books right now?

It was tempting, but I decided to confront Mom first.

I still had a few hours to kill before she got home to change for the Hilton, time I spent reading *The Race to Mars* and daydreaming. *Wouldn't it be neat if Tom lived in that world and I got to go to Mars!*

Right now I wanted only to get as far away from everybody as possible, and life in a Martian colony sounded cool. When this book was published, fifteen years or so ago, they had domed hydroponic farms and big plans to start "terraforming" the whole planet, giving it a breathable atmosphere and surface water. I wanted to be a part of that—part of something grand, instead of dealing with all these nasty arguments and my own uncertain future.

Even if I could get enough scholarships and student loans to go to college, what was waiting for me after that? If I was lucky, some cubicle job so I could repay those loans, and if I wasn't, the same sort of scrabbling to make ends meet that Mom did.

All the adventures had been lived, all the fights worth having were over, unless I could somehow escape from all this—and Gloria's Gateway Books offered a way.

* * * *

At last the click of a key turning in the front door lock. I stood up, clutching the bundle of letters from Dad.

Mom didn't see me at first—she was talking to herself as she walked in, sorting through the day's mail. She still had on her waitress uniform, that horrible short skirt that makes her legs look fat, the blue blouse with her name tag clipped to it, and the pink hairband holding back her curly black hair.

She must have forgotten that I'd stayed home from school, because she gave a start when she looked up.

"Teresa, oh! Are you feeling better?" She reached out to check my forehead.

I stepped back.

"Teresa, what the—what are you doing dressed in those clothes? You can't be planning to go out when you stayed home sick from school today!"

I silently held out the letters. Her eyes flicked to them, then back to me.

"What were you doing in my room?"

"How come you never gave me Dad's letters?"

She sat down suddenly and avoided my eyes.

"I didn't want you hurt," she said.

"What?"

"Your father left. He left! He wasn't coming back. He was out having his fun. All those stupid letters from him would have just confused you. They would have made you miss him all the more. It was simpler this way. I just wanted to make it easier for you." She raised her chin and looked at me with a gleam in her eye that reminded me of Nana. "I was going to give them to you when you were old enough to understand. Why else would I have kept them?"

"I don't know. Maybe you felt guilty about not letting me have them."

"That is not true! I just wanted to protect you, protect what was left of your childhood."

"Mom, I was fifteen! I think I was old enough to decide for myself. And Heather says Dad did send you money!"

"Oh, so it's 'Heather says' now. Fine, yes, he sent me a little something now and then. Might as well have been nothing. And Heather didn't have to struggle to keep the house. Heather didn't have to take extra jobs to make enough money to keep you fed and clothed."

"Well, maybe you'll be able to stop worrying about that soon."

"What's that supposed to mean? Where are you going?"

But I just slammed the door behind me.

6

I was crying as I made my way through the gathering dark toward Gloria's Gateway Books. I kept dabbing at the tears with the back of my stupid baby-blue mittens. Another example of how Mom thinks I'm still a little kid!

Did I want Tom to see me like this? His first glimpse of the girl who (I hoped) would be the love of his life to be an ugly snot-nosed mess? No, of course not. But I couldn't stop crying.

At that moment I hated Mom and Dad and Heather for making me so miserable, and I'd always hated my classmates for treating me like a freak. Kylie was the worst of the bunch. The only person in this world who had ever really cared for me was Nana, and she was dead.

As soon as I met Tom, I would beg him to let me stay in his world with him. I would seek asylum, yes I would, in his British America! I'd never go back, and instead of fighting over *me,* everybody could fight over who had made me run away. All they wanted to do was fight anyway, so *they'd* be happy. And Kylie and her gang could go on being shallow self-absorbed little b-words, but they'd have nobody to be mean to any more.

Relax and enjoy the walk, Gloria's note had said. There wasn't much chance of that, and the crummy neighborhood I walked through seemed grayer and more run-down. But somehow my feet knew where to take me even if my head didn't, and before it got completely dark I saw the welcoming light of the bookstore.

I ran to the door and pushed it open, startling Tiferet from her perch atop a stack of books that I hadn't seen before. *Maybe Tom's already here, and these are all the books he's going to buy!* Tiferet turned into an orange streak and disappeared into the back.

"Sorry, kitty," I called. "Tom? Tom, are you there?"

No answer. I followed the cat into the gloom, toward the secret back room. The doorway I'd made stood before me, and I heard someone moving around.

"Tom?" I called again, over the pounding of my heart. A hard rubber ball in my chest that kept bouncing against my rib cage.

Was that a muffled voice? I peeked into the hidden room, but no one was there. The bare light bulb dangled from its cord, casting sharp shadows on those heaps of incredible books.

The shadows shifted. I blinked once, twice. Could it be? Sure enough, the light bulb swayed, as if someone had just brushed past it.

"Tom?" I shouted.

A muffled voice said "Teresa?"

"Tom! Tom, where are you?"

"I am here in the back room!" the voice said.

"Huh? But I'm in the back room!" I said.

"Well, I am here as well. Right in the corner where the audio platters are."

Audio platters? Oh, he must mean records! I turned. A stack of vinyl records sat in the far corner, all right, but no one was standing there. Where was the voice coming from? It sounded like whoever it was, was standing right beside me, yet the voice seemed to come from everywhere at once, even from inside my body.

Suddenly I started shivering so hard that my teeth clattered together, even though the room was too warm. A cat yowled and I jumped. That noise too seemed to be coming from everywhere at once, but then Tiferet bounded from of the corner where Tom had claimed he was standing. She leaped into my arms. Then things got really weird.

* * * *

It was harder bidding everyone farewell on Sunday afternoon than I expected. A good deal harder. In fact, it had not been so difficult for me to part with them since I first left for boarding school three years ago. I even shed a few tears.

"Stop crying, big brother, you look like a total idiot," Jo whispered as she hugged me.

"I shall make you pay for that," I whispered as I hugged her back.

"You're not going to forget to send me that voicegram, will you, Tommy? So I can know if you found your Teresa?"

"Perhaps I shall," I said.

Dad pretended not to notice that I was crying, but he patted me on the back in addition to his usual handshake.

"You keep those marks up, Tommy," he said. "I'm holding a place open for you at the DRRAGON base. We're doing exciting research that I didn't have time to tell you about this weekend. And I have my own special side project as well. I just know you'll want to be a part of both projects."

"Thank you, Dad," I said softly.

A hug from Mum was what I needed most. "I do not know what is bothering you, Tommy boy, but remember we all love you," she said, softly so as not to give Jo ammunition or make me look unmanly in front of Dad.

And really, what was bothering me? I waved goodbye to the carriage as it moved slowly away down King George Boulevard, towards the Nanticoke Pike.

The question kept nagging at me as I carried my presents up to my room—of course Mum had insisted on buying me clothing that might have looked smart in the Home Islands around 1990, but was bound to make Curtis call me a ponce if I wore it. Maybe the trousers were salvageable. In fact, maybe I would wear them and my old Gingo Teag High blazer when I met Teresa tomorrow.

Was that what was making me nervous? The (admittedly small) chance that I was being played for a fool, and that Curtis would be waiting at the "bookstore" to laugh at me while Adams and his clique beat me up? It took me a long time to fall asleep that night.

* * * *

Which of course meant that I had trouble staying awake in class the next day. Mr Goldberg, the natural philosophy master, noticed me jabbing my wrist with a pencil to stay awake, and asked me to stay after class. My heart sank. His was the last class of the day, and I must leave soon if I was going to meet Teresa—or my ultimate humiliation.

"Tom, have a seat. Don't look so worried, I'm not going to give you detention," he said in his heavy Yiddish accent. (Even teachers use contractions without a second thought! Why is Mum such a stickler?)

The scuttlebutt around the school was that Kirkwood had hired him "fresh off the boat from Palestine," where the Emperor had decided that fewer Jews would make the Arabs happier and the province easier to control.

Of course His Royal Majesty Henri-Napoléon III could also have reduced the numbers of Jews pouring into Palestine by ordering his Russian provinces to stop imposing so many anti-Jewish laws, but the Imperial slogan these days was "local control," so we Britons gained the benefit of some very motivated refugees with an axe to grind with l'Empire.

"Tom, what's been bothering you lately? You seem distracted in class." Despite his accent, Goldberg speaks English with pedantic correctness. Except for those contractions.

I squirmed and could not look him in the eye. "I'm having trouble sleeping," I muttered.

"That may be the efficient cause of your distraction, young man—and you *do* remember what efficient cause means, yes?"

"The immediate cause, right?"

He gave an approving sniff and brushed his long brown hair back from his forehead—"young man" indeed, he cannot be more than five or six years older than me. "Very good, I think perhaps you shall not fail the final after all. And so, yes, the immediate cause, but I think there may be deeper causes behind this sleeplessness. Or am I off on the wrong track, as we English say?" Mr Goldberg became a naturalized British subject last year, and he is very proud of it.

All right, I would give him something to think about. I looked him straight in the eye, and said, "Mr Goldberg, what do you think the nature of reality is?"

He drew away, a puzzled frown on his face. His accent thickened even further. "Philosophical troubles you bring me?"

"You could call them that." I told him much of what I had already told Reverend Marks, except I framed it as a series of hypotheticals: "Suppose there was a place full of impossible things…"

Why was I was reluctant to tell Mr Goldberg everything? Perhaps because I know the pastor better, and I wanted to be careful in case Mr Goldberg should be inclined to laugh at me or report me to the school's Mental Hygiene Advisor. But he nodded thoughtfully.

"Tom, there is much about the world that our natural philosophy doesn't truly understand," he said, stroking his long, bushy walrus mustache. "And perhaps our history as well. Our minds are small and limited, and we must rely on the work of others who came before us, who had their own limitations. If I can inspire you and the others in this class to go beyond those limitations, to do away with some of the errors that hold men back—well, that is why I love to teach. So no, I don't think you're crazy to think there could be worlds that have taken a different path than ours. Or even communication with other—intelligences. I would warn you only to keep one eye on the ground while you're learning to fly."

I started. Did he know about Dad's work? I hadn't mentioned it. In fact, Dad had warned me not to talk about it in school.

"May I go now?" I asked after a pause.

"Oh, of course! Away with you," he said with a smile and a dismissive wave. "Enjoy your evening."

Outside it was already growing dark. I was going to be late, late to meet Teresa, and after I had taken the trouble of asking the pastor to agree to excuse me from advanced Bible studies! Which he had done without asking any awkward questions, but with a wink that made me blush.

I hurried towards the gate, but before I could get there Adams and two of his flunkies loomed out of the shadows.

"Where you going in such a rush, Purnell?"

"None of your business, Adams," I snapped. What had I said?

The flunkies ooh'd and ah'd and whistled. Adams smirked, stepped forward and pushed me in the chest. Something in my snapped, and I punched him in the jaw. He lost his balance and fell onto the flunky on his right, who I think is called Jack Madison.

Adams must have been surprised, since I am known for going to great lengths to avoid a fight. Yet I could hardly have avoided what followed, regardless of my actions. The other flunky, Jim Monroe, grabbed me from behind while Adams rose, murder in his eye, and punched me in the gut. All the air rushed out of my lungs. I fell to the ground, my mouth opening and closing like the striped bass Dad catches on week-ends. Adams and Monroe yelled at me to get up and fight like a man, while Madison asked if Adams was all right.

At that moment Mr Thiel, the deputy headmaster and Latin master, ran up and began his useless blustering—we call him Squeal behind his back.

I peered up at his toadlike face, my vision going in and out of focus. Madison grabbed my arm and pulled me to my feet with exaggerated politeness.

"Fighting on the campus?" Mr Thiel shrieked. "This is antithetical to the spirit of cooperation and unity we expect from students fortunate enough to be allowed to attend St George's!"

"Fighting? We weren't fighting, Mr Thiel, sir," Adams said, wiping away the blood on his chin. "Infernal here tripped, and we were just helping him to his feet. Isn't that right, boys?"

The flunkies nodded vigorously.

"My name is Thomas Jefferson Purnell, Adams," I growled, adding more softly, "And I shall give you a good reason to remember it!"

"This is unacceptable behavior!" Thiel said. "You are all confined to quarters for the evening! And tomorrow morning, you will *report yourselves* to my office for five strokes apiece!"

Rumour has it Mr Thiel was dishonourably discharged from His Majesty's Border Guards, the most corrupt and ineffective branch of the service, for being too useless even for mess-hall duty.

But he was still a master, and we all mumbled our yessirs and waited to be dismissed. As Adams headed off toward his dorm and I headed off toward mine, we looked each other in the eye.

This is only the beginning, mate.

Which still left me with the problem of getting to Gloria's Gateway Books in—I looked at Curtis's handcrafted silver alarum clock as I entered the room, and gasped—ten minutes!

"What's the matter, Purnell?" Curtis asked.

I turned, slightly startled—I had not even noticed anyone else was in the room, I was so flustered—to see him lying on the bed with Martha, their arms around each other. Entertaining a member of the opposite sex in one's quarters is strictly forbidden at all times at St George's, but people like Curtis assume the rules are meant for others, and it seems they are usually right.

Martha smiled at me, her brown eyes kind, and for a moment I forgot all about Teresa. I told them what had happened, and Curtis clucked sympathetically.

"Thiel's an ass. You need help getting over the wall?"

"Yes." Thiel had doubtless told whoever was on gate duty not to let me, Adams, Madison, or Monroe out.

"All right then, Tommy boy, follow us," Curtis said, rubbing his hands together. We all tiptoed out of the dorm and crept around to the back wall. Curtis helped boost me through the gap in the wall while Martha kept watch.

She winked at me just before I went through. "Have fun, Tommy. Bring Teresa back and introduce us to her when you have the chance," she whispered.

I nodded and climbed over the wall to freedom.

* * * *

It was a cold night, but I barely noticed the wind as I darted through the streets, hoping desperately it would not take me too long this time to find the strange, vague neighborhood around the bookstore. Even using Gloria's recommended method of not consciously seeking my way, it had never taken me less than an hour to get there before, and I was afraid Teresa would not wait.

But for some mysterious reason, this time the streets seemed to fall behind me as if I was an artillery shell in the Great War zooming straight to its destination, and I found myself standing in the doorway at one minute to five, stroking Tiferet's head as she purred.

My heart thudded in my ears as I walked toward the secret back room, calling Teresa's name. There was no answer. I had to duck my head to fit through the makeshift doorway through the bookshelves that led to the back room. A warm breeze scented faintly with oranges wafted from out of the darkness. On my previous visits, the back room had a warm orange glow from gas lighting, but now it was plunged in darkness.

Reaching up, I waved my arms around until I bumped into a gas sconce, on which I cleverly managed to scrape my hand. I muttered words that would have resulted in a caning at school as I fumbled around looking for the switch. At last I found it and turned it carefully to the left, striking the spark that lit the gas.

The shadows retreated. Was that a girl's voice calling my name?

"Tom! Tom, where are you?"

"I am here in the back room!" I said.

"Huh? But I'm in the back room!" the voice said.

"Well, I am here as well. Right in the corner where the audio platters are," I said.

She sounded as if she stood beside me, yet her voice seemed to come from everywhere at once, even from inside my body. I turned completely around, but no one was there except for Tiferet, who had wandered into the room in that offhand way cats have but was now trotting purposefully towards the opposite corner. I was looking right at her when she vanished.

I rubbed my eyes. *I must be seeing things.* In that instant came the sound of something heavy shifting, followed by a thump. Then *two* girls stood in the corner, a dark-haired, slightly plump girl my own age, and a tall, slim girl—no, a woman of about thirty, as far as I could tell in the shifting light—with long red hair and a mischievous gleam in her green eyes.

The dark-haired girl hugged the woman tightly, but then she yelped and did the most amazing double-take I have ever seen in my life, which made her lose her balance and go reeling backward toward the nearest row of bookshelves.

I leaned forward and caught her. She was out of breath and her skin was cold to the touch, as if she had just come in from outdoors.

"Teresa?" I said, my voice cracking on the second syllable. Her head was cradled in my arms and she looked straight into my eyes.

She nodded slowly. Her eyes were a much richer, warmer brown than Martha's. Suddenly it seemed to be very hot in the room. I released her hastily, after ensuring she was standing steadily on her feet. Then we both turned and stared at the flame-headed lady, who grinned broadly.

"Hello. I'm Gloria," she said, and curtseyed—she was wearing a long, bright green skirt, almost a gown. "I would ordinarily say how very pleased I am to make your acquaintances, but I feel we have already been on much too intimate terms for such formality."

She smiled again and brushed what looked like orange cat hair off her sleeves. Her voice was warm and confiding, like your oldest and best friend in the world. Her accent was vaguely Home Islands, but not quite like Mum's. It was impossible to place, I would have to say.

She began to chuckle, then threw back her head for a full-throated belly laugh, her arms clutching her bosom.

"Oh, my dears," she said finally, dabbing her eyes on a corner of her skirt. "Look at you! You have positively turned to stone! You must accompany me to the front room for your tea and cocoa. This chamber is propitious for traveling, but not for proper introductions. And you *must* be properly introduced to one another. Much depends on it."

7

I swayed and clutched onto Tom's arm, I hope not too hard, as we walked up to the counter where our drinks waited. *After all, he's a stranger. This is the first time you've met him.* Also, he wasn't exactly what I'd imagined, physically, though I'm sure I wasn't quite what he was expecting, either.

He did have an inch or two on me, with hair midway between sandy and a chestnut color instead of the straw color I'd imagined, almost Marines-short in front but over his collar in back. Later I saw that all the guys our age in his Philadelphia had that same hairstyle. He was also skinnier than I'd expected, with long, thin features and stick-out ears that made me want to grab them as handholds when I kissed him.

Okay, okay, cool out, girl, we're not quite there yet. His eyes were the one feature that really were more beautiful than I could have imagined, brown and dreamy with flecks of green, the kindest eyes I'd ever seen. Still, he looked a little frail to be holding up my big fat body, and I would never have done it if I hadn't been quite so wobbly.

It had been very fast, the trip from the bookstore *here* to the bookstore *there*, a trip that may not have involved any actual movement, if you know what I mean. Certainly the secret back room looked the same, or almost the same, except there were gaslights instead of a bare electric bulb.

The books and records seemed to be in the same places on the shelves, most of them, though I noticed another copy of the Beatles reunion album that hadn't been there in *my* world. I was sure I'd "bought" the only one. I think I saw it, but my brain was still trying to wrap itself around the impossible information I'd seen at the moment of passage.

I swallowed bile at the memory. Dizzy doesn't begin to describe how I'd felt, seeing everything turned inside out, exploded and sort of *flattened*, but in a three-dimensional way. Oh, I can't really describe it.

Picture an inside-out sports sock that you pull out of the dryer (this is always happening to me because I pull the socks right off my feet and toss them into the hamper, after much nagging from Mom). Okay, so you see all those loose threads and stuff, right, and the white stitching crossing over the colored bands. Not the view of the sock you're supposed to get.

So, ramp that up to three dimensions. Somehow I was able to see the inside pages of all the books in the room, books that were closed and standing on the shelves. Not only that—I saw both sides of every page, all at once! I could have read every page, except that I was only there (wherever "there" was) for less than a second, and I felt more like screaming than reading.

There were two reasons for that. One was that I got an exploded view of Tom as well, a moment before I actually got to meet him in the normal way. He looked like road kill, except that I could see his blood was still pumping, his lungs were expanding and it looked like everything was working the way it was supposed to. But the other reason I wanted to scream was that I got a full-on glimpse of Tiferet, or Gloria, or whatever her name really was.

A full-on, multidimensional view. Give me points for not fainting. There was the living road-kill effect stuck to a bunch of orange cat fur stuck to something that looked like a woman's head, with the brain fully visible…and then there were glimpses of other—

"Facets," said Gloria, who was watching me closely.

I jumped.

"What did you say?"

"You saw a lot of different facets of the world—and of me—that aren't normally visible to beings such as yourselves. That's why you look so green."

I gulped.

Tom said, "Huh?"

"Drink your cocoa, dear. I've put some chamomile and other herbs in it. It will settle your stomach."

"That sounds gross," I muttered, but I did as I was told.

Chamomile tea is my second-favorite drink, as Gloria probably knew. The concoction really did make the heaving waves in my guts calm down a little.

My head swam and I sank to my knees in my brand-new used patchwork skirt. This was supposed to be the high point of my life so far, and now just look. Tom made soothing noises and touched my shoulders gently, pulling his hands back at once as if he'd just touched a hot stove.

"I'm so sorry, hon," Gloria said. "I should have just given you a glass of water. The first trip is always really hard on you four-dimensional folks."

"Would you please explain to us what you are talking about?" Tom asked as he helped me to my feet. He immediately blushed.

Wow. Do I have that effect on him? Or is it Gloria?

But she didn't seem fazed.

"Certainly," she said, walking behind the counter and reaching down for two books. Well, two copies of the same book—sort of the same book—they *looked* like the same book—but not exactly.

"*Flatland, A Romance of Many Dimensions*, by Edwin A. Abbott," Tom read aloud, picking up one of the books.

He had an odd accent, something I couldn't quite place. Not like someone whose first language wasn't English. No, he sounded a little bit like someone from Australia, or maybe South Africa. Or maybe England, but not London, not like those English actors you usually see in movies. There was bit of a burr, some strangely rolled r's that didn't sound American.

Maybe he thinks I sound weird, too. I picked up the other book and read, "*Planeworld, A Romance of Many Dimensions*, by Theodora A. Abingdon."

"They're really the same book, sort of, and Ed and Teddy were sort of the same person," Gloria said with a smile as she discreetly handed me a peppermint. I sucked on it and found it helped settle my stomach. "I'm sorry I don't have two copies of the exact same version. But it doesn't really matter much. Here's the point," she said, flipping to a marked page in Tom's book.

"You see," she said, putting on a pair of very old-fashioned glasses that she wore on a silver chain around her neck. The lenses were flattened half-circles that even Nana would never have worn, although Gloria somehow made them look stylish. "This story, in either version, is told by a square, a two-dimensional shape who lives in a completely two-dimensional world. He cannot even imagine that a third dimension exists, or what it would look like, until one day a sphere appears in his house. Only, what would a sphere look like, if you could only see it in two dimensions?"

"I hate geometry," Tom groaned.

I said timidly, "A circle?"

Gloria beamed at me. "Excellent! A circle, yes. Here's how the sphere explains it: 'Your country of two dimensions is not spacious enough to represent me, a being of three, but can only exhibit a slice or section of me, which is what you call a circle. The diminished brightness of your eye indicates incredulity. But now prepare to receive proof positive of the truth of my assertions. You cannot indeed see more than one of my sections, or Circles, at a time; for you have no power to raise your eye out of the plane of Flatland; but you can at least see that, as I rise in Space, so my sections become smaller. See now, I will rise; and the effect upon your eye will be that my Circle will become smaller and smaller till it dwindles to a point and finally vanishes.'"

"Now, the square is talking," Gloria added. "'There was no "rising" that I could see; but he diminished and finally vanished. I winked once or twice to make sure that I was not dreaming. But it was no dream. For from the depths of nowhere came forth a hollow voice—close to my heart it seemed—"Am I quite gone? Are you convinced now? Well, now I will gradually return to Flatland and you shall see my section become larger and larger.'"

I thought about how, when I first heard Tom's voice, it seemed to come from everywhere and nowhere—and also from inside my own body.

"So you're saying that our worlds are connected through the fourth dimension," I said slowly.

Gloria smiled. "Not the fourth, hon. The fourth is what you call time. That's why I called you four-dimensional folks."

"Right. I knew that," I said, thinking that Miss Chen would be very disappointed in me, and also, *What you call time?*

"Not to boast, but I have quite a few more dimensions," she continued. "Let's see, there are—" she held up her fingers and started counting, and I swear for a second she had an extra one—"eleven. Eleven dimensions."

"So that explains why you are sometimes a cat and sometimes a—a person," Tom stammered. I squeezed his hand and he blushed again.

"Precisely. Different facets," Gloria said.

"And I could see the insides of things when I was in between our worlds because—"

"Mr. Abbott, or Miss Abingdon, explains that very well in the voice of the sphere, just before the part I read you," she responded, and quoted: "'In order to see into Space you'—that is, the square—'ought to have an eye, not on your Perimeter, but on your side, that is, on what you would probably call your inside; but we in Spaceland should call it your side.'"

"Okay," I said shakily.

"When you make the transition in the future, my dears, you might find it easier to keep your eyes closed," she said, closing the book.

"But how will we see where we are going? And anyway, how are we supposed to make these interdimensional trips without you?" I demanded.

Tom blushed again. It was charming. Gloria too seemed delighted.

"This is why you were chosen—because you both see the connections between things so quickly, and are quick to anticipate the next move. In other words, you're both super-bright."

Tom and I snorted at the same time.

"Also modest. Modesty is a great thing, but you should also know your own potential. And that is why you belong to—or belong *with* each other, I believe it is more socially appropriate to say."

Now we were both blushing furiously.

"You must each help the other discover what is strongest and most beautiful in the other. That is why you felt such urgency about this meeting."

"Speaking of urgency," Tom said, glancing nervously at his watch—a real, honest-to-God pocket watch—"my curfew is in less than half an hour."

"Oh, that. Now, if you've been paying attention, you'll notice I said that time is only another dimension, and for me, one of the lower ones," Gloria said.

"Yes?" Tom said blankly.

There were invisible spiders running down my arms. I gulped and turned to Tom. "She—it—she can control time," I said.

"Well, perhaps no more and no less than you can 'control' space by moving one object nearer to another," Gloria said. "But yes, I can do some modest manipulations. You don't need to worry about your curfew, Tom. Or the weather, Teresa," she said, glancing at my thin skirt and raising an eyebrow. "The end of November isn't the most pleasant time for a first 'date'—Tom, I believe you call it 'walking out with a girl,' right?"

"Yes, ma'am," he said softly.

"When you walk out the door, once you pass the in-between zone, you will find it is a warm May evening," she said.

"In-between zone?" I asked.

"You must have noticed that this place has no address, that the streets around it have no name and are a little—off-putting," Gloria said. "I call it the in-between zone, or the Zone for short. I don't want you to worry too much about it, but those streets aren't exactly real, and neither are the buildings. Your minds fill in the scenery for you, is the simplest way of explaining it."

"So what's really there?" Tom asked.

"Nothing terribly interesting, I assure you," Gloria said quickly. "Well, off with you then. Try to be back by ten o'clock by your watch, Tom. Why not take Teresa to Gerald's Gelato and Tea Room?"

"Mum and Dad always take us there in the summertime!" Tom exclaimed. "How did you—"

But she had already vanished.

8

Naturally I did not believe that it would in fact be summer when we walked out the door, with the cricket bats swinging under a warm sun. Other worlds and magically appearing and disappearing women and cats and books I could believe in—I did not really have much choice, after having been presented with the evidence, including the solid, breathing evidence of the girl beside me. But time travel? Everybody knows that is an impossibility. I saw an early kinetoflick once of Herbert Wells, the famous scientification writer, explaining why his novel *The Time Traveller* could never have worked in real life.

"Suppose my time traveller goes back into his own past to shake hands with his father as a young man, but accidentally pushes him in front of a speeding carriage so that he is run over and dies," Wells had said in his broad Boston accent. "Well, if the Time Traveller's father can never sire him, then he is not born, never grows up to invent time travel, never goes back into the past and pushes his father in front of a carriage...so his father *does* live to sire him, and he grows up, and invents time travel, and... Thus we ah trapped in an endless loop of paradox, which cannot be resolved by any means. Therefore, time travel—at least, travel into the past—is impossible."

So when I walked out the door, the heat and the faint scent of honeysuckle struck me like a punch in the nose. Teresa drew a sharp breath.

"I don't know what's scarier," she said in a near whisper, "the fact that it's now summer, or that we're walking through the Zone."

I took her hand. Her palm was cold and clammy and I suspect mine was no better. I needed comfort as much as I wanted to give it.

"Gloria has assured us there is nothing to worry about," I said, silently damning my voice for cracking. "Everything looks perfectly normal to me." I slapped at a streetlamp pole we were passing, just to show how solid it was. My hand passed right through it.

"Okay," Teresa said. "That was creepy. So what's behind this façade?"

"I for one," I said firmly, "do not want to know. We are merely passing through!"

Teresa rolled her eyes, but then she glanced at my face and sobered.

"I am simply trying to inform whatever is here that we are not a threat," I whispered.

She nodded, her eyes wide, and added, "And that we're not afraid, either."

"Right! It is as though we are strolling through Pitt Park!" I said, and even added a forced little laugh.

"Pitt Park? Where's Pitt Park?"

"Have you never been there? I thought you said you are a native Philadelphian. It is only the biggest and best city park in the English-speaking world!"

"Oh. We call it Fairmount Park, where I come from."

"Well then, I am sure it is just as lovely in your world as in mine, and there is probably no crime there at all, and if some brigand were to try to attack you I should give him a sound thrashing!"

"Brigand? Oh, you mean a mugger. I can take care of myself with muggers. Mom got me a little canister of pepper spray that looks just like a tube of lipstick."

"I don't know what pepper spray is, but do you have it handy?"

"Have it handy? Sure, it's right in my purse," she said, reaching into her small, bright pink handbag and pulling out a tiny metal cylinder.

"Capital! Now, would you please point its business end that way?" I said, indicating a point just behind her head. My finger shook.

Her eyes grew even wider, and she spun around quickly, jabbing frantically at the top of the cylinder with her index finger. There was a tiny hissing noise, followed instantly by a roar of anger and pain.

"*Run!*" I pounded pell mell down the possibly imaginary pavement, slowing a bit to allow Teresa to keep up. I compared notes with her later, and while she also had not seen the thing very clearly, the fact that its shadow passing over us seemed to be at least a city block long was really all we needed to know.

"Gads, that thing must have been bigger than Assa Teag Ashley," I gasped when we fetched up on an ordinary Philadelphia street and I could breathe again, or try to.

"Who?"

"Assa Teag Ashley? You know? The Belle Dragon of the Nanticoke? Could it be that she does not inhabit the island in your world? Or that there are no dragons at all?" I started to laugh, but it quickly turned into a coughing fit, and I bent over and pressed my palms against my knees to try to regain control. Some walking-out this was.

"Dragons? Are you serious?" Teresa gasped. It took her longer to recover, since I had been holding back a little when we were running. But when she did she stared around her in wonder. "Where are we?"

"Nowhere special," I said, glancing around myself. "This is the corner of King George Boulevard and South Street."

She shook her head. What was causing such amazement? True, she was dressed oddly, and attracting a few stares.

I moved to block her from view—we were standing in an alley. But she pushed me aside and stood out on the sidewalk, openly gaping at the scene before her.

Most of the women and girls walking by wore skirts at least as long as Teresa's, despite the warmth of the May air—certainly none wore the denim trousers that I later learned were so common in her Philadelphia. Carriage traffic was lighter than it would have been further down King George, because this was the intersection crossed by the cobblestoned South Street pedestrian mall, and seasoned Philadelphia drivers avoid the lengthy traffic stop by detouring around to 16th Street. Less seasoned drivers usually take advantage of the wait by plugging in at the recharging station on the corner, which must do a royal amount of business.

Teresa gawked as a Pontiac Warbird nosed its way out of the station and stopped to allow a gaggle of little children to pass, shepherded by a tired-looking teacher.

"What's that?" she asked, pointing at the carriage.

"A Pontiac Warbird," I said, looking a little enviously at its sleek lines and distinctive metal beak. Dad drives a Tucker Stallion, which is nice and dependable but a little dull.

"But how come your cars don't make any noise?" she asked.

"Cars? We call them carriages. And why should they make noise? There have been countless improvements in them since Sir Ben drove the first one back in 1790!"

"Sir Ben?"

"He may have preferred 'Dr Franklin,' but it is quite impossible that you would never have heard of him! When he donated that first carriage to His Majesty King George III he received his knighthood, of course."

"Oh, I've heard of Ben Franklin all right," Teresa said with an odd smile. "Early to bed and early to rise, and all that. But do you think we could get something to drink before we talk any more? I'm really thirsty after that run!"

"Of course," I said, "Gerry's Gelato is just a few blocks up South Street, towards the river."

"Well, let's go then," she said, marching straight off into the middle of King George Boulevard without a backward glance. She looked the wrong way when crossing the street, but fortunately there was no traffic at the moment, and she did not stop till she reached the other side. "Well?" she called. "Aren't you coming?"

I started after her, annoyed. "We drive on the left, unlike the Imperials. Do try to remember! And how can you not know that it is proper to offer a gentleman your arm, instead of just stomping on ahead of him?" Even Jo minds her manners that much!

She started to laugh, then said, "By God, you're serious."

"And do not take the Lord's name in vain, either!" The pastor is the nicest bloke I have ever met, but blasphemy is one thing that upsets him.

"I'm sorry," she said, looking genuinely abashed. "Tom, customs are really very different in my America. I promise I'll try hard to fit in here." She stuck out her right elbow awkwardly. "Is this what you meant by offering you my arm?"

I hooked my left arm through hers and smiled, forcing it a bit. "Good enough. It is strange to be walking out with a girl without a chaperone, though."

"Chaperones? Really? You all have chaperones?"

"Well, decent people do anyway," I muttered, looking at the ground and blushing. Curtis and Martha did not have a chaperone. Was I calling Martha indecent, then? Or even Curtis, for that matter? He was a little rough around the edges, but he had not actually peached on me as I thought he would. It was true, people were a little freer and easier in Philadelphia than back home in Gingo Teag.

"I don't mean to embarrass you, Tom," Teresa said. When I kept staring at the ground she reached out and lifted my chin with her hand, still cool to the touch. "Tom. Look. It's probably a little strange for you—it's damn strange for me, I mean darn strange—but why don't we just consider Gloria to be our chaperone? She seems to know everything that's going on with us anyway."

"True enough," I said. "All right, the gelato is waiting for us." On that at least, we could agree.

* * * *

Gerry's was over-crowded, and as we walked in I began to be afraid that I would see somebody from school. I could not decide what worried me more, my embarrassment about Teresa's strangeness or the danger of changing the past and destroying the entire universe. I glanced at Teresa. *The embarrassment.* But it was too late to turn back now, and there were so many people that I doubted we would receive too many stares. I ordered my favourite, Liberty Bean, and asked Teresa what she liked.

"I'm a girl. Chocolate," she said simply.

I hoped I had enough money for that. Chocolate is very expensive, since Mexico has been part of the Empire forever and the South American republics are always having wars and coups. Like the Florida "constabulary conflict" that poor Jason Marks died in—just a week before the armistice was signed, too. I have never had the nerve to ask Reverend Marks if that somehow makes it worse.

I said that to Mum once and she just shook her head. "Dead is dead, Tom sweetheart. Poor Reverend Marks and his wife did not deserve to lose their son, even if he *does* wear the dog-collar." Mum does not have much use for organized religion, thanks to all those "Goddess of Reason" services she attended as a girl in the Home Islands.

But I shook off the morbid thought, fished around in my pocket, and pulled out half-a-crown. We found a bench under a fenced-in beech tree outside and sat side by side, spooning our gelato out of the little paper dishes that resemble upside-down bells.

"This is really nice, but it seems more like ice cream than gelato to me," she said.

I frowned. "Ice cream? What is that?"

She giggled, displaying chocolatey teeth. "Now you're putting me on."

"Do you mean I am joking with you? Absolutely not! Ice cream? You mean to tell me your people take a bowl of cream, put some crushed ice in it, and drink the whole thing?"

She giggled again, covering her mouth with her hand. Her eyes sparkled. She was… Without allowing myself to think about what I was doing, I leaned toward her, pulled her hand away, and kissed her right on the lips. I could not seem to stop, either. When I did pull back, we stared at each other with big, astonished eyes.

"You do that in front of a chaperone?" Teresa asked softly.

* * * *

It was kind of a stupid thing to say, but I wasn't expecting him to kiss me. He looked terrified after he'd done it, too, so I had to grab him in a quick hug.

"It's okay," I said, trying for a husky whisper. "You taste like vanilla. I like vanilla, too."

"Come on, then," he said, glancing around nervously at the people walking past, none of whom seemed to be paying us any attention. "We had best be on our way."

I was really getting to like that oddball accent of his. The people in the ice cream shop sounded a little different from him, but not like any Philadelphians I'd ever met. Their vowels were a bit broader, almost Midwestern. *Thaank you*, they said. *Mooch obleeged.* It was cute. But South Street was almost the same; back home it's a funky shopping street, too, and closing it to cars—carriages, I guess I should say—seemed like a great idea.

I have to admit that the flag flying over their version of City Hall brought me up short, though. Also the giant statue of "Sir Ben" Franklin.

"What are you looking at?" he asked, following my gaze.

"The flag," I said.

"The Union Bars-and-Stars? It has looked like this for about one hundred and fifty years, when the design was adopted during William Seward's premiership."

I was hardly listening. The banner looked like the bastard child of my world's Union Jack and the Confederate battle flag, which still found a comfy home on the rear bumpers of pickup trucks everywhere. There were interlocking red crosses on a blue field, like the familiar British flag, but also quite a few white stars, like on the Confederate flag—sixteen or seventeen, it looked like.

My stomach did a slow somersault, as if there'd been something spoiled in my ice cream. I turned to Tom. He gazed back at me innocently.

"Tom, I need to ask you something," I said and bit my lip.

"Yes?"

There was no tactful way of putting this. "Tom, in your country you—well, what I mean to say is—you don't keep slaves, do you?"

He looked at me blankly, then began to laugh. "Slaves?" he chuckled. "Slaves? No, Teresa," he said. "We do not keep slaves. Not for more than two hundred years. Prime Minister Wilberforce made certain of that."

I giggled with relief. I'm really not cut out to be Abe Lincoln. Then what he had said sank in a bit and I stopped laughing.

"Now what is the matter?" he asked.

"It would take too long to explain. Some other time," I said, thinking of the battle of Gettysburg, and the civil rights marchers beaten on that bridge in Selma, Alabama. Whose world was ahead of whose?

"Right, then," he shrugged, and pulled out his watch. "We still have almost three hours. Shall we?" He bent his elbow outward this time, and I slipped my arm through his. I liked walking along beside him. After a while, he asked me why I was so quiet. I shrugged.

"Everything here is just so strange," I said. "I mean, I thought I had it figured out. You never had the Revolution here, so you stayed part of England—"

"Thanks to Sir Ben," he said as proudly as if he were the old goat's great-grandson. "Sorry. Do go on."

"And Napoleon conquered Europe for good. I got all that. And then you tell me there are dragons…"

"I grew up right across the water from Assa Teag Ashley," he said. He smiled as if she were a member of his family, too.

I returned his smile for a moment.

"It's just so strange," I said, and shivered. "A famous scientist in my world once said, 'The universe is not only stranger than we know, it is stranger than we *can* know.' I never really understood what that meant till now. And then there's Gloria, and you… How do I know you won't turn out to have twelve heads and exist in twenty different dimensions, like her?"

"I think it was eleven dimensions she said she had," he replied, and thumped his chest with his free hand. "And there is no need to worry about me. I am just plain old three-dimensional Tom Purnell."

"Okay then, I'll take your word for it."

He frowned. "You are prone to using that expression. What does it mean?"

"What? To take your word for something?"

"No. *Oh-kay*. What does it mean?"

I explained. It was the little things like that that made Tom's world so strange to me. But then there were a bunch of other things that were so normal, like when we arrived at the riverbank and I watched the clouds floating in a blue sky over the New Jersey shore.

The Garden State, or Garden Colony or whatever they called it here, looked a lot prettier on this side of Gloria's gateway. Camden was country-like instead of a huge slum—I could see a whole row of flowering dogwood trees on the opposite bank.

Landmarks weren't in the right places; for example, we should have been sitting almost in the shadow of the Ben Franklin Bridge, a few blocks to the north, but it just wasn't there. But old Ben had enough other stuff named after him in this world, it seemed, and we hadn't had to pass under the roaring, stinking mess of the Delaware Expressway to get to the river's edge, so all in all it seemed like an improvement.

As the hours went by I told Tom all about my screwed-up family life. About Nana dying suddenly of a stroke and Dad leaving us for Heathery pastures all in the same horrible year when I was in tenth grade.

About Mom working two jobs and how I admired her and pitied her and wanted to get away from her as fast as possible, all at the same time. About how I'd just found out about this awful thing she'd done, keeping Dad's letters from me.

Tom told me all about his family. His annoying little genius of a kid sister, Jo, who drove him crazy though he loved her more than anyone. His "mum" with her mysterious past. His dad with his mysterious research job that he expected Tom to follow him into, only Tom didn't want to. The closed little world of Gingo Teag Island, where everyone treated him like a "come-here" even though he'd lived there all his life, so that he'd been so eager to go to St. George's Academy in the big city, only everyone *there* treated him like an outsider, too. How his roommate Curtis was always bringing his girlfriend Martha over (Tom blushed and looked away from me), so that Tom ended up hanging around the library more than his own room, "though I have been repaid with excellent marks this year."

I did great in school too, I told him, but I also didn't have any idea what I wanted to do afterward. College seems so terrifying and expensive, and these days there's not necessarily a job waiting for you when you graduate. In a way Tom had the opposite problem: his future was all too certain.

"What does your dad actually do, anyway?" I asked.

Tom made a face. "Oh, that. Heavier-than-air travel, believe it or not. They think they can draw inspiration from working near Assa Teag Ashley's lair. Maybe they have, because Dad just told me when he was here last weekend that he will soon have big news for me."

"Heavier-than-air travel," I said.

"Yeah. Ridiculous, is it not? I mean, even if it was possible, why would anyone *want* to replace airships?"

I sprawled on the pier under the warm setting sun, giggling helplessly.

"What is so funny?" Tom said at last.

"Oh, Tom. We've had heavier-than-air travel for, like, over a hundred years where I come from. I've been on planes myself twice." Once when we went to Disneyworld when I was five, and once when Dad took me on a business trip to San Francisco. We had such fun. I stopped laughing.

"Planes?" Tom asked. "You mean you travel on giant flat surfaces, like flying carpets?"

"No, silly," I said. Maybe I still looked sad, because Tom leaned over and kissed me. That was *nice.* So nice I hated to pull away long enough to explain what an airplane is. It was surprisingly hard. Tom didn't quite believe me, and I began to doubt that giant metal machines could ever get off the ground, much less carry people thousands of miles without even stopping to refuel.

I mean, when you stop and think about it, most of us don't have any idea how most of the stuff we use works. Even the computer geeks I sometimes hang out with can't really explain how pressing a bunch of plastic keys on a keyboard can send words around the world. I certainly can't explain it, or tell you how a television works—and I started to wonder if Tom's world had those things, either.

"There's an airship right now," Tom said, pointing at something float-ing high above the river.

I looked up. Through the swirling bands of orange and rose that decorated the sunset sky, a silver object like a stretched-out football was drifting southward, toward Delaware Bay. I couldn't tell how big it was until I glanced down at the river's surface. An enormous shadow that seemed to take up most of the river's width moved swiftly downstream. I shivered. It looked like the shadow of that thing that had been chasing us back in the Zone. A better name for that would be the shadow land, but no doubt Gloria had wanted to keep us from being afraid. Another grown-up assumed she knew what was best for me! Just like my mother. I took a deep breath and turned back to Tom.

"It's beautiful," I said. The airship drifted lower. A flag was painted on its side, three thick vertical bands of blue, white, and red with a golden eagle in the center.

"It would be beautiful, except for that flag," Tom growled.

"Oh, that's the French flag, isn't it?" I said.

"There has not been a country called France in more than two hun-dred years—just the Empire," Tom said. "You should hear Madame Dantès go on about it. She is my French teacher, a Parisian lady through and through, but she is a refugee here because the Empire does not like dissidents. They called her a traitor, which puts her in some very fine company, like Victor Hugo."

"Well, the sky is sure beautiful," I responded. Lame, lame, lame. But I didn't really want to talk politics. It sounded just as awful as in the real world.

"Not just the sky," Tom mumbled.

"Hmm? Not just the sky what?"

"Is beautiful."

"What?"

He smiled a little and kept staring at me.

Oh. "Oh, no. No, you can't mean me." Me, with my fat butt and tucked-in chin, and pimple scars all over my face, beautiful? It was too ridiculous. I shook my head.

But Tom shut me up with a kiss. I could get used to that. Everything around me, the bright orange sky, the silver river, the pier and the people walking past were doing the old tilt-a-whirl, as slowly and steadily as that "airship" was flying across the sky. I closed my eyes and let the slow spin continue in my head.

Then the warm, firm pressure of Tom's lips stopped. I opened my eyes.

"I think," he said, clearing his throat and patting his hair—had I messed it up?—"that we had best be on our way. It is growing dark, and my watch indicates that the time is…half-past-nine in real time," he said.

As he studied his pocket-watch he reminded me of a drawing I'd once seen of the White Rabbit in *Alice in Wonderland.*

"I don't think there is any such thing as real time," I said as we walked hand in hand toward South Street. "This is just as real as the time we left, isn't it? I mean, I *hope* so. It's like relativity. Miss Chen explained in class last year…"

A tall, thin, middle-aged man stepped into our path. He looked like a fussy old teacher—glasses, wrinkled face, thinning gray hair even messier than Tom's.

"Tom, my dear boy," he said, putting his hands on Tom's shoulders. He turned to me and smiled, a little grin that started out at the left corner of his mouth and rapidly spread across his whole face. "And dear, dear Teresa," he added. "How wonderful to see you both." His accent sounded more like standard British than anything I'd heard so far, but still not quite right. "I say, good show that I ran into you two. I'm afraid *our friends* are up to no good once again. Meet me at my offices in the university tomorrow morning. If you don't have school, that is!"

"Your offices at the university?" Tom echoed.

"Yes, didn't you know? I am now a guest lecturer at Franklin University. Here is my visiting card," he said, drawing a little leather case out of the pocket of his beige sport coat and handing us business cards that looked as if someone had hand-printed each letter. "Ramsey Urquhart, Ph.D., Guest Lecturer in Biology, Franklin University." There was an address and a "voicegram" number.

There is no Franklin University in Philadelphia in the real world. I knew that for sure, since I'd been researching local colleges.

"Must run along now," the stranger said. As he was walking away he turned and said, "I—I don't think I ever properly thanked you for what you did, Tom, Teresa. I owe you my life!" Then, with an odd little salute of his right hand off his forehead, he was gone.

Tom and I looked at each other. "I have never," said Tom, "seen that man before in my life."

I shook my head. "I suppose it goes without saying that I haven't, either."

"I think we had best get back," Tom said again, glancing around nervously.

"Good idea," I said, and we started to walk faster. "Tom," I said after a moment, "you presumed earlier that Gloria had sent us back in time, right?"

"Ye-es," he said, drawing the word out. "Just a minute." He stopped at a newsstand, which was made of dark, polished, sturdy-looking wood, and bought a copy of the *Philadelphia Bulletin*, a paper I'd never heard of.

"Hey, what do you need another copy of the paper for?" the newsstand owner said.

Tom looked at him, and they both shrugged. The headline said something about "dragonets." We stared at the date. It was six months in the future. Tom dropped the paper as if it was on fire, and the pages blew away in a sudden gust of wind. There was a rumble of thunder, and the newsstand owner reached up and pulled down his shutters. We began to run, still holding hands, as a downpour started. A downpour with hail that hurt when it hit.

"I know about this!" I shouted over the noise—it sounded like we were inside an enormous metal garbage can full of gravel.

"What?"

"I know about this! What's happening! I've read about it! We're not supposed to travel in time! The universe will stop us! We're going to get hit by a bolt of lightning or something!"

"Not if I can help it!" he shouted and pulled me into a doorway. We were both sopping wet. He grabbed hold of me and kissed me again.

I tried to pull away. "Don't you ever think of anything else?" I said, but then I grabbed him with both arms. Our lips met again. I used my tongue.

Someone cleared her throat.

We pulled apart and looked around. We were back in Gloria's bookstore! She was looking at us and smiling. Now her gown was a midnight blue, and her hair was up in an elaborate 'do that looked like it took hours to create.

"Well," she said after a moment, "it appears you two have now been properly introduced."

9

I was so busy daydreaming about Teresa the following morning that when I was called to the deputy headmaster's office it came as a surprise. Allowing one's mind wander in French class might be ordinary behaviour for some, but it certainly is not for me. I am Madame Dantès' star student—not that there is much competition.

We were reading The Count of Monte Cristo (*je suis désolé, madame*, I meant *Le Comte de Monte-Cristo*), Alexandre Dumas' great adventure novel, which Madame Dantès has insisted is not real literature, "though the poor man did suffer so, so many years in prison at the Emperor's command." Besides, she likes to huff, after he was released and exiled to Louisiana, his French became quite corrupt, being polluted with the dread "Créole jargon." I never quite dared ask her whether he should therefore have stayed in prison in France.

But my mind was not occupied with Dumas at the moment, neither *père* nor *fils*, it was occupied with Teresa and when she and I would have our next "date," as she called walking out. We were both "freaked out," another useful expression I had learned from her, by our encounter with the mysterious Professor Urquhart, and we did not wish to use Gloria's time-bending abilities again. She had loved visiting my world, and I could not wait to visit hers, but seeing our own pasts and futures? Frightening.

Even Gloria had seemed worried about tinkering with time. "You didn't see anyone you knew while you were out, did you?" she asked as I sat in front of the bookstore counter in a fluffy white bathrobe while my clothes dried on a radiator.

I forced myself not to look at Teresa. "No," I said truthfully, "no one I knew."

Gloria visibly relaxed. "That's good," she said. "I was taking a bit of a chance sending you into what you would call your own future. Higher dimensional beings like me have no trouble, of course, but you 4-D folk are liable to trip over your own feet."

The visiting card still rested in the pocket of my trousers, but I said nothing, leaving it to Teresa to ask shyly when we might see each other again. Gloria smiled and said that was up to us.

"But we can't get back and forth to each other's worlds without you," Teresa pointed out.

"I can be here whenever you need me to be," Gloria said.

Teresa glanced at me. I shrugged and said, "Saturday morning, immediately after flag-raising? About nine o'clock?"

"Okay," Teresa said. "This time, can I show you my Philadelphia, Tom?"

"Nothing would give me greater pleasure."

She smiled—she had already confessed she thought I "talked funny," but she found it charming. "You might be disappointed when you do," she said.

"Impossible, if you are to be my tour guide."

"All right, kids, that's quite enough for the first date, I think. Your clothes should be dry by now anyway," Gloria said. "Now, I did move you just a little bit in the fourth dimension—about an hour backward, you would call it—so it's only nine o'clock the night you left. Early enough that neither of you will get in trouble, I hope."

We agreed that was fine, and after dressing—I ducked behind some bookshelves—Teresa and I hugged quickly. Our lips brushed.

"You take care of yourself," Teresa said, fingering my palm. I blinked as her touch sent tiny electric shocks through my body.

"Until we meet again," I said.

Gloria ushered her toward the back. I turned and walked quickly out the door, not wanting to hear the odd sounds of Teresa being taken back to her world. Outside, the November chill had returned. We had forgotten to tell Gloria about the thing that had chased us. Was it still around?

"No, I am not afraid," I said to myself, then said it aloud, for all the world like the Fraidy Lion. "I am off to see the Witch, the Wondrous Witch of Oz!" But I was cold, that was certain. I had left my coat in the bookstore before setting off into next summer, so it had remained dry, but the cold settled into my bones.

Shadows flickered at the edges of my vision as I marched along. I recited the climactic scene with Dorothy and Glinda, the Good Witch of the North: "So you mean the wondrous witch I've been searching for all along is me?"

"That's all it is, my dear," I said, in Glinda's saccharine voice. "When you help your friends and they help you, you are as powerful a witch as any ever seen in the Land of Oz!"

But the flying monkeys were after me, and I hurried my footsteps. Gloria had been as good as her word; I crept into my room with a good twenty minutes to spare before lights-out and bed check, in time to say good night to Martha.

"So when are you bringing Teresa around?" she asked with a smile.

"Yeah, when? I must see this girl who's crazy enough to walk out with Purnell," Curtis said, earning an elbow in the ribs from Martha.

"I meant to this time," I said, "but we were out far later than I thought we would be." *True enough, Tommy.*

* * * *

None of this, of course, was enough to save me from the Wrath of Squeal the next morning. He stalked into my French class with blood in his eye and crooked a finger at me, ignoring Madame.

I winced, as did the rest of the class, not because of what was going to happen to me but because of what was going to happen to *him*. Madame's tongue could thin-slice beef at fifty paces.

"To what," she asked icily, "do I owe the pleasure of this visit, *Monsieur* Thiel?"

He started. Had he forgotten that she was there?

"My pardons, Juliette. Master Purnell here is required to report to the office for punishment."

"I will not pardon your rudeness and insolence, *Monsieur* Thiel. I do not barge into your classroom and interrupt your veni-vidi-vicis, do I, my little Nero of the Delaware?"

"What? Um, no," Thiel said, as suppressed laughter ran through the class. We sounded like a pack of squirrels up in the attic. Both teachers favoured us with fisheyed glares and we stifled our chuckles.

"Master Purnell was just about to explain to the class, in French most perfect, the theme of last night's reading. After he is finished, you may have him for your disgusting little caning."

"Um. Thank you?"

"Which as we all know, gives you *such* pleasure," Madame said.

There was a muffled gasp at this; even amongst ourselves we scarcely dared say such things above a whisper. Thiel turned a sort of pale brick color but didn't move. Madame turned and looked at me, but then she glanced to her left where Thiel stood rooted to the spot.

"Are you still here, *Monsieur* Caesar manqué?"

"I—I—I am just waiting for Master Purnell to finish reciting so that I can escort him to my office."

"When Master Purnell finishes, he can find his own way to your… den," Madame said. "You may go there now yourself, *monsieur*."

Squeal squeaked and scurried away. He would make me pay for his humiliation, but it was worth it.

* * * *

Satisfaction must have shown on my face as I stumbled out of his office, because Adams, passing by in the hall, demanded to know why I was looking so pleased.

"I've never seen anyone hobble and smirk at the same time," he said. "What gives, Infernal?"

I scowled and tried to walk past, but he reached out and pushed me in the chest again. I stood still.

"Something the matter with your hearing, Infernal? Thiel cane you on the head or something?" As if by magic, Madison and Monroe appeared at his side. Monroe was walking almost as stiffly as me. Adams sneered.

"Kind of a shame for you and Jimmy, isn't it? I mean, Thiel wouldn't dare touch me or Jack."

I gritted my teeth. Half my classes were in the brand-new Adams Building, largely paid for by my tormentor's father, and I walked to them on the Madison Pathway, named in honor of Jack's grandfather, a big manufacturer and longtime benefactor of the school.

I had heard enough. "Pity about the election, *ne c'est pas,* Adams, old boy?" I said. "Looks as if Daddy has gone from being 'the next prime minister' to looking for a job."

Adams Senior had lost his own riding in the general rout the Tories had suffered in September. Adams Junior knocked me over with a single punch. I hit my head on the floor and lay there, my ears ringing.

* * * *

Now Thiel leaned over me, his ugly face twisted in annoyance and—could it be fear?

What was he saying? I couldn't hear. Oh, he was asking if I was all right. His concern was touching if a bit self-interested.

I sat up, still dizzy; questions might be asked if one of his whipping boys walked out of a session with him and promptly lost consciousness.

"Quite well, thank you," I said, allowing him to pull me upright with his clammy hands. "Just slipped and fell. They must have put on too much floor wax, I think."

"A bit too much ear wax, more like," Thiel growled. "Get along with you!"

"Yes sir, Your Hypocrisy," I muttered as I slouched away toward my next class. I paused under the fancy archway dedicated by Geoffrey "Mad Battery" Madison, who had gone quite as mad as his own workers from the mercury he used in manufacturing carriage-batteries. The school logo was painted on its keystone, a shield with a stylized depiction of St George running his sword through a dragon that looked nothing like

Assa Teag Ashley. Why was I studying at a school that defined itself as the enemy of my home town's guiding spirit?

When I returned to my room Curtis sat on his bed, alone, studying, and a voicegram waited for me. I have always wished there was some way to tell who is sending them, so that one could avoid all the people one does not wish to hear from in the first place. Maybe if each voicegram made a little chirping noise before it was opened, for instance. Chirp, chirp, I am a voicegram from Mum! Chirp, chirp, I am a voicegram from the King! Chirp, chirp, I am from your bratty little sister! But of course they do not do that. And this one was just an ordinary voicegram, oblong, six inches long, and gunmetal gray, with my name scrawled on it in erasable marker. I sighed and broke it open. Of course it was Option Number 3.

"Hey Tommy boy, you broke your promise to tell me what it was like walking out with an alien girl!" Jo's voice said. "Does she have purple skin and three eyes? Does she slither instead of walk? Or did she have an attack of good sense at the last minute and stand you up?"

I poked the reply button in the capsule's belly, wishing it was Jo's belly, and said, "I had a great time walking out with Teresa, thank you very much. She looks like a kinetoflick star and has more class than you shall ever have, sis!" Then I closed it up and shoved it back in the tube. The pneumatic hiss-whine sounded as it started on its journey back to Gingo Teag.

"That's no way to talk to your little sister," Curtis said. "I handle mine with threats."

"Your expertise with girls is unquestioned, Curtis," I sighed. "So where is Martha?"

He waved a dismissive hand. "Off shopping on South Street, I think. I'm sure she'll look fabulous when she gets here. Perhaps she could give *your* girl some fashion pointers. I have little doubt she needs them."

"How can you insult someone you have never even met?" I demanded.

"Easy," he smiled, "her taste in men tells me everything I need to know about her. So why was your sister babbling about her having three legs and purple skin, anyway? Your girl got a complexion problem or something?"

"Curtis, why not pay your books some attention. I know they are starved for it," I snapped.

Then I frowned. I still had to give the pastor the book I had found for him. I did not want him asking me questions of whose answers I was unsure. I grabbed the book, which I had wrapped in leftover wrapping paper (I am like Dad that way—I never throw anything out) and hurried out the door.

As expected, Reverend Marks was in his rooms behind the chapel, watering his plants and checking the grow-lights before heading home for the evening. He raises orchids and certain rare breeds of roses back there, sometimes with the help of favourite students, who are always teased for being suck ups, though I have never understood why—having Reverend Marks in your corner does not count for anything at St George's, despite the school's name. Still, I was almost as proud as he when his Royal Blues took third place in Parliament's famous annual flower show last February, though all I received for my pains was having my books and papers drenched in weed killer, no doubt the work of Adams & Co.

Mr Marks greeted me affably enough. "I've missed you this week and last, my boy," he said, straightening up and dusting off his trousers.

"Yes. I am sorry about that. I brought you a present to make up for it," I said, handing him the wrapped book. He almost dropped it when I put it in his hands.

"What could possibly be so heavy? Is it an addition for my rock garden?" he smiled.

"No, sir. I bought it at the bookstore I told you about."

He tore at the paper with an eagerness undignified in a clergyman. The poor man cannot help himself when it comes to books. He fumbled out his Franklin lenses.

"*War and Peace*, by Leo Tolstoy," he read aloud from the cover, then opened it to read the jacket copy. "How extraordinary! It says here that this Tolstoy was a Russian count! Have you ever heard of such a thing? The first Napoleon abolished the Russian aristocracy as soon as he had subdued the country, you know."

"I know, sir, I do pay attention in history class."

"Quite. Sorry, my boy. What an extraordinary idea! I can only assume that 'Count Leo Tolstoy' is a pen name."

"Perhaps," I said. "The book is a crazy fantasy where the Emperor lost his war against Russia. Maybe the author is a French dissident, like Madame."

"Could be, yes. I'm sure I'll know more once I read it. Well, young Thomas, tell me how much I owe you for the book, and I shan't keep you any longer. Unless you'd care to come back to our house for dinner?"

I could not risk the questioning that would come with the meal, so I said I had too much studying to do. "But you must not pay me anything for the book, sir," I added.

"That's very generous, Thomas, but I know schoolboys are always short on cash. How much do I owe you?" he asked, jingling the coins in his pocket.

I looked at the floor. "Nothing, honestly," I mumbled, as the tips of my ears caught fire. How could I possibly explain to him about Gloria, and Granny's comb? There was no way of doing that, and Reverend Marks did not pursue the matter. The book would keep him occupied and distract him from questioning me too closely for a while, though, and if after he finished it, he still wanted to visit Gloria's Gateway Books—or wanted to visit it all the more—well, I could worry about it then.

My chief problem now was to make it to the end of the week. If only I could send Teresa a voicegram to tell her how much I missed her. I counted down the hours, falling asleep Friday night to a droning voice in my head saying, "Six hours, thirty-seven minutes *and counting...*"

* * * *

As soon as I opened my eyes to sunlight I dressed and hurried down to the square for flag raising, after which I raced off campus so fast I no doubt left a cloud of dust behind me. Gloria was standing there smiling at me when I burst through the door of the bookstore.

"Catch your breath," she said, "I'm not going anywhere." She handed me my tea, and I sipped it.

"All right then," she said, "are you ready?"

"Of course," I said.

She looked me over thoroughly, from head to toe and back again, then stepped toward me and adjusted my collar. I was wearing my St George's blazer with a white shirt under it, a pair of freshly pressed trousers—I had ironed them myself last night, ignoring Curtis' teasing, which was jolly decent of me, considering that I would have been within my rights to make him do it—and my best pair of shiny black loafers, which I had polished myself.

"Do I look all right?" I stammered.

She stepped back and looked me over again. "Honey, you are *cute*," she said.

It is a wonder I did not melt into an embarrassed puddle on her floor.

"Come on," she said, holding out her hand. I hesitated, and she cocked her head and peered at me. "What's the matter?"

"It is not right for me to embrace a woman other than Teresa," I mumbled

"Oh," she said. "All right. Hold on a second." She vanished toward the back, and a moment later reappeared as Tiferet, rubbing herself against my legs and purring.

I must admit I flinched, but then I reached down and scratched behind her ears. She leapt up on the countertop so I could stroke her head, but that only made me more uncomfortable.

"I do apologize," I said, "but I keep thinking of how you look in human form and you are, well, you are quite attractive." I could only get the words out because I was talking to a cat, after all. "It would not be proper of me...*you* know."

At that Tiferet put her nose up, jumped back to the floor and padded off. I followed her through the doorway in the bookshelves into the darkened back room, only to be hit in the face by a furry cannonball. I grabbed at it wildly, and then I lost my senses. The books on the shelves all turned inside out, the shelves themselves reassembled themselves in impossible positions, I saw my own insides red and pulsing and connected to each other in impossible ways. My screams sounded wrong, rolling out flatly as if I was standing on an open plain at night.

I lost consciousness, coming to on my back on the floor, Teresa leaning over me. Teresa frowned, and Gloria stood further back, her hands behind her back, looking half abashed and half mischievous, as if she had planned the whole thing. Which she probably had.

"Are you all right?" Teresa asked.

I groaned.

She put her right hand behind my back and her left hand on my chest and helped me sit. I clutched my stomach and groaned. I had *seen* my insides.

Teresa flinched but held onto me.

"Don't worry, I'm not going to vomit," I said, and turned what I hoped was a reproachful glare on Gloria. "No thanks to her."

"I'm sorry," she said, the corners of her mouth twitching. "You didn't want me to hold you in this form, so what else was I supposed to do?"

"You could have meowed or something," I said, leaning heavily on Teresa as I stood up.

"Next time I shall try to remember that," Gloria said, clasping her hands together as she favoured us with a wide-eyed gaze. "I am sorry, my dears. I forget sometimes how limited you poor four-dimensionals are. But come, adventure awaits you!"

"Come on," Teresa said, tugging on my hand. "Unless you want to wait for her to play some other dirty trick on us."

She immediately released my hand, however, and stalked ahead of me through the Zone. Could it be that she was jealous of Gloria? I hurried after her. What could I say? But why was she piqued? After all, we would never even have met each other without Gloria, would we?

I hurried to catch her when a shadow passed low overhead. I grabbed Teresa by the shoulders and pushed her to the ground as something flew low enough to ladle a hot, stinking wind over us. We both began to gag.

"Crawl forward," I said between coughs, "and hold your shirt over your nose and mouth."

Teresa nodded and we both began to crawl along the street. This close to the ground, there was something not quite real about the pavement. What had appeared to be ordinary, slightly worn cobblestones felt rough beneath the palms of my hands, like sandpaper, and yet somehow yielding, as if a thin layer painted to look like cobblestones had been laid over a gigantic bowl of gelatin. Rotten gelatin, at that—a smell like spoilt food mixed with the stink of low tide back on Gingo Teag made me start choking all over again.

"We'd better get out of here," Teresa wheezed, "I think that thing is using chemical warfare on us."

I nodded. What on earth was *chemical warfare?* It was growing darker and darker, the light blocked by something large. *Like giant wings?* With a burst of effort I crawled ahead and caught Teresa's hand in mine. Her palm was cold and clammy.

I wanted to tell her it was all right, I would protect her from whatever was after us, but my throat was too dry for me to speak, so I contented myself with squeezing her hand. She squeezed back.

And without warning, it was finished and we were lying side by side, gasping, on the sidewalk in Teresa's Philadelphia. People stepped right over us, without even asking who we were, why we were crawling on the ground, or whether we needed help. I was shocked when Teresa told me this was nothing to be surprised about. Fortunately I was fine, and I quickly got to my feet and helped Teresa to hers.

"Where are we?" Everyone and everything seemed to be moving at once. Someone bumped into me and walked on without even begging my pardon. Despite the overcast sky there was light everywhere—not a single bright light but thousands of lights of all sizes and colours, in the shop windows, on the fronts of the moving carriages, in the tiny black or silver slabs like miniature cigarillo cases that everyone seemed to be holding in their hands or pressing up to their ears. Perhaps they were trying to block out the noise, which would make sense because the din was awful—a roaring, shrieking, bleating, beeping, shouting, trilling, shrilling cacophony that made me want to press my hands to my ears. I did so only to find that I had no hand free to block the stench from my nose—a smell of burning that was all around, inescapable even inside the shop Teresa quickly dragged me into, though she claimed she didn't smell anything.

"How can you not?" I gagged. "It's almost as bad as it was in the Zone."

She shook her head and asked the figure behind the counter for a bottle of water. A girl our age stared openly at me. I stared back as she handed me my water, then blushed and looked away. She had obviously suffered some kind of horrible accident, judging by the metal shards embedded in her lips, nose, and tongue. Also, her hair stood up in uneven spikes, with stripes the colour of the rising sun. In a flash I understood what was wrong.

I leaned over and whispered in Teresa's ear, "Chemical warfare."

She gaped at me. "What?" she whispered back.

"That chemical warfare you mentioned. That must explain the smell! And this poor girl is a victim, is she not?"

Teresa stared at me a moment longer, her mouth slightly open. Then she shook her head and said, "Come on," grabbed hold of my hand and dragged me out into the street. "There a T-shirt place down the block. It'll be quiet enough in there to explain a few things to you."

"What is a T-shirt?" I asked, picturing a jersey with a giant capital letter T stenciled on it. I was wrong again, of course. At least Teresa was right that there were few customers for the flimsy, trashy-looking clothing they had for sale, seeing that it was almost winter. She pulled me to the back, where a rack of denim trousers were so badly made they all had rips in the knees. I pointed this out in wonder and she shook her head again.

"No, they're supposed to be like that," she said. "They actually cost more than if they weren't ripped." She scowled and stuck her hands in the pockets of her own denims. Why was she wearing denim trousers instead of a skirt when we were walking out together? Never mind. "Mom won't let me buy anything like that, of course. If she had the money, she'd send to me Catholic school and I'd have to wear a stupid uniform instead."

I frowned. "D-does your mother not know that I am walking out with you?" I asked.

Teresa avoided my gaze. "Umm, not exactly."

"And your father?" I could not understand what Teresa mumbled in response.

She stared fixedly at the shop floor.

"What did you say?" I asked as gently as I could.

She raised her head and glared at me. "I said, my parents are divorced! Divorced, okay? I'm a freaky girl from a broken home!"

"Divorced?" I echoed stupidly. So few people get divorced where I come from. But poor thing, she looked so miserable I drew her close and hugged her as hard as I could, apologising over and over again, kissing the tears off her pale, soft face.

Far from pushing me away, she hugged me back. Then she tilted up her face and we kissed on the lips. I glanced toward the street. Was someone watching? No.

So you can kiss in public in Teresa's world and they will not bother you, or you can lie down in the street and die and they will not bother you, either.

"What are you thinking?" she asked, looking up at me. I told her, stammering a little.

"Yeah, I guess things are sort of different here from what you're used to," she said.

"Yes! Exactly. That is why I was so confused—you see, back home on Gingo Teag, if I wanted to walk out with a girl I would have to talk to her parents first, and they would have to give permission, after meeting with my parents first, of course."

"Of course," she said, smiling. "And they do this in your version of Philadelphia, too?"

"Well, matters are a little less formal in the city," I admitted, offering her my arm. "Shall we go?"

Outside the sky was clearing, and a beam of sunlight lit Teresa's face as she explained how matters worked in her version of Philadelphia. It was too much to take in at first. Nothing but overwhelming chaos. I may not have wished to adhere to all of my parents' rules or those of St George's, but would I really want to make up all my own rules? It might be amusing, but it also sounded frightening. Not that I was going to say that to her, of course. She probably thought that I was a timid soul.

So I changed the subject and asked her about the strange-looking carriages in the street and those cigarillo packs everyone seemed to be carrying. Petroleum-burning automobiles? And that was what a cell phone looked like? Teresa repeatedly apologised for her poor explinations. Her explanations were not poor, yet how I could ever grow accustomed to the choking fumes from the petroleum-burning *cars*, even if they were faster than carriages?

"Cars are a lot better than they used to be," she said defensively. "Some of them are even part-electric now."

"*Our* carriages have been electrical ever since Dr Franklin invented the carriage-battery more than two hundred years ago," I pointed out.

She stuck out her chin. "Well, in our world Ben was too busy helping write the Constitution," she said. "Not to mention posing for the hundred-dollar bill and partying in Paris." Then she had to explain about the "American" Constitution and "American" money. It was hard to fathom and utterly unexpected, except for Sir Benjamin's (who was just plain

Ben Franklin in Teresa's world) naughty behavior in Paris. That was true in the real history I learnt, too.

10

I didn't want Tom ever to leave, especially after he told me about his scariest run-in yet with what we called "the Zone monsters."

"Come to my house," I begged him as it started to get dark. We were walking along Broad Street—King George Boulevard, to him—trying to ignore the bitter wind leaking in through our jackets. I snuggled closer to him and said, "I'll hide you in my room. Mom doesn't come in anymore."

But he shook his head. "I have to get back, and so do you. Your mum will be quite irate if she finds out you were walking out with a boy, right?"

"Well yeah, but you're going to be really *dead* if one of those monsters gets you, right?"

"Somehow I doubt Gloria will let that happen. Please do not worry on my account, my love. Go on home."

My love? I blinked, repeating the words to myself. I looked up. Tom was walking quickly away, toward the Zone.

"Hey!" I yelled, but he didn't turn around. His cap, a bright cheery red one he'd said his "mum" had knitted for him, disappeared around a corner. That cap was a perfect target. I ran after him. But I couldn't find the Zone! Everything was just ordinary Philadelphia streets. Frantic, I wandered as night fell and the streetlights came on, but there was no sign of Gloria's bookstore. I couldn't do anything but go home, hoping that Mom was running late and wouldn't have noticed I'd gone out.

I had no such luck, of course, and we went at it for a good half hour—

"You are grounded, young lady!"

"Oh, yeah? You can't 'ground' me! I'm going to be eighteen in January!"

Finally the Peruzzos started pounding on the wall. As Mom tore open the front door to start yelling at them, I slammed my own door and pushed a chair under the knob.

Sure she's right that I'm an ungrateful, disobedient, useless, lying little tramp of a daughter. But at least I've got an actual life, *unlike her.*

I threw myself on the bed and buried my head in the pillow and ignored Mom pounding on my door. A fly tickled my cheek and I swatted at it, but it wouldn't go away. I turned on my side. Tiferet sat there, nuzzling me with her salmon-colored nose.

"What are you doing here?" I whispered, scooping her up in a hug.

"Mwowr," she explained as she wriggled free.

Mom rattled the doorknob, threatening to ground me till June if I didn't open up this instant, missy.

Tiferet blinked at me as she moved her head slowly back and forth. What was wadded up under her collar? I pulled it out. A piece of notebook paper with something written on it. Another note from Gloria.

Dearest Teresa, Tom got safely back to the bookstore and from there to his school. I knew that unfriendly powers would try to get at both of you when you passed through their domain, but that you were reluctant to ask for my help lest I think of you as scared children. But there is nothing to be ashamed of. The "Zone monsters" are scary, even for me! I will do my best to protect you, but it is your own courage that truly keeps them at bay. Please don't let them scare you from going to Tom's world tomorrow—I know you have a date—or from helping him when he needs your help. And he will need you sooner than you know, more than you can know.

Courage, my friend. Gloria.

"Gloria?" I called out softly, as soon as I had finished reading the note. But the cat-woman had already vanished.

"Furious? Of course I'm furious!" Mom shouted, and started banging on the door again. Eventually she gave up and went away.

I waited for what felt like hours before sneaking out to the kitchen to make myself a sandwich. Then I went back to bed and lay staring at the ceiling. If only I still knew how to pray.

Dear Jesus, please protect Tom and keep him safe from the Zone monsters. And please make Mom and Kylie and Mrs. Weddell and everybody stop being so mean to me.

Did I really think He was listening? I don't know, but I did fall asleep soon afterward. And I dreamed I was flying: not by flapping my arms or anything stupid like that; I was just walking down the street when I found that I could walk on the air, and soon I was taking big steps high over the trees and rooftops. *There's nothing to it—I'm really flying!* Floating along beside me was a huge silvery cigar, one of Tom's "airships," which looked at me with huge amber cat's eyes and puffed out a lazy tongue of orange flame. But I wasn't scared of it at all. I waved at it. And next thing I knew, it was morning and Mom was already gone, so I jumped out of bed and showered and dressed to go "walk out" with Tom.

As I ran off down the street, I wondered why I hadn't been able to find my way to the bookstore the night before. Did it only appear at certain times, like Brigadoon? Or was it up to Gloria? Or were the Zone monsters able to interfere somehow? No. I wouldn't think too much about that last possibility, because if that was the case they could trap me in the Zone as soon as I walked into it. So I just bulled ahead, whistling loudly and acting unafraid, until I came to Gloria's shop. I banged open the door and saw Gloria. Luckily she was a person this time, not a cat.

I started shivering, and then stupid, fat tears rolled down my cheeks. She opened her arms and I ran to her.

"Shh, it's all right," she whispered, patting my head while I sobbed. "They can't get to you in here. And I'll make sure they can't get to you out there, either."

I pulled away. "How are you going to do that?"

But she wouldn't answer me, just smiled and told me to drink my cocoa, Tom was waiting for me.

So I pushed my fear aside and did what I was told. *I'm going to have a good time no matter what.* And we did have a great time, then and the next two Saturdays, getting to know each other and each other's worlds. On the second Saturday, Tom brought me to a diner where his roommate Curtis was having lunch with his girlfriend Martha. He'd told me to say I was from Alaska, which was apparently a separate country where they spoke some weird combination of English and Russian, since that would explain my "strange" accent. I didn't think that was a very good story, but Curtis and Martha seemed fine with it.

* * * *

I felt so bad for Tom. His manners were too perfect for his own good, even in his own world. In my Philadelphia, everyone was always asking where he came from with his funny accent, and we decided to say New Zealand. A couple of times we got funny looks from people who maybe knew better, and when that happened we always got away as quickly as we could. Luckily we never met anyone I knew, except for Miss Chen. And that was my fault.

I bumped into her in the hall at school one day, knocking her iPad and neat little black attaché case right out of her hands. Instead of yelling at me like any other teacher would have done, she smiled as I picked up her things and tried to apologize.

"It's okay, it's not so long since I was distractible teenager myself," she said. "Those floor tiles must be really fascinating, considering that Kevin McCabe just walked by and you never even looked up."

"Oh, Kevin," I said, wrinkling my nose. I was *so* over him. "Not only is he not the only fish in the sea, the sea is much broader than he and his buddies ever dreamed of."

Miss Chen cocked her head. "That's almost poetic. Reminds me of what Isaac Newton said. Remember?"

A lot better than I could remember any of the math from her class. "He said that he was like a little boy playing with pretty seashells on the beach while the great ocean of truth lay all undiscovered before him."

"Very good! And you can't be accused of brown-nosing either. Not after the grades you got in my class. Solid C's that I know you had to work hard for." But she was still smiling, and I couldn't help doing the same.

A devil must have gotten into me, though, because the idea I'd had that first time in Gloria's Gateway Books came back into my head and wouldn't leave me alone.

"So I suck at the math, but what if I had experimental proof of the many worlds theory?" I blurted out. For once, Miss Chen looked totally baffled.

"Meet me at 10:00 Saturday morning in the Starbucks on Market Street and I'll being my proof!" I said, trying to smile mysteriously.

She paused, then gave a quick nod and said, "Okay, I'm looking forward to it." I stared after her when she turned around, walked back over to me, and murmured, "If you're playing a practical joke on me, you'll live to regret it."

* * * *

When Saturday arrived she drove up to the Starbucks in her scratched-up green Geo Metro. Tom and I sat at a corner table as she walked in. Her long, glossy black hair was held in place with a barrette, and she looked cool as a cucumber when she shook Tom's hand and asked him straight out where he was from. He and I exchanged glances. He'd confessed to me that he'd sort of told one of his teachers about the bookstore and the "other world," but this was the first time either of us had given ourselves away to anybody from the real world.

"That's a little complicated to explain," he said.

"I guess so, with that accent," she said. She turned to me and raised an eyebrow. "So where's this experimental proof you were telling me about, Teresa?"

I pointed to Tom. "He is."

"Excuse me?"

"Tom is the proof. He is. He's from a p-parallel world."

Miss Chen's right eyebrow rose almost to her hairline. But she turned and studied Tom through narrowed eyes, taking in his odd, overly formal clothes and weird haircut. But it was his gold watch chain she zeroed in on, reaching forward and pulling the watch right out of his school blazer to examine it. After staring intently at it for several seconds she let it go, looked into his eyes and asked calmly, "What's it like, being from another world?"

Tom slowly smiled, blinked his brown eyes once, and replied, "I could ask you the same thing."

"Miss Chen, please! *Everybody is looking at us,*" I hissed.

But the thing was, they weren't. The woman at the next table worked on a laptop, earbuds in her ears. A man sitting at another table was on his cell phone. Sounded urgent. On the other side of the room, a couple sat across from each other, both engrossed in games on *their* cell phones. Come to think of it, every single person in the room, including the barista and except for the three of us, was using some kind of electronic device.

Tom glanced at me, then at Miss Chen and said, "Looks to me like everybody here comes from *their* own world."

That broke the ice, and from then on Tom and I were practically shouting each other down in our eagerness to tell her how we had met, who and what Gloria was, and what Tom's world was like.

When we paused for breath she had just one question. "Can you take me to the bookstore?"

We couldn't say no. But we hadn't mentioned the Zone monsters.

* * * *

We dodged among the run-down buildings of the Zone while menacing shadows flitted by overhead. None of them came as close as they had that other really scary time, though, and we arrived at Gloria's bookstore safe and sound, if a little out of breath. Tiferet dozed atop a pile of books. She woke up sleepily, stretched and meowed. I bent down to scratch her behind the ears.

"This is Miss Chen," I explained. "She was, uh, my AP Physics teacher last year."

"How do you do," Miss Chen said gravely, scratching Tiferet under her chin. Tiferet purred and rubbed against her. After a moment Miss Chen looked up at me. "So where's Gloria?" she asked.

"Er, this *is* Gloria," I said.

She raised an eyebrow and I looked at Tom for help. He tried to explain, with some lame-o help from me.

"Oh," she said at last, "it's just like in *Flatland.*"

"MWOWR!" Tiferet agreed. She darted off into the back room and came back a moment later in human form. "Pleased to meet you," she said, curtseying to Miss Chen.

"Nice place you've got here," Miss Chen said calmly, like she met eleven dimensional beings every day. "And I do have a first name. It's Susie. So, Teresa and Tom told me you exist in eleven dimensions."

"Eleven and a half, you might say."

"Really? Does that mean that string theory is correct?"

"Not exactly," Gloria said. A moment later she and Miss Chen—Susie—were talking math, and my head began throbbing.

Tom sidled over and asked me in a whisper what string theory was. I sighed.

"You're asking the wrong girl," I said. "I suck at math and physics. It's some new physical theory that's been around for a few decades now, but nobody's been able to prove."

Tom frowned. "Physics? Physical theory?"

"The branch of natural philosophy that deals with the motions of objects, light, electricity, and so on," Gloria said, then resumed her conversation with Susie.

"Oh, that. I 'suck' at that too," Tom said. "If suck means to be really bad at."

Miss Chen turned to us and said, "It's decided, then."

"What is?" I asked.

"She's going to visit Tom's world with you," Gloria said. "Don't look so worried. Tom's an old hand at guiding alien women around, aren't you, Tom?" She winked at him.

How could I bring up the fact that Miss Chen would look, well, exotic in Tom's Philadelphia? I hadn't seen any Asian-looking people there. There was no good way I could think of, so instead I asked, "How are you going to get all three of us there? You've only ever taken Tom or me by ourselves."

"Not to worry, it actually gets easier with more people," Gloria said.

"Oh, of course, because the manifold phi epsilon square root of negative 42.378," Miss Chen said. Or something like that.

"More or less," Gloria smiled. "Everybody ready?"

We crowded into the back room, and Gloria linked arms with me and Tom, with Miss Chen completing the circle.

"Better shut your eyes," I warned her. "Those higher dimensions are a little—confusing."

Tom nodded but Miss Chen shrugged.

"Seriously you guys, you think I would miss this show for anything? I'll see enough in one second for my doctoral thesis at Caltech."

"Well, don't say we didn't warn you," Tom said, closing his eyes.

"Yeah, and don't throw up on me," I said, squeezing my own eyelids shut so hard I saw little red spirals.

"Ready everyone?" Gloria said. There was a moment of dizziness. I staggered and my shoulder hit something hard—the bookshelves to my right. A whole shelf load of vinyl records came down on me.

Tom leaped to my aid, and as we started picking up the mess I could hear Miss Chen chattering breathlessly about the higher dimensions. I might've known she wouldn't barf.

Unfortunately Gloria couldn't respond very well as she was now back in Tiferet form, but she rubbed up against Miss Chen's legs and purred.

"What are all those?" Miss Chen asked, wandering over to help us pick up the last few records.

"What do they look like?" I snapped. I'd been so looking forward to showing her everything, but now my shoulder hurt. "They're records. Ever heard of them? Just plain old records, like this one… *Buddy Holly and Elvis, live onstage in Las Vegas, 1965…*"

"Buddy Holly died in a plane crash in 1959," Miss Chen pointed out. "Ever hear of *The Day The Music Died?* Looks like somewhere he didn't die. I think there may be some treasures here, don't you?"

Tom rolled his eyes. "Oh no, not another one like my sister," he groaned.

"Whatever you take, you have to leave something of value in exchange," I added.

"Hmm?" Miss Chen said. She was intent on the liner notes. "Sure, I have some money with me."

I gently took the album from her. "Not money," I explained. "You have to leave an object that means something to you."

She looked from me to Tom and back again. "Like what?"

I shook my head. "I can't tell you that. Me and Tom had to figure that out for ourselves. It's like a kind of test, isn't it, Tiferet?" She meowed agreement. "But don't worry about it right now. Just leave the record here and you can pick it up when we get back."

Miss Chen seemed reluctant to put it down, but at last she nodded and laid it on the countertop by the cash register. "Okay, let's go," she said. "What's the matter?" she added when she saw Tom and me exchanging glances.

I explained about the Zone monsters.

To my amazement she just laughed. "Shadows? You're afraid of shadows?"

"They're not just shadows," Tom said. "Gloria says they're real…but she's also told us not to worry about them."

"Well then, we won't worry about them," Miss Chen said firmly. And marched straight out the door. She was already half a block ahead when we saw a shadow pass over her and took off running, yelling to her to wait.

"What?" she said, turning around as we caught up to her, out of breath.

I blinked. The shadow was gone, and the Zone with it. We were standing on the busy corner of King George Boulevard and South Street. Carriages drove slowly past, and the people walking by were throwing us curious glances—at Miss Chen instead of me. *What a relief. Oh, but poor Miss Chen!*

She didn't seem bothered, though. She stared around in wonder. Christmastime isn't as big a deal in Tom's world. Since the street lighting comes from gas lamps, they don't string colored lights everywhere the way we do. Even Christmas trees aren't so popular, except, Tom told me once, among people with German or Scandinavian ancestors. They call them *tannenbaums*, as in "O Tannenbaum." The gift-buying they do in his Philadelphia is also less frenzied than in our world. Still, the people seemed a little happier than they had a few weeks before, at the gray end of November. Street stalls sold roasted chestnuts—really!—and navel oranges, which seemed to be a real treat, judging from the way Tom eagerly fished out his funny sorta-British money and paid for one for each of us.

"Come on," he said, peeling the fruit with his thumbnail as he walked, "we had best finish up before we arrive. There is someone I would like to introduce you both to, but I do not want him to see we have been eating oranges."

"Who? And why shouldn't he know we've been eating oranges?" I asked.

"St. George's pastor, Reverend Marks. And as for the oranges—have you not heard of 'blood oranges'?" he said darkly.

I shook my head.

He blinked. "Oh. You must not have had a war with Florida, then."

"A *war*? With *Florida*?"

"Yes. Some people said we were just going to war to conquer the orange groves for Royal Fruit. The Marks' only son was killed there."

I exchanged glances with Miss Chen. What could we say? Maybe I'd been wrong to think of Tom's world as a more innocent place.

"I'm full anyway," Miss Chen said, tossing Tom hers. "Why don't you two share mine?"

"Thanks," Tom said, fielding the extra fruit and quickly peeling it and handing me half. I love how graceful he is. Me, I'm always such a klutz. I can barely work the buttons on my cell phone.

We walked a little way west on South Street, then waited at a trolley stop. Miss Chen stared as the brightly painted green and orange streetcar squealed to a stop, the other passengers stared at her more as soon as we got on and Tom paid our fare. I was starting to sweat inside my coat, but he didn't seem worried.

"This is nothing," he whispered, "compared to what it would be like if she visited Gingo Teag."

She was still too busy watching everything around us to notice how *she* was the center of attention, or maybe she just didn't care. I must have been like that, the first time I visited Tom's Philadelphia.

Fortunately, we didn't have far to go. Tom pulled the cord beside our seat and the trolley came to a stop on a street with a lot of big, bare trees. I didn't recognize the neighborhood, but it looked fancier than where I usually hung out. We walked up a flagstone path to a white-framed two-story house with a holly wreath hanging over the door. Tom pulled a cord, which rang a clanking bell inside the house. After a moment a gray-haired lady with a wrinkly face came to the door. She smiled a big smile when she saw Tom.

"Jeff, it's Tom and, uh, two young ladies!" she called over her shoulder.

A man's face appeared over her shoulder a moment later, and then he squeezed around her. He and Tom shook hands like they really meant it.

"Good to see you, my boy," he murmured. He looked too skinny, somehow, for such a big man. And there was a spiderweb of wrinkles around his eyes like my grandfather's face—but the pastor didn't look old enough to look so old.

"Come in, come in!" he said. "I haven't had the pleasure of meeting these young ladies." When he saw Miss Chen he nodded and said something in a musical-sounding foreign language.

"Oh. That's Mandarin, isn't it?" she said. "I'm sorry. My Chinese is terrible. I've been here in America since I was six. I barely know enough to say, 'Bad girl! Put away your toys this instant!'"

I never saw anyone look so confused and embarrassed. Miss Chen laughed and tapped him lightly on the arm. "Oh, it's all right. I wish I could speak Mandarin! But when I was a kid all I wanted to do was study English, and now I'm too busy with teaching and postdoc applications." She smiled and held out her hand. "Susie Chen. Pleased to meet you." He shook, looking even more bewildered.

I had to introduce myself, since Tom was tongue tied.

Reverend Marks cleared his throat and asked us where we went to school. We looked at each other, trying to figure out what to say, but Tom spoke up. "Sir, they're *from the bookstore*. Remember what I told you?"

"Oh," he said. "Oh!" He peered at us over the rims of his glasses. "Yes. Do forgive me. You're from a place, er, where America and Britain are two separate countries, right?"

"Right. Our America goes all the way to the Pacific, and includes Alaska and Hawaii, too," Miss Chen said.

He shook his head. "Amazing. I've been to Alaska and Hawaii myself, when I was younger. Proud people, very independent. I can't imagine them wanting to be part of the same country as Pennsylvanians and Virginians."

"Were you ever in China?" Miss Chen asked.

The reverend shook his head. "Since Emperor Song came to the throne, they don't allow missionaries in, I'm afraid."

"I see," Miss Chen said.

I didn't. In our world the last emperor of China was kicked out, like, a hundred years ago. I suddenly wondered if my family was back in Sicily squashing grapes for some feudal landlord. Everything seemed so backward here compared to home, like history had stopped sometime in the nineteenth century.

That wasn't really so, of course. There was a clattering noise from the far wall. Mounted about four feet off the floor was what looked like a wooden Scrabble rack, filled with honest-to-God Scrabble tiles. The rack was slightly tilted, and at the moment the tiles that had been resting on the top row were sliding off into a square hole through a miniature trap door. Beneath the rack stood a varnished wooden cabinet. I tapped Tom on the shoulder.

"What the heck is that?" I asked, pointing at the rack.

"That? That is a communication panel for a babbage, of course. Have you never seen a babbage-station before?"

"What's a babbage?"

"I though you said Teresa's world is more advanced in natural philosophy than ours," the pastor said.

"Wait a minute, a babbage? As in Charles Babbage's difference engine?" Miss Chen exclaimed.

"Of course, young lady. Though 'difference engine' sounds so clumsy, we always call it after its inventor."

She had joined me in examining the Scrabble tiles, which spelled out, "P.M. CONCERT CHOICES: BEETHOVEN 9 OR BRAHMS 3"

"Excuse me, ladies," the pastor said. He plucked a series of tiles from a small basket hanging beside the rack and spelled out the word BEETHOVEN on the empty bottom row. The tiles slid off and fell through a second trapdoor, closely followed by the top row of letters.

A moment later a full orchestra began playing a symphony right there in Reverend Marks's living room. At least, that's what it sounded like, though of course the sound was coming from the wooden cabinet below the Scrabble rack.

"I'm sorry, I'll turn it down," he said, adjusting a knob so that it sounded as if we were in the lobby of a symphony hall rather than in front-row seats.

Trust me, you have never heard recorded music coming out of a stereo or a TV set, no matter how new and shiny, that sounded half as good as that did. I stared at the cabinet, half expecting to find a lid I could lift up to uncover an actual miniature orchestra playing inside, like in a "Far Side" cartoon I once saw. I looked for a slot for CDs or vinyl records, but there was nothing. There wasn't anything like a digital panel, or a radio tuner, or an antenna.

Miss Chen was even more amazed. "You mean to tell me this thing's a computer?" she murmured as she stroked the wood grain.

"I don't know what you mean by a 'comp-you-derr,' but it's merely a station," Reverend Marks said. "There are thousands just like it across the city. The babbage itself takes up the whole basement of the British Library out in Brandywine."

"And he pays a pretty penny for his telegraphic link to it, too," Mrs. Marks said, walking into the room with a tray of tea and cookies. "But he must have his concerts!"

I listened to the music. Was there someplace I could go and listen without everyone talking? Guess not. But Nana used to love classical music. She used to take me to Philadelphia Orchestra concerts, and then for ice cream afterwards. This music sounded very familiar and yet completely different and weirdly beautiful.

"Is it really Beethoven?" I asked.

The pastor smiled at me. "Of course, my dear. It's the opening movement of his Ninth Symphony, the one he composed when he was already deaf."

Well, it was but it wasn't. Above and around the strings and woodwinds a mischievous saxophone played, sometimes harmonizing with what the rest of the orchestra was doing and sometimes setting off on its own, though somehow it always belonged with the rest of the music— I don't know how to explain it. I closed my eyes for a moment. Why I couldn't be more like that saxophone, instead of always acting like everyone around me was my enemy? When I looked over at the pastor I had to blink away tears.

"It sounds pretty different from the version I know," I managed to say.

"Amazing, isn't it?" Reverend Marks said. "But you really should go hear it live in Nouvelle Orleans."

I remembered that "*nouvelle*" means new in French.

"Why there?" I asked.

"Because that's where he wrote it, of course! You must know the story, a bright and cultured girl like you. Just two years after he fled the awful tyrant Napoléon…his hearing and his country taken away from him…then does he breathe the free air of the République du Louisiana, and the genius within him arises…"

I looked at Tom and smiled slightly.

We stayed till the end of the concert (the famous chorus "Ode to Joy" was in Cajun French instead of German), talking and sipping Mrs. Marks's tea. Miss Chen didn't want to go, but it was past dark already and Mom would be getting back from work, so we said goodbye and took the streetcar back downtown. The Zone was lit up like a football field for a night game, brighter than I'd ever seen it before, though I still couldn't see any streetlights. *Gloria must have fixed it up for us somehow.* She was waiting for us in the doorway of the bookstore.

"Did you three have a good time?"

"Amazing!" Miss Chen exclaimed. "Do you have a book about the 'babbage' they have here?"

"I can do better than that, Susie," Gloria said as she ushered us inside, "I have a copy of the blueprints Charles's grandson drew up for the giant difference engine out in Brandywine. As well as that record you wanted."

Miss Chen's eyes widened. "I have to give you something of value in exchange, right?" she asked in a small voice.

Gloria smiled at her. "That's right. But if you don't have anything with you now—"

"No, I do, it's just hard to let it go," Miss Chen said. She reached into her pocket and took out an ordinary-looking pebble. It was smooth, pale white with orange stripes, and less than an inch across. "It used to have mica flecks on the surface, but I think I must have rubbed them off from carrying it around for so long," she said, holding it out to Gloria, who held it up to the light.

Gloria flicked the pebble with her fingernail, which was painted hot pink, and said, "I think it's still got some shine to it." And sure enough, it was alive with silvery sparkles.

"How did you do that?" Miss Chen gasped.

Gloria smiled again. "I know it came from the beach behind your grandparents' house back in China," she said. "It will have a special home here too." And she reached up to some pigeonholes just below the ceiling—she didn't look tall enough, and her arms didn't seem to stretch—but somehow she reached without even standing on tiptoe and pulled down a tightly rolled-up bundle of papers, which she handed to Miss Chen along with the record. "Here you go," she said, while I rubbed my eyes. What had I just seen?

Miss Chen unrolled the plans, studied them for a moment and whistled. "Thanks, Gloria," she said, and hugged her.

"Susie, there are some aspects of these plans I'd like to talk with you about. Maybe we should go into the back room, the light's better in there," Gloria said.

"Huh? Oh, sure!" Miss Chen said, and they walked down the hallway, leaving me and Tom alone. Our eyes met and we both smiled at the same time.

* * * *

Miss Chen—all right, Susie—drove me home after Gloria brought us back to our Philadelphia. It was late and my street was quiet, so I had her drop me on the corner. I meant to sneak in the window to my bedroom, which I'd left unlocked while leaving the door locked and my light on in case Mom was home.

"That was the best time I've had in years," Susie said seriously. "Maybe ever. I hope you'll take me back to the other Philadelphia soon. I promise I'll find my own way around so you and Tom can have time to yourselves."

"Sure," I said, and we actually hugged. I never knew a teacher could be so cool! It was hard to go home after such a great day, and especially when Mom might still be waiting up to catch me. But the house was quiet when I climbed through the window, and I was suddenly so sleepy that I could barely shut the window and kick off my sneakers before falling into bed. I didn't even turn off the light

I woke suddenly after what seemed like only a few seconds. Tom stood over my bed.

"Tom?" I gasped, sitting up. "What are you doing here?" I peered into his face. "What's wrong?"

His lips moved without making a sound.

His knees gave way and he fell onto my bed, his shoulders shaking.

"What is it?" I asked.

He turned to face me. His soft brown eyes were wet with tears.

"My father," he choked out. "Disappeared!"

Part II

Of Dragons and Devils

11

Teresa held me as I cried on her shoulder. I was ashamed of my un-manly behaviour, and I made an effort to pull myself together, or at least not to make noise while I wept. Teresa's mother was probably in the house, and I certainly didn't want to alert her to my presence.

"It's going to be all right," Teresa whispered as she rocked me. When I was calmer she pulled away, gave me a little smile and smoothed down my hair. "How did you know where to find me, anyway?"

"Gloria gave me your address," I said. "I have to catch a train back home in a couple of hours. I just wanted to come tell you that I am going to have to leave school for a while, until we find out what is going on. I did not mean to worry you—and I *certainly* did not mean to start weep-ing like a baby."

"Wait here," Teresa said, and went to the door. She opened it a crack and peered out, then slipped through the door. I heard quiet rustling and the sound of cabinets being opened and closed softly. She was back less than a minute later with a loaf of bread, a jar of something labeled "pea-nut butter," several apples in a bag made of a crackly material Teresa had once told me was called "plastic," some bottles of water, also in "plastic," and a large canvas sack.

I took one of the water bottles and gulped it down. "What is that for?" I whispered, pointing to the sack.

"For me to pack my clothes in, silly," she whispered back, opening a chest of drawers and taking out several shirts, which she stuffed into the sack.

"Just a minute—who said anything about you coming with me?" I asked, putting my hand on her arm.

She shook me off. "I'm coming with you," she said, "you're not go-ing to face this alone."

"I will not be alone." I had to raise my voice due to the large lump that had suddenly formed in my throat. "I have my mum and Jo to look after."

"And who's going to look after you? I'm coming," she said, throwing in a few of those denim trousers people from her Philadelphia are so fond of, along with a skirt, undergarments, and socks.

I opened my mouth to argue, but we both froze when we heard the sound of footsteps on the stairs.

"Teresa?" a woman's voice called, and the doorknob rattled.

I dove out the window, and Teresa followed a moment later, zipping up the sack as she climbed over the sill. We ran down the street. The sky was already grey with dawn as we stumbled out into what was King George Boulevard in my world.

"Stop," she gasped, reaching for my arm, "I need to catch my breath."

"Teresa, you cannot come with me!" I said. "You must not! What about your school?"

She flung out her arm. "Hell with that. Sorry, Tom, bad language and all. But I can always make up my schoolwork. You need me now."

What could I say? That I did not need her? I turned away and watched the noisy, fast-moving traffic. I did not want her to see me cry again. She touched my shoulder and kissed me lightly on the cheek.

"I have to call somebody quickly, okay?" she said. "Then we can go catch your train."

"Teresa," I said, turning, but she already had her cell phone in her hand. I cannot get used to the way people call each other all the time in her world. You cannot receive a voicegram anywhere, or at anytime the way you can with a phone call. These phones ring in the middle of the night, when you are in the water closet, apparently even when you are deep in the country, far away from everything. It is rather appalling. I love my family but I would not want them to be able to reach me all the time. Besides, I have overheard Teresa's people chattering away into their cell phones—not that I want to eavesdrop, but it is impossible to get away from their voices—and they seem to have so little that is truly worth saying.

Except that this time, Teresa did.

"Hello?" she said. "Heather? Oh—I'm sorry I woke you. Look, I'm really sorry. Is Dad there?" A pause. She bit her lip. "All right, then. I'll tell you this and you tell him, okay? Look, I—I left Mom's house. But it's not what you think! No—no, I'm not coming to stay with you. You don't have to worry about that." Another pause. "Well, sorry! I didn't mean to be all sarcastic. Look, I don't have time. I need Dad to tell Mom that I haven't run away from home—not for good, anyway—I, I have to go help my boyfriend with something. I'll be back when it's done." Another pause. "I don't know, okay? I don't know! A few days…a few weeks… I don't know! But I don't want her to worry. Or Dad either!"

A tinny voice shouted from the little device so loudly that Teresa held it away from her ear. After a moment she brought it close to her mouth.

"Look, don't pretend like you care. I have to go now." And she silenced the voice and put the phone in her pocket.

She stared at the ground for a long moment, then looked up at me. "I'm sorry you had to hear that," she said quietly, "I know you've got more than enough of your own problems to worry about right now. Let's go, okay? We've got a train to catch. Oh!"

I grabbed her in a bear hug.

We ran down the street. The "cars" soon vanished, except for a few derelicts rusting by the kerbside. It had been a sunny but chilly morning in Teresa's Philadelphia, but the sky faded back to grey as we ran pell-mell along the crumbling pavement. She panted just behind me. Then she cried out.

I whirled. Teresa thrashed on the ground, her face, chest, and legs above the knees covered by something black and oily-looking. She scrabbled at it with her fingers, trying to pull it free.

I yelled and dived, trying to pull the thing off. But it was impossible, because it didn't seem to be solid. When I plunged my fingers into it, it felt cold and slimy, like February mud. Teresa's fingernails started to turn blue as the thing smothered her, and her struggles grew weaker. I went down on my knees and hammered at it with my fists.

Suddenly there was snarling behind me, and before I could turn a flash of orange crossed my field of vision. I had an impression of claws and teeth, and a sudden sharp pain across the back of my hand made me cry out and jerk away. It was Tiferet, of course, only she was no longer a gentle house cat but something larger and fiercer, like a mountain lion. Above her and around the struggling forms on the ground came a vague flickering, like heat lightning on a summer night, except that it made my eyes hurt. I blinked, and it was over.

Teresa lay gasping on the ground, and Gloria lay across her, her red hair tangled and mussed and her clothes ripped. I helped them both to their feet and grabbed Teresa's canvas sack, which had been thrown to one side in the struggle. Gloria and I each took one of Teresa's arms and together we hobbled to the bookstore.

Gloria repeated over and over how sorry she was. She seemed to be on the verge of tears.

"I didn't think they would dare try a direct attack," she said softly as she fetched her magical compresses. She placed them over Teresa's arms and neck where her clothes were torn, and handed me one for the back of my hand, which had a long, deep scratch. The colour slowly returned to Teresa's cheeks and fingernails.

"What was that?" she gasped.

"They don't have a name. Not a proper name. You can just call them the Grey Ones. They aren't supposed to invade the lower dimensions!" Gloria said, raising her voice as if she was talking to someone beyond the room.

"Please don't be upset, Gloria. It isn't your fault," Teresa said, sitting up and putting her hand on Gloria's arm. At that Gloria began to cry big, silent, crystalline tears that didn't soak into the carpet but instead rolled around like little glass beads.

I picked some up, looked at them, and put them in my pocket. They felt warm, rolling around in there. Gloria smiled and hugged Teresa.

"Thank you, dear," she said. After a moment the three of us rose and walked into the back room, where Gloria placed her hands on our shoulders and told us to close our eyes. It was the gentlest transition we had been through yet.

I leaned down to stroke Tiferet under her furry chin.

"Will we be all right out there?" Teresa asked, glancing toward the door.

Tiferet meowed in a reassuring sort of way, and I led the way out. *I'll die before I let them hurt Teresa again.* The sky over the Zone seemed a shade brighter than it had been on the other side, and no shadows followed us as we walked quickly out into the real world. Maybe Gloria had frightened them off.

Once we were back on King George Boulevard we caught a streetcar that took us near the school so I could pick up my bags. Teresa waited outside the gate of course, but I pulled her behind the big plane tree that stands there and stole a quick kiss. Fortunately nobody stopped me as I ran up to my room to grab my things. As I dashed back out Mr Kirkwood, who had woken me up with the news a few hours ago, called out to wish me good luck. I waved as I ran, and Teresa and I jumped on the next streetcar to Penn Station.

* * * *

Only when I was settled in my seat on the train with Teresa beside me did I finally have a chance to catch my breath. She snuggled up to me, put her head on my shoulder and was asleep before we left the station with the familiar white chuff of steam.

I stared out the window as the train left Philadelphia behind, rumbling its way south over the wide, still waters of the Chesapeake-and-Delaware Canal into Nanticoke Colony. I wasn't home yet, but as the city gave way to scrubby woods and the woods to flat fields of stubble, I began to feel I was returning to my own country.

Half an hour into the trip we passed Dover House, the modest Edwardian mansion where the Duke and Duchess of Nanticoke live. They were a young couple and popular with most people. She had begun life as a commoner from a fishing family in Fenwick Island, not far from the village of Spence Landing, where we were headed to catch the eleven o'clock ferry to Gingo Teag.

Despite my worries and fears, I was exhausted, and I too fell asleep. I woke up when the train pulled into Spence Landing. I nudged Teresa awake so we could get off before the train pulled out again on its long trip down the peninsula and across the causeway-and-tunnel system at the mouth of Chesapeake Bay to Norfolk, Virginia.

While we stood shivering on the dock waiting for the ferry, Teresa asked me what had happened to my father.

I shook my head. "I do not know much. The headmaster told me only that he did not come home last night, and Mum went to the police about midnight. It was the sheriff who telegraphed the school."

She scratched her head under her cap. Her cap was bright pink with white stylised snowflakes and a cherry-red fuzzy ball sewn on top. I had never seen anything like it before, and I would wager that it was a novelty to most of the other people staring at her whilst waiting for the ferry. I knew them all, of course. Billy Jones, Ginny's brother, waved to me.

"Home early for the holidays? And with a lady friend?"

Billy is a decent bloke, three years my senior and already a veteran hand on the *Miss Marie*, his father's fishing boat. How could he be so tactless? He must have been out of town. Indeed, Joe Thompson elbowed him and whispered in his ear, and Billy turned a little green. "Sorry—sorry Tom, I didn't know…"

"No worries," I called back. "This is my friend Teresa, from Philadelphia. She will tend Jo while I help Mum."

Teresa glared, as if she wanted to object. Then she shrugged. What else could I say? I needed to explain what she was doing here.

"Why didn't your mom call you herself?" Teresa asked quietly.

No doubt the juicy new piece of gossip that I had a girl with me caused the whispers and nods, which soaked through the crowd like the tide coming up the beach.

"You know we do not have phones like you people use," I responded, equally quietly. "And the school shuts down the voicegram network after lights-out at ten o'clock."

"Oh." She was silent for a moment, watching the grey water of Gingo Teag Bay fluff up in the breeze. "Even if your 'mum' accepts me as a babysitter, how are we going to explain who I am?"

"I have been thinking about that," I said. "St George's has a sister, all-girls' school—Cleodolinda Preparatory." She looked at me blankly and I rolled my eyes. "The princess? You know? The one who St George saved from the dragon? I thought you said you were a Papist—sorry, I mean a Catholic."

She failed to take offense. That certainly spoke volumes about how little people in her America cared about religion.

"Sorry, they didn't teach me that one when Mom was still making me go to Sunday school. Not that they didn't try to teach me a lot of other bull—uh, unbelievable stuff. So, fine, I go to Cleodolinda Prep. What else?"

"You are an Alaskan, like we told Curtis and Martha. That should go a long way towards explaining your accent and why you do not know things that everybody knows. But try not to say more than you have to, oh-kay?"

"Okey-dokey," she smiled at me. "Good use of the word, Tom." She gave me a quick hug. "It's going to be all right, Tommy, I promise," she whispered in my ear.

I nodded.

A moment later the chuffing, whistling ferry pulled up to the dock. Teresa stared at it in disbelief. "A steamboat? Really? You people still use steamboats *and* steam locomotives?"

"Where do you come from that people don't, missy?" a voice growled.

I groaned inwardly. It was Dean Greene, who fancies himself the saltiest old waterman in Nanticoke. Mum calls him Mean Greene and has been working for years to get him removed from the Tourism Advisory Council. But thus far she has not been successful, because when you're as from-here as the Greenes are, you cannot be removed from any official position by any force short of Assa Teag Ashley's fiery breath.

Teresa stuck out her chin and met his gaze. "I'm from Alaska, Anchorage born and bred, and we haven't used steamboats there in a hundred and fifty years!"

"Really. How do y'all get about, then? On kayaks, or on the backs of polar bears?"

Teresa looked flummoxed for a moment. Would she spin an unlikely yarn? And just where was this Anchorage, anyway? However, she merely laughed and said, "Come up north some time, and I'll show you around! Though I have to admit your weather is nicer."

Greene blinked, and you could practically see the neural firings attempting without success to cross his barnacle-encrusted synapses. He turned away, muttering, and I let out a relieved breath, but then Billy wandered over and bowed slightly.

"Pleased to meet you, miss. Any friend of Tom's is a friend of mine. And don't mind ol' Mean Greene there, he's just that ornery to every-body who crosses his path. So you're from Alaska?"

Teresa executed a clumsy curtsey and promptly produced a line of flapdoodle such as I never hope to hear again in my life. Alaska has a "network" of babbages that can talk to each other by radio, without any telegraphic connections! Alaska has buildings a thousand feet tall! Alaska put a man on the moon almost fifty years ago, if you please, but people thought it was so boring there they never went back! And on and on...

Billy looked slightly stunned, but he smiled at Teresa's enthusiasm. Would I have to "accidentally" elbow her to quiet her?

* * * *

Once we were safely on board the ferry I grabbed her arm and steered her behind the boiler. It was noisy, of course, but luckily the day had turned out mild so there were no other passengers huddling back there.

"What was that about?" I demanded.

She shook me off. "I thought you said to say I was from Alaska."

"I did, but I also told you to say as little as you can get away with. Do you actually *want* to attract attention?"

She stuck her tongue out at me. "Maybe I do! I'm sick of being the shy, nerdy girl all the time. I like the idea of being from out West, with a big personality and biiiiig hair!" She grabbed her brown curls and bunched them high atop her head.

I had to laugh, but I said, "All right, but could you keep the reins on the tall tales? Not everybody here is an ignorant rustic, you know. Some people might have read about Alaska or even been there, and they would realize how ridiculous the things you said are."

She planted her hands on her hips. "Oh, yeah? What's so ridiculous?"

"Men on the moon? Really, Teresa!"

"For your information, Mister Stick-in-the-Mud, *my* America—"

A blast from the ship's horn drowned out whatever silly tall tale she was about to tell. We were pulling up at the Gingo Teag town dock. Now to get her down the half-mile stretch of Main Street to get to our house on Davis Street before every gossip-mongering old biddy and good-for-nothing slouch in town got wind of her arrival and skittered up like a flock of sand pipers to start asking a lot of nosy questions.

So I grabbed my bag in one hand and Teresa's hand in the other, and, after making sure she had her bag as well, jumped to the dock and doubled back into the marsh. It was unlikely that people would bother to follow us back there.

Teresa followed me, gasping and complaining. I could not blame her for complaining, with the cattails flapping in our faces and the rich mud sucking at our shoes and that rotten-egg smell of decay and regrowth all around us.

I took us along a twisty path I knew, startling a snowy egret into flight. In the distance stood the peppermint-striped pole of Assa Teag Lighthouse—I was on the right track home.

Not that I could ever get lost amid the tufts of tough green marsh hay and the narrow brackish creeks we from-heres call guts. I spent my whole life before boarding school running around back here with my mates and Jo, so I knew it better than the lines of my own face. This smelly paradise of crabs and clams, mosquitoes and blue herons was my own backyard, and we were at my own back door in less than five minutes.

I raised my hand to knock on the door and it was opened from within. Mum smiled when she saw me, her face pale from lack of sleep, but her eyes widened and then narrowed when she saw Teresa. I gulped.

12

I don't know exactly what I was expecting Tom's mother to look like. Since he had said something about looking after her and his little sister, I guess I expected her to be a teary wreck, the way my mom would be if anything ever happened to me—the way she probably *was* right now, a thought I quickly pushed away.

Anyway, that wasn't Mrs. Purnell. She looked pale and tired, but who wouldn't be after staying up all night? She wore a mid-calf-length skirt and a bright red sweater. She had the figure for it too, though she was a head shorter than Tom and had only an inch or two on me. Her hair was blond, shoulder-length, and neatly combed—unlike my mom, who'd stopped caring what she looked like after Dad left. Mrs. Purnell's eyes were hazel with bright flecks, like the mica in Susie's pebble, and they were fixed on my face.

Tom said that I was a friend of his who went to Cleodolinda Prep, and would she mind letting me in so I didn't freeze to death out on the stoop? His voice was a little shaky. What *was* I going to do if she didn't let me in? All the confidence I'd shown on the ferry began to melt away under her stare.

"Well," she said at last, "I suppose we must not have frozen, young, prep school girls out on our stoop, the neighbors might start talking about us, might they not?" The accent was pure Beatles.

A mischievous voice in my head dared me to ask her to sing "Yellow Submarine" as we walked in.

"Tea will be ready in a moment." Unlike Gloria she made quite a ceremony of it, starting by warming up a white china teapot with little blue cornflowers painted on it over the gas range for several seconds before adding the water. Then she got out a matching china canister and a dark gray pewter teaspoon.

"I learnt how to make a nice cup of tea from my best friend Violet Blair's grandfather when I was a girl," she said. "Old man Eric, we called him. He was always in and out of jail for printing up leaflets denouncing the Empire and that sort of thing. Rumor was he'd come to Liverpool from London to live further from the Imperial authorities. They disappeared him back in 1984, though."

There was an awkward silence. Mrs. Purnell shook the pot, waited for a minute, and then carefully poured into three china cups that matched the pot and the canister.

Tom finally broke the silence. "Where is Jo?" he asked.

"I sent her to school," his mother said. "She was only under foot here. And frankly, you belong back in school too, Tommy. It was a mistake asking you to come down. The police are doing everything they can, and I can shift quite well for myself and Jo, just like when your father was at that conference in Manahatta last summer."

Tom stepped over and hugged his mother. She spilled tea on the counter and sighed.

"But I *want* to be here with you, Mum. I want to help out. I couldn't concentrate on my studies anyway, worrying about Dad."

"*Contractions,* Thomas. Your sister says the same thing, but all she does is ask a lot of questions. The sheriff finally told her to sit down and shut up!"

Tom smiled, his eyes swimming.

As for Mrs. Purnell, her eyes were as dry as a Sahara summer. Did she ever cry? *Tom's dad must be the emotional one.* All Mrs. Purnell seemed to care about was how I took my tea.

"You must not spoil it with milk or sugar. Old Eric always used to say tea should be drunk down straight and strong."

"Actually, I like both," I confessed.

She clucked disapprovingly as she got down a sugar canister and took a pitcher of milk out of an odd-looking squat metal box that must have been the refrigerator—or maybe an actual icebox with a big chunk of actual ice in it. "Colonial habits," she grumbled.

"Mum! We are just as British here as Home Islanders like you," Tom said.

She ruffled his hair. "Well, you and Jo are, Tommy, because I raised you right. But Teresa, now—you cannot be a native Philadelphian with that accent."

Of course I am, I almost said, but Tom was already explaining how I came from Alaska at the beginning of the school year and was still learning about life down here.

"Well, you are most welcome, my girl," Mrs. Purnell said. "The realms of His Britannic Majesty are the freest and best in the world."

"Mum, you are going to offend her," Tom complained.

"It's all right," I said quickly, "I'm really enjoying it here, it's true. And Tom has been so nice, showing me around Philadelphia."

"Has he, now? Has he indeed," she said, sitting down at last and taking a sip of her own black tea, which was almost the color of Gloria's cocoa. Tom and I looked at each other. "Tommy boy, please run upstairs and bathe. You need a bath after that long trip."

My guts turned to ice. *Don't leave me alone with her,* I silently begged Tom, but he just stood up.

"Yes, Mum," he murmured, throwing me a look of apology.

I glared at him as he slouched out of the kitchen. *Coward!* Sure enough, water ran upstairs a minute later. I stared at the wallpaper, which was creamy white printed with a faded rose pattern.

Mrs. Purnell smiled when I asked about it. "I picked it out after I married Mike. This house has been in his family for a hundred years, and do you know, when they stripped the old wallpaper off they found the walls are made of plaster mixed with horsehair? That is how they used to build them here."

I nodded and took a deep breath. Maybe she wasn't as scary as she seemed.

"Enjoying your tea, dear?" she asked.

I nodded. "This Eric Blair must have been quite the tea expert!" I said.

"Oh, he was quite a bit more than that. Fancied himself a writer, but of course he could not get his work published in the Home Islands, so I suppose we shall never know. More tea, dear?"

"Yes, please," I said. Why was she calling me "dear?" *She's not really very motherly.* She poured me another cup. If I ran into her on the street back home, I'd have thought she was a tough, successful businesswoman, or maybe a cop.

But why did I think that? Was it just because she didn't yell at Tom and try and spread guilt all over the place, the way my mom did? *I should be happy meeting a mother like this. After all, if I ever have kids, the last thing I want to do is to act like Mom.* But my stomach filled with butterflies as Tom's mother brought me my tea.

"Thanks," I said.

She smiled widely, showing off a gold false tooth, and said something in a foreign language.

"That's Russian, isn't it?" I said. "I know a girl at school called Marina who's from Moscow and who talks Russian with her parents on her cell—that is, she talks Russian with them."

"Yes dearie, very good, it is Russian," Mrs. Purnell said. She grabbed my right wrist, taking the cup from me with her other hand and placing it carefully down on the table.

I stared at her, my heart thudding, as her fingernails dug into my skin.

"Ow! You're hurting me," I said.

"Indeed. Now, my girl, what sort of person grows up in Alaska but does not even know enough Russian to understand a simple joke about a samovar? Hmm?" She gave my wrist a vigorous shake, and my hand flopped loose, useless as a wet rag. She leaned in close enough that I could smell a hint of something alcoholic under fresh mint—I know the smell well enough, from Mom's nights out. *Must have been a long night in Gingo Teag.*

"Tell me who you really are, girl, and what you are doing with my boy! And why you show up now, when my husband has just been kidnapped by the Imperial Intelligence Directorate! Here to check out the family's reaction, are you, you—"

The words that tumbled out of her mouth hadn't been covered in my French class, which I barely passed last year, but I was sure they weren't compliments. I stared into her glittering eyes. What could I say?

Then I heard footsteps behind her.

13

When Mum began shaking poor Teresa like the hawk with a muskrat in its talons I saw once, it was time to step out of the pantry. I'd been hiding there all morning. With everything going on at home, did she really think I was going to sit in school being bored by old Gassy Grant's droning on and on about the causes and effects of the Texas War?

Not even fear of being caught by the assistant headmaster, Mrs Withers, could keep me away. She thinks she's such hot stuff just because her husband's a solicitor. Big deal! Anybody with half a brain can draw up wills and bail drunks out of gaol. It's a well-paid job for a lazy fellow like Sam Withers.

I have to admit Teresa's appearance disappointed me at first. I was expecting someone tall and glamorous, with flowing blond hair and a dazzling smile. I'd never admit it out loud, but Tom's a handsome fellow and I expected him to do well for himself. So what was he doing with this mousy-looking girl with curly brown hair and a slight overbite, barely taller than me? But she had those puppy-dog brown eyes that boys go mad over—girls too, I guess, considering how every girl in my form is mad about Billy Jones. Not *me* of course, I'm *serious* about school instead of thinking about a boy who works on his dad's fishing boat and looks good in short sleeves. Even if he does have puppy-dog eyes.

Anyway, I was so interested in Mum's reaction to Tom's bringing Teresa home (I almost fell out of the closet when I saw her—I can't believe nobody heard my squeak) that I almost forgot to worry about Dad. Of course, Mum didn't, not for one second. She thinks the Frogs snatched him—I heard her say as much to Sheriff Watson, after they kicked me out of the room last night—though I have to say I couldn't quite understand why. Dad's an engineer, for pity's sake. What were they going to do with him, torture him until he bored them to death? I can just see it:

"You weel give us zee plans, *monsieur*, or we will stuff snails down your throat!"

"Oh. Well, you see, the surface of an airfoil must be designed in such a way as to permit the air to flow in a fashion that—here, let me draw you a diagram…"

"Aiieeee! Shut up, *monsieur*, *s'il vous plait*! We will give up on zee heavier-zen-air flight forever if only we do not have to listen to you talk anymore!"

Still, I couldn't let Mum torture poor Teresa, so I stepped out of the closet and walked right up to them. Teresa saw me first and her eyes went wide. Mum half turned, saw me standing there and said tightly, "Jodie Marybeth Purnell, go to your room this instant. We will talk about your truancy later."

I gritted my teeth when Mum said my middle name, which she *knows* I hate, but stood my ground. "Mum, leave Teresa alone. She's not a Froggy spy."

"Really. And how would you know that?"

"Because she's an alien," I said cheerfully.

"She's a *what?*" Mum said, letting go of Teresa's wrist.

Teresa rubbed it and I gave her a wink.

"She's an alien, Mum. You know? Like the monsters in Jules Verne?"

She sniffed. "I do not care for scientification, and especially not for that Frenchman! Even if the Emperor did exile him to Louisiana." She glanced over at Teresa, who was still rubbing her wrist and sniffling. "Though this so-called Teresa does not seem to be much of a spy!"

"She isn't one, Mum," Tom said, coming up behind me. He was still dripping wet and wore nothing but a towel around his waist.

I smirked at him and at the look on Teresa's face. *Wow, he and Mum are so upset they're* both *using contractions!* (She gave up on correcting my grammar years ago.)

"She's not a spy!" Tom said again, his voice cracking. "She really is from another world. Though the other world is Earth…just a different Earth."

"Did that train trip scramble your brains? Because you are not making much sense," Mum snapped.

"No, it is the truth. I have actually been there," he said, and began describing all the different times he'd walked out in "American" Philadelphia with Teresa.

I scowled at him. He'd promised to tell me everything! All right, I didn't want to know *everything* everything. He could keep all the kanoodling to himself. But he might have told me at least a little about the "cars" and the "planes" and the huge tall buildings!

While he was talking, I darted up to my room and grabbed the books about the colonies on the moons of Jupiter and the unknown Mozart symphonies. I'd hidden them under a pile of dirty laundry and dog-eared schoolbooks, knowing they'd be perfectly safe from discovery there since Mum has also given up on trying to get me to clean up my room. I ran back downstairs and shoved the books at Mum.

"What are these?" she asked, looking at me.

"Just look at them!" I panted.

She did as I asked, and slowly her scowl faded to a thoughtful frown, and finally to open amazement. I elbowed Tom.

"Ow!" he complained. "Do you have to be an annoying little shite even at a moment like this?"

"Thomas Jefferson Purnell!" Mum boomed, but without taking her eyes off the books, as if they might vanish into thin air if she stopped looking at them. "Your people have been to Jupiter?" she asked Teresa.

Teresa licked her lips. "No, just the moon," she said. Mum raised her eyebrows. "I think those books are from *another* parallel Earth," she explained.

"Oh, that makes *so* much sense," Mum said.

"Look, I know it sounds crazy, but—here," Teresa said, reaching into her pocket.

"Ah-*hah*!" Mom shouted and pounced on her again, bending her wrist back until she yelped with pain.

"Mum!" Tom yelled.

Fortunately, Teresa had already managed to pull out the thing in her pocket, and when Mum grabbed her arm it clattered to the floor. Without letting her go, Mum bent down and picked it up. It was a slim black rectangle about three inches long, with little keys on which numbers and letters were printed. When Mum touched them, a grey piece of glass lit up with colourful words and shapes.

"This does not *look* like a weapon," she said.

"It's not, honestly," Teresa said. "It's like a miniature, uh, voicegram generator that you carry around in your pocket."

"Really. And can you demonstrate how it works?"

"Well, it won't work here," Teresa said. "Except—push that little green button, yeah, then that red one and—"

"Why should I do that?"

"It'll bring up a game."

Eventually Mum satisfied herself that neither Teresa's "cell phone" nor Teresa herself were cleverly disguised weapons from Imperial intelligence, and let go of her wrist. Teresa jumped up and ran over to Tom, who patted her on the shoulder—I'm sure he would've hugged her, if he wasn't wearing nothing more than a towel.

"I can*not* believe you would do that to a friend of mine, Mum! Or to any guest," he said.

Mum sighed and stood up slowly. It was one of the few times I've ever seen her age catch up with her. I mean, she must be at *least* forty, though she never will tell. "I am sorry, truly I am, but this is such an awful time, and it would be a lot to take in under any circumstances," she said. "More tea, anyone?"

"I'll have some!" I said. Mum always gives me my tea with two sugar biscuits, but she fixed me with a glare. "No tea for you, Jodie. Not till we have a little talk about you skipping school and eavesdropping. What do *you* think an appropriate punishment would be, young lady?"

I was saved by a knock on our front door. When Mum opened it Sheriff Watson was standing there, along with a strange man in a grey suit and tie. Mum nodded to the sheriff. She stiffened when she looked at the other man.

"Viv, as you can see we've already called in outside help to find Mike," the sheriff said. "I don't like to admit when a problem's beyond my abilities, but the last time we had a kidnapping here was clear back in the nineteenth century. So I figured it was best to call in the R.C."

The Royal Constabulary. Someone was taking Dad's disappearance *very* seriously. Had it really been Sheriff Watson's idea to call them in? If I had gone to school I could have weaseled the information out of his daughter Tracey, who was two forms ahead of me. But something else was upsetting Mum. Did she know the man in the suit? She was not very happy to see him.

While I stood there, Sheriff Watson pushed past Mum casually, as if he lived here, making a beeline for Teresa. *Uh-oh.*

Mum spoke up. "Excuse me, sheriff, but I have *not* invited you in, and you have *not* shown me a warrant," she said frostily.

He looked startled, then sheepish, and stroked his mustache. "Now Viv, there's no call to act that way," he said, "I just wanted to meet this famous girl with the funny accent who ran through the marsh with your Tom."

The man in the suit said nothing.

"Well, here she is," Mum said crossly, "and there, now you have seen her. She is a school friend of Tom's who had planned her visit long before all this happened. And she is from Alaska, so please refrain from asking her a host of absurd questions. Tom, why not take her down to Smitty's for a nice cup of tea so the sheriff and I can talk?"

"But we just had your tea, Mum," Tom protested, earning himself one of Mum's fiercest glares.

"And take your little sister with you," she added.

Neither of us bothered protesting. I fetched my jacket while Tom ran upstairs and dressed. Then the three of us squeezed past the man in the suit and headed for Main Street. Smitty's is the only teahouse in town that bothers to stay open all winter. Tom is right, though, their tea is like dishwater. I was not going to drink it.

As soon as Tom and Teresa turned the corner onto Main Street, talking to each other in low voices, I turned and darted in the other direction. Unlike my idiotic big brother, I had no intention of parading through the marsh like a ridiculous egret. I ducked until my head was at least two feet below the tops of the cattails (to be fair, I do have the advantage of being a good six inches shorter than Tommy) and tiptoed along. Even in midwinter, animal noises surrounded me. A flock of gulls squabbled loudly, probably over a dead muskrat.

When I came closer to the house I slowed and moved carefully, following the same route I'd used earlier that morning. I crawled through a stand of bright green salt marsh hay until I reached the underside of our house, which is up on stilts in case of flooding. When I was seven I'd found a place right under the kitchen pantry, where the boards were loose. This time I scraped my forehead climbing up, I was so eager to listen in on Mum, the sheriff, and the R.C. agent. I didn't even realize it until much later, when I ran my hands through my hair and they came away wet with blood.

I eased the door open. The first surprise was that the sheriff was gone. Only Mum and the stranger in the suit were sitting there, and now it was obvious they knew each other.

"Viv, believe me when I say we want him back as much as you do. Maybe more."

"Oh, so 'we,' want him back. Is that so, Agent Connery? You yourself have no unofficial feelings about it?"

Peering through the crack in the door I got a better look at this bloke. He was tall and skinny, with a sharp nose and dark brown eyes. His hair was brown too, with a bit of grey around the sideburns.

"That's not fair, Viv. You know that I'm the one who plumped for your being a genuine defector rather than a spy. But we're wasting time. After Mike is back safe and sound the three of us can drink to old times. Right now, you must tell me what you know."

Mum sank back in her chair. "I expect you know more than I do, Dan. Certainly more about what he was working on at DRRAGON. He followed regulations to a T. It is a wonder I even know he was working on heavier-than-air flight."

So it's true!

"But he wasn't working on Saturday, was he?"

"Of course not! He walked over to Assa Teag, which is what he always does on the week-ends. I think sometimes he is more in love with Ashley than he is with me."

Agent Connery smiled, or rather the corners of his mouth turned up, but his eyes stayed fixed on Mum. "Yes. According to Ranger Rogers' statement, Mike arrived on foot over the bridge from Gingo Teag before first light, about six o'clock."

"He loves to watch the sun rise over the beach, even when it is as bitter cold as it was Saturday morning," Mum said. Was that a tear I saw in her eye? Surely not. "Besides which, the dragon is most active early in the morning," she added. "If you want a good look at her aerodynamics, that is the time to go. In winter she must fly far out to sea for food."

"Indeed. But you expected him back for lunch."

"I did, yes. He should have returned about one o'clock. I began to worry when he had not returned by two."

"But you didn't go to the sheriff first."

Mum's cheeks flushed. "Is this an interrogation, Dan? Should I retain a solicitor?"

"Don't be silly, Viv." He stood and refilled his teacup. "I simply have to know everything that happened. It will aid in the investigation."

"What more information do you need? The Imperials grabbed him. Ransom him for some Directorate spies, or whatever it is you people do." Agent Connery didn't reply, and after a few seconds Mum sighed and said, "No, I did not go to the sheriff. I did not see the point of sending the entire village into an uproar. As would inevitably have happened in a place this small. I took the boat over to Assa Teag myself."

"Which boat is that?"

"Our boat, the *Lady Vivian*. I wish Mike had not named it that, but I always keep the batteries fully charged for an emergency like this. I wanted to get there as quickly as possible."

"Of course you did." He stood again and pulled open the curtains on the bay side of the house. "Is that it?" he asked, pointing.

"Yes. Mike gives it a fresh coat of paint every year."

"It's large for a motorboat, isn't it?"

Dad and Tom had built the boat's wooden cabin six years ago.

"Mike takes the children fishing in it. The engine is more powerful than you would think. I was over at the lighthouse in ten minutes. The Assa Teag Royal Dragon Refuge has its headquarters there, and Ron— Ranger Rogers—lives in a little house beside it. You walk through pine woods to get there. Well, as soon as I motored to the dock in Dragon's Cove, I could see something was wrong."

I'd have expected the R.C. man to be writing in a little notebook, but he was just listening. "This cove, does it face the open sea?"

Mum shook her head. "You must sail around Fishing Point to get out on the open water. I came into the cove that way." Suddenly she smiled. "Sometimes we call the place Tom's Cove, because Tommy loves it so much." Her smile quickly faded. "When I pulled into the docks opposite the lighthouse, I could see they were damaged."

"Damaged how?"

"As if a boat that was too big had come in too fast and rammed right into the pilings. There was a gash and several splintered boards floating in the water. I tied up to the first undamaged pier. Then I found *this* floating on the water. Luckily the cove is so calm it had not drifted far."

I leaned so far forward I almost fell out of the pantry. Mum was handing a dented tin to Agent Connery, who held it in both hands, examining the label.

"Why didn't you give this to the sheriff?"

"I gave him another one just like it. There were several of them floating around."

"Part of the label's torn off, but the rest is in French. Clearly Imperial Navy rations," he said grimly. "It looks as if they sent a launch from a submersible standing off the coast."

Mum nodded. "As soon as I saw that, I ran down the path to the lighthouse. Ron met me halfway. I asked him what had happened and where Mike was, and he said he did not know. They had been out observing the dragon early in the morning, but Ron had to go check on the oyster beds—blokes from the village are always sneaking over and taking too many—and he was up to his waist in the muck when he heard a loud noise from the docks. He ran over there as fast as he could. He was just in time to see a fast boat of some kind disappearing around Fishing Point. It looked as if there was a struggle going on onboard. And when he went over to the spot where Mike had been observing Ashley, he saw a lot of trampled vegetation but no sign of him. I made Ron take me over there. I recognised the place because I have been there several times with Mike."

"Could you point it out for me?" Agent Connery asked, pulling a large fishing map out of his brown leather valise. Mum pointed, but I didn't need to see the map to know where she meant.

Dad had taken me there several times too, always in the hour before dawn when the world is at its quietest. All you can hear are the waves tumbling over the sand on the other side of the dunes, an occasional distant whinny from a Gingo Teag pony, the wild horses that live in those parts of the island that Ashley doesn't frequent, and the small rustling noises the dragon herself makes in her den, prowling around as she waits for morning. I could smell the salt air and Dad's aftershave just thinking about it.

Agent Connery studied the map a moment longer, then nodded. "All right, that fits what Ranger Rogers told us," he said.

"Yes. His description was correct. But he had overlooked Mike's wallet, which had fallen behind a bayberry bush."

Mum held it up. Maybe he didn't know her well enough to notice, but her self-control was wearing thin. Her nostrils flared and she was breathing heavily.

He took the wallet and examined it carefully, removing Dad's carriage-license. "I'm going to have to hold onto this," he said.

She nodded.

"All right, I'm going to be honest with you, Viv," he said. "The situation looks very bad, but we shall do our best to find Mike. Right now our agents are out rolling up all the known Imperial spy networks to interrogate their agents and discover what they know about this operation. But, um, there's one thing I haven't told you, or perhaps that you haven't told me." He was looking at the floor. Mum and I both leaned forward. "What? What is it?" she asked.

"We've intercepted some letters your husband sent recently to Professor Urquhart."

Mum recoiled. "What! Writing to Ram!"

"So you didn't know."

"I do not believe you," Mum said. She got up and collected the teacups, clattering them together. "Mike would never take such a foolish chance!"

"I can show you the pictograms we took of the cancelled envelopes," he said, taking a piece of paper out of his valise.

Mum turned her head away. "I suppose you could show me pictograms of the letters themselves," she said bitterly. "It is so very good to know we have His Majesty's government's full attention, after all these years. Expecting one's letters to be private is so *very* old-fashioned."

"Come on, Vivian. It would be irresponsible of us not to sample the mails that go back and forth to the Empire. Especially letters to and from the Home Islands, and especially to centres of Imperial research like Université Louis-Napoléon."

"Oxford University, if you please, Dan! Give it its proper name, not the false name the invader forced upon it!" Mum was silent for a moment. "You are waiting for me to ask what Mike was writing to Ram about, just so you can tell me it is classified, are you not?"

"It is classified, but if anyone has a right to know, it's you."

My breath was coming so fast I was afraid I wouldn't be able to hear the secret when Agent Connery revealed it. *I'm about to become a real spy, hearing real government secrets!*

"Now, I suppose you know that Ashley hasn't laid any viable eggs in over thirty years," he began.

"How could I not know? I am the head of the Gingo Teag Tourism Advisory Council," Mum snapped.

"Yes, of course. But it's not widely known that the problem is general."

"What do you mean, the problem is general?"

"None of the other female dragons in any of the other lairs along the Atlantic coast have been able to lay, either," he said.

"Really?" Mum's face screwed up in surprise. "So, no new dragonets are being born anywhere, eh? Come to think of it, the last time I heard of one being born, Tom was still in nappies. But what does Ram have to do with this?"

"You didn't know? He happens to be the world's foremost authority on dragon biology. Mike wrote to him back in October about some observations he'd made of Ashley's nest. He said she is laying eggs, but their shells seem to be defective—they break easily. He even tried to send Ram a sample, but it appears to have been confiscated in the mail."

"Whoever by? His Royal Majesty's dunderheads, or His Imperial Majesty's buffoons?"

"We haven't been able to work that out yet, and that's a fine way to speak of loyal civil servants!"

Mum didn't rise to the bait. "Mike took the risk of writing to Ram because of a reptile's fertility problems." She stared off into the middle distance a moment longer. "If that bastard gets home alive, I am going to kill him."

"Viv, I must protest. This is serious business here! We're talking about the security of the Realm!" He actually waggled his finger under Mum's nose. It was all I could do not to laugh.

"You are quite right, this is serious business. My husband has just been kidnapped, and there will be royal and imperial hell to pay if I fail to get him back. Oh, and if you wave your finger in my face once more? I am going to break it off and stick it in your bum."

I nearly fell on the floor. Language like that coming out of Mum's mouth? And she wasn't done yet.

"Now, you listen to me, you pettifogging little clerk. I expect Mike to walk through our front door as if nothing happened in time for New Year's Eve dinner."

"Vivian, you can't be serious. These things can take months to sort out."

"Well, this particular 'thing' is going to take all of—" she glanced at our wall calendar, which showed Ashley soaring majestically over a herd of Gingo Teag ponies—"nine days to 'sort out.' Or I shall travel to the Empire to sort it out myself!"

"Vivian, you cannot give ultimatums to the British government!"

He wasn't going to get anywhere with Mum, and I'd heard enough anyway. I wriggled back out through my secret trap door and began squelching through the marsh. Wait til Tommy and his girlfriend heard what I'd just learnt.

14

It was amazing how quickly Tom's face shifted from loving to annoyed when Jo ran up. Me, I always wished I had a younger sister. And what she had to say showed one of the advantages of having one: two pairs of ears are better than one.

"Darn it, Jo, you are going to get me in as much trouble as you! More, because I am supposed to be watching you!" Tom snapped. He actually said that, *darn it*. It was so cute.

I was working on watching my mouth around him, but I'd already caused him quite a bit of embarrassment. In his world, he said, nobody used language like I did except soldiers in live combat.

"All right then, I guess you don't want to know what Mum and the R.C. agent were talking about," she said cheerfully.

"You were eavesdropping? Jo! What did they say?"

Smitty's was what might have been called a bed and breakfast back home, though here they just called it an inn. Without a causeway from the mainland to Chincoteague like there is in the real world, Mrs. Purnell's efforts to bring the tourists in could only have limited success, so the inn was pretty small. There were only four little round tables in the dark, cramped little dining room.

Edna Smythe, the owner's wife, hadn't looked any too pleased when we showed up asking to be served, since they normally only opened on the weekends in winter. She made a big production of banging around the tea kettle and throwing us dirty looks.

"Don't pay her any mind," Tom had said, "you would be grumpy too, if you were married to Jack Smythe."

Luckily she had stomped off to her house and left us alone. I guess she must've trusted Tom not to steal the teaspoons or anything.

Jo filled us in on what Dan and her mother had said to each other. "We already knew of course that it was Ranger Rogers who last saw Dad," she said, glancing at me, "but Mum didn't tell me any of those details about the torn-up pier and the dropped wallet."

Tom stared at the floor, as if the unpolished boards would stop his tears. "This is my fault," he suddenly.

"What? How could it be your fault?" I said.

Jo reached over and touched his shoulder.

"He told me when I last saw him that he was about to make some kind of breakthrough in heavier-than-air flight and he would tell me about it next time we got together. I should have made him tell me then."

"He didn't tell me that," Jo murmured.

"I still don't see how that makes it your fault," I said, throwing Jo a look. *Come on, this isn't the time to fight with your brother.*

"But if he *had* told me, maybe we would have a better idea why the Frogs grabbed him."

"The Frogs?" I said.

"The French Empire. That is what we call them," Tom said.

"That's not all we call them, those lousy backstabbing—"

"Jo, please," I said. I frowned. Wait a minute. One thing she'd said seemed familiar, which was pretty weird considering that everything she was talking about was so strange. "What did you say the name of that professor was, again? The one your father was writing to in England?"

"What do you mean, England? This is England, right here!" Jo said, stamping her foot. I made an effort not to smile.

"I mean in the Home Islands."

"Oh, that guy. Urquhart. What a strange name."

Tom and I looked at each other. "It's not just his name that's strange," I said. "I think we've met him."

"Met him how? You haven't been to the Home Islands, have you?" Jo said.

"No, it's not that. It's a little hard to explain," I said.

Tom frowned at me. "Are you sure we ought to tell her?"

"Why? Because it might cause a paradox and make us vanish?"

"No. Because she is an annoying little git," Tom snapped.

"That's the thanks I get for telling you everything?" Jo said.

"Tom, Jo, *please!* Your dad's just been kidnapped! Are you more interested in rescuing him or in fighting with each other?" They both looked at me, and I explained about our weird encounter with Professor Urquhart. Jo wasn't confused and she got it right away.

"You mean you met someone you haven't met yet? That's *wizard!*" she yelled. "Why don't we just take the train back to Philadelphia, get Gloria to take us to the same point in time, and ask him where Dad is now?"

Her logic was hard to beat, but I shook my head. "I don't think it works like that," I said.

"No? Why not?" she demanded.

"Well, it might cause a paradox, like I said. Like in that story by Ray Bradbury, 'A Sound of Thunder.'"

They both looked at me blankly. Guess Ray Bradbury didn't exist in this world, or he'd becoming something other than a science fiction writer. I sighed. "It's about a guy who goes back into the past to hunt dinosaurs—"

"What's a dinosaur?" Jo interrupted.

I gritted my teeth. "You don't know about those either? You know, those huge lizard things that lived 65 million years ago—"

"Oh, you mean terradracos," Tom said.

"What?"

"Earth-dragons. Their fossils were discovered long after Englishmen found that the Atlantic coast of the New World was bristling with winged dragons. The Louisianan natural philosopher John James Audubon figured out that dragons evolved from a winged form of terradracos."

"I see," I said. *So dragons are pterodactyls that survived the extinction of the dinosaurs. That takes some of the mystery out of their existence.* "Anyway, so this story is about a man who goes back in a time machine to hunt terradracos—"

"Oh, like in the Herbert Wells novel," Jo said.

"Yes. I guess so. Please stop interrupting, Jo!" I said. She looked hurt, so I patted her arm. "Well, they only hunt dinosaurs, I mean terradracos, that they've found fossils of, so they know they're going to die anyway. But the guy in the story steps by mistake on a butterfly that wasn't supposed to die, so when he returns to the present everything's all messed up."

"I see," said Jo. "But it seems that you met Professor Urquhart in the future. So you wouldn't be messing up our past by asking him where Dad is."

"Yeah, but we'd be messing up *his* past, that is, Professor Urquhart's," I said. "And we'll know where to rescue your dad only as a result of our having rescued him in the future. It's an endless loop."

"But—" Jo said, scratching her head.

"There is another problem," Tom said. "We would need Gloria to take us into the future again, and she did not seem to think that was such a good idea, either. She asked Teresa and me whether we had spoken to anyone we knew in the future, and we could honestly say we had not, since we had never met Professor Urquhart before. But she is bound to be suspicious if we ask her to take us there again."

"Oh, fine. You just don't like my idea because *I* was the one to think of it," Jo said, folding her arms and pouting.

"No! It's great thinking, Jo. We should save it in case we run out of other ideas," I said.

"Oh yeah? What are your other ideas?" she demanded.

I looked at Tom, who shrugged. "The most obvious person to talk to first is Ranger Rogers," he said. "There is always a chance of learning something that the police and Mum missed."

"Great, let's go over there now," I said, standing up.

Tom and Jo both shook their heads. "He is sleeping now," Tom explained. "He rises before dawn every day to observe Ashley at daybreak, since that is when she is most active. So he retires late in the afternoon."

"Well, maybe he's still up," I said, glancing out the window at the reddening sun. "We can go knock on the door of his house, can't we?"

This time Jo replied, "He doesn't live here in the village. He's not *from here*. Anyway, he lives in a little house beside the lighthouse."

"So, we'll go over there and wake him," I persisted.

They both shook their heads again. "You cannot travel to Assa Teag without an escort," Tom said.

"Why not?"

"Because of the dragon," Jo said in a *duh* tone of voice.

"Oh. Guess we'll have to go see him in the morning." If I was going to have stay in Gingo Teag overnight, I had to figure out where I was going to sleep.

Tom was thinking the same thing. "You will have to lodge here, with Smitty," he said.

"Oh great," I groaned, "and you say he's even worse than his wife?"

"They have their good points," Tom said.

They may have, but the only one I saw was that they let me stay there without Tom having to pay. Okay, that's not nothing, though Mr. Smythe made a big deal of letting Tom know what a huge favor he was doing him and his family. He was a big man with a tangled gray beard and hands that were a mess of cracked, dry skin. He grunted when Tom explained that I was a school friend from Alaska.

"Didn't know your dad was as *advanced* as all that," he rumbled at Tom. "Don't believe in coed education myself."

"St. George's is not coeducational. Teresa goes to our sister school, Cleodolinda Prep," Tom explained, somehow keeping a straight face as Jo stuck out her tongue at the innkeeper behind his back.

"And yer from Alaska, are yer?" he said, turning to me as Jo stuck her thumbs in her ears and crossed her eyes.

"Er, yes," I said, trying hard not to crack up.

"So is it true yer all live in igloos and eat whale blubber?"

"Er, I think that's just the Eskimos," I said. *Please, God, don't make me have to keep this conversation going all night.* Jo was doing everything but standing on her head.

Luckily Mr. Smythe had lost interest, or perhaps he'd reached the limit of his knowledge about Alaska. He told Tom that Edna would keep me out of trouble and make sure I was in bed by eight. I wouldn't have dreamed of arguing. Dinner was a piece of fried flounder that tasted like it might have been quite good when fresh, six months or so ago. If they really were still using iceboxes here, I didn't want to think too hard about how well that fish had been preserved.

Since Tom would be coming to get me long before sunup and there wasn't any light in my room anyway (or more likely, the Smythes didn't want to burn their precious gas so I could stay up knitting or whatever it was they thought girls did at night), I climbed straight into bed, shivering under the thick quilt. But I was too excited to sleep. Here I was on my first night in another world! Granted, it was only Chincoteague Island, and a much less comfortable version of it at that, but still! Mom wouldn't be waking me up in the morning with her clattering around and grumbling to herself. Instead I was going on a real, bona-fide adventure. Except that this wasn't any fun for Tom, Jo, or their mother. And God only knew what was happening to their father.

Still, I might get a glimpse of a real, honest-to-goodness dragon in the morning! What did pterodactyls look like? I'd seen pictures when we studied them in eighth grade biology, but that was a long time ago. And Ashley would be at least 65 million years evolved from them, anyway. Maybe she'd look like a giant, winged crocodile, with teeth the size of my shinbone. I shivered and wished Tom was sleeping here with me.

Tom, sleeping with me. My gut knotted, and I felt mushy, tingly, and confused, all at the same time. Was I really ready for *that*? All Tom and I had really done so far was kiss. Well-brought-up boys in this Gingo Teag probably didn't do much more than that, at least not before marriage, but I sort of wished he would. Though the thought scared me too.

I did fall asleep. My dreams were confusing too. I had the flying dream again, but this time Tom was up in the sky with me.

"Better keep up, Teresa!" he called out from way ahead of me, as he strode directly into a big bank of puffy white clouds. I yelled for him to wait up for me and ran as fast as I could to catch up. But when I reached the clouds, they didn't part and turn to mist like they should have. Instead they closed over my face, leaking oily black over my eyes and into my nose and mouth, just like when the Zone monster had attacked me. I tried to scream but I couldn't even breathe.

"Ow! Stop biting me," Tom's voice said. Something—his hand?—was over my mouth. "Shhhhh."

It was still as dark as the inside of a closet, except around the fringes of the curtains. I sat up and squinted; a smaller shape stood beside Tom.

"Jo? You let Jo come, too?"

Tom waved his left hand. "It was easier than trying to keep her from coming."

"Plus I know where to find Ranger Rogers better than you do," Jo said in a loud whisper.

We both shushed her, and Tom asked how she knew that.

"Because I go over there all the time by myself to watch Ashley."

"You do *what?* I am going to tell Mum!"

"You do that and I'll—"

"Tom, Jo, please! Save it for another time. Give me a couple minutes to get dressed and I'll meet you outside."

It was very cold in the unlighted street. I was shivering so hard my knees were knocking together, despite my warm jacket. Tom and Jo stood waiting for me, each carrying a small flashlight (torches, they called them).

Tom handed me an extra sweater and I put it on gratefully, while Jo skipped up and down muttering, "Let's go! Let's go!" Tom gave me an apple to eat as we walked.

Even in the predawn darkness I could see that Gingo Teag was still a working fishing and crabbing village in this world, instead of being full of miniature golf courses and gift shops like I remembered from my trip down here in the real world—okay, in *my* world. Which way was better? Certainly Mrs. Purnell seemed like she would have been happier if her Gingo Teag was more like my Chincoteague. And a nice warm motel room would have been better than Smitty's. But it sure was quiet, with no cars on the island and only a handful of those battery-powered carriages, none of which was out driving around at this hour. I told Tom that the place was like a ghost town and he nodded.

"The fishermen are already out on the water," he said. "Nobody else has to get up before first light."

"Except Ashley!" Jo cried happily. We shushed her again, but she paid us no attention.

After ten minutes' brisk walk, we reached the marshy eastern edge of the island. There were no more buildings, either, except for a deserted guard booth. We were walking on a boardwalk through the salt marsh. Tame little ripples lapped at the pilings below our feet. I could hear gulls calling over the water, and a chorus of trills and peeps. Something big splashed in the water a few yards off to the left.

"Was that a fish? But it's so cold!" I said to Tom.

He smiled. "The marsh is always alive."

The boardwalk continued out over a narrow channel that marked the end of Gingo Teag. Ahead of us loomed a wall of dark pine trees. "Assa

Teag," Tom said. He shined his flashlight on a plain wooden sign planted in the narrow sandy bank beneath the pine trees. It said, in black letters six inches tall:

ASSA TEAG ISLAND ROYAL DRAGON REFUGE
CAUTION
HERE THERE BE DRAGONS

Tom glanced at me. "There is nothing to worry about, Teresa. We are perfectly safe."

"You sure?" I asked, hating how it came out in a scared-little-girl voice.

"Trust us. Jo and I have been coming here all our lives. By now, Ashley is probably far out to sea."

"Well, all right then," I said, and took a step off the boardwalk, into the cold sand. Suddenly there was an angry shout, and the sound of hurrying footsteps.

15

A man about Tom's height came running out of the pine woods. He was a sturdy-looking guy wearing an official-looking broad-brimmed hat with a tan jacket and matching pants.

"What do you kids think you're doing?" he demanded. "Oh—oh, it's you Tom. Jo." He gave me a look, then turned to speak to Tom as if neither of us girls counted. "What are you doing here? You know better than to go wandering around the refuge on your own."

Tom introduced me again as a school friend from Alaska. Ranger Rogers nodded at me. "Pleased to meet you, miss," he said, offering his gloved right hand.

I envied him his gloves as I shook—they looked warm and waterproof. His grip was firm and he looked me in the eye. Maybe he wasn't so bad after all.

"I am here about my father," Tom said. "I know you have already told Mum and the police what you saw, but still…"

"Oh, of course. What a terrible thing," Ranger Rogers said, shaking his head. He pushed his hat back and ran his hands through his hair, which was starting to go gray. "Who would believe the Frenchies would have the nerve to kidnap an Englishman on English soil?"

"They do it all the time in the Home Islands," Tom said drily.

Ranger Rogers nodded. "Of course. You know what I mean, though."

"Can you show us where he was the last time you saw him?" Tom asked.

"Of course, but we'll have to be careful. Ashley hasn't taken flight yet."

"Really? I thought she was always up before sunrise," Tom said, as we followed the ranger down the path through the trees. The sky between the high branches was beginning to show a daytime blue.

"She sometimes sleeps in a bit when it's as cold as this," Ranger Rogers said.

"Aren't dragons cold-blooded?" I asked. "How can she fly in the winter at all?"

"That's a common misconception," Ranger Rogers said. "It's true Linnaeus classified *Draco americanus* as a reptile, but we've learned quite a bit since the eighteenth century. Dragons are more similar to birds in that they are warm-blooded, despite their scaly-looking reptilian skin. I'm with those natural philosophers who think dragons need to be placed in a separate class of their own, of which they're the only surviving genus and species."

"That's all really fascinating," Jo said sarcastically. "Are we going to get a look at Ashley or not?"

Ranger Rogers ruffled her hair, and she glared at him.

"Maybe, if you're good," he said.

The trees ended after about a hundred yards and we crossed a barren patch of sand behind the dunes. On the bayward slope of the nearest dune, a patch of tender green shoots of dune grass had been trampled. I'm no Sherlock Holmes; I might not have noticed it at all if the ranger hadn't pointed it out to us.

"The sheriff and the RC were already here, not to mention your mother, so any evidence that might have been here is already gone. You can't even see any footprints since it's so dry back here."

"What about the docks?" Tom asked.

Ranger Rogers pointed toward the crest of the dune. "Let's walk up there so you can see the cove. Also, you'll be able to see Ashley waking up. Stay low to the ground and keep your voices down." He leaned over as if he was walking into a strong wind, though the morning was calm.

When we reached the top of the dune, the open ocean lay beyond a wide stretch of clean white sand. The sun was just climbing up over the waves, looking like a strangely pointed reddish-orange triangle that turned rapidly into a flattened semicircle and then a roundish oval. I thought of the Circle in Flatland and what Gloria must really look like and shivered. Tom put his arm around me and held me close. Not that I minded.

Ranger Rogers gestured bayward, toward a cove protected by a long spit of sand that stretched away into the distance before curving in toward the mainland. "That's Dragon's Cove," he said. "People used to think Ashley had actually dug it herself, but we know now that the sandy hook of Dragon Point was really deposited by currents moving southward along the shore."

"Where are the docks?" I asked, shading my eyes against the glare of the sun. Tom put his hands against the sides of my head and turned it slightly. I leaned into his touch and said, "Oh. *Oh.*"

Even from this distance it was obvious that something big had rammed into the pier. There was a huge pile of wrecked timbers on the beach, big enough to make a bonfire for the entire village. None of us said a word. Somebody had meant business.

A long minute passed while a cold breeze blew in off the ocean. Finally, Ranger Rogers said. "As long as you're all here, do you want to see Ashley?"

"Well, we have seen her many times, of course—" Tom began.

"*I* never get bored of it," Jo said.

"—but for Teresa it is a first."

Ranger Rogers looked at me. "It's a good thing you've come now, then, miss. Ashley and Carolina Joe down Hatteras way are our best prospective parents, and they're both pushing the five-century mark, which is old even for a dragon. If they don't have some dragonets soon old *Draco Americanus* is going to go the way of the dodo bird."

I nodded solemnly, though the whole thing still seemed unreal to me. I mean, dragons? Honest-to-goodness, fire-breathing, scaly green dragons? What if Tom had to rescue me? I glanced at him and imagined him wearing armor and waving around a lance while riding one of those potbellied Chincoteague ponies into battle. That would be a sight!

Ranger Rogers suddenly glanced toward the marsh and said softly, "There's the dragon, behind that islet." It looked like he was talking about a shallow pond a couple of hundred yards away, in the middle of which was a tiny island covered with low brush.

For several minutes the only sound was the waves rolling in on the beach below us, the ragged sound of my own breath, and the chittering, piping and squalling of small island creatures. A whinny in the distance made me start. I would have expected Jo to be squirming the whole time, but she hardly moved, and Tom and Ranger Rogers were like statues. Something flickered behind the dead tree crowning the islet. Had I imagined it? But then I saw it again, a flash of deep green that could have been mistaken for a loblolly pine branch waving in the wind.

I stopped breathing. It was the top of a huge, scaly green head, which reared up over the tops of the trees. We were so far away it was hard to say how big it really was, but I guessed that the dragon's head alone was taller than I was, with a pair of shiny black eyes the size of dinner plates and a blunt, curved tan horn with a roundish nozzle at the tip that looked big enough to stick your head into.

"Get down!" Ranger Rogers whispered, and I threw myself flat on my stomach. The dragon's head bobbed back and forth like a pigeon's when it walks, and the water in the pond sloshed back and forth like bathwater when you stand up. Then its whole body surfaced.

I crossed myself, which I haven't done since I took my first (and, I had vowed, my last) communion. Ashley must have been fifty feet long from her beak to the tip of her tail, a mass of shimmering scales in all different shades of green, with legs as wide around as small trees. She had stripes of a delicate light green like leaves unfurling in April mixed with a deeper summery shade and huge dapples the color of a pine forest at night—a complete rainbow, if rainbows came in all green. She opened her mouth and roared so loud the dune seemed to shift under me.

"Don't cry, Teresa, she does this every morning," Tom whispered. "You can almost set your watch by it."

"I'm not crying," I said, but I let out another whimper as Ashley lumbered out of the pond and headed for the beach. Headed to the north, away from us, or I might not be here to tell the tale. She picked up speed at a surprisingly dainty trot, then pole-vaulted with her wing joints—the elbows, I guess you'd call them—to take off. I don't know how else to describe it. It happened very fast, but since she was moving away from us I could see clearly that her rear legs pushed off first, while her front joints were planted firmly in the sand to give her leverage.

Then she was soaring through the air, her wings stretched out at full length, catching the wild salt wind and the bright early morning sunlight, and I shouted with the wonder of it as she made a wide, curving right turn out to sea. Later Ranger Rogers took us up the beach and I walked around one of her footprints near the waterline. It was almost big enough to lie down in.

First, though, he took us for a walk around the pond, which he said Ashley had made wider and deeper. A stiff breeze ruffled the water, and with Ashley away shorebirds probed its shores, looking for whatever smaller creatures she might have stirred up in waking.

Tom explained that we didn't know much about dragons up in the frozen north, so Ranger Rogers lectured about the history of English contact with the dragons.

"By the end of the sixteenth century, most people in Europe thought dragons were just an old legend," Ron said. "That changed in a hurry in August 1590, when Sir Walter Raleigh stopped off to see how the Roanoke Colony he had founded was faring. His men found the burnt remnants of the village, with a dragon gnawing on what they took to be a human leg bone. Today of course we know that dragons rarely eat anything as large as human beings and the colonists had probably fled at the dragon's first approach, but Raleigh's expedition didn't know that. After fleeing to their ship they turned their guns on the poor beast. That was the beginning of a centuries-long dragon slaughter that only ended by order of Queen Victoria in 1867."

"But what about the houses in Roanoke Colony? Did the dragon burn them down?" I asked.

Ron shrugged. "Dragons don't actually breathe fire, Miss Angelov. The front of a dragon's beak is a sort of test tube. To make 'fire,' they combine fatty acids with hydrogen peroxide."

I wrinkled my nose. Ugh, chemistry. But he kept going on and on. It was almost as bad as school.

"The combination burns at a few thousand degrees, hot enough to produce a huge blast of air which in turn can set things on fire. It also burns the dragon's beak, which is actually made of a seashell-like material. That doesn't hurt them, but it takes time to grow back, so they tend to use the ability infrequently. It's no match for modern weaponry, of course, or even for a seventeenth century ship's cannon. By 1700 the dragons were gone from most of the Atlantic seaboard, except for isolated places like Assa Teag Island and the huge nest of them on Manahatta Island."

"Manahatta?" I asked. *Oh of course, Manhattan.*

"But then of course we captured Manahatta for England in 1776, under the great General Sir Benedict Arnold. Why are you coughing, Miss Angelov? Are you sick?"

"No no, I'm all right." *The great hero Benedict Arnold?*

Ranger Rogers gave me a curious look before continuing. "The general founded the famous Order of St. George, which adopted the symbol of the red cross on the field of white, like the flag of old England, and did a very efficient job of hunting dragons all up and down the coast. It wasn't until Victoria's reign that people began to appreciate how rare and wonderful our American dragons are. Charles Darwin played an important role in this, speculating on their ancient origins when he was developing the theory of evolution. By the time Prime Minister Teddy Roosevelt made them a protected species, there were very few of them left. And now it seems they are going to die out altogether, since no dragonets have been born in so many years." He shook his head sadly.

Jo asked if we could stop by the lighthouse and warm up. Maybe Ranger Rogers had some cocoa?

I visited it in the real—all right, in the *other* Assateague. Would it look any different here?

But Tom elbowed her. "Jo! You cannot simply invite yourself into someone's home! And you know how expensive cocoa is!"

"That's all right," Ron smiled. "But the place is such a mess I'd be embarrassed to have any guests over."

"Can you show Teresa one of Ashley's old nests?" Tom said after an awkward pause.

By now we'd walked all around the lagoon and traced her footprints out to the beach. I breathed in the cold, fresh air, and began softly singing a line from one of Nana's favorite songs—not the Beatles, Bob Dylan,

I think—"Out to the windy beach/Far from the twisted reach of crazy sorrow."

Ranger Rogers smiled and ran his hand through my hair just as he had done with Jo. "That's very pretty. I never heard it before. Sure, Tom, I'll do anything for your pretty girlfriend."

Pretty, he was calling me pretty? Really? But I didn't much care for him touching me. By the look on Tom's face, neither did he. I forgot about it when Ranger Rogers took us down a twisty path through the trees to a hidden freshwater pond.

"This was Ashley's nest until about ten years ago," Ranger Rogers explained. "She got tired of it and moved on. As you can see, the trees are just starting to grow back here. Watch your step there, it's marshy."

"What are these?" I asked, bending over to pick up something that looked like an oversized, broken clam shell.

"That? That's a fragment of one of her eggs. They seem to break easily these days, nobody knows why."

How could they break so easily? They were a good half an inch thick, with smooth mother-of-pearl insides. On the outside they were brown speckled with baby blue. But the broken edges were sharp, sharp enough to cut my finger.

"Ow," I said, sucking on my fingertip.

"Better put those pieces down before you hurt yourself," Ranger Ron said. "Also, you never know, Ashley could notice that someone's been messing with her eggs. Dragons can be cranky that way."

"Okay," I said. *That doesn't make much sense, if she abandoned the nest so long ago.* But I dropped them to the spongy, pine-needle-covered ground.

"What's that mean, oh-kay?" Ranger Rogers asked.

"It is an expression they use in Alaska that means 'all right,'" Tom explained.

"Well then. I think we'd better start walking back toward Gingo Teag, before Vivian starts worrying about you lot," Ranger Rogers said.

As soon as his back was turned, I bent down, picked up the broken bits of shell and put them in my jacket pocket. Jo saw me doing it and winked at me. I winked back.

* * * *

Although it began sleeting before the Purnell children and the foreign girl had reached the other side of the bridge, I avoided walking back to my home, instead dawdling around the smashed-up pier as if I was looking over the damage. I was being ridiculous, of course, but better to err on the side of caution.

The sleet stopped after about a quarter of an hour. I pulled out my binoculars and made a quick sweep of the cove, which was deserted. The docks were going to take a lot of work to repair, but it couldn't be helped—it was lucky I'd had on hand some black powder rockets I'd confiscated from a bunch of hooligans who sneaked out to the island to set them off for Guy Fawkes Day last month. Then I turned my binoculars toward the bridge and watched as my three visitors left the guard booth where they'd taken shelter against the storm and headed back to town. Only then did I climb the hill to my house, which is really just a snug cabin where the lighthouse keeper used to live. One hundred years ago the lighthouse was right out on the beach, but the same currents that built up the hook around the cove also left the lighthouse stranded high and dry. The Nanticoke Burgesses voted money to build a new one a few miles further south at Assawoman Inlet back in the 1960's, and the Assa Teague Lighthouse was turned over to the Dragon Refuge. Sometimes I took visitors up to the top for the view, though it would be a long while now before I'd be able to do that again.

I puttered around the kitchen, fixing two cups of tea and two chicken salad sandwiches, tidying up as soon as I was done. I like everything just so.

"You're such a fussy bachelor, you're like an old woman," my mates used to say, back before I got the ranger job and moved out here to the edge of nowhere, with nothing but potbellied ponies and a horrible green monster for company. Sure it's lonely, but most of the girls I've met wouldn't put up with my particular ways. Out here, I don't have to answer to anyone but myself. Or I didn't until last week.

When everything was ready, I covered the tray with a tea towel, ducked out the door, and unlocked the lighthouse. It's a solidly built stone structure, with a winding staircase leading up to the old oil-burning light, which sits 154 feet above sea level. Of course, I wasn't climbing up there—I headed in the other direction. I put the tray down on the floor and unlocked the trap door leading down to the cellar where they used to keep the kerosene and other supplies. The stairs are old and a little rickety, and I don't mind saying I was a bit nervous carrying all that weight down there last week. But the steps held up well enough—they built things to last back in Queen Victoria's day.

"Mike? Are you awake?" I called as I carried the tray down. There was a faint clanking. The kerosene lantern I'd left burning out of his reach had gone out, so I turned on my torch. He was half-sitting up on the mattress I've set up for him, holding his arm in front of his eyes. The smell from the bucket I left down there for him was pretty bad.

"What day is it?" he croaked.

"Christmas Eve, Mike. Happy Christmas!"

He swore an oath.

"Now, come on, Mikey. Everybody knows how Viv hates hearing you curse. You should avoid developing bad habits for when you get out of here. Chicken salad sandwich?"

"I hate chicken." But he snatched it from me anyway, and said around a mouthful of food, "You're not ever letting me out of here. Just admit it, Ron."

"Now that's not fair, Mike." I brushed aside the hair over his right temple to check the bruise from where I'd hit him. He flinched. "I'm not going to hurt you, Mike! I just had to stop you interfering with my mission."

"Your mission?" he said, reaching out for his tea. "Is that what you call it? Fancy yourself a soldier, do you?"

"A knight, actually." I smiled. "When Pierre LaWayne re-founded the Order of St George in 1977, he assigned everybody ranks. I was just a boy then. I never would have dreamt of the honour which is now mine."

"Ron, this is insane," he said. "Ashley and Old Hatteras Joe are no threat to anybody. They are an endangered species, under royal protection. A law you have sworn to uphold, I might point out."

I shook my head. "I have sworn a prior, greater oath. Dragons must be extirpated from the face of God's green Earth. But the wily worms are too smart to openly slay human beings these days, so we must match their cunning. That is why I was doing what I was when you unluckily happened upon me."

The old anchor chain I'd secured around Mike's leg rattled as he threw the tea in my face and lunged. Fortunately the tea had cooled, and I easily ducked his wild punch.

"Don't upset yourself, Mike," I said as gently as I could. I really hated having to do this. "The Order's chief biologist Dr Kovarkian has assured me that by next year—or the year after at the latest—the steps I have taken will make it impossible for the worm ever to lay a viable egg. And then I can leave and let you go."

16

I was so discouraged by our visit to Assa Teag that I fell silent on the walk back to Gingo Teag. Teresa held my hand and snuggled against my shoulder, leaving the chatter to Jo, who babbled on and on, telling Teresa all the local legends about Ashley.

"Our granny lived here all her life, but she hated Ashley. 'Filthy scaly green worm' she called her, isn't that right, Tommy?"

I grunted, which Jo took for encouragement. She takes everything for encouragement when it comes to hearing the sound of her own voice. If somebody else is talking, she takes that for encouragement. If somebody is trying to read, she takes that for encouragement. If it is a cloudy day, she takes *that* for encouragement. If it starts pelting down sleet, which it did as we crossed the bridge over Assa Teag Channel, she takes that as additional encouragement. We all huddled in the guard booth as she kept on chattering.

"...people said Ashley stayed in her lair and refused to come out the day old King Edward the Ninth died, but I *know* that one's not true, I was eight years old and I saw her flying around the marshes myself. I think she's secretly a republican, like me."

"A Republican?" Teresa said, with a puzzled frown. Oh yes, I remembered her saying that was one of the two parties they had in her America, like our Whigs and Tories.

"She means she hates the monarchy," I explained. "A real bomb-throwing radical, is our Jodie."

She shoved me so hard that Teresa and I nearly fell off the bridge. "Don't *ever* call me Jodie!" she shrilled. "Just because I think hereditary royalty is a ridiculous idea!"

Teresa smiled. "In my world, we Americans had a revolution against that very idea," she told Jo. "But that was more than two hundred years ago. Now lots of Americans seem to love the British royal family—who live in London, not Philadelphia—and for the life of me, I can't understand why!"

Jo laughed and gave Teresa a hug, much to my surprise. My sister isn't usually a very demonstrative sort of girl. "I like your girlfriend better all the time!"

"I am glad you approve of her," I said. "What about finding Dad? I mean, I know you are busy and all talking about dragons and politics and anything else *but* finding Dad, but…"

Jo burst into angry tears, and Teresa started scolding me for being mean to her. "She was just trying to take our minds off things, that's all," she said. "I didn't hear you coming up with any brilliant ideas."

My face heated. "What are we supposed to do? Maybe Mum is right and we should all just go back to school and let the police look for him. Maybe we are simply in the way down here." There was a sudden pressure behind my eyes, and tears started dribbling out before I could cover my face.

Teresa hugged me. "Okay, calm down," she said. "Let's think. Is there anybody else who might know what happened to your father?"

"Maybe the people at DRRAGON," Jo said hesitantly. "It's just the other side of the marsh, but would they even talk to us? You can't even get in unless you work there."

"I think they would let me in, though. Dad took me there often enough," I said.

"Better hurry," Jo said. When I looked at her blankly she said, "Have you forgotten? It's Christmas Eve today!"

Teresa and I both gave a start. Christmas Eve?

"Jo, could you take Teresa to Mum and ask her to please, please allow her to stay over tonight and tomorrow?" I said. "Tell her I shall sleep at Smitty's if needs be, and Teresa will take the first train back to Philadelphia on Boxing Day."

"All right, but I'll have to wait till school's over. I'm supposed to be in class, remember?" Jo said.

"Fine with me too, but what is Boxing Day?" Teresa asked.

This time we both stared at her. "The day after Christmas. When servants and employees receive their Christmas box. It is one of the oldest holidays in England," I said at last.

"But I'm not from England. I'm from America," Teresa retorted.

By this time the sleet had stopped, so we left the guard booth and started walking back to the village, deserted under the dark sky. Jo walked off in a different direction so that if Mum asked I would be able to answer truthfully that I had no idea where she was. When we returned home, though, Mum was taking a nap. I thought it best not to wake her, so I made Teresa a cup of tea (not as good as Mum's, but after being out on the beach we would both have drunk plain hot water to warm us up), wrote Mum a note, and headed around back to get the boat. Teresa was not happy about being alone in the house with Mum, but it would be slightly less dangerous than trying to sneak her onto a high-security military base.

* * * *

Once I was out motoring around the familiar tidal creeks I began to feel better. I could have navigated these waters on a cloudless, moonless night without hitting anything. A blue heron stood motionless in the still water not five yards from the boat as I passed by.

I waved and called out, "Hi, Max!"

It was an old family joke not much appreciated by the bird, who took off with a slow flap of his wings. Max Powell had been a Coastal Patrol friend of Dad's who came by once a year, usually in June, to go fishing and swap tall tales with Dad. Mum used to pretend to be irritated by these visits, but I think she was actually quite fond of him.

"If I have to listen to you blokes tell one more story about how you kept Floridian privateers from raiding the coast," she'd begin.

Max would wink at her. "The only exaggerations here are old Mike's," he'd say. "I was the one protecting his bum from the pot shots of those gomezes, not the other way around!"

"Oh yeah? Who almost drowned in the storm off Hatteras that time?" Dad would tease right back.

I joined them in the boat after I turned ten, when Max decided I was "old enough to be able to sit still and stay quiet." I am not much of a fisherman myself, but I enjoyed the quiet out on Dragon's Cove on those early summer mornings. I even trained myself to ignore the whine of the mosquitoes, which Mum's insect repellent did little to keep away.

Dad never had much time for fishing except when Max came to visit. More than three and a half years had passed since our last outing. Max had disappeared the winter I turned fourteen. Many people thought Ashley had eaten him, though Dad defended her honour. Since then all egrets and herons were Max to us.

These days the fellows at DRRAGON Base saw more of Dad than we did. I tied up to the public dock at Wallops Island. The entrance gate to the base was fifty yards from the docks, down a slate path through a well-manicured lawn that looked as if it belonged in Philadelphia rather than lower Nanticoke. The actual gate was not as attractive. It was made of tempered steel, with an armed guard posted outside. Fortunately I knew the chap on duty. Fred had graduated high school just six months ago. We both used to play for the school cricket team, the Gingo Teag Hawks, until I left for boarding school.

"Tommy, I'm sorry about your dad," he said. I shook hands and straightened to my full height. If only I could forget how, when I was thirteen, he would bawl me out for missing the wicket on those rare occasions when I was batsman.

"Thank you, Fred," I said, looking at the ground.

Fred had talent and could have become a professional, but his dad was dead and he wanted to stay at home and look after his mum, at least till his sister was old enough to marry. That was the trouble with growing up in a place like Gingo Teag; it sucked you back in until, before you knew it, you had started a family of your own and were too old to escape. Jo and I were alike in that—we were determined to escape this dreadful fate, especially since our *from-here* status was considered a little questionable thanks to Mum being from the Home Islands.

"So, you come back here to pick up some of his stuff just in case, uh, just in case he's a while getting back?" Fred asked.

"Something like that," I mumbled, still looking at the ground, my ears heating up. I was fortunate compared to Fred, who had lost *his* dad before he was out of high school.

"You know how to get to your dad's office?"

I nodded, still not looking up. "I should. I have been there often enough."

It was only a few minutes' walk from the gate, though with enough twists and turns to confuse any outsider. Most of the buildings were large, low structures with enough space inside for short test flights, but Dad worked in an ordinary office, much to his disgust.

Many of the people I passed on the way there knew me, though I did receive a few funny looks. At Dad's building I was stopped by another guard, this one a stocky fellow in plainclothes whom I did not recognise. This was something new—normally there was only the one bloke on duty at the outer gate, a fact that amazed Teresa when I told her about it afterwards.

"In my world," she said, "you'd have to show picture ID and go through a metal detector to get into some fancy government research lab."

It seemed His Majesty's men also thought they had been a little lax, because the plainclothes guard gave me a hard look. His face did not soften even when I told him who I was and why I was there.

"You've no business wandering around a closed government facility," he said. He had a harsh drawl from somewhere down in the borderlands, West Florida or Franklin.

"But my father—"

"Probably wouldn't have been kidnapped if anyone around here cared a rat's arse about security," he snapped. "Oh, don't give me that look. Come with me to Major Frost's office."

Was he from the R.C.? He was nasty enough.

At least I was getting somewhere. I followed him inside and up a metal staircase. I had only met Dad's supervisor a handful of times, but he knew me. Dad had never had anything bad to say about him, at least not around me.

Frost's office door stood half open and he leaned over a draughting table working on some blueprints. The guard cleared his throat.

Frost looked up. He was a tall man with a slight paunch, a bald spot, and a grey mustache, and he was dressed as if he was about to go fishing.

"Sir, this boy here," the guard began.

"It's all right, George, this is Captain Purnell's son," Frost said, nodding in my direction while deftly rolling up the blueprints. It was odd hearing my dad referred to by rank. We never thought of him that way at home. He was just Dad, and was no more military than I was.

"So he told me, sir, but he really shouldn't be in a restricted area like this," the guard said.

"Oh, take the stick out of your bum, George," Frost said.

I stifled a started laugh. Mum would have tanned my hide if I used language like that around her. "I've known Tommy here since he was hardly any bigger than a sand piper, isn't that right, Tommy?"

At least he did not ruffle my hair.

"Yes, Major Frost," I said.

"So it's quite all right, George. Well done. Return to your post and keep me informed if any more suspicious schoolboys or sand pipers show up." He glanced at me and winked.

The guard snapped off a salute before stalking out of the room, not quite slamming the door behind him.

Frost winked again and said, "Pull up a chair, Tommy."

I did, and he did the same. The chairs were not what you would expect in an office. They were overstuffed and comfortable. Had he bought them at a jumble sale?

His office was certainly unusual. One whole wall was decorated with a mural depicting the Wright Brothers' famous blimp flight over the royal palace at Valley Forge, while the opposite wall displayed the Peace Bridge across the Mississippi River to St. Louis, Louisiana. Come to think of it, Frost did have a Western accent. Dad had mentioned he was an amateur artist. If he had painted these murals, he was very skilled. Perhaps I should not have been surprised. There is something artistic in the design of a graceful flying wing.

He looked at me keenly with his grey eyes and asked how boarding school was going.

"Fine. Look, I hate to be rude, Major Frost, but I did not come here to make small talk."

He nodded and sighed. "Since your dad disappeared, I've wasted more time with that martinet George and the other R.C. men than I want to think about," he said. "We've gone over and over the blessed business. It's obvious that even the R.C. has no idea what happened."

"But he was kidnapped by the Frogs, surely," I said.

"Things aren't always what they seem. But you didn't come here for me to tell you that. You came here to tell *me* something, didn't you?"

I hesitated, but after all, what was the use of coming here if I did not trust him? "Well, Dad said something to me the last time I saw him, back on Union Day weekend."

"Yes?"

"He said he was going to show me 'some really exciting stuff' you lot are doing here."

"Now Tommy, you know I can't talk about our work, and your father shouldn't either," Frost said, frowning. "In this case, I have no idea what he was talking about."

"None? Really?"

"Truly," he said, frowning harder. "We've been rather on our heels, actually, since the crash down at Roanoke a few years ago."

"I remember that," I said. It was hardly a secret when DRAGGON's latest attempt at powered heavier-than-air flight at Kitty Hawk in the Outer Banks had ended up an expensive wreck. It was fortunate no one had been killed, though the pilot was probably never going to walk again.

"Everyone has been discouraged since then, including myself. Your father has been one of the few exceptions. He keeps saying the dragon holds the key. The real dragon, that is—Ashley, in all her glory. He's taken to spending all his free time out there on Assa Teag, even with the weather turning bad. He'll take his boat out there during his lunch hour on occasion. It's becoming a bit of an obsession."

Oh dear. "Did he ever talk about consulting with experts? Experts in dragon biology, I mean?"

If Frost had frowned any deeper, his chin would have detached itself from his face. "Yes, now that you mention it. He told me he was writing to some academic type about his theories on how dragons fly. That might be the key to the breakthrough we've been looking for all these years, he said. The chap he was writing to had an odd name. Earhart, maybe?"

17

I dozed off with my head on the Purnells' kitchen table less than five minutes after Tom left for the DRRAGON base. When I woke with a start, Mrs. Purnell stood not three feet away, holding the note Tom had written and staring at me silently, her lips pursed.

I flinched.

The corner of her mouth turned up and she said, "Don't worry, Teresa, I'm not going to rough you up again."

"That's a relief," I said.

"My Tommy obviously believes you are someone quite special. He is a young man now and I must trust his judgment. Besides, I had a steady boyfriend by the time I was sixteen," she said, pulling up a chair across from me.

I didn't know what to say. She still scared me, but she put the note on the table and ran both her hands through her hair with a sigh, which made her seem a lot more human. Still, she was dressed better for a day at home, in a rich purple blouse, matching skirt and stockings, than Mom or I ever were, except maybe for my First Communion. My eye was drawn to a large mother-of-pearl brooch that hung on a silver chain around her neck. She followed my gaze and smiled.

"That's one of the few things I was able to bring with me from the Home Islands," she said, taking it off and handing it to me. "Have a look inside."

It held one of those funny photographs they had in Tom's world. It was black and white and the lines were all blurry, like a charcoal drawing, but it was obviously of her and Tom's father long ago, maybe just after they met. She was grinning hugely, but there was something tough about her eyes and the set of her mouth, while Tom's dad looked like the softy. In fact he looked a lot like Tom; I had to squint really hard to see that his nose was a little broader, his hair a shade darker than Tom's.

I handed the brooch back and said, "It's a nice picture."

"It was taken just after we came to America," she said.

What had she called this place?

She continued with a grin. "Hah! At least I can call this country America around you. The natives are offended if you call them anything but true-blooded Englishmen."

"Where I come from, we had a little revolution that took care of all that confusion," I said, adding hastily, "but England and America have been friends for a long time now. We fought in two world wars together."

"Two world wars?" she mused. "It took your people that long to defeat the disgusting Bonapartes?"

"Er, not exactly," I said. "But I don't think you really want to talk about history right now, with everything that's going on."

"No, it is true, I do not," she said. "May I examine that cell phone of yours for a moment?" I handed it over and she took her time inspecting it. "Remarkable," she said when she handed it back. "The weapons your people have must be remarkable too."

My guts clenched. I could see where she was going with this. "We don't have ray-guns or anything like that," I said. "My mom does have a handgun since she got mugged eight years ago, but she keeps it locked up in her dresser drawer. I don't have the key and I wouldn't know how to fire it anyhow."

"Oh, we have all the pistols and shotguns we need," she said with a dismissive wave of her hand. "I was just thinking…never mind. A gun is not much use if you do not point it at someone, is it?"

Her grin made me nervous. Those French people who kidnapped her husband were luckier than they knew. If they had tried to take him when she was around…

"Oh, do not look like a frightened rabbit," she said, leaning forward and patting my hand. "I am simply a harmless housewife…and not a very good one, either, seeing that Christmas Eve dinner is in three hours and I have not fetched the goose yet. Would you be a dear and get it for me?"

"Er, sure thing," I said. "Where's the supermarket?"

"Super-market? What's that? No, just run down to the Kelvins' farm. Make a right on Main Street, a right on Maddox Boulevard, then a right on Chicken City Road. Shouldn't take you more than twenty minutes, there and back. Jake or Betsy will have one set aside for us."

"That's kind of funny," I said, as she handed me a two-pound note and two shillings, which were heavy yellow coins about as big around as Kennedy half-dollars, but much thicker.

"What's funny?"

"That they live on Chicken City Road but raise geese, not chickens."

She rolled her eyes. "Oh, you will get on just fine with my Michael," she said. "Run along with you, now."

There was only one small problem with my being sent on this simple errand—the fact that I have no sense of direction. The only reason I was always able to find my way back to Gloria's bookstore is that it didn't actually have a specific, real location. Maybe the bookstore always found me, in some strange way. The Kelvins' farm sure wasn't cooperating. I found Main Street all right, but not Maddox Boulevard, let alone Chicken City Road, and within ten minutes I was no longer on Main Street either, but on an unmarked dirt road winding through the pine trees.

Even when I was still in the village no one had been around to ask for directions. Maybe they were already in their houses roasting chestnuts over an open fire, toasting the King, and doing whatever else proper British Americans did on Christmas Eve.

When I tried to retrace my steps I only got more lost. Then the pine trees petered out into reeds and the road dwindled to a muddy track that ended at a sluggishly moving gut. Crabs scuttled sideways through the muddy water, and I shivered with disgust more than cold; spiders don't bother me, but creepy crawlies that can pinch you really bug me.

Where the hell was I, anyway? There was no one in sight except for a blue heron eyeing me suspiciously.

"Don't worry, I'm not going to try to pass you off as a Christmas goose," I said.

It opened and closed its long, sharp beak, then took off with slow, powerful strokes of its wings. A pair of seagulls that had been playing tug-of-war with something decaying dropped it with an abrupt splash and took off, cawing loudly.

"Great, even the birds think I'm for the birds," I said. A blast of cold air hit me and my eyes teared up. I blinked, trying to clear them. The day had suddenly darkened. Was I about to find myself lost in a blizzard?

That would have been just my luck, except that luck had something even bigger and scarier in store for me. After another blast of cold air, it finally got through to my dumb old brain that the wind wasn't coming from north or south or east or west—it was coming from straight overhead, as if something enormous was creating the wind as it came in for a landing. Well, there was no "as if" about it—something enormous *was* coming in for a landing.

It was too late to run; the treeline was a good fifty yards behind me, and I was always famous in my class as The Slowest Girl In The Fifty-Yard Dash. *Maybe I should throw myself flat, like you're supposed to do if you're caught out in the open during a thunderstorm. But that might just attract her attention.*

Coming in for a landing right in front of me, on wings as wide as a fighter jet's that kicked up huge waves in the marsh all around me, was Ashley, the Assa Teag Dragon.

I stared and almost forgot to be scared out of my wits. Almost, but not quite.

But I didn't scream "eek!" and go running away, so I had that going for me. Though a knight in shining armor would have looked really, really good right about now. Or Tom—Tom here with me, even if all he could do was tell me to run, would have been great. I closed my eyes for a moment. Maybe when I opened them again I would be in my own bed at home. No such luck, though. Not only was Ashley still there, she was looking right at me.

Her shiny black eyes were enormous, maybe more like dinner *platters* than dinner *plates*. They were set in the sides of her head, which she swung slowly back and forth as if trying to give each eye a chance for a good stare. This also meant that she kept pointing the nozzle of her horn right at me. The thing curled over and over on itself, like the horns of a ram I'd petted once on a visit to a farm, though it must have measured a good three yards from the tip to the point where it was attached to her skull.

Tom later told me I could have counted the coils to see how many years it had been since Ashley had last used it to breathe fire, which I guess would have been somewhat reassuring if I'd known it at the time. A strong smell reminded me of a grease fire I'd started the morning I tried to make Mom and Dad breakfast in bed for what turned out to be their last anniversary together. A secret corner of my mind still insists that that's the real reason they got divorced.

Ashley blinked twice. Was she trying to send a message? ("Hi! You look nice and tasty!") I was close enough to see that the camouflage patterning that covered her body was made up of overlapping scales, each as large as a tabletop, with edges that looked sharp enough to cut your fingers on. Maybe all she had to do was roll over on her victims to make herself some nice, pre-sliced cold cuts.

WISH THAT LIFE WAS THAT EASY.

Wait a minute. When did I shout in my mind? I never shouted in my thoughts, unless I was thinking about Kylie or Osama Bin Laden or somebody else really bad. Besides, the thought hadn't sounded angry, just loud.

LOUD AND GREEN.

Now that really made no sense. How could a thought be green? Unless a tree thought it. A tree or…something bigger…

AH, YOU FIGURED IT OUT, DID YOU? I COULD TELL YOU HEARD ME, BUT I THOUGHT I WAS GOING TO BE STANDING HERE TILL SPRING WAITING FOR YOU TO CATCH ON.

I planted my hands on my hips. "Since when are dragons sarcastic? Is that some kind of survival mechanism?"

The head reared and the nozzle of the horn swung in my direction. I flinched.

DON'T WORRY, I'M NOT GOING TO ROAST YOU. I SPENT FORTY YEARS GROWING MY HORN OUT LIKE THIS. YOU KNOW HOW HARD IT IS TO GET THESE CURLS RIGHT?

So I was talking telepathically with a dragon. Two impossibilities at once! How could I hear a dragon's thoughts—was it because I was a virgin? No, that's unicorns. Could she hear everything I was thinking? My head throbbed, so I shut my eyes and rubbed my fingers against my temples.

"Do you have to shout? My head is really starting to hurt!"

MOST PEOPLE CAN'T HEAR DRAGONS AT ALL. IT DOESN'T MAKE ANY DIFFERENCE WHETHER OR NOT THEY'VE MATED. THERE HAVE ONLY BEEN A HANDFUL WHO COULD HEAR US SINCE YOU ENGLISH CAME AND TOOK AWAY THE CHINCOTEAGUE INDIANS' CLAM BEDS.

I stamped my foot, splashing cold mud all around me. "I am *not* English! I'm an American!"

WHAT DIFFERENCE DOES IT MAKE WHAT YOU CALL YOURSELF? YOU'RE STILL A CLEODOLINDA, AREN'T YOU?

"A what? No, no—we don't even have dragons where I come from! You're a mythical creature!"

At that, Ashley also stamped her foot, drenching me in mud. I must have looked like a chocolate soldier.

IS THAT SO? WAS THE MANAHATTA MASSACRE A MYTH, TOO?

"The Manahatta *what?*"

The marsh around me faded and disappeared, and suddenly I was flying, just as naturally as in my dreams. All around me flowed the cool evening air, alive with the graceful forms of other swimmers, or rather other flyers, dipping and soaring along with me. Two of my sisters were racing. Lo'purea gently teased Er'yitro as she soared past, toward the northern tip of the large wooded island below us. The summer air carried the muddy-clean smell of the large river that flowed from the deep green forested country to the north and the salty tang of the ocean to the south. It fell behind as I followed my sisters north. The setting sun to my left picked out dramatic shadows across the face of the dark cliffs that marked the edge of the mainland to the west. This beautiful scene was my home; my sisters and I lived in a sandy valley in the southern part of the island, between rocky hills to the north and south. I flipped lazily onto my back, fixing my wings in position for a gentle glide as I looked at the glowing orange and rose-colored sunset clouds and daydreamed.

Maybe if I'd been watching the river more carefully I would have seen the ships coming around a bend where they'd been concealed by the dark cliffs and I could have sounded a warning. I would always blame myself for that in the long, lonely years ahead, though it might not have made any difference.

I suddenly heard something whizzing past me, much too fast and heavy to be a bird. Could it be a meteorite? There was a legend that an elder, a hero of our people, had been killed by one, struck down in his sleep thousands of years ago. There was an epic ballad about it, "Ge'ohan and the Falling Star," which our parents had taught us when we were just hatchlings. Another object whizzed by, much closer this time.

White sails glimmered in the sunlight far below; we were facing something much more dangerous than mere falling stars. These must be the invading humans who had come from across the ocean in their huge artificial seabirds to take away our nests and the lands of the local humans, who had long ago learned to live in harmony with us.

I roared and dove toward the ships, which rapidly grew from looking like tiny seagulls that wouldn't even make a decent snack to looming before me like wooden cliffs. There was a series of loud bangs and more whizzing noises. Something struck my right wing, something that burned like a lightning strike. Far above and behind me I heard a scream. Lo'purea? She had just celebrated her hundredth birthday and was engaged to be mated with shy Ki'thot, who lived with his family in a separate band far to the north.

I roared again as my horn discharged reflexively. I was barely fifty years old myself and mine hadn't even a full curl. The whole thing melted down to the nub and fell off.

A huge flapping white sail sprouted an orange flame brighter than the setting sun. It spread rapidly. The humans on the ship shouted; a few pointed long straight sticks at me, and tiny pellets flew past, but they were too small to harm me. Other humans dove into the water, their heads bobbing like seaweed.

As I banked sharply and flapped my wings to go higher, another ship let off a blast that ripped past me. My right front foot felt like it was on fire, and I roared. I wheeled around to attack again, but my father gently knocked me aside and I sailed off toward the western cliffs, watching helplessly as he dove straight toward the biggest ship. I roared and screamed, but he couldn't hear me or anyone else; a meteorite had struck him in the soft spot above his horn, and he trailed a red mist as he slammed into the deck. The ship wobbled and rolled over like a fallen log.

But all the other ships were firing now. I landed hard on the cliff's edge and rolled, knocking over small trees. I wept at their fall.

When I had caught my breath I got to my feet. The pain in my wing and my foot was even worse now. I hobbled back toward the cliff's edge and tried to take off, but my right wing had been badly hurt, and I couldn't get off the ground. I did, however, have a clear view of the slaughter going on in the river below.

Just minutes later it was all over, though those minutes seemed to last years. The green and gold bodies of my mother, my sisters, and everyone else I knew drifted seaward in waters stained purple and scarlet by the setting sun, while the ships fired cannons and muskets in wild celebration. Not even in the times of Ge'ohan had there been so much bloody death. I sank to the ground.

* * * *

When the darkness lifted I stared at my two tiny stubby legs and mere hands instead of graceful wings. I cried. I cried harder than I ever had since Nana's funeral. I cried until sparks swam before my eyes, sparks that reminded me of the setting sun flashing on the Hudson River as it flowed toward the sea carrying "Sir" Benedict Arnold's cruel ships and the broken bodies of my dragon kin—of Ashley's family. How terrible if she could never have hatchlings, if there were no dragonets to carry on the memories of her parents and her sisters. I lifted my aching head. I was alone in the marsh.

How I found my way back to Tom's house I'll never know. I knocked feebly at the door and his mother opened it. She stood there looking me up and down, from my filthy, ripped socks—my shoes had disappeared in the marsh—to my scratched and bleeding face. She let out a slow breath.

"I take it you did not bring back the goose," she said.

18

"The dragons are obviously the key to everything," I said.

For once, Tommy didn't disagree with me. Teresa sat slumped in a corner. I felt sorry for her, looking at the rumpled shirt and torn denim pants she had changed into—was her family so poor she couldn't afford a decent skirt? At least she had thought to bring an extra pair of shoes with her from her home, though they were ugly, scuffed off-white things she called "sneakers."

I had to fetch the goose from the Kelvins and the plum pudding from the Birches, since Teresa needed a bath after getting lost in Wildcat Marsh and Tommy took his sweet time returning from the DRRAGON Base. It's *so* unfair how I must always run the boring errands! I had to help Mum cook, too—Tommy came in wearing a face like a nor'easter and went straight to his room, slamming the door. I was certain Mum was going to kill him, but no, all she did was tell me to light the oven! Unfair, I tell you. But then Tommy came out of his room and started setting the table. He looked so sad I wanted to hug him—but something told me I'd better not. Anyway he now has Teresa to give him all the hugs he needs, and smooches too.

She came out of the bathroom, her hair all tangled, and offered to help, but Mum shooed her away, saying she was a guest. The smell of roast goose filled the house, and my mouth watered.

It seemed wrong to be hungry and to enjoy Christmas Eve dinner when Dad wasn't here with us. He was probably in an Empire dungeon right now, with a torturer shoving needles under his fingernails and forcing him to eat snails and whatever else it was the Froggies did to people. Guilt kept gnawing at me, making a hole in my stomach till I wasn't hungry anymore.

When Mum called us to the table I told her I couldn't eat. Her face darkened and I braced myself for a smack. Instead she took a deep breath and said, "Honey, your Dad would want us to enjoy our Christmas Eve dinner, even though he is not here." She stroked my arm with a hand warm from the oven.

I burst into tears and buried my face in her sleeve as if I was five years old. I was so ashamed I couldn't stop crying. What was the matter with me? I cried and cried until I started hiccupping, which made me even angrier with myself. After drying my eyes I looked up to see both Tommy and Mum struggling to hold back tears of their own.

Teresa took my hand and looked at me with shining eyes. "It's all right, Jo," she said, "I remember how I cried and cried when my grand— well, when something bad happened in my family, too."

"Come on everyone, we must eat now or the food will get cold," Mum said. "Jo, I will not be angry if you cannot eat, I promise. But please stay with us through the meal."

The fact that she *wasn't* punishing me was one of the scariest things that had happened so far. And I did try to return the favour by eating a couple of forkfuls of roast goose. I might as well have been eating wet sand. What was happening to Dad? What did Tommy find out at the DRRAGON Base? I never dreamt that Teresa had made the most amazing discovery of all.

She wasn't about to tell us anything with Mum there, of course. But luckily, as soon as we were finished eating Mum said she was exhausted, apologised to Teresa and asked Tommy and me to clean up while she went upstairs and took a nap.

The three of us talked quietly while Tommy washed, Teresa dried, and I put things away. Teresa rubbed plates with our familiar green dish towel while telling us calmly that she'd swapped thoughts with Assa Teag Ashley. Very, very odd.

Tommy stared at her as if she'd suddenly grown horns. "Teresa, that is quite impossible," he said. "Nobody has ever spoken with a dragon. They cannot speak!"

"I didn't say she talked to me," she said. "I said her thoughts just appeared in my head, telepathically."

"You mean like using that cell phone of yours?"

"No, telepathically," she said. "Don't tell me you don't have that word."

"She means mindspeaking, Tommy," I said.

"Like in the Herbert Wells story? Go on, that is just a silly story."

"But there are stories about the Manahatta Indians talking with dragons," I pointed out.

Tommy scowled. "Ridiculous! Mindspeaking is impossible!"

"Like travel between worlds?"

"It happened, Tom," Teresa said, handing me a dry plate. "Ashley told me about the battle of Manahatta. She *showed* it to me. It's like I was in her memories!"

Tommy opened his mouth, then stopped and looked thoughtful. "If you talked to Ashley, did you ask her if she saw what happened to Dad?"

Teresa looked embarrassed. "I'm sorry, Tom. First I thought she was going to kill me…then when she showed me the Battle of Manahatta, I was too overwhelmed to think about anything else."

That's when I said the dragons were the key to everything. "Dad was obsessed with them," I said. Managing not to cry when I said "Dad" was a real achievement. "It looks like the Imperials grabbed him to find out what he'd learned…like the secret to heavier-than-air flight!"

"Maybe that's what he wanted to tell you, Tom," Teresa said. "That he's been talking to Ashley just like I did! And maybe he wrote about that to his friend Ramsey Urquhart, and the French secret police opened the letter. It wouldn't be that hard, since they control the Home Islands and all the mail that goes there, right?"

"Major Frost did say Dad was always writing to Professor Urquhart," Tommy said.

"We have to talk to him. To the professor, I mean," I said. *And I do mean "we." You're not leaving me behind!*

"But he's in the Home Islands, Jo," Tommy said.

"I have an idea—" I began, but Teresa got a faraway look in her eyes. The bowl she was drying slipped out of her hands and shattered on the floor, and she didn't look down or even flinch.

"Teresa! What's the matter with you?" Tom said.

He looked at the broken shards at her feet, peered into her face, then took the towel out of her hands and waved it in front of her eyes. She didn't blink or react when Tom put his hands on her shoulders and looked in her eyes. The black pupils of her eyes expanded, crowding out the warm brown irises.

Then she shook her head, her curly hair flying around, rubbed her fists in her eyes and said, "Hey, who turned up the lights so bright? Oh— Tom. Tom, that was Ashley."

"What was Ashley?" Tom said, taking his hands off her shoulders and stepping back. He can be so stupid sometimes!

"Ashley was just talking to Teresa, you big idiot," I explained helpfully.

"Yes, that's right," Teresa said. "And she said—and Ashley's not really her name, you know, it's actually Ir'befunzu, which means—"

"Yes?" Tom said. "I think I shall just stick with Ashley for now."

"Well. She said she's sorry, but she was fishing far out at sea Saturday morning and she didn't see what happened to your father. But she didn't see any big ships near the island. Nothing but the usual Gingo Teag fishing boats."

"That is strange," Tom said, frowning, "although not quite as strange as the idea that you have been speaking with a dragon in your mind!"

Teresa's face crumpled up as if she was about to cry.

"Look, I apologise," Tommy said. "I—I suppose mindspeaking must be possible, if parallel worlds and eleven dimensions and heaven knows what else is real. I just wish she could help us!"

"But she is helping!" I said. "She's helping prove my point about how the dragons are the key to everything, and that we need to go see Professor Urquhart, like I just said."

"Brilliant as always, Jo," Tom said. "But how are we going to travel to the Home Islands and see Professor Urquhart?"

"By airship, big brother, how else?"

"And what are we supposed to use for money, little sister? Or passports?"

"You have almost fifty pounds in your bank account," I said. Tom's eyes bugged out of his head as I continued, "I opened your mail, so shoot me. Mum and Dad said they were going to give you spending money, Tommy, but I think fifty pounds is a bit much!"

"I need that money for books and food and all these fees and *what business is it of yours how much money I have*?"

"Tom!" Teresa said. He shut up, but then she turned on me. "You open your family's mail, Jo? What the hell kind of thing is that to do?"

She said *hell*? Tommy's eyes grew wide.

"We need to do something," she said, turning to Tommy again. "The police in your world don't seem very sophisticated. No offense or anything Tom, but what exactly have they accomplished?"

"Nothing more than we have," Tom pointed out. "We are at a dead end. You are not taking Jo's idea seriously, are you?"

"Why not? What's the big deal about going to England—the original England, I mean? And we have to meet Professor Urquhart. We did meet him, or will have met him, and we know he's going to help us, or we're going to help him."

"Well first of all, it *is* a big deal going to the Home Islands," Tommy said. "It takes weeks—"

"Only one week by airship," I pointed out.

"—it takes weeks, I said, and you have to get a visa, and for that you need a passport, which neither of us has."

"Hey, what about me?" I said. "I haven't got one either!"

"I do have a passport!" Teresa said. "I got it when we went on a big trip to Italy, my parents and Nana and me, for Nana's sixty-fifth birthday seven years ago."

"Great, a passport from a nonexistent country," Tom said.

"Mum and Dad have passports," I said. Teresa and Tom both looked at me. "I know where they keep them. In the old dresser in the attic crawlspace, in the middle drawer under some old papers."

"So what?" Tom said. "We cannot use them. We are not Mum and Dad!"

"We could change the names and put our own pictures in," I said.

Teresa and Tom both gaped at me like a couple of dead fish washed up on the beach after a big storm.

"Well, why not?" I said. "I'll use Mum's passport, you'll use Dad's, Tom, and Teresa can use her own. I'm sure it looks similar to a proper British passport."

"First of all, you are not to go anywhere. You have to stay home with Mum," Tom said.

While I was still opening my mouth Teresa put in, "He's right, Jo. It's much too dangerous. Besides which, if we go, you'll need to stay here with your mother and keep an eye on her. We have to make sure she doesn't try to go to the Home Islands herself. She'd be caught, and then both of your parents will be captives of Napoleon, and what good will that do us?"

"Henri-Napoléon, you mean," I said.

Tom scowled. "The whole idea is mad. Changing Mum and Dad's passports? How are we supposed to do that? And tampering with passports is a crime."

"Only if we get caught," Teresa said. She looked at me and winked, while Tom gaped.

19

It was tricky, getting Jo to agree to stay in Gingo Teag while Tom and I went to England. She had to actually *want* to stay, because otherwise she might spill the beans to Mrs. Purnell, and then all hell would break loose.

So I asked Jo to get her parents' passports for us. That way she'd feel like she was really part of our conspiracy. "You should do it, Jo, the whole idea was yours to begin with," I said. "We'd never have thought of it without you!" Boy, did she grin at that!

While we waited for her to come back downstairs with the passports Tom asked to talk to me outside. I gave him a look. Even without poking my nose out I could hear sleet rattling against the windowpanes.

"Really, Teresa, it is important," he said softly, so I sighed and reached for my coat.

It was just as bad as I thought outside. Maybe worse. The wind carried the salt tang of the bay on it, which made me sneeze, and my fingertips were going numb inside my worn-out gloves, so I shivered and pressed close to Tom.

"What is it? Quick, before Jo gets back or I freeze to death."

"There is another reason I do not wish to travel to the Home Islands, besides all the obvious ones."

"Yes? What's that?"

"Well, we met—*will* meet—no, we already *did* meet—good heavens, you know what I mean! We *met* the professor in Philadelphia six months from now, and he already knew us. He hinted that we had saved his life!"

"That's pretty cool, isn't it?"

"Cool? I thought you just said you were freezing."

"No, I mean it's pretty exciting to think we're going to save some guy's life, right? And save your father too, I'm sure!"

"Exciting?" He frowned. "Well, yes, I suppose it would be exciting, if we not for the fact that already know what we are going to do!"

"But we don't," I said, "not really."

"Yes we do," he said. "And I do *not* like it. We are *not* characters in a story that has already been written. We do not lack free will."

"Free will? You mean, like, choice?"

"Yes, exactly. I want to choose what I am going to do, and I do not want anybody else to decide for me! Not my parents, not Gloria, not even you. I do not want to know what shall happen to me in the future, even if it is something good."

I leaned forward and kissed him hard on the mouth before he could say another word.

"Did you choose that? Did you know it was coming?" I asked when I came up for breath.

"Umm, uh…"

I kissed him again. "How about that?"

"N-no, but I did enjoy it."

"All right then, stop worrying about it. Now, I *choose* to go back inside before my butt turns into a block of ice."

I looked up at the sky before we stepped through the doorway. The constellation of Orion the Hunter shone through a break in the clouds. Nana taught me to pick it out, though she and I used to agree you'd have to have a pretty good imagination to see a hunter in it. But the belt of three stars in an almost straight line was easy enough to make out. I gave them a hard stare. *Whoever's trying to control me better cut it out! Or I'll show* them *who the real hunter is.*

Back inside, Jo was standing waiting for us, her hands on her hips. "Jeez you guys, can't you go five minutes without sneaking out for a quick snoggle? It's disgusting."

"Did you get the passports or not?" Tom snapped.

She handed them over and we crowded around. Like the picture in Mrs. Purnell's brooch, Tom's father's passport picture looked so much like Tom that it really did seem we could get away with him using it and going by his father's name. But Mrs. Purnell was so much better looking than me that even the blindest, or kindest, cop couldn't possibly mistake me for her. We were obviously going to have to replace the picture, but how?

I squeezed my eyes shut. On the one hand, these passports were just paper folders with grainy pictures in them. They couldn't be too hard to forge. On the other hand, Tom was such a goody two shoes that I doubted he had the kind of friends who might even possibly have the kind of friends who make fake IDs. As for me, Kylie's gang went out drinking on fake driver's licenses all the time, but I couldn't exactly ask her for help. Maybe someone who was good at messing around with computers and printing… I opened my eyes and smiled at Tom.

"I know who can help us," I said. "Miss Chen!"

"Who?" Tom and Jo said together.

Then Tom said, "Oh, you mean Susie!" in a way that made me give him a hard look.

* * * *

Once we'd made the decision, we were both impatient to get back to Philadelphia, but there was no ferry until Boxing Day. Just as well, since we were both so tired we slept away half of Christmas morning. I blinked at the sunlight in my eyes when I finally woke up. I'd been sleeping on the sofa, and was amazed that everyone had been so quiet tiptoeing through the living room that I hadn't woken up all this time.

Tom greeted me in the kitchen with toast, eggs, bacon, and a cup of strong tea. It smelled so good my knees went weak.

"Where's Jo?" I asked around a huge mouthful of food.

"Who cares? Out with Marcia or one of her other stupid friends."

I frowned. Why did he talk about her like that all the time? I mean, I could understand that having a little sister could get annoying some-times, but Jo was really all right. And she had already helped us a lot. But Tom had a lot on his mind. I'd talk to him about it later.

"And your mom?" I asked.

Tom slumped and looked at the table. "Still in bed," he admitted. "It's not like her at all."

I bit my lip, remembering all the days *my* mom had stayed in bed till afternoon, which was pretty much every day she wasn't working. I never could figure out how to cheer her up. It had gotten so bad lately I even wished she'd find a boyfriend, even though the idea creeps the hell out of me.

And then I'd run away and left her to worry, which made me feel guilty, which made me angry and restless.

"Come on, let's go for a walk," I said, gulping down the rest of my tea and jumping to my feet.

"Now? But it's even colder out than yesterday," Tom complained as I tossed him his coat.

"So? It'll be good practice for us. We're going to England in the middle of winter, remember?"

"Why do you keep calling it England?" he said, puffing after me as I ran out the door. "This is as much England as the Home Islands. Maybe more! Parliament's been in Philadelphia for almost two hundred years, after all, even if the original Houses of Parliament are still in London. And our king is the *genuine* king and not the stupidest member of the Bonaparte family, who they always seem to give charge of the Home Islands."

"Tommy, this is America, love it or leave it!" I snapped.

"But not *your* America," he said quietly.

I hate it when other people get the last word. I stomped down the wooden sidewalk. A wooden sidewalk, for God's sake! How primitive could you get? I half expected some guy in a cowboy hat to swagger up holding two six shooters. Instead, a few families walked back from church, staring at me. Great, I would be the subject of gossip in Gingo Teag for weeks, if not months. The wild Alaskan girl. Kind of cool, come to think of it. Maybe I could bite the head off a whole fish just to show how tough I was.

Tom caught up with me. "Where do you think you're going?"

"To swallow some raw oysters," I said, deciding not to be too gross. "Is there any place open?"

"On Christmas? You must be joking."

"Do you people roll the sidewalks up at night?" Tom shot me a confused look. "Isn't there anything to *do* in this town?"

"Not really, not today. You should come for the pony swim in July."

"I have." He stared at me. "In the other Chincoteague," I explained. "The crowds were enormous. Probably bigger than anything you ever get here, because there you can drive to the island."

"Here we pick out the healthiest and best-looking ponies and keep them so Ashley cannot eat them," he explained.

"Ah. They don't have to worry about that in the other Chincoteague."

I DO NOT EAT THE ASSA TEAG PONIES, the voice in my head objected. *THAT'S JUST A MYTH.*

"Teresa? Are you all right?"

I repeated what Ashley had just told me.

"What about people? What about Max Powell?"

"Who?"

"An old mate of Dad's from the Coastal Patrol who disappeared three and a half years ago. He went out in his boat early one morning during striped bass season and was never heard from again."

WHY DON'T YOU ASK THE FLORIDIANS ABOUT THAT, the voice in my head said. We'd stepped onto a side street and there didn't seem to be anybody around, so I repeated what Ashley had said to me. Tom's eyes widened.

"You mean he was kidnapped and taken to St. Augustine? Maybe that's what happened to Dad!" He clenched his fist. "Though I wouldn't think El Presidente would dare, after the licking we gave him!"

The Marks' son had died for the sake of this "licking," but I said nothing.

MAX'S BOAT WAS SUNK BY A FLORIDIAN U-BOAT, Ashley explained. *BUT AS I TOLD YOU, NO BOAT PUT OUT TO SEA FROM ASSA TEAG SATURDAY MORNING.*

I told Tom what had happened to Max. He nodded with a frown.

"But we sank Forida's entire U-boats fleet, so it had to be the Frogs," he said after a moment. "I am sure that is what Professor Urquhart will tell us. Remember how he said *our friends* were at it again? Must be more trouble with the Empire, five months from now." He brightened a little. "Five months after we brought—*will* have brought—Dad home."

I hoped so. He made it all sound so easy.

* * * *

The rest of the day just dragged. "We usually exchange Christmas presents in the morning, but none of us want to open ours without Dad here," Tom said, avoiding my eyes. I tried not to tear up myself. "I understand, Tom," I said, taking his left hand in both of mine. But his right hand was behind his back. "Thomas Jefferson Purnell, what are you hiding back there?" I demanded.

"Well, I couldn't very well let you go without a Christmas gift," he said, still not meeting my eyes as he brought his right hand out and opened it to reveal a miniature duck decoy, no more than two inches long, carved and painted in careful detail down to the barbs on the feathers.

"I made it last night after you went to sleep," he said. "I know it's not mmmm—!" He couldn't say anything else, not with my lips covering his.

There was a party in the town hall that night, and Mrs. Purnell insisted I go with Tom. I hoped it would cheer him up a little. Jo stayed home with Mrs. Purnell, who had washed my clothes while we were out earlier.

"Your skirt is too thin for a respectable young lady to wear, but you *are* supposed to be a foreigner," she said with a little frown. "I would lend you something better, but we are not really the same size, dear." Which was probably just as well—Tom might've freaked out if I put on one of his mother's outfits!

The party wasn't as bad as I thought it might be, but while everyone was really nice to us, it was exhausting having to b.s. about Alaska and answer everyone's questions over and over again by saying we didn't know anything about what had happened to Tom's dad.

In Tom's world they didn't seem to care much about the legal drinking age—maybe they didn't even have one—so I had too much eggnog, which left me with a queasy stomach. The wooden walls danced oh-so-slowly around me. I was glad when Tom took me home early.

I collapsed on the couch without even getting undressed, and the next thing I knew the sun was in my eyes and Tom was brushing his hand over my cheek, telling me I'd better get moving if we wanted to catch the morning ferry. I sat up too quickly and winced as my head throbbed. Fortunately everybody was talking in really soft voices. Mrs. Purnell joined us for breakfast and even fixed us tea, but she didn't say much of anything.

"Mum, I think I should stay with you," Tom said around a mouthful of toast.

Mrs. Purnell shook her head. "There is nothing you can do here. We shall have to wait for the police and the RC to do their work. As soon as they discover anything, I shall let you know, I promise. And you," she said, turning to Jo, "will be late to school if you do not get out the door right now."

"But Mum, it's Boxing Day."

"So it is." Mrs. Purnell hugged herself and looked so sad *I* wanted to give her a hug. Instead Tom did, and as he turned to go, Jo stood up, draped her right arm over his shoulders and gave him an awkward squeeze.

"Take care of yourself in Philadelphia, Tommy," she said.

Tom startled everyone by throwing both his arms around her. "Do not get in Mum's way," he growled, but he wasn't fooling anyone. Mrs. Purnell's eyes gleamed.

Jo asked if she could go see if her friend Marcia was around, and as soon as Mrs. Purnell gave her permission she dashed out. Mrs. Purnell stood, tightened the sash of her bathrobe and started clearing the table. Tom and I both offered to help but she shook her head.

"You had best move now, if you want to catch the ferry. Take a few rolls with you, and I think there are still some good apples in the basket."

"Mum, I—"

"Tommy, you must not worry about me. I shall manage until your father returns. I shall go back to work for the Tourism Council, and I suggest you apply yourself to your studies. Dad will *not* be pleased if he finds your grades have suffered. He will *not* accept any excuses."

Mrs. Purnell was probably the one who wouldn't accept any excuses. "He'll do fine, Mrs. Purnell. I'll make sure of it," I said.

She gave me a long look. Had she figured out what we were up to? Or would she ask me something really embarrassing? But instead she smiled, a genuine smile that warmed my stomach even more than the tea.

"I know that, Teresa. You are good for him. Tommy, she is a fine young woman. Make certain you treat her with respect."

"Yes, Mum."

Now I was the one tearing up. I couldn't bring Tom home, even if he was just a boy from the neighborhood. Mom wouldn't be able to handle it. I was supposed to be Miss Perfect, doing my chores and my homework and generally making her crappy life as nice and easy as possible. Boys didn't fit into her schemes. And if I did bring somebody home, I'd get an earful about what a mistake she'd made with Dad and how I'd better watch myself. At least I was a universe away from her.

"What is the matter? You are being so quiet," Tom said once we were on the ferry.

"Oh, you're a right one to talk."

"Sorry! It is simply that you usually talk so much and now you are not saying anything."

How could I tell Tom what was really bothering me? I couldn't. Instead I started poking holes in the crazy plan Jo had hatched.

"Even if we come up with convincing forged passports and you have enough money, I still don't understand how we're supposed to just get on a plane—sorry, an airship—and fly to London," I said.

"What do you mean? You said you have already been to Europe. I am the one who ought to be nervous. I have never been any farther than Nouvelle Orleans."

"No, that's not what I mean. I mean, uh, well, don't you think we look a little young?"

He blinked at me. "Young for what?"

"Well, won't they ask where our parents are, or if they know where we're going?"

"I, I just assumed that we would pose as a married couple."

"*What*?" But I could see the logic of it. It would make a lot of things easier. There'd even be less need to mess with the passports if we left the same last names on them. But still… "Tom, I'm not ready to get married. Not by a long shot! I haven't even graduated high school yet!" *And I might never graduate at this rate.*

He looked hurt but said, "I was not, I mean, I am not *proposing*. This is just *pretend*."

"Oh. Just *pretend*." Then why was I disappointed?

* * * *

Once we boarded the train, I immediately fell asleep on Tom's shoulder. He dozed off too, so when the train pulled into Philadelphia the conductor had to wake us.

We blinked, stretched, got our bags and walked off the train. Penn Station in Tom's Philadelphia was a lot smaller than 30th Street Station in the real Philadelphia. The place was mobbed. We had to squeeze between, like, *thousands* of people to get to the exit. Most of them were unbelievably polite though. They even apologized when *we* stepped on *their* toes! That made me feel like I really *was* in a foreign city, even though it was called Philadelphia and the good old smelly Delaware River ran through it.

As soon as we were out in the cold, damp air I asked Tom, "You know the other river in Philadelphia, besides the Delaware?"

"Sure, the Shale-keel."

I giggled. Every true-born Philadelphian calls the Schuylkill the Skookle River.

"What is so funny this time?" he asked. I told him, and he scowled at me. "You Americans do not know how to pronounce *anything* correctly, do you?"

"Maybe you really are an Englishman, Tommy."

"How many times have I told you so? And please stop calling me Tommy. That is a baby name."

"Tommy, Tommy, Tommy!"

He made a grab for me, and we took off across the street, past slow-moving battery-powered carriage taxis and people dragging their luggage here and there. I almost tripped over a small dog on a leash, which growled at me and snapped at Tom as he raced past. I dodged through an alley, with Tom right at my heels. Then I stumbled over my own bag and crashed into a brick wall. My right shoulder got the worst of it, and my arm went numb.

"Are you all right? Let me kiss it and make it better," Tom said, taking me in his arms. Large flakes of snow drifted down from the gray sky and collected in his hair as we kissed and he massaged my arm.

"Did you ever think about becoming a doctor?" I said when we finally moved our faces far enough apart to talk. "Because my arm feels all better."

"This treatment is only for you," he smiled.

I wanted to keep smooching, but the air was cold and the alley gave me a familiar chill.

"Tom, I think we're already in the Zone," I said reluctantly.

"Hmm? Oh, indeed," he said, glancing around. "Come along, we had best find Gloria."

"Yeah," I said. "Stick close, please? I—I'm a little scared."

"How can you merely be scared? Personally, I am terrified," he said, gripping my hand. "Come, we had best get out of this forest before the Three Little Boars come and eat us."

Boars instead of bears? Alternate, scarier versions of fairy tales? I shivered and gripped his hand as we tiptoed out the far side of the alley.

We agreed in a whisper that I would watch our backs, Tom would look out ahead and we'd both keep an eye on the sky, which had stopped snowing and taken on that awful blankness. But for several blocks, nothing happened. There were no shadows or scary noises. Maybe we would reach the bookstore without anything happening.

"There it is!" Tom exclaimed, pointing.

I shouted with relief and we both took off at a run. Tom shoved open the door and I paused. Weird. The letters on the sign looked faded compared with the last time we had seen them. But then we were inside.

"Gloria?" we both called out at once.

Silence. It was dark in the store, with only the gray outdoor light coming in, dimmed further by dirt and grime on the plate glass window. I frowned. The window had always been clean before. Then I drew in a breath and started coughing.

How can I describe what the room smelled like? Once when I was little, Mom, Dad, and I went on a weekend trip to Atlantic City. Mom and I hung out on the beach while Dad spent most of his time and too much money in the casinos, at least according to Mom, who yelled at him all through the 60-mile-long traffic jam back to Philadelphia.

Then we got back to the house and found that a thunderstorm had knocked out the power for the past three days. Mom opened the refrigerator and all the food had spoiled. I coughed and started to retch, while Mom turned around and yelled at Dad as if it was his fault, and he started yelling at her as if it was *her* fault, and I kept retching on the floor. *That* was what the bookstore smelled like now.

I gagged and let go of Tom's hand to cover my face while the smell overwhelmed me, like a wave that knocks you over at the beach and you feel like you're going to drown. Beside me Tom doubled over and started retching too. He straightened, still retching, and staggered over to the counter where our tea and cocoa were usually waiting for us. He grasped hold of it for support and it collapsed under his weight with an enormous crack, letting loose a cloud of sawdust that made us both start coughing again. Everything spun as I stretched my hand out to Tom to help him to his feet.

His palm was cold and clammy. "W-what happened here?" he gasped.

I shook my head. If I opened my mouth I'd throw up. We began poking around the room. Many of the shelves had collapsed, dumping books onto the dusty floor. We climbed over them, stepping carefully as we made our way toward the back room. Maybe we would find Gloria there and help her—I was sure she needed help. But it got darker and darker the farther back we went, and the bad smell got even stronger, even when I pinched my nose shut and tried to breathe through my mouth. I stepped on some loose, crumbling pages and almost slipped. Tom steadied me and I bent over until I could just make out the words *New Almanack* on a torn shred of paper. I pointed at it, and Tom nodded.

"We must be near the gateway," he said.

I nodded, then clutched his arm and pointed. "Look," I whispered.

Over the fallen shelving, where the back room should have been, shone a little light. We scrambled over the ruined books. Something crunched underfoot. A shattered black vinyl record lay beneath my feet. *Janis Joplin Sings The Blues, 1970-1990*, it said.

What had I just destroyed? I started to cry silently. Tom looked shaken but he pulled me gently along toward the light. It came through a hole in the ceiling.

I screamed. A skull, a human skull, lay on the floor, with some small bones that looked like they might have come from an animal, like a cat. I sobbed and pressed myself against Tom, who was crying too.

"Let's get out of here," he managed to say.

I nodded, took a step and slipped. I fell, twisting my ankle and cutting my hands on the broken record. I scrabbled around, clutching uselessly at the crumbling books as I tried to get to my feet. Tom helped me up and I leaned against him.

Suddenly he stiffened.

"What is it?" I said. His face was frozen in an expression of horror. He was staring at a book I held in my hand. I looked at it too. Printed in ugly block letters on a page that flaked away beneath my fingers it said: **ALL THE WORLDS END HERE. ALL CHOICES IN THE END LEAD TO DEATH.**

Thirteen words repeated over and over again, filling the page. I ripped it out and it turned to dust in my hands, but the next page was also covered with those awful words. And the one after that, and the one after that. I threw the book aside.

Tom let go of me and sank to his knees, his hands over his face.

"No," I whispered. "No." I stood up and shouted. "*No!* It's a lie! Tom. Tom, get up! On your feet!"

He rocked back and forth, moaning softly, so I reached down and grabbed his right hand. He was much too heavy for me to lift to his feet, but somehow I did it. My shoulder popped, but it didn't seem important.

"It's not true!" I shouted. "Do you hear me? It's a lie!"

I grabbed Tom's head in both hands and drew his face close to mine, and I kissed him. And I kissed him, and I kissed him. At first his lips felt cold, wet, and lifeless, as if I was kissing a dead fish. But not for long. He held me tightly. I gasped at the pain in my shoulder, but it didn't matter. I closed my eyes as the room spun slowly, then with increasing speed. I held Tom tighter, a solid anchor against the spin, which gradually slowed and stopped.

The warm pressure of Tom's lips finally left mine.

"That was some kiss," he said.

I opened my eyes to bright sunlight gleaming off the spotless plate glass window of Gloria's Gateway Books And Records.

20

I staggered into the bookstore with Teresa leaning heavily on my arm. Gloria opened the door for us, and her eyes widened when she saw Teresa's pale face, her cuts and bruises. Together we helped her to a red velvet-covered settee that stood against the wall opposite the counter.

"She's hurt," I said.

Gloria nodded, then yelped as I grabbed her in a quick embrace. It lasted less than a second but her skin was hot to the touch, and her pulse was as rapid as the broken-winged blackbird that I had saved when I was twelve. I pulled away in surprise. Those other times I had touched her, when she was helping Teresa and me through the gateway, I had not noticed this strangeness. Well, there had been other things to notice. And how forward I had just been! It was one thing when Gloria had to hold me to cross the dimensional divide, but for me to grab her… I must explain myself.

"We—we thought something terrible had happened to you," I said hoarsely.

She nodded. "Yes, but it's not true." She went behind the counter and brought out her salves, lotions, and bandages. "I'd hoped when I fought the Grey Ones myself that they'd leave you alone from then on, but it didn't work."

"We saw…we were in the store, but it was all different," I said.

Gloria shook her head and put her finger to her lips. "Some things don't need to be spoken aloud," she said. "At least, not now. They've tried their worst, but you've frightened them away for the moment."

"You mean they might return?" I said. I squatted by the settee, caressing Teresa's good shoulder while Gloria worked on her.

Gloria shook her head again and flashed me a smile. "Not any time soon. You gave them a good swift kick in the pants. I've never seen the Zone looking so bright and hopeful."

"But those things I saw. And *smelt*." I bit my lip.

Gloria wound a bandage around Teresa's ankle, but she glanced at me. "It must have been awful."

"It was," I said.

When the smell first struck me, I had a vision of the day of Granny's death. Dad was slumped over the kitchen table crying into his hands, but when Mum came over and rubbed his shoulders he turned on her with that silly accusation that she had killed his mother with the fried oysters for her birthday party. Sure, it turned into a family joke afterwards, but at the time it was pretty awful. Mum's face turned as pale as the sun-bleached seashells you find out in the marsh. When she walked out of the kitchen without a word, I wondered whether she or Dad needed to be comforted more. Poor Jodie was in her room sobbing—she was only seven years old. I was the only one who could hold the family together, but how?

I pulled myself back to the present. Gloria was looking up at me with those huge sea-green eyes. She looked so *alive*.

"I need to know one thing," I said slowly. "Was what we saw—what the Grey Ones showed us—was it *real*?"

She hesitated. Would she tell us a reassuring lie? As if, because we were not quite adults yet, we were too fragile to handle the truth. When I have children, I will never do that. Well, all right, I suppose I wouldn't tell a four-year-old all the gory details of life, but when you are seventeen you deserve to be treated like a grown-up.

Gloria sighed, brushed a stray strand of red hair off her forehead and said, "They show you the worst aspect of things, Tom. Because that's what they see. That's what they *are*."

"So it is true. I mean, it is real."

She shook her head slowly. "It's a distorted version of reality. There are other versions of reality—other, stronger versions. Stronger and better."

"But we thought you were dead," Teresa said, clutching at her arm.

"Well, I'm not. Never more alive," Gloria said firmly. "Now tell me, how's your shoulder? You dislocated it. I put it back and gave you some medicine but I'm not sure…"

Teresa rolled both shoulders and smiled. "Better than ever. I could get on the parallel bars in gym class. And I freakin' *hate* the parallel bars."

"Well, don't go doing that just yet," Gloria said.

"We've got to get back to my Philadelphia so Miss Chen can help us," Teresa said, and hopped off the couch before Gloria or I could stop her.

I braced myself as she put her weight on her sprained ankle, and sure enough she toppled into me.

"You have to take it slowly," Gloria said, as she and I helped Teresa stand up straight, leaning only some of her weight on me. "This isn't a marathon, dear. Luckily you'll have lots of time off your feet when you're on the airship to England."

"We already are in England," I pointed out.

"Sit back down, Teresa. You too, Tom. You're not going anywhere before you have your tea and cocoa." And she sashayed off behind the counter to fetch our drinks.

Teresa elbowed me and whispered, "Stop staring at her ass!"

"Her what? Teresa! I was not staring at her, uh, behind."

"Were too! Just remember, she's got eleven dimensions and is sometimes a cat, so that's kind of sick, right?"

"Teresa, I'm, I'm, I mean, I'm all yours! Always!"

"Aren't you two sweet!" Gloria said, leaning over to hand us our drinks. "Tom, you're blushing again!"

"Don't mind him, he always does that," Teresa said, reaching up and ruffling my hair. My face burned as they both burst out laughing. When we'd finished drinking Teresa leaned over and gave me a hug. She whispered "I love you" in my ear so quickly and softly I was not sure I heard correctly at first.

"What?" I said. Suddenly Gloria was nowhere to be seen.

"You heard me," Teresa said, leaning away from me and twisting her hands in her lap. Nervous? Of me? What did she have to be nervous about, this girl who had stood up to the most frightening nightmare ever? Then I had to respond.

"I luh, that is, uh, I love you too," I said.

* * * *

A long minute later footsteps sounded, and a throat was delicately cleared.

"Come on, kids, I think we'd better get moving," Gloria said. "And remember Tom, her shoulder's still healing."

I helped Teresa to her feet.

"We'd better get going," she said, leaning lightly on my left side so that I served her as a crutch. I did not mind at all.

"Are you sure you'll be all right, Teresa? Tom?" Gloria asked as Teresa shrugged her coat on. I hoped she had enough changes of clothes in her canvas bag with her, after losing one to Assa Teag Ashley and another to the Zone monsters! Mum has trained me well, I always pack extra.

"We'll be fine," Teresa said firmly. "Let's do it."

Gloria looked at each of us in turn, then nodded and led us to the back room. As we walked through the clearing in the shelves I checked to see if the *New Almanack* was back in place and smiled with relief when I saw that it was.

In the back room itself, the records were all in their usual places on the shelves, and I wished we had time to take them down and play them. Maybe we would, some day soon. The three of us joined hands, and Teresa and I closed our eyes. The transition was an easy one. When we opened our eyes, the gas lights had been replaced with electric bulbs, and Tiferet was twining herself between our legs, mewing. Teresa reached down, scratched her behind the ears, then turned her over and rubbed her furry belly while she purred. I smiled but kept my hands off, after what Teresa had said.

The cat followed us out through the shop, watching with her big amber eyes as we went to the door. I stopped and looked back, and she let out a tiny peep, almost a trill.

She's lonely.

Suddenly Teresa bent over and picked up Tiferet, then limped out the door.

I followed her. "What are you doing?"

"What does it look like?" Teresa lifted her chin defiantly.

"Teresa, I do not think this is a good idea. I think Tiferet—Gloria—whoever she is, belongs in the bookstore."

"She went out to save me from the Grey Ones that time," Teresa pointed out.

"That was an emergency. Maybe she needs to stay to protect the shop—the gateway—from the Grey Ones."

"It's more like she needs to be protected *from* the Grey Ones." Teresa and Tiferet both looked at me, a pair of soft brown eyes over a pair of amber ones.

There was only one way to know for sure if this was right. "Put her down," I said.

"No! Tom!" Teresa said, clutching Tiferet as if I was about to yank the cat away.

"What I mean is, put her down, and let her decide for herself whether she wants to go back to the store or come with us."

"Oh. Okay." She looked doubtfully at Tiferet, who looked back at her and meowed softly. "All right, puss. Tiferet. Gloria. Whoever you are," Teresa said, leaning over and putting her gently on the ground. "Which way?"

We both looked intently at the cat. When she was a cat, did Tiferet have a cat's mind? When she was a woman, did she have a woman's mind? Or was she always the same being, an eleven-dimensional being (whatever that meant), so that the cat and the woman were just extensions of herself, and were no more independent creatures than my hands were separate from me? She had hinted that was the case, but perhaps we had misunderstood her.

Tiferet looked up at Teresa and meowed, then looked over at me and blinked. No, she winked. Only her left eyelid flicked down, then up.

I knelt down and asked her, "So which is it? Home, or with us?" And she jumped into my arms. "Umm, Teresa," I said, a little nervously.

She smiled. "It's all right. I'm not jealous. I was just teasing you earlier. Come on, there isn't any time to waste." And she hobbled on ahead as if she knew exactly where she was going, though we were still in the Zone. I thought I heard her mutter under her breath, "But she really *does* have a nice ass, when she's a girl."

This time our exit from the Zone was signaled by a darkening of the sky. I looked up, the blank blue sky was now covered with clouds sifting a light, chilly drizzle on our heads. That was a bit puzzling since it had been snowing when we departed the train in the real Philadelphia.

I mentioned it to Teresa and she nodded knowingly. "Global warming," she said.

"What?"

"Never mind. I know where we are. We have to catch a bus up Broad Street to get to Miss Chen. You like Miss Chen, don't you, Tiferet?" she said, ruffling the cat's fur. Tiferet licked her hand.

"But I thought she was a teacher, and you said Boxing Day isn't a holiday here. Why would she be at home in the middle of a weekday?"

"It's winter break, silly."

"Winter break? You mean you get a long holiday this time of year?"

"Yeah, till after New Year's. Don't you?"

"That is not fair," I sulked. "Here, you can carry Tiferet for a while if you are going to gloat."

"Gladly. Come here, baby."

Oh, good grief. I rolled my eyes. Had it been a good idea to bring Tiferet with us? I had not been given much choice in the matter, however.

We walked half a block through the insane din of what Teresa assured me was just an ordinary winter morning in Philadelphia. Tannenbaums stood in the shop windows, strung with gaudy little coloured electric bulbs. We never had one in our family. I doubt anyone in Gingo Teag did; we were all descended from settlers from the Home Islands, after all, not a German or a Swede among us.

The people appeared in a bad mood as they pushed and shoved their way along the sidewalks. The crowds were not nearly as dense as in Penn Station in my world, but woe betide you if you got in their way. A big scowling woman ploughed right into Teresa and almost knocked her over.

"Why don't you watch where you're going?" the female—I won't say lady—snarled.

I looked back and forth between them, confused. I mean, if it had been a bloke, I would have been all over him, but I could not fight with a woman, even if she had all the feminine grace of an alligator.

"Why don't you shove it up your—"

I blocked my ears and watched helplessly as Tiferet wriggled out of Teresa's arms.

"Now look what you've gone and done!" Teresa yelled at the woman as she scooped up Tiferet.

"That's the most horrible looking cat I ever saw! Ow! She bit me! The stupid animal bit me! I'm gonna sue you for everything you're worth! I'm gonna—"

"There's our bus!" Teresa yelled over the din, as an enormous, hideous metal box on wheels pulled up to the kerb and sneezed black fumes all over us. I clambered up after her, coughing and choking, while she fished in her pockets for a card she showed to the driver.

He was not amused. "This card expired two weeks ago, and you can't bring a cat in here, and where's your boyfriend's fare, and—"

Something happened then, something so quick and so subtle I wondered if I was imagining it. Tiferet turned her head and looked at the driver, a big muscular guy with grey stubble on his chin. She opened her amazing amber eyes wide until they were yellow circles with obsidian circles swimming inside them. The ancient Greeks thought circles were the perfect shape, and they must have been onto something, because the driver's eyes widened. He shook himself, then turned to look out his windscreen, humming a little tune as he pulled his monster machine away from the kerb.

I followed Teresa as she found empty seats for us toward the back of the bus, holding my tongue till we were sitting down. "Did I just see…"

Teresa was stroking a purring Tiferet and did not even look up. "Don't question a miracle when one happens, Tom. Just enjoy it. That's what I learned in Sunday school."

"Is that what the Catholic Church teaches?"

"That's what I learned."

"I see," I said.

Tiferet blinked innocently at me, then turned it into a sly wink. I was not even startled anymore. I merely scratched her behind the ears.

* * * *

It was not long before Teresa nudged me. We got off the bus and found ourselves in a neighbourhood of joined-together houses that

Teresa called rowhouses, like the one she lived in. However, the paint looked fresher and the gardens tidier than on her street. The rain had almost stopped, but Tiferet still shook herself every few seconds, making us all the wetter. Teresa quickly handed her to me.

Fortunately we were soon standing before the right house, painted a bright purple that Teresa said reminded her of blueberry yoghurt.

"It's pretty funky, isn't it?" she said as she rang the bell.

"I suppose so, whatever 'funky' means," I said, sneezing. "How do you know where she lives?"

"Because she used to have the whole class over for parties at the end of the semester," she said.

Imagine that. I snorted as the door swung open.

Susie Chen was dressed in those denim trousers that everyone wears in Teresa's world, as well as a short-sleeved, lavender-coloured shirt with some complicated mathematical formula on it and the words, "And there was light."

She barely reached my shoulder blades. Her black hair was cropped even shorter than the last time I had seen her, and a pair of enormous black-framed glasses seemed to take up most of her face. She pulled Teresa inside quickly, gesturing me to walk in with Tiferet.

"The police are looking all over for you! There's an Amber Alert," she said to Teresa.

"I can explain everything. But you can't call my mother, or the police."

"Oh, really."

"I never knew you wore glasses," Teresa said.

"I use contacts in class. Don't try and change the subject. Why did you run away?"

"I didn't," Teresa said, and told her about our trip to Gingo Teag.

Susie's thin black eyebrows rose so high they almost disappeared. By this time we had all made our way over to a cluster of comfortable, mismatched chairs.

Susie held up her hand when Teresa mentioned the passports. "Excuse me. You want me to do *what?*"

"Help us fix them up," Teresa said.

"Umm, and you think I'm an expert in counterfeiting for *what* reason, exactly?"

"You were always great at designing computer graphics to help us understand physics. Remember the one you did about Schrödinger's cat?"

Tiferet meowed so loudly we all started. We had forgotten she was there.

"Who's Schrödinger and why is his cat important?" I asked.

Susie reached out and began stroking Tiferet's back. "It's a thought experiment to illustrate a concept in quantum mechanics, in which a cat is placed in a box and has a 50-50 chance of being killed if a subatomic particle triggers a device that releases poison gas," she explained. "But until you open the box, the cat is half-alive and half-dead, because whether the particle is released or not can't be determined until you make an observation. Only once you open the box does the cat become completely alive or completely dead. Get it?"

"Umm, no," I said.

Teresa smiled. "Never mind, neither did I."

"In any case," Susie said, still stroking Tiferet, "there is no actual cat being threatened with death. It's just a thought experiment!" Tiferet fluffed up her fur until there seemed to be twice as much cat in the room.

"What is quantum mechanics?" I asked.

"Never mind," Teresa and Susie said together.

"Look," Teresa said, "can you help us or not?"

"Well," Susie said, standing up and grabbing Tiferet off a battered but dust-free side table filled with framed pictures that were so sharp and realistic I expected the people in them to start moving around and talking to us, "I wouldn't be breaking any laws *here*, because the passports aren't actually American or British passports, as far as *this* world's governments are concerned. But the question is, should I? What do you think?" She bent over Tiferet, slowly stroking the fur on top of her head. Tiferet meowed on a rising note. "Oh," Susie said, "true, it's kind of difficult for you to answer that question when you're a cat. But if I just—"

She reached behind Tiferet's neck. The cat made a startled yowl, immediately followed by an enormous thump. I blinked, then shut my eyes tightly. Gloria was sitting on the floor, completely naked.

"How did you *do* that?" Teresa, Gloria, and I said all at once. "And can you please get me some clothes before poor Tom spontaneously combusts?" Gloria added.

"My things may be a little tight on you, but sure," Susie said. "As to how I did it, well, it's no more complicated than origami. Remember those paper cranes I used to staple to your tests when you did well, Teresa? And Gloria, isn't it obvious how I did it, given the fact that you are eleven-dimensional?"

"It's not obvious to ordinary human beings," Teresa said.

I had turned my back and luckily spotted the water closet, where I hid until Gloria should be decently clothed.

"It's obvious to me how it's done, but not how one of you four-dimensionals could do it," Gloria said. Her voice came from just the other side of the water closet door.

My skin crawled with embarrassment. She was inches away from me, naked. I heard another door close and Teresa called, "You can come out now, Tom."

21

Poor Tom! I thought he was going to faint after seeing Gloria pop into existence buck-naked on Miss Chen's living room floor. When I finally coaxed him out of the bathroom he shied away from me, as if I was going to kill him just for getting that glimpse. I'm really not crazy jealous. But when Gloria came back out dressed in a skirt and blouse of Miss Chen's that were at least two sizes too small for her, his eyeballs practically hit the floor and rolled away. A grinning Miss Chen was right behind her.

"All right, let's see these passports of yours," she said.

Tom had them, and he handed them to her with a dazed smile.

Miss Chen went back to her chair, flipped them open, and frowned at the pictures inside.

"These look pretty makeshift to me," Miss Chen said, putting a finger to her lips. "Well, I guess you're planning to just go as your father, since you look enough like him, right?" Tom and I nodded. "Good, that means I only have to print a new name and picture page for Teresa," she said. "Well. The paper will be a problem. It feels like a cross between packaging paper and a burlap bag. And this gray color! What do you people do to make paper, Tom? Use hand presses?"

"I do not know," Tom said. "All I know is it is very expensive. We are taught from the time we are small children not to waste it."

"Probably is handmade, then," Miss Chen nodded. "All right. There's a craft store down on South Street that might sell stuff like this."

"Why do you need paper anyway?" I asked. "Aren't you just going to use what's already there?"

"I wouldn't want to try cutting out and replacing Tom's mother's picture. It would be obvious. I'll have to replace the whole page."

So we all followed after Miss Chen and squeezed into her tiny car. I sat next to Gloria in the back seat so that Tom could have the front passenger seat to himself. He swallowed hard and hung on to the handle, so I asked Miss Chen to go slow. Anyway, it wasn't a long drive.

The rain had stopped by the time we got there, and the street was crowded with kids our age out enjoying winter break. Miss Chen walked into the art supply store to get what she needed while Gloria went into a funky used-clothing store next door, so Tom and I had a few minutes to ourselves. We held hands as we crossed the street to a coffee shop, where I bought us each a hot cocoa with a few dollars Miss Chen had slipped me as we got out of her car.

I stirred the whipped cream slowly into my cocoa. "Do you really think this is going to work, Tom?" I said, without looking at him.

"How should I know? I have never been outside British territory— well, except for that journey we took years ago to Nouvelle Orleans. But British subjects do not need a passport to enter Louisiana, which is why I do not even have one."

"What'll they do to us if they figure out we've messed with your parents' passports?"

Tom's cheek grew pale. Soft downy stubble covered his chin, and I touched it. The skin pulsed under my fingertips. He put down his cocoa and took my hand in both of his warm ones.

"Depends who you mean by 'they,'" he said at last. "If the authorities catch us here in Philadelphia, I should think nothing too awful will happen. They will shout at us, and sooner or later they will call Mum, and I shall be grounded until I am eighty years old." I giggled, picturing Tom as a little old man. "But if Henri-Napoléon's men capture us in London, well…"

"I'm sure Susie will do such a good job there's no chance of that happening," I said quickly.

"Thanks for your faith in me!" Susie sang, bustling in with one of those bright little paper shopping bags under her arm. She sat down beside us. "I think I've got everything we need. The only question is, where has Gloria gotten off to…"

Just then Gloria swept in through the door on a gust of damp air. Everyone in the coffee shop stopped talking and turned to stare at her. She couldn't have drawn more attention if we'd been able to see all eleven of her dimensions.

First of all there were her boots. To say they didn't match would be like saying my parents don't get along—true, but hardly a full description. On her left foot she wore a crinkly black leather thing with a heel that looked sturdy enough for hiking, while the top extended way past her knee, ending somewhere up under her skirt. The right boot was made of some light tan material that looked flimsier than a pair of flip-flops and barely came up to her ankle, leaving her right leg bare. As for her skirt, had it really been meant as clothing? It looked like a wild abstract mural someone had dyed on chiffon. The colors were so bright and deep they made my eyes water. The pattern of the blouse was also showy and bright, but it didn't go with the skirt (as if anything could). It hung off her left shoulder, leaving her right shoulder completely bare.

"Why does she have to do things like that?" Tom groaned. "And what did she do to her hair?"

Normally I'm the last girl to pay attention to anyone's hair—I leave that to Kylie and her crowd—but now her curly, tangled, shoulder-length, red-orange locks had been woven into what looked like a basket atop her head. This left her ears uncovered, and there was something odd about their shape. In any case we had more urgent problems, like leaving this coffee shop before we were all arrested for excessive weirdness.

"Did I do something wrong?" Gloria asked as we walked out.

"Of course not, dear," Susie said, patting her on the arm, "but you do attract a lot of attention, dressing like that. Especially with those ears. Let's get to my car."

"My ears?" Gloria said, rubbing one absently. "But I thought they were so convincing—I mean, what's the matter with my ears?"

"They're so pointy they look more like a cat's ears than a person's," Susie explained.

"Well, that's your fault for origami-folding me out of *n*-space that way," Gloria said.

* * * *

Back at Susie's apartment Tom and I sat on her threadbare sofa while Gloria went upstairs to change so poor Tom wouldn't keep getting attacks of the vapors (he would probably have spelled that "vapours"). Susie sat at her desk fiddling with her computer and cursing softly at the laser printer.

She'd taken a quick snapshot of me with her cell phone as soon as we stepped in the door—"It doesn't have to be that great, it's supposed to look all blurry anyway," she pointed out when I protested—and then she took scissors to the artsy-fartsy notebook she'd bought at the craft store. There was plenty of paper to print up my passport, but the printer kept crunching every page. Tom winced every time, as if he was paying for it. He winced even more at the words she was using, though they were kind of creative.

"Listen here, you misbegotten offspring of a leaky pen and a pepper grinder, if you don't print me a usable page, like, right *now* I am going to heave your worthless carcass out the window, let a bus run over it, and then stomp the pieces into unrecognizable balls of—"

Tom clapped his hands to his ears, startling me. I jumped to my feet, knocking my knees into the scratched-up glass coffee table, which overturned and shattered with an ear-splitting crash. In the silence that followed, the printer hummed contentedly and turned out a perfect page for my fake passport.

Gloria came down the stairs and covered her mouth with both hands when she saw the wreckage.

"You know," Susie said after a long, long moment, "there must be some parallel world where that did *not* just happen."

"But in *this* world," Gloria said, tiptoeing daintily around the shattered glass in her mismatched boots, "there is a big mess to clean up. Teresa? Is your knee all right?"

"Uh, I think so," I said, rubbing it. "It'll go nicely with my sprained ankle."

"Never mind, you sit down, I'll clean it up, it's my fault anyway," Tom said. "Susie, we'll have to replace your tea table—"

"It's all right, I didn't really like it anyway," she said with a wave of her hand. "There's a dustpan and brush in the kitchen, and trash bags under the sink."

While Gloria and Tom cleaned up the mess and Susie found a needle and thread to sew the page into Mrs. Purnell's passport, I curled into a ball on the couch.

Couldn't I do anything right? Everywhere I went people thought I was some kind of freak, because I *was* some kind of freak. Even in a whole other universe I couldn't fit in. Now just look what I'd done!

And a glass splinter in the cushions cut the palm of my hand. I let out a yelp and started to cry. Susie took me to the bathroom and cleaned the cut with soap and water, holding my hand like Mom used to when I was little. I cried harder.

"Teresa, what's the matter?" Susie asked. "I mean, I know it sucks cutting your hand on broken glass, but it's not really worth all these tears, is it?"

"I destroyed your coffee table and ruined your floor!" I wailed.

"Seriously, Teresa? That coffee table? It was a piece of junk that the previous tenant left and I was too lazy to get rid of. You practically did me a favor. And don't worry about the floor either. The wooden floors in these old rowhouses are already all scratched up, so there's not much you can do to make them look worse. What's really bothering you?"

"I'm the clumsiest idiot in the world, that's what. Tom said he luh-luh-loves me, but he won't for long when he realizes how stupid and useless and ugly and fat I am."

"Uh-huh. Lucky for you, Tom seems to be a much better judge of who you are than you yourself. Look in the mirror. Just look!"

I did. A plain girl with an acne-scarred round face, swollen and red from crying, with mousy, curly brown hair tangled into knots stared back at me. I mean, shallow twerps like Kylie worry about their hair, but only an idiotic dreamer would think a nerdy, messy, clumsy girl like me could ever find a boyfriend. Plus, how would anybody in Tom's world ever be fooled into thinking I was his w-w-wife for one second, let alone for the couple of weeks we would have to keep on pretending so we could get to England and figure out how to rescue his father? They'd take one look at me and throw me in prison forever. Or worse, just start laughing their heads off.

I sat down on the closed toilet lid and stammered all this to my teacher, beautiful, composed, brilliant Susie Chen. She nodded and smiled. Then she pulled up a stool and sat facing me, our faces so close her warm breath tickled my cheeks.

"Teresa, why do you think I became a teacher?"

"What? I don't know."

"You know, with my degree from Caltech I could have done almost anything. I had offers to do postdoctoral research at CERN, the big particle accelerator on the French-Swiss border that I talked about in class, or the Argonne National Laboratory in Illinois. Cutting-edge research on string theory. But I told them they'd have to wait a couple of years, because I wanted to teach high school in my home town."

I stopped crying and stared at her. "Are you nuts?"

She smiled again, a wider smile this time. "I don't think so, though my parents sure do! I wanted to help kids like you discover the excitement of learning science. And let you know that you can get through high school without dying of embarrassment. Some time I'll show you pictures from my high school yearbook. The way I dressed back then… well, you're a glamour queen next to how I was."

"You have *got* to be kidding me."

"Nope, not at all. You know the book *The Little Prince*?"

I nodded. "My Nana used to read it to me when I was little."

"Well, remember when the little prince says, 'The eyes are blind. One must see with the heart'?"

I nodded again.

"Well, sometimes all those blind eyes out there need a little extra help to see properly. Come with me and I'll give you a makeover before you have to face the world again—even if it's a parallel world."

She shepherded me out the door and up the stairs to her bedroom, where the housekeeping was only a little better than in my own room. There was a collection of empty containers of Ramen noodles on the bedside table, and messy heaps of books and school papers strewn on the bed. Just like home.

* * * *

I tried not to blink away the mascara she was putting on my eyelashes.

"And now there's one other advantage of being a teacher that even I never expected," Susie said.

"Oh? What's that?"

"If I'd never become a teacher, how would I ever have met Gloria? I only know her because of you. I'm learning more about the eleventh dimension from her than I ever could smashing protons in Switzerland. There now, I think we're ready to go back downstairs."

"Can I look at myself in the mirror first?"

"Nope. You need to see how everyone else looks at you first." She pushed me out the door and down the steps to the living room. Tom and Gloria had finished cleaning up all the broken glass and were sitting on the sofa watching TV with fascinated puzzlement (Tom) and something like horror (Gloria).

They both did a double-take when they saw me.

Tom said, "Wow, you look great!"

Gloria tried to smile but her heart wasn't in it.

"What's the matter?" I asked.

"Oh, you look great. Tom is right. It's just that you look so…normal."

I beamed at the compliment.

"Come on, Gloria, we can't all dress as flamboyantly as you!" Susie said, punching her lightly on the shoulder.

"It's not *that* flamboyant. If you could just see how I look from a seventh-dimensional perspective or higher…"

While they joked I limped over to Susie's desk and picked up the passport she had made for me. When I compared it to the original page, the font and layout was close to perfect. And I could see what she had meant about my picture. It almost didn't matter what you put there, though it was still better to have my head there than Tom's mother's because my hair is darker and my face rounder.

I stared at the name. My name. Teresa Purnell. I said it softly to myself a few times, just rolling it around on my tongue for the feel of it, wondering what it would be like if I had that name for real. Tom would say that "D'Angelo" was a prettier name than "Purnell" and I should stick with it. But I was sick of being a D'Angelo, however much my parents liked the name, Mom stubbornly keeping it after the divorce, as if it was a cross she could bear. But they used to call me "danger-girl" out on the playground, right before somebody would kick dirt in my face.

Tom and Susie put on their coats and Gloria threw on a shawl that sparkled with silvery threads, arranging it so it covered the pointy tips of her ears.

"So we're going?" I said.

"Yeah, I think we should. It's already dark out," Gloria said.

I blinked in surprise at the black rectangle of the window. Already?

"I'll drive you," Susie said, and when Gloria shook her head and said her car wouldn't be able to enter the Zone, Susie said she could still get us as close as possible. So she dropped us off where we'd caught the bus on South Street.

I wished she was coming with us, but how could I say so, especially with Tom right there? He'd think I didn't trust him to protect me. I leaned on his shoulder as we set off on foot, almost glad I'd sprained my ankle because it meant I could be close to him.

The cold drizzle had stopped and a full moon appeared with a halo around it. Gloria looked up and I swear she gave it a wink. And it actually followed us through the Zone, lighting our path right up to the door of the bookshop.

Gloria opened the door for us, and Tom went in first. I followed him in, and Gloria made a strange, high-pitched trilling noise. When I turned around, she was facing the moon.

Who are you? I shivered.

She winked and smiled. "It pays to have friends in high places."

22

Since the banks and the airship ticket office had been closed for hours, we stayed overnight in the bookstore. Gloria and I insisted that Teresa sleep on the settee, while I borrowed one of the cushions and curled up alongside it. The next thing I knew Gloria was gently tapping my shoulder. I sat up and rubbed the sleep from my eyes. Daylight (or the Zone imitation of daylight) streamed through the plate-glass window.

Gloria was dressed in a navy-blue ankle-length skirt, printed with little white flowers, the sort of thing Mum wears to town council meetings. She still wore that weird basket hairdo, though curls were springing out of it.

Teresa's hair was disordered, as well. She sat up and rubbed her eyes. I leaned over the couch and kissed her good morning, but she wrinkled her nose.

"Ugh, your breath stinks."

"Ah, young love," Gloria grinned, clapping her hands. "Well my dears, ready for breakfast?"

"Yeah, I'd say so," Teresa said as Gloria handed her a mug of cocoa. "And then I need to use your bathroom."

While she freshened up, a mysteriously lengthy process even Jo has started doing lately, I browsed a book of scientification tales. There was a thrilling story called "Zap-Gun Jack Flash and the Dame-Eating Monsters of Venus." Teresa finally came back out and Gloria handed us each a round roll with a hole in the middle. I looked at mine curiously and asked what it was.

"Jeez, you people never heard of bagels?" Teresa said, rolling her eyes at me.

"Jeez, you people never heard of manners?" I mimicked.

"Hey lovers, keep it cool," Gloria said. "You're gonna be sharing a tiny cabin in a blimp for a week, remember?"

I had been trying not to think about that. Teresa's eyes widened. Perhaps she had not fully understood the situation.

"But it's an adventure!" Gloria added. "The adventure of a lifetime, as they say. And you're in it to save Tom's father's life. What could be better than that?"

"Sitting safe and comfortable in a bookstore reading about other people's adventures," Teresa said ruefully.

But we had no time to lose, so as soon as we finished our breakfast—the tea was even better than Mum's, though I wouldn't admit that even under Froggie torture—we picked up our bags and trooped to the back room with Gloria. Teresa's limp was almost gone. What magic had Gloria worked?

Before we made the transition Gloria handed us each a coin. They had both been minted in the "United States of America," though Teresa said they couldn't have come from her world, because the "presidents" on them had never held that office.

Her coin was bright silver and had the profile of "President Robert F. Kennedy" on one side and a strange spindly house on stilts surrounded by a group of four figures wearing bulky helmets that covered their entire heads on the other. That side was captioned, "Mars Landing, July 4, 1976. COURAGE."

My coin was golden and depicted "President Norman Thomas." The other side showed a man in overalls holding a baby. The caption was a quote from Mr Thomas, about a decent society and a father's love. A lump rose in my throat.

"Keep them safe," Gloria said unnecessarily. "Ready?"

We nodded and joined hands with her. With my eyes closed I pictured my dad sitting beside me with his fishing pole on a quiet morning out on the bay.

We shall get you back.

There was a moment of dizziness, and when I opened my eyes the gas lamps were back and Tiferet, with oddly curvy ears, rolled on her back and meowed at us. We both knelt and rubbed her belly, then set off hand in hand out the door and into the Zone.

Whatever magic Teresa and Gloria had worked between them was still active, because the sky was a blank but not unfriendly blue. It remained clear as we arrived in the genuine Philadelphia, where the snowstorm we had walked through the day before had left two or three inches of light fluffy flakes on the ground. My fingers itched to form it into snowballs, but I refrained. We had best look respectable.

First I went to the Royal Bank of Philadelphia to withdraw my money. My account contained 49 pounds, 8 shillings, and 10 pence. The teller was a middle-aged lady with deep frown lines. She reminded me unpleasantly of my natural philosophy master from last year. Not all of us are fortunate enough to have Susie Chen for a teacher.

"See here, young man. We will need your parents' written permission to withdraw all your funds and close your account," she said.

"Oh. Well, what amount can I take out and still leave the account open?"

She sniffed. "If you leave one shilling thruppence in the account it will remain open. Though I shall have to send a letter to your parents informing them of this unusual withdrawal."

"That is in order. Quite proper of you," I said. Maybe Adams is right and I am a suck up. But it worked, even though I thought I heard Teresa snickering behind me. I had little enough choice. We would have a difficult time and could use every penny, though I did not know just how difficult until we reached the airship company office.

Montgolfier Lines has the monopoly on flights to the Empire. That fact was reflected in the prices they charged.

"What do you mean, 23 pounds a ticket?" I squawked. "Can we not receive a discount for being a married couple?"

The ticket seller was even more unpleasant than the bank teller, but then, she was French. My apologies, Madame Dantès. Her name tag identified her as Marie-Claire Le Petomaine.

"Obviously, monsieur has not been out of the so-called British Commonwealth recently, or monsieur would understand about taxes and fees."

This was bad. Would we have enough money for the train to Oxford, not to mention little extras like food? Teresa elbowed her way to the counter.

"Listen, don't you have any specials?" she asked.

"I am sorry, mademoiselle. Special what?"

"Deals. You know, discounted tickets? And call me madame, if you please. I am married."

"My apologies, madame. Discounted tickets." Mme. Le Petomaine's sneer was so powerful, if we could have harnessed it, it would surely have taken us all the way to Oxford. "I am afraid not, madame. If one does not have the money to travel at popular times, perhaps one should wait until a *saison* when there is less demand. Such as February."

Or any flight with you on it.

Teresa leaned over the counter. "What about a combination ticket? You know, airship plus train?"

I had not thought of that. Mme. Le Petomaine was none too pleased at having to check. "Where do monsieur and madame wish to go in *l'Angleterre*?"

Call them the Home Islands if you please, Froggie lady.

"Oxford," I said.

"Ah. The home of Université Louis-Napoléon. Not nearly so fine a university as the Sorbonne, but still, I can understand why young British subjects like yourselves would wish to partake of the knowledge His Imperial Majesty generously offers his subjects there."

Lady or not, if she failed to sell us our tickets soon, I might be tempted to punch her a one-way ticket. But she did seem pleased that we would soon be worshipping at the stinky feet of the Bonaparte family, and she found us a package that only set me back another five shillings ha'penny. Leaving us with all of four pounds and change for food—and heaven alone knew how many francs I could get for that—but without Teresa's help we would not have reached Oxford at all.

She smiled when I told her that. "Mom taught me well," she said. "We may be angels, but call us hard-bargaining ones."

"You are an angel," I said, kissing her hair.

We were now queued to have our passports stamped, and I braced myself for more obnoxious comments from the consular clerk, a pudgy but dapper little man with a neat black mustache. While my heart pounded he examined our passports and consulted a ledger, running his finger down some columns until he nodded. He raised a rubber stamp that looked big enough to cover a whole sheet of paper. It made a satisfyingly solid thwack as it came down on our passports.

"Enjoy your honeymoon in *l'Angleterre*, my friends."

"How do you know we are just married?" Teresa said.

He smiled. "I can see how in love you both are, the way you hold hands."

Teresa blurted out, "You're so nice, you can't be French!"

I gasped, but the clerk only smiled. "Ah, but I am not French, Madame. Permit me to introduce myself. I am Hercule Poirot, and I am from Wallonia." He shook hands with both of us while I gaped at him. For any Imperial subject, much less a diplomatic official, to talk as though Wallonia is not a part of France was…well, it was very surprising, to say the least.

We had a few hours spare, so we went for a walk. The day had turned out surprisingly warm, and the snow was melting all around us, so we had to step over many puddles and streamlets as we walked. Teresa was quiet at first, but at length she said, "Tom, assuming we get to Oxford, what are we actually going to find out about your father's disappearance?"

I frowned. "Well, remember what Major Frost told me. Dad has been writing to Professor Urquhart very frequently. So the professor should be able to give us a clue about why Dad was kidnapped."

"Maybe," she said, frowning. "But do you think he's actually going to be able to tell us where your dad is?"

"Well, no, I suppose not."

"I mean, Tom, we're not exactly the F.B.I.—I mean the R.C. We can't follow every lead or go wherever we think your dad might be—and if we do think we know where he's being held, we can't go rushing off there to try and rescue him, we might only get him and ourselves killed. We'll have to come back and tell the police or the R.C. whatever it is we find out. We can't do it all on our own."

"And when we do that, we shall have to live with the consequences," I said slowly, "after Mum discovers what we did. I understand that, Teresa."

She squeezed my hand. "I want you to know that whatever happens, I'll be right by your side."

I looked into her eyes, and my heart skipped a beat. Gloria might have those unearthly green eyes concealing who knows what kind of powers, but Teresa's eyes were even more beautiful. I squeezed her hand back, and she jumped up.

"Come on, let's get rings!" she said.

"What?"

"Rings, silly. We're supposed to be newlyweds, remember?"

"Oh. Right. There should be a jewellery shop on South Street," I murmured. And there was—we found a costume jewellery store that could have been a twin of the clothing shop where Gloria had outfitted herself in the other Philadelphia. I bought us plain brass rings for tuppence each.

"Someday we'll have money for better ones," Teresa said as we walked out of the shop, headed for the airfield. I stared at her and she laughed.

By now, dark grey clouds had moved in. We rode the streetcar, and I turned to Teresa.

"We might not be able to take off with the increasing cloud cover."

"Your old blimps can't take off if it's *cloudy?*"

But when we reached the airfield, four or five other airships were boarding. The ground crew hauled on the guide ropes that held down each craft, clearly preparing them for takeoff. I sighed with relief.

It was not at all difficult to find our airship, the *Maid of Orleans*, which was painted with the tricolor and a giant grinning replica of Henri-Napoléon's face. Maid of Orleans, indeed. The Emperor would have burnt Joan of Arc at the stake. Never mind that one of my countrymen had lit the fire.

Teresa stared at the gondola as we queued. "That's really big," she said quietly.

"Indeed. I thought you would say one of your jet planes could swallow it for a snack and still be hungry."

"No, seriously. That's, like, really big. Maybe Susie was wrong, and we'll have a nice big room to ourselves?"

"Probably not," I said.

The bobby checking passports had a quick, well-practiced routine. He'd open each passport with a flick of his wrist, glance from the picture to the face of the person in front of him, ask the passenger where he or she was going, compare that with the stamped visa, and wish the person "a pleasant journey, sir," or "a lovely trip, ma'am."

I already missed good old British manners.

23

Tom and I sat out on the airship's observation deck enjoying the view of South Jersey. It seemed that the whole state was a lot more rural than in the real world.

We passed over the coastline. Wasn't that the site of Atlantic City? I'd spent enough time staring at maps during all those family trips down the shore, and knew the coast. Looking out the windows of the airship, though, I didn't see anything that looked like casinos and high-rise hotels and condos, only a few small villages and unspoiled beach. I asked Tom and he'd never heard of a place called Atlantic City. *Wow.*

Darkness fell not long after we sailed out over the open sea. We ate cheese sandwiches and an apple each—our tickets covered basic food, though better-dressed couples were enjoying chicken and steaks in a restaurant we passed—and we would have stayed in the observation lounge all night if we could have, making small talk and avoiding our cabin, but it closed at ten o'clock.

Now what were we supposed to do? We picked up our bags and made our way up a metal staircase and down a long, narrow corridor lit by electric bulbs that cast a weak orange light in search of our cabin, number 407.

The gondola swayed gently beneath our feet. I clutched Tom's arm as we turned a corner and found the right room. Tom took the little key from his pocket and opened the door, which was so low even I had to duck my head.

We both groaned. The "cabin" couldn't have been much more than seven feet long and five feet wide. More than half the floor space was taken up by a narrow shelf with a thin foam mattress. This shelf was molded from the walls, so there was no room underneath it.

How could both of us fit on the bed? Lying on the floor was next to impossible—the strip between the bed and the outer wall looked no more than a foot and a half wide. Luckily there was a little wall cabinet with room for our backpacks, although if we'd been normal travelers I don't know how we could have fit our stuff in there.

Before I could say anything Tom said cheerfully, "Well, good night!" and wedged himself into the space at my feet.

"Tom! How can you even fit in there?" He pretended he'd already fallen asleep, so I climbed onto the bed. The same thing happened the next three nights, and Tom was walking around stiff and sore all day. How could I convince him to share the bed without seeming like…someone he wouldn't respect?

There was only one way. The next night, as we sat in the observation lounge waiting for them to kick us out, I said I needed to use the toilet, but instead went straight back to our cabin, let myself in and wedged myself into the floor space. It wasn't easy! How had Tom done it for the past three nights? There was barely enough room for me to stretch out.

When Tom opened the door a few minutes later, he almost stepped on me. "Teresa? Good heavens, Teresa, this is terrible! You must not sleep on the floor!"

"Why not? I got the bed three nights in a row," I said.

He backed out into the hallway and put his hands on his hips. "Absolutely not. I forbid it. I am a man, and I will *not* permit my wife to sleep on the floor."

I tried to fold my arms, but there wasn't enough room for my elbows. "Well, I'm not moving, so that's that."

People stared and murmured as they walked past. Tom glanced around and lowered his voice. "Teresa, please be reasonable."

"No, *you* be reasonable," I said. "We'll just have to share the bed."

Tom's eyes grew enormous and he took a deep, shuddering breath.

"It's all right. I mean, really it's all right." I tried to smile. "I won't let you do anything improper."

"Teresa, I was perfectly comfortable on the floor," he said. He was a terrible liar.

"Look, it's only tonight and two more nights, right?" I said. "I think we can behave ourselves for three nights."

He looked around again. "Well, we *are* supposed to be a married couple. People will think it odd if we are *not*, um, sharing the bed."

"There you go," I said, reaching out my arms so he could pull me to my feet. I didn't let go and tugged him into the bed, so he wouldn't get any funny ideas about diving down onto the floor. We squirmed around as we tried to get comfortable, or anyway, the least *un*comfortable that we could manage. Tom did fall asleep surprisingly fast—poor thing, he hadn't slept much the past three nights. It took me a while, though.

After all, what's the big deal? So we have to share the same bed. It isn't as if we're, well, sleeping together.

Actually, this must sound weird, but it was the best thing ever. When you trust someone enough to fall asleep beside him, it means *everything*.

* * * *

The next day was New Years' Eve, and the crew handed out little cakes and cookies to all the passengers. There was a party in the observation lounge, which stayed open till one in the morning. I even had a taste of champagne. But that wasn't as amazing as the fact that we'd shared a bed last night, and we were going to do it again tonight, and tomorrow night too! Was Tom thinking the same thing?

That was the best New Year's Eve ever. After midnight (and a slow, dreamy kiss), we danced—although dancing probably isn't the right word for what I do, "shuffling my feet around and hoping I don't step on Tom's feet" is more like it—until we were both so tired we bumped into the walls and other people.

We stumbled back to the cabin, where it took Tom three tries to get the key into the lock. Would they charge us for the scratches he left on the door? That was my last clear thought, because we both fell on the bed, barely even managing to kick our shoes off. We didn't even have to squirm around as much to find good positions. And I was much too tired to be embarrassed about anything—or to have any dirty thoughts. It was good to be next to Tom's solid, warm body as the airship rocked us back and forth. Was *he* embarrassed? He began to snore just before I passed out myself.

* * * *

Waking next to him in the morning was fun, if a bit strange. He'd thrown his arm over me, and I ducked out from under it. He mumbled something and went on sleeping. I smiled and left to find breakfast. When I came back with a couple of rolls and a mug of tea, he was sitting up, blinking and yawning.

"Happy New Year, Tom," I said, handing him a roll.

"Happy New Year," he said.

We kissed. Nothing seemed to have changed since we had left Philadelphia, except that we were both smellier (there were no showers on the *Maid of Orleans*).

I gave him a quick hug, and we walked out hand in hand to find the crew rushing around getting ready for landing.

"Really? But I thought that wasn't till tomorrow," I said to one crewman.

"We got some nice tailwinds south of Greenland," he said, shrugging. "Sorry miss, must run. We'll be on the ground at Thermidor Aerodrome in less than two hours."

Tom and I found a seat as close to the windows as possible. The airship drifted over the south coast of England. I had never visited England in the real world, but it was almost as rural as this world's South Jersey.

A lot of small farms were separated by stone walls, with brown dots of cows out grazing in the frosty fields.

"It's beautiful," Tom said.

"Does it feel like you're coming home?" I asked, squeezing his hand.

"Of course. It's the Home Islands," he said, a little crease between his brows.

* * * *

An hour later we were over the outskirts of London. Houses, buildings, and streets passed below us.

The few times I'd flown over a city, the scenery reminded me of a circuit board, all those neat lines hiding the grime you'd see at ground level. But these streets curved or headed off at odd angles, the houses looked all crooked, as if they'd been added onto over hundreds of years, and instead of cars and trucks, there were horse-drawn carriages and teams of pack animals, with only the occasional modern battery-powered carriage.

I kept my mouth shut. I didn't want to hurt Tom's feelings, but he voiced my thought.

"It's so primitive compared to Philadelphia," he said. "Are the Frogs hogging all the good stuff for themselves back in Paris?"

Just then a crewman tapped Tom on the shoulder and told him we'd better get ready for landing. That didn't take us long—we grabbed our bags from our cabin and lined up with the other passengers. Now was the big hurdle: getting through immigration control with our counterfeit passports in an unfriendly country. My hands grew clammy.

"Never fear, Teresa," Tom whispered, "I shall protect you no matter what!"

The airship touched down with a gentle bump. There were so many people in front of us I thought we'd be waiting all day, but actually the line moved pretty quickly. When we boarded in Philadelphia we hadn't passed through anything like a metal detector or those fancy new X-ray machines everyone complains about. Looked like the Imperials didn't have anything like that, either. Nobody worried about terrorism, then. Which world was backward?

We were almost at the front of the line. The customs inspector, a pudgy man with a salt-and-pepper mustache, was going through people's bags. Once in a while he would take something out and put it behind his desk before stamping people's passports. Nobody complained. I guess nobody dared.

"Don't worry," Tom whispered, "We do not have anything worth stealing."

Indeed, the agent gave our bags a very quick look and actually sniffed. He gave our passports an even quicker, more bored look before stamping them. I took a deep breath.

"*Bienvenue a l'Empire Français,*" he said.

Tom stiffened, stood up straighter, and opened his mouth. I elbowed him and he said "oof," which earned him a quick, curious look from the customs guy.

"You're welcome," I murmured as we walked on, Tom holding his stomach and glaring at me.

"I would not have said anything," he grumbled.

"Right, I'm sure you were just about to say how wonderful it is to be in Bonaparte-land. Which reminds me, how are we going to get a train to Oxford on New Year's Day?"

Tom wrinkled his nose. "That is no difficulty. New Year's Day is not a holiday in the Empire. They use that stupid, ridiculous calendar they made up during the French Revolution. That was the one thing I could never remember on Madame's tests, otherwise I would have received outstanding marks. Who calls a month 'Fructidor?' It sounds like a bath soap. Anyway, their New Year is in September."

"Okay, so where are the trains?" I asked.

Tom didn't say anything.

"All right then, we'll have to ask someone," I said.

Tom plucked at my sleeve. "Please, no."

"Why shouldn't I ask for directions? What are we supposed to do, wander around until we find ourselves on the train platform by accident?" His ears turned red and I laughed. "Seriously, that's what you'd prefer we do? I guess some things are the same in every world. Well, I'm a girl, so I'm not embarrassed to ask for directions. Excuse me, sir." I addressed a tall, thin, middle-aged man walking past with a briefcase and an old-fashioned-looking black bowler hat. He looked at me. "Can you tell us where to get the train to Oxford?"

It was a natural mistake. After all, if you know nothing else about England, what's the one thing you think you know?

24

If you know nothing else about England, what is the one thing you think you do know? Why, that they speak English there, of course.

I knew better. True, when we were growing up Mum always made an effort to speak proper English and not *patois* around me and Jo. But sometimes she slipped, usually when she was tired or upset. Then she would speak like she did whilst growing up in Liverpool.

It gave me a head start in French class, though even Madame, unshockable as she was, raised an eyebrow at some of the words I asked her about, especially the ones Mum used when we had been really bad, or to describe the DRRAGON management that was so stingy about giving Dad the pay and honour he deserved.

In any case, Madame used to sniff, I was in her class to learn proper French, not backstreet *patois*. I did not repeat that remark to Mum. Imagine a showdown between her and Madame—it would be truly brilliant.

So of course the poor man Teresa asked for directions had trouble understanding her. I stepped up and did my best, but the Liverpool version of patois differed from the London version. Still, with a lot of pointing and gesturing and finally grabbing my elbow we finally understood the correct direction. The vast, bustling floor of the Aerodrome looked as if it could swallow two Penn Stations and still be hungry for more.

"So, was that a Frenchman?" Teresa asked as we pushed our way through the dense crowd. "I mean, I couldn't understand very much of what he was saying, but I really suck at French."

I grimaced. "No, he is as English as me, although he was speaking *patois*."

"What's pat-wah?"

By this time we had managed to elbow our way onto what I hoped was the right train platform. "Well, the Frogs have been running things here in the Home Islands for two hundred years, right?"

"Right, but I'm not sure you said it loud enough for that gendarme over there to hear."

I glanced at the uniformed figure directing foot traffic several yards away and lowered my voice. "So, for all that time, if you want to apply for a job in the government, say as a teacher, or you need to understand the official forms the French love so much—even something as simple as an apartment lease, Mum says—you have had to learn French. So naturally French has come to pollute the English language." I scowled and glared at the gendarme's back. "The English language is endangered in her own homeland!"

Teresa chuckled.

"What's so funny?"

"Just that in the real world—sorry, I mean in *my* world—the French feel the same way about English corrupting *their* language."

"I think I would rather live in your world," I said.

She smiled and gave me a quick hug. "I want to live in any world that has *you* in it."

Just then the train pulled in. I started. It made so little noise! The engine was sleek and clean, and no cloud of steam rose over it.

Teresa smiled. "This is more like the trains in the real—in *my* world," she said, taking me by the hand and leading me into a carriage. "Except a lot nicer!"

"Yes, it is indeed very *fine*. The wood-paneled walls and the velvet-upholstered seats, for instance. The wine dispenser at the front of the car with a choice of two, no, *three* kinds of champagne, and a polite little note asking passengers to 'please take care of the crystalware.' And the little icebox with a choice of smelly cheeses. Yes, I said *smelly* cheeses!" I coloured and lowered my voice when a grey-haired, thin-faced woman looked down her nose at me. "The good old Nanticoke Limited is much finer any day!"

"Of course it is, Tom, because it goes to your home," Teresa said soothingly. "Let's sit down and enjoy the trip, all right?"

"There must be something wrong with my hearing. Did you say 'enjoy the trip?'"

"You're right, I'm sorry, what I actually said was, 'let's be miserable the whole way there,'" Teresa said and patted my arm.

"You won't have to endure it for long," the long-faced woman said with a chuckle. "We'll be there in fifteen minutes." She had a French accent but spoke English—English, not *patois*—perfectly.

I had looked in an atlas before we left. True, Oxford was less than 60 miles from the Thermidor Aerodrome, but still, we would arrive there in *a quarter of an hour*? It took almost four hours for the Nanticoke Limited to make its slow way down the peninsula from Philadelphia to Spence Landing, a distance of less than 150 miles.

Teresa patted my arm again and kissed me lightly. "I'm going off to find the bathroom while you sulk, okay?" she said.

"Bathroom? Even Imperial trains do not have full baths in them," I objected.

She sighed. "I mean the water closet. Try not to get into any fights while I'm gone, all right, baby?"

The thin-faced lady smiled at me after Teresa disappeared through the door at the end of the carriage. "Your girlfriend is delightful. And such an adorable accent. Where is she from?"

"Alaska," I said as rudely as I could.

"*Vraiment?* But I didn't hear even a trace of Russian in her voice."

I opened my mouth to reply when Teresa came back.

"That was fast," I said, as she stopped in front of her seat. "How did you get to the front of the train? You went toward the back."

"This seat, is it occupied?" she said in an accent I had never heard before.

All right, so she wanted to be silly. I could play along. I smiled and patted the cushion.

"Not for a pretty girl like you," I said. "Please, do sit down."

She did, but she looked at me strangely. Her expression was almost bored.

How strange. Is this some sort of game? And is her change in clothing part of it? I did not really want to play, however.

"Why did you change your clothes? And how did you do it so fast?" I asked.

Instead of those ugly but useful denim pants she always wore, she was dressed like some of the lady teachers at Cleodolinda Preparatory, in a long bright dress and court shoes. She wore powder and rouge, and her hair was tied back. I scratched my head. How *had* she found time to do all that? She could not have been away more than a minute or two. Not that the effect was bad. Not at all. *She must have changed just to please me.* I grinned, put my arm around her shoulders and brushed her cheek with my lips.

She jumped to her feet and out into the aisle, after landing a slap on my face that left my head ringing. What in heaven's name—

"*Signore*, I shall thank you to mind your manners!" she said, loudly enough that everyone in the car turned to look at us. "I am used to such behavior from the boys in my own unhappy country—they are pigs, *Italiano* men—but I expected better in *l'Angleterre!*" She looked me up and down, as if I was something they had just scraped off the tracks. "Much less from an actual *Englishman*," she added with a sneer and a toss of her head.

My mouth opened, but nothing emerged. Teresa had never shown evidence of a taste for practical jokes—and if she had been such a joker, this was hardly the right time and place for such a prank.

I managed to hiss, "Teresa! The gendarmes!"

"Yes, I shall certainly call the gendarmes on you, and that without hesitation, *signore!* And I am sure they will be most interested in how a—a—a *hooligan* I have never met before knows my name! Perhaps you have been following me with intentions dishonourable, *signore?*"

My heart raced and perspiration dampened my back. The thin-faced woman, who had been watching with as much fascination as everyone else in the train carriage, suddenly turned to look at the back of the car.

"*Incroyable!*" she gasped.

What was she looking at? *Who* was she looking at?

Teresa stood in the aisle, in her denim pants and her messy, curly hair, frowning.

"Tom? What's going on?" My mouth still refused to work. "And who," she asked, pointing, "is *that?*"

Along with everyone else in the train carriage, I turned to look at Teresa—the *other* Teresa, who stepped forward with a sudden smile and addressed my Teresa.

"I am afraid there has been a slight misunderstanding, *signora.* Permit me to introduce myself." She curtseyed. "I am Teresa D'Angelo, of Palermo, Sicilia. At your service."

25

She was better dressed than me. She had a better complexion than me. She had a better figure than me. She had more poise, more style, and more self-confidence than me. Only took two seconds to see that Palermo Teresa was a better *me*.

Had Tom had mistaken her for me and "gotten fresh with her," as Nana would have put it? If so, should I be flattered or jealous? Everyone was staring at us, and I couldn't try my ridiculous parody of a curtsey in my tatty old jeans. I settled for smiling back.

"I'm Teresa D'Angelo of Phil—of Anchorage, Alaska at your service."

She raised her eyebrows. God, even her eyebrows were better than mine, shaped and tweezed.

"Really? I traveled to Alaska when I was fourteen and I never heard of a place called Anchorage."

"It's a new town," I said quickly.

"And your accent—"

"It has been a pleasure meeting you, but we had best go now, Teresa," Tom said loudly.

"Right! Yes! Gotta get our stuff together. Excuse me," I said, pushing past the other Teresa.

Luckily, the train was already slowing on its approach to Oxford Station, so people were no longer paying us much attention. But Palermo Teresa only had a shoulder bag, and a curious glint in her eye. She leaned over the seat back while I rummaged through my pathetic luggage.

"What did you say your last name was?"

"D'Ang—ow!—Purnell," I said as Tom elbowed me.

Palermo Teresa smiled. "Newlyweds, *si*? But your maiden name is actually D'Angelo? That's odd, because we look so much alike!"

"Yes, what an extraordinary coincidence!" Tom said with a forced laugh. "Well, we would not wish to keep you from arriving at your destination—"

"I'm traveling also to Oxford," Palermo Teresa said as the train pulled to a stop with a barely noticeable bump. People started piling out the doors. "I'm a medical student at the university. You're headed that way, too, are you not?"

"Yes, we are," I said firmly, before Tom could insist that we didn't need directions. "We're looking for a Professor Ramsey Urquhart. I'm afraid we don't know which of the colleges he's in. Can you help us?"

"*Si*, no problem. I was in his first-year biology class in the autumn." She scowled. "He is much too enthusiastic about *rettili* for my taste. You know, scaly green *animali*. What do you want with him?"

"We're thinking of sitting in on his course," I said. By now we were out on the platform. "Tom and I aren't students at Oxford ourselves, of course—I mean, we're not students at Université, uh, whatever-it-is Napoléon—"

"Don't call it that around me, or any other student," she said firmly. "Oxford is Oxford. We don't name things after any smelly old Bone-a-fart."

It took a moment for what she had said to sink in. I gulped when it did. "Maybe you'd better not talk like that, Teresa."

"Ha!" She tossed her head back. "You think I am afraid of these ridiculous *flics*?" she said, wiggling her fingers at a cop who had his back to us.

The street we were following her down was so narrow it was as crowded as the train platform. Most of the people seemed to be about our age. They were better dressed than the students I'd seen around the campus at Temple University when Mom dragged me there last year, and because most of them were speaking *patois* I could barely make out one word in three, but they acted a lot like college kids anywhere, flirting, teasing, and talking about their classes, sometimes at the same time. Oh, except that nobody had a cell phone, of course.

The sky was overcast and the air was damp and freezing, but we were walking so quickly and had so many people around us that I hardly noticed. I was in England for the first time. Jolly old England! And ahead of us I could see the gray, Gothic towers of the university. Our business here might be deadly serious, but I'd be damned if I wasn't going to have as much fun as I could along the way.

Palermo Teresa stopped so suddenly when we came to a big fancy gate that I almost collided with her. "I shall take you straight to Dottore Urquhart's office, but I want you to do a small favor for me."

"Of course," I said. If you can't trust yourself, who can you trust?

"Teresa, would you take some homework to my friend Geoffrey Watkins, over at All Souls' College?"

"Why can you not just give it to him yourself?" Tom asked.

I shot him a dirty look, but Palermo Teresa only laughed and patted his cheek. "Because, *bambino*, All Souls' is a men's college, and I am not permitted there any more than Geoffrey is allowed to visit me in the Women's College."

"Oh," Tom said. He thought for a moment, then asked, "But what about Professor Urquhart's office? If it is in a men's college, will Teresa—I mean, my Teresa—not be able to go there with me?"

Palermo Teresa rolled her eyes, just as I would have done. I was starting to like her. "No, *bambino*, the faculty offices are open to men and women both. It wouldn't be very practical otherwise, would it?"

"I suppose not," Tom said. Palermo Teresa turned and walked through the gate, past a uniformed gendarme who nodded at the ID card she flashed him. I braced myself to do some fast talking—or rather for Tom, Mister French Expert, to do it for us—but Palermo Teresa said a few quick words and he waved us through.

"What did you tell him?" Tom asked.

Palermo Teresa raised an eyebrow again. "I said you are possible students here. Is that not so?"

"Of course it is," I said quickly. "Thanks, Teresa."

We cut across a lawn, and Palermo Teresa pointed out an impressive library—"the Bodleian to all true scholars, not the '*Bibilothèque Impératrice Josephine*,'"—and told Tom to wait there for us there, which he agreed to do, a little sulkily.

She then led me down a winding path to an only slightly less impressive building—a sort of mini-Gothic castle. We climbed a staircase so dusty and deserted I half-expected to see the ghost of Anne Boleyn pass us on the way down, her cut-off head held under her arm. Instead the other me led the way to a battered wooden door, which she unlocked.

Her room was surprisingly ordinary despite the gas lighting. I shivered in the chill air. It was not all that different from how I imagined my own dorm room would be if I decided to go to college—filthy and messy, with books, papers, and clothes strewn all over the place. Palermo Teresa threw herself on the bed, grabbed a pack of cigarettes from under a pile of dirty laundry, and lit up.

I took one breath and spluttered and choked. I mean, I can't get Mom to stop smoking, so I'm used to the smell. These things, however, were really nasty. They stank like rotting garlic might, if you wrapped toilet paper around it and set it on fire.

"You don't smoke, I take it," she said, waving the pack lazily in my direction.

"No, thank you," I coughed. "Where's that homework?"

"Not so fast. I want to talk to you first. Have a seat."

"Where?"

"There's a chair right over there, can't you see?"

Well no, I couldn't, not until she pointed right at it, because it was buried under a pile of drying panties and bras. I moved the clothes and sat down, trying to breathe through my mouth.

Palermo Teresa sat up and grinned wickedly. "Now, my dear double, do tell me where you're really from," she said, stabbing her lit cigarette at me, "because if you're from Alaska, I am Henri-Napoléon's latest mistress."

I sighed. But as I said before, if you can't trust yourself, who can you trust? I told her the whole story, not forgetting to whip out my cell phone for a demonstration. Of course the battery was long dead, but the teeny-weeny keys and the pearl-gray screen might do the trick. She examined it cautiously, as if it might explode in her hands, then shook her head and tossed it back to me.

"I don't know, Teresa Americana. Let me ask you something. What are your parents' names?"

"Frank and Celine. But they're not married to each other anymore."

"Strange. My parents' names are Celine and Francesco," she mused. "And they *are* married to each other, but only because Henri-Napoléon in his imperial wisdom has decided that legalizing divorce is contrary to the interests of *l'Empire*." I never heard anyone pronounce a word so contemptuously. It sounded like "lump-ear." Like a lump of some really, really nasty earwax.

"You mean they don't get along?"

"'Get along'? My dear, if a week goes by without one of them black-ing the other's eye or introducing an interesting new dent into the other one's skull with a thrown frying pan, we consider it a good week."

"We?"

"We. Me, my little sisters Anna, Allegra, and Concetta, and my broth-ers Gianni, Roberto, and Sergio." So it seemed Francesco and Marie got up to more than just fighting, and birth control was also forbidden by *l'Empire*. I shook my head in confusion. But Palermo Teresa wasn't done yet. "And you mean to tell me in your, um, world, there is no ump-ear?"

"No what? No, there's no empire. Napoleon was defeated two hun-dred years ago. They exiled him to a desert island. And yes, Italy is an independent country. Has been for, like, a hundred fifty years."

She murmured something to herself, then looked up at me. "Listen, Teresa Americana, can you do me a really big favor?"

"What is it?" I asked. I needed to get back to Tom so we could do what we'd come here to do.

She scrabbled around in the mess until she came up with some blank notebook paper and what looked like a leaky old fountain pen. "Write down history as you know it for me. Can you do that?"

"Excuse me?"

"Just what you told me, about Napoléon I's defeat and exile, and Italia's liberation, and the wonderful things she has done in the world." She held the pen out to me, her eyes shining.

"Oh, I see. All right," I said. This was going to be a tough one. I didn't actually know that much about Italian history, and some of what I did know wasn't going to make Palermo Teresa very happy. Could I get away without mentioning Mussolini?

I did my best, filling up several pages with a scrawl that no one else can ever read, but another version of *me* ought to be able to. I went heavy on composers like Verdi and Puccini and filmmakers like Fellini and Di Sica, and managed to completely leave out Benito Scumbag-olini.

Could I work in something about the afternoons I used to spend making "red gravy" with Nana? No, this wasn't supposed to be about me. Besides, what would Palermo Teresa tell me about *her* version of Nana—like, what if she was actually still *alive* back in Sicily? How would I choose between helping Tom and going to see her?

In any case Palermo Teresa was delighted with my scribbles. "*Belissimo*," she cried, kissing me on both cheeks. I coughed, because she still stank like a rotten garlic fire. "*Bene*," she added, "I have kept you long enough, Teresa Americana. You and your Tomaso must speak with *Dottore* Urquhart about freeing his father."

She handed me a bundle of her homework, took my hand, and led me back down the stairs. How was it possible to have so much homework, even at Oxford? There must have been a hundred pages in the bundle, all neatly typed and folded in thirds. It was in French, and it said something about a "struggle" and "revolution." Suspicion began to gnaw at me and I asked Palermo Teresa what it was.

"My term paper on the French Revolution, what do you think?" she said. "I want Geoffrey to make sure it is not too, how you say, provocative?"

Before I could ask anything more, she swept me into the library. Tom was leaning against the wall in the outer lobby looking bored, since of course he didn't have a student ID to enter the main reading room.

"What took you so long?" he asked.

"You shan't be bored anymore, *bambino*," Palermo Teresa responded. "Teresa, give to him my homework to take to my good friend Geoffrey Watkins at All Souls."

I was only too glad to hand over the bundle. Tom took it with a grunt. "What is your homework? Writing a new medical textbook?"

Palermo Teresa chuckled. "Very droll, Tomaso. It isn't far you have to go. It should be no trouble for a big, strong boy like you, I am right?"

"Well—"

"Very good, then. All you have to do is turn right outside the library, follow the flagstone path across the lawn, turn left when you see the clock tower, left again, and you'll see the gate to All Souls. Geoffrey's room is in the third building on the right. You can't miss it."

He grumbled, but he did as she said. Palermo Teresa and I sat on a bench. She got out one of her horrible cigarettes, and this time I had to say something.

"They cause cancer, you know."

"What do, dear?"

"Cigarettes. They cause cancer. Also emphysema," I said, coughing as the smoke wafted my way.

"Oh, these aren't tobacco," she said. "It's you Americans or English or whatever you want to call yourselves who grow and smoke that dreadful stuff."

"So what the hell are you smoking?"

"Garlic leafs," she said.

I stared at her, but couldn't tell whether she was joking or not. "What are you going to do when you become a doctor?" I asked. "Go back to Italy to practice?"

"What else?" she scowled. "The Bone-a-farts have made sure Italia has stayed poor and backward. I have to help my people—*our* people. You know what cholera is?"

"Um, a disease?"

"A disease spread by dirty water. So many little babies die in Sicilia each year because of this. My own brother Alfonso did, before his first birthday. Maybe he got to grow up in your world?"

I shook my head. "I'm an only child," I said.

Palermo Teresa stared at me in amazement. Then her face grew serious again. "Of course, in your America, people don't need to have so many children, since more will live to become adults. Is that not so? It must be so."

I shrugged. "I never thought about it that way."

She suddenly grabbed my hands, startling me. Her hands were warm, the same size as mine, but with calluses where I had none. What kind of life had she had back in Sicily?

"It doesn't have to be that way, Teresa. My Sicilia is poor and backward because Henri-Napoléon doesn't care about Italian peasants. But when Italia is free of *l'Empire*, it won't be that way anymore. A free Italia will care for all her people!"

Nana had told me things she had heard from *her* Nana about life in Sicily. Things that would not please Palermo Teresa. Would it work out the way she planned, if she got her way and *l'Empire* went the way of Rome? But she was so excited, all I could do was smile and squeeze her hands in return. Maybe if there were enough people like her, things would work out better than in the real world.

"And what about you, Teresa Americana?" she asked. "What will you do, when you get back to *your* country?"

"Oh, I don't know. First I gotta finish high school," I mumbled, looking at her knees. "My grades aren't good enough to get into a school like Oxford. And I don't really know what I want to do, anyway."

Her intent gaze drew my own. "But there must be things you want to do, Teresa. Things you want to change in your world. Or is everything so perfect there?"

I looked away. It was like being lectured by the face in the mirror— even though her face was *not* a mirror image of mine, because when you look in the mirror, left and right are reversed from the way other people see you.

I was seeing what Tom saw when he looked at me—except better, wiser, sexier, and more sophisticated, with neater hair and good makeup. And she had asked me a question. Were things so perfect, back in the real world?

"Hardly," I said. A man with a ragged wild beard stood holding a torn scrap of cardboard every day at the corner of 9th Street and Snyder Avenue. PLEASE HELP GOD BLESS. Mom would never give him anything when we drove past.

"Bum," she'd spit. "Give him change I can't afford and he'll use it to go shoot up."

She might be right, but what if he was just hungry? So many men and women standing on the traffic islands at every busy intersection.

I looked into Palermo Teresa's eyes, the same muddy brown as mine. If she could be so brave and fight to make things better, then so could I. "Yes," I said, "there's a lot to be done." She smiled and squeezed my hands again.

Just then Tom rushed in, breaking up our weird little moment of togetherness. "Well, I gave it to him," he puffed. "You did not tell me he was French!" Palermo Teresa just looked at him. "French! With a name like Geoff Watkins," he complained. "How can that be?"

"His father is from *l'Angleterre*, somewhere up north I think, but he grew up in Paris," Palermo Teresa said, pronouncing it *Paree*. "What difference does it make?"

"What difference?" Tom spluttered. "What *difference?* He is French, for heaven's sake! How can you be friends with a Frenchman?"

Palermo Teresa smiled and raised one brow. "Not all French people love Henri-Napoléon, Tomaso," she said. "You should not be so quick to judge."

"But—but—he called me a cute American boy!" Tom said.

Palermo Teresa and I laughed the same laugh and said, "Oh dear!" in unison. Tom grew red.

"If you are both *quite* finished laughing at me, perhaps you could be so good as to tell us how to find Professor Urquhart?"

"I shall do better than that, Tomaso. I shall accompany you there," Palermo Teresa said, jumping up and taking his arm.

Oh no, you don't. I scrambled to my feet to take his other arm. *So there!* Poor Tom looked from one me to the other.

Outside, the wind had shifted and a hard sleet was falling. At least we were almost the only people out in it, otherwise I'm sure the three of us would have attracted curious stares. Teresa guided us through a twisty alleyway or three to another mini-castle. A plaque by the doorway said this building was the home of the Natural Philosophy Department. She led us up two flights of stairs and pointed us down a long corridor.

"*Dottore* Urquhart's office is down there, fourth on the right. He is almost always in when he's not actually lecturing. I think the poor man actually lives there."

"Aren't you coming with us?" I asked as she turned back into the stairwell.

She smiled, shook her head and gave us both a hug and a peck on the cheek. "I must return to my studies. The *dottore* will be of great help to you, I am sure. Good luck! *Ciao* for now!"

As her footsteps faded away Tom murmured, "It is good to see the last of her!"

"You don't have a crush on Palermo Teresa, do you?" I asked innocently.

"A crush?" he said blankly. Then he colored. "Teresa! I do not have a crush on anyone but you!"

"But she *is* me," I pointed out, "in a way." We walked down the hallway in thoughtful silence for a few moments before I said, "You know, there might be a parallel version of *you*…in my world."

Tom shuddered as he knocked on the professor's door. "If he is anything like Garlicky Teresa, I think I had rather not meet him."

At first there was no reply to Tom's knock. Then, just as he was raising his hand to knock again, a man's voice said something grumpy in *patois*.

"I am not here about my marks, professor," Tom called. "I am not a student."

There was the sound of a chair scraping against the floor, followed by a loud thump and some very unprofessorial swearing. The door was yanked open, and there was the man we had last seen *five months from now*, looking just the same as he would in May except that his tie was crooked and his graying hair was all messy, as if he had just woken up from a long nap. He squinted at us as if he'd forgotten his glasses.

"Mike? What are you doing here? No, wait, you can't be Mike…you must be his son…and Miss D'Angelo? Why are you dressed like that?"

"My father has been kidnapped," Tom blurted out. "May we come in?"

26

"Kidnapped? Michael Purnell? But why?" I exclaimed. "Who would do such a thing? Come in, come in both of you. You poor things. You came all the way from Nanticoke for my help, Thomas? It is Thomas, right?"

"I am usually called Tom," the young man who looked so much like Mike said. *Good Lord, what bloke his age talks so correctly, so pedantically? That must be Vivian's influence. I've seen it many times in young men and women who come up from the provinces and want so desperately to be taken seriously. No more patois for them!*

"All right, Tom then," I said. "I don't know what I can possibly tell you. But come in, sit down and tell me what happened, while I fix you some tea. You take it with milk and sugar, like your father, Tom?"

"No, Mum always says milk ruins a nice cup of tea," he said.

Well, Vivian would have a strong opinion even about how to drink tea!

"And you, Miss D'Angelo?" I asked.

What on Earth is Michael Purnell's son doing, running around campus with a notorious Italian radical like her? Surely Mike would have warned him against things like this! I gave her a hard stare.

"Why are you speaking with such a strange accent, and dressed like a workingman? Is this some sort of joke?"

"No, professor," she said. "I'm not who you think I am... I mean, I *am* Teresa D'Angelo, but not the one who goes to school here." She looked at Tom, who shrugged. She shrugged back and reached into her rucksack for something—a small black oblong made of some unfamiliar smooth material, with a grey side and a collection of tiny letters in a square.

"It's a miniature computer," she explained. "What you people call a babbage. Combined with a voicegram transmitter."

I looked from one to the other. "Is this some sort of prank? I tell my students at the start of each term, I have no tolerance for pranks! Whoever has put you up to this is going to regret it!"

"It is no joke, sir," Tom said, with those big earnest eyes that were so much like Mike's. "Please let us explain. Teresa is from another world...

not like Herbert Wells's scientification Martians, but from another version of Earth."

I sat down on my desk, barely hearing the sound of term papers being crushed beneath me, and put my head in my hands. "I think I'd prefer if it *were* a prank."

"But it isn't, professor, we swear!" the strange Teresa said. And she began to tell me how there were other versions of Earth out there, which one could reach through a used bookstore...

"This *is* a prank," I said, standing up. They didn't smile and admit the game was up, however. *They are tough, I'll give them that.* "Oh come now, it's the very plot of *Le Lion et la Sorcière Blanche*, the work that nearly got poor Professor Clive Lewis guillotined! Only instead of a wardrobe, you find your way to the other world through a bookstore!"

"It is no children's story, sir," Tom insisted. "It is very real. And the woman who runs the bookstore—well, sometimes she is a cat—said we should get your help!" To my astonishment, large tears started rolling down his cheeks. His next words, though, froze my guts. "And my father, he's been seized by Imperial intelligence because he is working on heavier-than-air flight, and because of all those letters he has been sending you about Assa Teag Ashley..."

"How do you know about those?" I whispered.

"The British police intercepted them," he said. "Probably the Imperial gendarmes, too. But we're certain the Imperials are the ones who grabbed him!"

I shook my head. This story was even more illogical in its way than the Clive Lewis business. "That doesn't even make any sense. You obviously haven't heard the news. On New Year's Day the first powered heavier-than-air flight was held outside the palace in Versailles. They're calling it a *dragon mécanique*."

"No!" Tom gasped.

If he's acting, he's doing a better job of it than the All Souls Players. Reason help me, am I going to take these children at their word?

"I'm sure your country will catch up, Tom," I said. "It's in the nature of these things, you know. Science doesn't keep secrets very well. And that being the case, why would the Intelligence Directorate resort to kidnapping and risk provoking an international incident just to preserve what's doubtless a lead of a few months, if that? No, no, something doesn't add up."

I took a deep breath. "All right, then. Let's leave aside your bookstore-wardrobe for the moment. Yes, you are quite correct, your father and I were exchanging letters about Assa Teag Ashley. *Draco americanus* is my passion, my life's work. It's why I met your father in the first place."

"Really?" Tom exclaimed, wide-eyed.

"You don't know the story? Can this be true?" I said. "How astonishing! What have Viv and Mike told you then?"

"Only that Mum was a dissident and Dad helped her escape from the Home Islands," Tom said.

"I see. Well, I suppose I can't really blame them, though their caution seems a bit excessive, after all this time."

Tom scowled. "Doubtless they were afraid Jo—my little sister, Jodie—would go blabbing it to everyone."

"Oh, a younger sister, eh?" I said. "Bet she's a chip off Viv's block… So she can't keep a secret? Well, be that as it may, you're practically grown up. Not to mention, with this horrible kidnapping business, you'd best know everything, just in case the Directorate *is* mixed up in it. Though that's quite unlikely, as I said." I shut my eyes and massaged them. It had been long ago when poor Mike and Viv had been in such trouble. It was not possible that their son could be involved in anything nefarious, not even a prank.

Yes, I'm going to trust them.

"Make yourselves comfortable," I said, "this is a long story."

* * * *

Tom's father went up to Oxford on an Imperial scholarship more than twenty years ago. He was reading aerodynamics and theory of heavier-than-air flight, a fact which shocked Tom, though it shouldn't have—relations between the Empire and the British government weren't always as bad as they were now. And heavier-than-air flight wasn't as sensitive a matter then. People used to say that heavier-than-air flight is twenty years off—it's *always* twenty years in the future. Miss D'Angelo interrupted me with some scientification prattle about cheap passenger travel in heavier-than-air craft, but Tom elbowed her into silence.

Mike's scholarship was from a longstanding Imperial program, the Prix Les Routes, which every year awards annual grants to 500 non-Imperial subjects to study at Oxford, the Sorbonne, and a few of the other top Imperial universities. The idea is to spread Imperial values and friendliness to the Empire itself among those not yet fortunate enough to live under its dominion.

The Emperor was wasting his money on young Michael Purnell. He was completely apolitical—he seemed to care only about the structure of insect, bird, and dragon wings, and what these might tell us about "the mystical secret of flight." He spent all his time studying. Didn't go out drinking and partying and looking to pick up *anglais* girls, like so many other British Routes scholars. They promise the poor girls the world, say they'll marry them and take them back to Philadelphia or Charleston, but then they have their fun and leave.

One such blackguard put my sister Oona in the family way, then took the next airship back to Britain when she told him she was pregnant. My nephew Stephen is a fine young man, but Oona had to work hard to bring him up alone...

As for me, when Mike came to Oxford I was just starting out my career as Professor Galsworthy's research drudge, which meant many late nights dissecting newts from bogs in Scotland in search of the species that was eventually named *Lissotriton galworthicus*. Mike was a student in Galsworthy's "Introduction to the Age of Terradracos" class, and I a teaching assistant who had to mark all the papers.

I discovered Mike was a fellow dragon enthusiast, and we started chatting after class about these creatures, their habits and evolution, and why they were endangered. I'd never had the chance to actually see one, of course, so I reveled in his descriptions of growing up right across the water from Assa Teag Ashley. He'd traveled many times to the Musée National in Nouvelle Orleans to see the terradraco fossils from the Far West of Louisiana, a country no Imperial subject could ever hope to visit.

The more time I spent with Mike, the more I realized that I was the only friend he'd made in Oxford. Poor fellow. At times I would borrow a carriage from the department and take him on tours of the countryside, such as the site of the Battle of Dover in which the first Napoléon's troops put the British Army to panicked flight after the Duke of Wellington was killed. Mike was greatly moved then, and also when I took him to see the ruins of the Houses of Parliament. I never did understand why Henri-Napoléon insisted on following his predecessors' policy of refusing to allow the site ever to be cleared. We *anglais* understood the message, after two hundred years.

Viv was another story. She wasn't particularly interested in dragons, but that was only because she was interested in *everything*. Not only wasn't she a student; she had no legal right to be in Oxford. Her *permis de domicile* didn't allow her beyond the Liverpool city limits for more than a week at a time, but she'd already been living in Oxford for over a year by the time I arrived from Glasgow to begin my own graduate studies.

I explained to Tom and Teresa what a *permis de domicile* is. They were outraged at the idea that one needed permission from the Imperial government before changing one's residence. Of course the *flics* aren't equally strict about enforcing the law everywhere, and in a university town like Oxford they usually don't bother illegal residents, so long as they mind their own business and don't cause problems. But if they pick you up for something else, you can be in real trouble.

Not that Viv had to worry about that much; she'd made herself too useful to the faculty, particularly the natural philosophy profs at All Souls, whom she served as an assistant, marker, tea maker, and general dogsbody. Galsworthy in particular took shameless advantage of her. He loved her tea and had her bring him endless cups during class. Viv put up with it just so she could sit in on the classes. She learnt far more than most of the registered students, although she never took a test or received a mark and had no prospect of ever being awarded a degree.

I was raging about the unfairness of it all to Mike one day in the tearoom we frequented. "Here you have these toffs whose families have been attending Oxford since before the Invasion, if not since the Norman Invasion, with brains inversely proportional to the length of their titles, and they garner all the honours while brilliant *anglais* girls like Viv can't even apply for admission!"

"Why not?" Mike asked.

"They have a quota, you see, with fifteen percent of the seats set aside for *anglais* boys and only five percent for the girls. There are barely enough for all the toffs, let alone for lower-class girls with strong accents like Viv. The authorities certainly do not care if people such as her are the ones who should be running this country!"

Mike gazed at the far wall. "Is she the blonde with the nice legs who's always running errands for Galsworthy?"

I nodded. "That's the one. Maybe I'm oversensitive because I'm a Scot, but—"

"You mean to tell me she's not even a student?"

"That's right. I suppose I should be grateful I was admitted here myself, being a *terroriste écossais*, a Scottish bomb-thrower, don't you know, but it just burns me up…"

"Is she seeing anyone, do you know?"

"I shouldn't think she has the time," I said. His face grew ruddy. "Michael Purnell, you're not thinking of asking her to walk out with you, are you?"

"I've seen her looking my way a few times," he said. "She has the most beautiful hazel eyes."

I chuckled. "Don't let her looks fool you, that girl is tough as nails! Don't come crying to me if she rejects you!" But of course, she didn't. It wasn't long before they were walking hand in hand down by the river, gazing into each other's eyes in the tearoom, snogging in doorways, and generally being disgustingly happy. Fortunate souls, and yet unfortunate souls. It couldn't last. It was already spring by the time their relationship grew serious, and Mike had to leave for home in a matter of weeks.

I was dreading the coming conversation. The moment arrived when Mike plucked at my sleeve after class one day.

"I need to talk to you, Ram," he said. "Please. It's really important."

I sighed and pushed aside the enormous stack of papers screaming to be marked. "I'll meet you in the tearoom in twenty minutes."

Once there, I heard him out and shook my head. "Ordinary Imperial subjects can't apply for a tourist visa to the British dominions," I said as gently as I could. "The Empire doesn't want emigrants spreading 'seditious' ideas about liberty back here. And even if she could get out to Britain, they'll never accept her as a student over there. She's not registered anywhere."

"I'll wait," he said. "If it's a matter of time, I'll wait. I don't mind staying here for however long it takes for a visa to come through. Even if it's years. I'll get them to extend my own student visa—I love Oxford anyway…"

I leaned forward. "Mike, they will *never* give Viv a visa. You could wait here till the crack of doom and that won't change. Worse, they'll probably arrest her for violating her *permis de domicile* if she even applies."

"And the Empire boasts about having invented '*liberté, egalité, fraternité,*'" he said bitterly.

"The first Napoléon corrupted those words a long, long time ago, Mike," I said. "But you're no fool. You knew all that when you asked Viv to walk out with you."

He glared at me as if I were the one denying Viv a visa. "Then I'll stay here, legally or not. Viv has lots of friends back in Liverpool… I'm sure I can find a place to live and work…"

"With your accent? The *flics* will pick you up within a week," I said.

"I don't care. I'm staying with Viv regardless. Let them put me in prison. No Empire can prevent true love."

"Perhaps not, but they can certainly ruin both your lives if they want to," I said. "All right, Mike. Let me see what I can do. I know some people back home who might be able to help." He was intelligent enough not to ask questions.

Viv understood what I was up to, as well as the risks I was running. She caught up with me at the railway station. "I'll never forget this, Ram."

I grimaced. "I only hope we don't all end up in gaol. Or worse. Scotsmen aren't very popular with the authorities to begin with, you know."

"I know," she said, and gave me a hug and a peck on the cheek, which fortified my determination all the way to Glasgow.

Once there, though, I wondered if I'd truly taken leave of my senses. Just then the Rebellion was at a low simmer, but you never knew when the S.C.A.R., the Scottish Army of the Republic, would stage a spectacular bomb attack and there'd suddenly be *flics* everywhere, checking everyone's papers and demanding a detailed accounting of your business. True, I was from Glasgow and my parents still lived in town, but I hadn't told them I was coming. If questioned by the police I'd have had a hard time explaining why I'd left Oxford in the middle of term.

They would have been very interested indeed to know that my business was actually with S.C.A.R., though their tactics of setting off bombs in cafés, kinetoscopes, and other places where gendarmes or Imperial troops are known to gather—no matter who else might be there—disgusted me. My cousin Angus was one of them, and had been for a long, long time. We were only six months apart in age, and he lived around the corner with his mother—my mother's sister—when we were growing up. We used to play together, especially since the other boys all shunned him since his father had left the family when he was two years old. He always maintained that his father was working secretly to bring down the Empire and would bloody anyone's nose who dared suggest different. By the time we were eleven he was daubing nationalist graffiti on walls, and I hid him in our cellar for three days once when we were fifteen and he set fire to the local gendarme station.

I tracked him down and called in a very big favour, in the shape of a counterfeit passport with a British visa already stamped for one Vivian Purnell. (When I reached that part of the story, Tom and Teresa exchanged an uneasy glance. *History repeats itself.*)

There were still three weeks till the end of term, but we all agreed that Mike and Viv should leave immediately, since the phoney documents were too risky to hold onto for very long. I dared not accompany them to Thermidor, so we took our leave at the railway station in Oxford, and I'm not ashamed to say Mike and I shed just as many tears—more, even—than Viv.

* * * *

"That's the entire story, and more than I should be telling you. You see how very unlikely it is that the Empire is behind Mike's disappearance," I said to Teresa and Tom. "From their point of view, all he did was to smuggle a very unimportant Imperial subject from a backwater city into British territory. Your parents have kept their heads down over the years, Tom, so it's not as though the Intelligence Directorate needs to shut them up. As for your father's involvement with heavier-than-air flight, even if he was the head of the project at DRRAGON, they would not risk kidnapping him just to throw a spanner in the works. After all, we have all seen the Emperor shake hands with the first *dragon mécanique* pilot."

My new young friends drooped, as though Father Christmas had just stolen their last *sou*. They had run an incredible risk to see me—only a young person would be that headstrong—and what had it gained them? Nothing at all, unless I could use my all-too-academic brain to help them work it out.

"So who could have taken him? Did he have any enemies?" I asked.

"With respect, sir, the police and the R.C. have already been all over that ground," Tom said.

"True, my boy, true enough. But don't look so glum. Let's try and think. What were his other interests outside work, apart from the dragon life cycle and evolutionary biology? Could it have something to do with the dragons, after all?"

Teresa leaned forward. "You know, professor, when I went to Assa Teag Island with Tom and Jo, I picked up some pieces of broken dragon eggshell."

I jumped to my feet. "You did *what*? Excuse me, but you must be teasing. I'd sooner believe your dubious tale of being from another world than I would that Ashley would allow you to take her eggs."

"But I have them with me," she said, and reached into her rucksack again.

Along with the miniature babbage? She held out genuine fragments of dragon eggshell. I took them gingerly. The only specimens I had ever seen before were behind glass in the Sorbonne. Teresa's samples were much thinner than I would have expected, but perhaps my memory was playing tricks.

"I have an idea," I told her. "But first, I shall ask one of my colleagues to test these fragments."

"Now?" Tom said, glancing out my window. It was already as dark as midnight out there.

"Jacobsen always works late in his chemistry lab," I said. "Can you both please wait here until I get back? Here are biscuits to go with your tea, and I'll bring back food from the faculty canteen. Poor things, you must be starving."

27

The professor was gone for hours. Eventually we both dozed off on an uncomfortable little sofa, my head in Tom's lap. Then Urquhart burst back into the room, his hair and eyes wild.

"I knew it!" he shouted. "I knew something was wrong with those eggshells!"

"What is it, professor? What are you talking about?" I asked, standing up and smoothing down my shirt.

"The eggshells," he said again. "Which reminds me, I bought you both some eggs mayonnaise and a couple of croissants. They're probably stale, but I was fortunate to find anything in the faculty canteen at this hour."

We ate as we listened to the professor—I couldn't think of him as "Ram" any more than I could call Susie Chen by her first name.

"Mike and I both thought the dragons' failure to spawn might not be due to some complex problem with their reproductive systems—which is fortunate, because if it was, there would be nothing we could do, since there isn't a veterinarian in the world who would try to operate on the cloaca of a fifty-foot fire-breathing flying reptile.

"We think the problem is with the actual eggs, once they are laid and fertilized." He took a deep breath, then held out the shell fragment he'd taken with him. "This," he said, "is only two inches thick, less than half what the ones at the Sorbonne measure. I had Jacobsen run some chemical tests. Mike and I were right. Jacobsen confirmed our theory, though the why of it still escapes me." He paused. "Dichlorodiphenyl-trichloroethane."

Tom blinked at him. "That is easy for you to say, professor. What is it?"

Something clicked in my mind. "DDT," I said simply.

Tom shot me a puzzled look, but Urquhart nodded. "Yes, that's its common name. It was invented at the Sorbonne twenty years ago and was at first hailed as a miracle breakthrough in controlling disease-spreading mosquitoes in the Empire's African territories, but it was banned by Imperial decree last year because—"

"It poisons a lot more than just mosquitoes," I finished his sentence for him. "Among other bad things, it kills off birds because when they eat it, they lay eggs whose shells are so thin they break before they can hatch."

Tom was looking at me as if I'd grown an extra head, or turned into Palermo Teresa. "How do you know that?"

"In my world there was a famous book written about DDT more than fifty years ago, called *Silent Spring*," I explained. "I wrote a book report on it and on the life of its author, Rachel Carson. Thanks to her, it was banned in my world more than twenty years before it was even invented in your world, professor."

"I have never even heard of it," Tom said.

"Which means," Urquhart said slowly, "that someone went to a great deal of trouble to bring the stuff to Assa Teag deliberately, just to poison Ashley so she can't lay viable eggs. But who would do that? And why?"

The pieces finally fit together. I looked at Tom. "There's only one man who could possibly have done it, Tom. The same man who kidnapped your father when he thought he was under suspicion."

He stared at me. "You cannot be serious. Ranger Rogers loves Ashley. He is the one who protects her and keeps people away from her nest on Assa Teag."

"I don't read a lot of mysteries, but in my world we talk about 'motive, means, and opportunity,'" I said. "The ranger's certainly got the means and opportunity to harm Ashley, and to kidnap your father if he found out what he was up to."

"That leaves motive," Tom said firmly, "and he lacks any motive to do such a horrible thing. True, he is not actually a from-here—"

"Neither am I," I pointed out drily.

"—but he is the next best thing. He comes from a little chicken-farming town called Salisbury, just fifty miles from here, and he has been coming to Gingo Teag for the pony roundup since he was a kid. He knows everyone in the village, Dad especially, and he would never do such a thing!"

"It does sound a little unlikely, Teresa," the professor said. "Perhaps someone else has been sneaking onto the island to poison Ashley? From what Mike writes, there isn't actually a fence around the island, is there?"

"No, it's too big for that," I agreed. I sat thinking for a moment, my chin resting on my clenched fist. "Didn't he mention something called the Order of St. George when he was giving us a tour?" I said suddenly.

The professor and Tom both exclaimed at once. "That is quite ridiculous," Tom said. "The Order was merely founded by Sir Benedict to help raise the money for the fleet that drove the dragons out of Manahatta.

True, they did exterminate most of the other dragons, but all that ended more than one hundred fifty years ago."

"What if it didn't?" I insisted. "What if the Order still exists, and Ranger Rogers is a member of it? What if he became a ranger at Assa Teag so he could stop Ashley from having more dragons?"

Tom opened his mouth, but the professor spoke first. "It may not matter," he said. "Now that we know that *someone* is poisoning Ashley with DDT and most probably kidnapped Mike to cover up the crime, it should be much easier for the police or the RC to find both your father and the criminal. At least they won't be looking in the wrong place, and increasing the chances of a global war to boot."

"Besides, Tom, it's better if it does turn out to be Ranger Rogers," I said softly.

"Oh? Why so?"

"You said he's known your father for many years. That makes it more likely that he wouldn't want to hurt your father. He'll just keep him locked up somewhere until his plan succeeds and Ashley can't lay eggs anymore."

Which must have been cold comfort for him, because no one knew exactly how old was too old for dragons to lay eggs, and if Ranger Rogers *wasn't* the one behind the plot, then…

"I think," the professor said suddenly, "that I'd better return to Amer—to Britain with you."

"Why? I shall go straight to the police as soon as we get there," Tom said.

The professor shook his head. "They might not believe you. And I'd like to assist in rescuing one of my oldest friends."

"But what about an exit visa?" I pointed out. "You said the Empire is pretty stingy with those."

"I'm a professor at 'Université Louis-Napoléon,'" Urquhart said drily. "That ought to count for something. And I already have a passport for internal use, that is, within the Empire. It shouldn't be too difficult to get a visa for Britain. I'll just say I'm doing some research on dragons. That will even have the virtue of being true. I shall go first thing in the morning when the Ministry of Security opens."

Tom and I agreed with this plan, since it was much too late to take a train back to Thermidor. The only question was where we would sleep. Palermo Teresa had been right—Urquhart slept in his office most nights.

"I do have a flat in town, but it's in no condition to entertain others," he said. "I'll sleep there and you young people can, er, make yourselves comfortable here. I should be back with my passport well before lunchtime, but if you are hungry there's a student café just 'round the corner. You do have money, don't you?"

Tom and I shrugged. In all the excitement we'd forgotten to exchange our pounds for francs at the aerodrome. Urquhart handed Tom a twenty-franc note.

"Now I know for certain that you're absent-minded Mike's son!" he said. "And Tom, do try not to spit on the bill even if it does have Napoléon I's picture on it. The shopkeepers here frown on that sort of thing."

Tom insisted that I take the sofa, which was only wide enough for one of us, while he slept sitting up in the professor's padded "thinking chair." He may have got the better deal, but anyway we were both so worn out from lack of sleep on the airship—I called it blimp lag, a term that puzzled Tom—that we had no trouble dozing off.

Tom was snoring from the moment his head hit the blotter on Urquhart's desk. I couldn't tell what time it was when we woke up, since Tom had forgotten to wind his watch, but the sun was high enough to reach us through the narrow alley outside the professor's grimy office window.

"Where is he? I thought he would be back by now," Tom said.

I shrugged. "Who knows, but I'm getting hungry. Why don't we go find that café?" I made him turn his back while I wriggled into sort-of clean panties and a skirt, my last clean piece of clothing, and he rummaged in his own bag for clean underpants. For good luck I slipped the Mars landing coin Gloria had given me into my pocket.

"If he does not return in the next couple of hours, we should return to England by ourselves," he said as we went down the stairs.

I frowned. "Can we do that? I mean, we *know* Professor Urquhart is coming back to Philadelphia with us, because…"

Tom rubbed his forehead and groaned. "It is too early in the morning for paradoxes," he said. "I refuse to try to think until I eat."

We found the café with no trouble. It was like a grimy diner back home, only without the chrome-plated charm. Still, I didn't see anybody keeling over from food poisoning, and the portions were big and cheap, so we got ourselves big plates of bangers and mash—sausages and mashed potatoes—though there was a hint of something Mediterranean in it, oregano maybe. Everything was lukewarm, but we gobbled it up and washed it down with tea.

Just as I was passing from hunger straight into stomachache territory, a tall skinny boy wearing taped-together glasses rushed up to us and started jabbering away in *patois*. He kept pointing at a folded, printed piece of paper that looked familiar. I shook my head.

Tom said something to the guy, who looked puzzled, then sheepish.

"I *regrette*," he said to me. "To Teresa, you look so alike. I did not know you are merely her écouter—'ow you say—cousin."

"She's the one who looks like me," I said, patting him on the arm.

He looked even more confused and turned to go. But he left the folded piece of paper on our table, where it rapidly soaked up a puddle of spilled tea. Tom snatched it up. Oh, that was why it looked familiar.

"That's Palermo Teresa's homework," I said, frowning. "It was in that bundle she gave me. What was that guy doing with it? And what did he want from me?"

Tom was silent for a moment, his lips moving as he read. Then his face went pale. "This is no homework assignment, unless she is taking a class in inciting a riot," he said. He began translating aloud. "'Students and faculty of the great Oxford University! The time has come to rise up against your oppressors!'" He belched, somewhat spoiling the effect. "'No longer shall we pay tuition to the tyrant in Paris! No longer shall our research go to benefit the evil Empire! Join us for a rally today, 13 Nivôse, on the lawn in front of the Library!' Er, '13 Nivôse' is the Imperial date...'"

"Never mind that. We're not going anywhere near there." I smacked my fist into my palm. "Damn, but the other me is devious! Homework, my foot! She thought it was too dangerous to take these pamphlets to her friend Geoff herself, so she tricked us into doing it for her!"

"That was not quite cricket of her," Tom agreed. "If not that she looks just like you and has an even sharper tongue, I think I would go find her right now and tell her just what I think of her! Come on though, we had best go back to the professor's office before anyone else mistakes you for her." He stood up.

"Just a minute," I said, staying firmly in my seat. "What do you mean, 'an even sharper tongue?' Are you saying I have a sharp tongue, you stuck-up little fake Englishman?"

Before he could apologize Professor Urquhart rushed into the café, looked around frantically, and darted over to our table.

"Thank God I found you here," he said. "I've got some bad news."

"So have we," I said. "Sit down and tell us."

He shook his head. "Can't, sorry. I must run off again. I've a train to catch in twenty minutes." When I raised my eyebrows, he hastened to explain, "The bastards wouldn't give me a visa, and when I complained to the snotty little clerk, he actually took my passport away and said I would have to undergo a security review before I could have it back."

I sighed. "Sounds just like home. So why are you off to catch a train?"

"I'm, er, going to use the same solution I did last time. You know, what I told you about last night. Don't worry, I checked the train schedule and I can be back by tonight, as long as I can find my cousin."

Tom spoke up. "If you do not come back by tomorrow morning, sir, we shall have to leave regardless." And he told him about the pamphlets the other me had printed up calling for a rebellion in Oxford.

The professor shook his head. "I always knew that girl was trouble. Sorry, Teresa. Look, just go back to my office and sit tight. I'll be back as soon as I can." And he ran out the door. I never saw an old guy like him run so fast.

I got up and Tom and I did a little fast walking of our own. Soon I was way ahead of Tom, and I heard him calling me to slow down. But he wasn't the one being mistaken for a dangerous radical. I was running flat out by the time I reached the doors of the Natural Philosophy building. As I pushed my way in, a strong hand gripped my shoulder. I turned around, annoyed.

"Tom, don't you think you could bother to try to keep up…"

It wasn't Tom, however, but a uniformed gendarme wearing a navy-blue jacket with polished brass buttons, a cap with a little visor, and a gun at his waist. He had an even taller friend dressed the same way.

"Teresa D'Angelo?" said the one with his hand on my shoulder.

I blinked. "Yes—I mean no. No, I'm Teresa Purnell."

The taller gendarme smirked and said something in Italian. I caught the word for "slut." Nana didn't always have the cleanest mouth.

"I'm afraid you have me mistaken for someone else," I said, but by that point they'd already yanked my hands behind my back, painfully twisting my shoulders as they handcuffed me. The cold metal cuffs hurt as they pinched into my wrists, but I was afraid I might fall helplessly on my face. They marched me out of the alley and into a street where a police van waited, unmistakable even though it was battery-powered and had a weird curvy front.

They shoved me into the back seat, where I suddenly developed a terrible itch on my nose. I wriggled around, wrinkling my nose, then rubbed it on the seat back in front of me. They must have thought I was crazy. As the van pulled away I spotted Tom's face in the crowd, and hoped the cops didn't see him. I couldn't handle him being arrested, too.

The cop in the passenger seat turned around and snarled something in French, or maybe it was *patois*. I shrugged.

"Do either of you speak English?" I asked.

For an answer, he leaned over and slapped my face. I was too shocked to start crying. *Cops aren't allowed to do that, are they?* It was probably safer to keep quiet until we arrived at the police station and hopefully found someone who could speak English.

I sat back, my cheek still stinging. At least the itch in my nose had gone away. But something was dripping onto my skirt. Blood. I had a moment of dizziness, then my fear suddenly disappeared.

I looked up and yelled, "You bloodied my nose, you bastard!" The cop who had hit me looked at the one who was driving and sniggered. "You get off on hitting girls who can't hit back, is that it?"

He turned and raised his hand to hit me again, but the driver caught his arm and said something, and he settled back, though not without growling something really nasty about *tua mama*.

"Oh yeah? Well your mother made damn sure to count the money *twice* after your father was finished!"

Lucky for me, he didn't understand. I sat back. Where were they were taking me? I hoped that it was at least in Oxford or somewhere nearby, because if not, how were Tom and the professor ever going to find me?

No sooner had I thought that, than the van came to a stop. The driver got out, opened the door and pulled me out. I stumbled and almost lost my balance, but the one who had hit me came up on my right side and yanked me to my feet.

"Thanks, you're a real gentleman," I said as they hustled me into the police station.

I didn't see anything that looked like a front desk, only a corridor lined with cell doors, each with a barred window set high up near the ceiling. The man who had been driving took out a set of keys and unlocked one, shoved me inside, and locked the door. I fell on my knees and hit my head against the metal frame of a cot.

It took a while for the sparks to stop dancing in front of my eyes, but when they did I yelled, "Hey, what about the handcuffs! Come here and take off these damned handcuffs!" There was no answer.

Maybe I shouldn't have mouthed off to them. I wriggled up onto the cot.

There was nothing else in the room but a rusting, stinking metal bucket. I groaned and turned to face the wall. There was an outside window high up, set with bars like the one that faced the corridor, and at first the fresh air that came in through it was good. But as the day crawled by and the light began to die, it got colder and colder. I began to shiver, and the muscles in my arms cramped up.

When I had to get up to use the bucket, it felt like a million pins and needles were sticking into my arms. I was only able to stand up by pushing myself against the wall. It was a good thing I was wearing a skirt, but even so, it wasn't easy pulling my panties down and then back up while still handcuffed.

I threw myself facedown on the cot, too tired and sore to cry anymore. Besides, if my jailers were looking in, I didn't want to give them the satisfaction of seeing me cry. I tried to remember some prayers, but none came to mind.

I closed my eyes. Tom. He'd be worrying. *Please God, don't let him do anything stupid that would get him into trouble.* Why couldn't Gloria just pop out of the eleventh dimension and rescue me? What would happen to Mom and Dad if I never came back? It would all be my fault. I was turning eighteen in just a few more days, and it looked like I'd be celebrating in a dungeon on another world. Tears tracked down my cheeks. *Stop it.*

The light from outside had almost completely faded when the cell door suddenly swung open. I winced at the bright light from the hall and tried to sit up but ended up falling on my face.

A big gendarme strode in—I wasn't sure if he was one of the ones who had arrested me—and unlocked my handcuffs. I yelped as the blood rushed back into my tortured arms.

"Never allow people like that to take away your dignity," Nana had said to me after Kylie and her gang beat me up on the playground when I was in third grade. "They are the ones who have no dignity, Teresa, for treating you like that."

So I walked, head high, as the gendarme led me down the hall to a plain wooden door. He opened it, pushed me inside and shut it behind me. The room was bare, the walls piss-yellow. There was nothing there but a wooden table, which was bare except for a small cardboard box, and two hard wooden chairs. In one of them sat a man with a hard face, a thin nose that looked like it had been broken long ago, iron-gray hair, and gray eyes. He was not in uniform. Was he from the Intelligence Directorate? But he stood up, smiled slightly and made a stiff bow.

"Monsieur Geraldo Paglioni," he said.

Not knowing what else to do, I curtsied back. "Teresa Purnell," I said.

He gestured at the empty chair, and I sat gratefully. He tilted his head and looked at me for a moment, then made a long speech. In Italian.

I sighed and said, "Listen, Mister Paglioni, like I told the other policemen, you've got the wrong Teresa. I don't speak Italian. Or French, or *patois.*"

He sighed in return and switched to lightly accented English. "Fine then, Miss D'Angelo, I will play your game for the moment. Though why you should wish to put on the worst imitation of a British accent I've ever heard, I cannot imagine."

"I'm not British," I said, "I'm Amer—I mean, I'm from Alaska."

The man snorted and said something fast in Russian, just like Mrs. Purnell had. Damn, I was trapped again. I shook my head helplessly, and he switched back to English.

"I am sorry these local *flics* were so rough with you, Teresa," he said, all friendly-like. "I would have been here sooner to take you out of their hands, but I had business in London that couldn't wait." He picked the box off up the table, opened it and casually handed it to me. "I understand they didn't feed you, either. Here, I picked this up."

My mouth watered at the sight of a croissant with sliced ham and cheese and an apple. Before I gulped it down I said, "You can't hold me, I haven't done anything."

"You haven't done anything, eh? I've been following your career since Palermo, Teresa, and I think you're being far, far too modest."

And he went through my double's rap sheet. I couldn't help but be impressed. The girl could have given the professor's terrorist cousin Angus a run for his money. Starting out in the same way, with anti-Imperial graffiti, Palermo Teresa had quickly moved on to the big time. She had lots of experience writing pamphlets like the one she had Tom deliver for her, starting at age thirteen when she boldly handed one out to recruits waiting in line to join the *carabinieri*, the Italian arm of the Imperial gendarmerie, begging them not to "take up arms against your brothers and sisters." She was almost expelled from school, and she quickly learned to be a lot more careful, but her pamphlets were soon popping up as far north as Naples.

Soon Sicily was as rife with unrest as Scotland and Ireland, and they suspected Palermo Teresa of being involved in firebombing the Imperial naval base at Syracuse. Two ships sank and a dozen sailors drowned or burned to death. As if by coincidence, Sicily quieted down a good bit after Palermo Teresa was accepted as a premedical student at Université Louis-Napoléon, "for which I am sure you have some perfidious *anglais* to thank. Furthermore, this pamphlet," he said, waving around Palermo Teresa's homework, "is in your usual awful style. One might think you would have learned here that 'crush the stone heart of Tyranny with the fire of Revolution' is a mixed metaphor."

"Sounds like you have a problem," I said, "but you know I am not Teresa D'Angelo."

Paglioni smirked. "Then why did you tell Inspecteur Laforge that you were when he arrested you?"

"It's my m-maiden name," I stammered. "My married name is Purnell, like I said. My h-husband is Thomas Purnell, and he's a British subject, and there's going to be hell to pay if you hold me here any longer."

Paglionis started to lose his temper. "Let's cut out the nonsense, shall we? You are Teresa D'Angelo, a well-known terrorist troublemaker in Sicily, and you have brought your trouble here to *l'Angleterre*. Or are you going to deny you wrote this garbage?"

"I'm Teresa Purnell," I insisted.

"Then explain this," he said, and held up the silver coin Gloria had given me. The *flics* must have taken it from my pocket when they arrested me. I grabbed for it but he held it out of reach. "What is this? A model of the coins you plan to mint after your revolution? But why in English? And why on earth would you rename Italia 'the United States of America'? What a ridiculous name for a country!"

He was holding the coin so I could see the Mars lander, the four astronauts, and the motto COURAGE, and suddenly I found some. I folded my arms and shut my mouth.

Paglioni shook his head and rubbed his eyes with the palms of his hands. "Listen, D'Angelo, if you start cooperating I can try to see they go easy on you. No more than five years' hard labor and deportation back to Sicilia. If you don't," he shrugged, "there's always Devil's Island."

"But how can I cooperate when I'm not Teresa D'Angelo," I said, hating myself for whining.

"Oh, I grant you, you did a great job learning English and faking a peculiar accent, though how you have the time between your classes and your, ah, extracurricular activities, I can't imagine. Your disguise is damn good too. You look like a seasonal fruit picker or something. Why, you even put on a lot of weight—"

That was when I jumped him. It took three gendarmes to pull my hands off his throat. He gasped for breath while they put the handcuffs back on me and kicked and punched me so hard I could barely breathe.

Paglioni smacked me in the mouth. I tasted blood. "Murdering slut," he snarled, "now they'll take you to the Tower of London for the treatment you deserve!"

And with that two of the gendarmes dragged me out of the room. I went limp and heavy to make things as hard for them as I could.

What would happen to me in the Tower? Wasn't that where they used to lock up traitors to the Crown in the old days, before they cut off their heads, like Henry VIII's wives? Poor Anne Boleyn. I liked my head right where it was, on my shoulders. *What if they do other things to me first?*

I struggled, and the policeman on my right yanked my arm so hard something popped in the joint. The other one walloped me on the side of the head. Sparks swam before my eyes, and my ears rang. By the time they stopped, the cops had dragged me almost back to the outside door. But suddenly they stopped.

"Did you hear that?" one of them said. (I could understand that much French.)

"What is it?" the other one asked.

A low rumble came from outside. A low, rhythmic rumble that was gradually getting louder, like a lot of people chanting the same thing at the same time. I strained my ears. It sounded like babbling.

Uh-BAH with lump-EAR! Uh-BAH with lump-EAR! Uh-BAH with lump-EAR!

What? No, lump-EAR was *l'Empire*. And they were saying bah with it. *A bas* means "down with" in French. My French teacher had explained the phrase, when she taught us about the fine old Parisian tradition of building barricades, tearing up cobblestones to throw at the police, and generally giving the authorities a hard time. Well, it seemed that here they'd taught the English, or rather the *anglais*, a thing or two about that.

"Down with the Empire," I murmured, raising my head and spitting bloody mucus on the gendarme to my right. Had they knocked my teeth loose? *If I ever get back home, poor Mom's going to have to spend a ton to get my braces fixed!* "That's what they're chanting. Down with the Empire!"

"We'll see about that," he growled. He let go of my arm, drew his gun, and reached for the door handle.

28

I was actually far less nervous about the fact that I was about to do something wildly illegal than I was about seeing Gus again after all these years. I hadn't been back to Glasgow at all since my parents died in a carriage accident ten years ago. I had nothing really to go back *for*. Oona had lived in London since she was eighteen, and I had no close friends back in Scotland. My life was in Oxford.

After Gus made that counterfeit passport for Viv (with an artistically smudged picture based on my description of her), I avoided him, and I did not want to know what else he might be involved in. Even twenty years ago, he was almost a stranger, and he frightened me. The wild boy I'd grown up with was already changing into someone altogether more sinister. His language grew increasing violent. What would he be like now, after more than two decades of underground life?

The train took less than an hour and a half. I caught a cab back to the old neighbourhood and walked up to Gus's parents' old house, my breath catching in my throat. The rooms inside were arranged like those in the house I'd grown up in. The furnishings and paint colours were of course different—and that was a strange parallel world for you, if you like.

But the red-haired young lady who answered the door was definitely not Gus's mother, and the interior of the house had been completely gutted and redone, with more open space and brighter walls. The place appeared much pleasanter, of course, but Gus's parents must be long gone, perhaps long dead like mine. All the woman could tell me was that they had moved out several years back.

"So you wouldn't know how to get in touch with Angus McIntosh then," I said.

She shook her head.

"I'm terribly sorry to have troubled you, then," I said.

"Not at all. What did you say your name was, again?"

"I didn't. I'm Ramsey. Ramsey Urquhart." In this part of town, it wouldn't do to go calling myself professor and saying I taught at Oxford. They'd only think I was putting on airs.

Something flickered in the young lady's brown eyes, but she shook her head regretfully. "Sorry I can't help. Come a long way looking for him, have you?"

"Yes, from the south of *l'Angleterre*. Thank you all the same." And I turned to walk back to the railway station. I was thankful I'd left Glasgow so long ago. I love Scotland, but to live with smoldering resentment all the time... The French have made themselves more hated in Scotland than even the *anglais* were before the Invasion, and that's saying something.

I shall have to tell Tom and Teresa that I have failed and they must go back to Britain without me. I trudged down the deserted wintry street, the early darkness already falling. The old neighbourhood was still paved with cobblestones. A cold, damp wind blew, and I turned my collar up as I passed under a streetlamp.

Someone tapped my shoulder. I whirled around, my heart firing cannonades in my chest. A short, stocky, down-at-heel man about my own age looked at me, his face almost completely hidden behind a bushy mass of grey whiskers and a tall, shapeless hat. I squinted in the dim yellow light.

"Gus?" I whispered.

"Rammy boy. What brings ye so far from the hallowed halls of Oxford, to visit your kin that ye barely ken anymore?"

"Gus, I—how have you been?"

He made a rattling noise like a dancing cloud of dead leaves. "Ah, Rammy boy, ye clearly don't care a whit about that. Ye haven't even tried to find me for all these years, now have you? Much too comfortable in your cushy professor's chair, no doubt."

My face burned. "I've been terribly busy."

"I'll wager," he said drily. "All those papers to mark, all those skirts to chase."

"I'm not much of a skirt-chaser, Gus, you know that."

"Aye," he said, and began to cough.

He raised his fist to cover his mouth, but the cough wouldn't be restrained, and soon he was doubled over with both hands clutched to his stomach. I didn't offer to help—it would only make him angrier. Eventually he straightened and glared at me.

"Ye might at least have visited when Peter was guillotined. I couldn't be there myself, nor would I allow Kate to go—she was only fifteen. But someone from the family should been there for him."

"Guillotined?" I whispered. The last time I'd seen Gus's son, at my parents' funeral, he couldn't have been more than nine years old, a solemn-faced, towheaded little boy.

"Aye. The Imperials murdered him for running messages before the Hotel De Ville bombing."

I closed my eyes. "Oh, Gus, don't tell me he was mixed up in that affair."

One hundred sixteen people had died when Glasgow's swankiest hotel, which also contained the headquarters of the district gendarmerie, had been blown up two years ago. Thirty gendarmes had died, but so had seventy-five hotel guests and eleven passersby. The death toll included forty women and ten children, three of them under age five.

"Aye, why shouldn't he have been mixed up in it, when I planned it?"

Was there a trace of *pride* in his voice? I said nothing.

"Don't ye dare go judging me, Mr. Université-Louis-Napoléon Professor," he spat. "All that blood is on the damned Imperials' heads. We voicegrammed in a warning half an hour before the bomb was to go off…"

"…but they ignored it, and your fuse was faulty and the bomb went off twenty minutes early," I finished.

"Aye, and don't go a-weepin' to me about little Jean-Claude L'Enfant," he growled. The appropriately named youngest victim. Three years old, killed along with his Swiss nanny. "He would only have grown up to be a filthy *flic* anyway. 'Tis only the Scottish victims I mourn for."

"What about the *anglais*?" I said tightly. "There were thirty or forty of *them* dead, too, if I remember rightly. Are they not just as much victims of the Imperials?"

"No. Ye have it soft, south of Hadrian's Wall," he snapped. "But surely, ye didn't come with me to debate the morality of the De Ville operation, did ye now?"

I closed my eyes again. "No," I whispered, and told him what I had come for.

He was silent for a long moment. The wind blew down the empty street, and the dusk deepened. Did he think I was a deserter for fleeing Scotland? No doubt he recalled with perfect clarity what he had said when he'd produced the counterfeit passport for Viv all those years ago: that his debt to me was paid, and paid in full, and I was to ask for no more favours. Still, there was nothing I could do but tell him the truth.

"Mike's in trouble," I said desperately, "the same man whose girl you helped escape to Britain. I need to help him. If he dies, Viv will too. So you'll be helping save her life, too. If you look at it that way, it's not really a new favour I'm asking."

Gus gave out a rattling, terrible laugh. "Ah, Rammy boy, truly you are a droll one. I'm almost tempted to help you out of sheer admiration for your gall." Almost, but not quite. So I played the only card I had left.

"Mike's the top man in the British effort to develop heavier-than-air flight," I said, stretching the truth just a little. "It's thought the Imperials kidnapped him to ensure their little air show at Versailles wasn't upstaged. But he was writing me before he vanished, and he had something much more...spectacular, in mind." Well, dragons *are* a lot more spectacular than the little flying machine the Emperor had hailed last week as "proof of France's eternal superiority."

That did the trick. "Wait here fifteen minutes, then walk to this address," he said, taking out a torn cigarette carton and scribbling on it with a pencil stub. "And for your own sake, Rammy, don't ever show your face again in Glasgow until Scotland is free. Maybe not then, either." He paused and stared at me, his eyes glittering in the dim gas lighting. "Ask yourself, laddie, what ye have done for Scotland," he said softly. "I have damned my own soul to eternal torment for what I have done, and my punishment has already begun. I deserve what I have suffered from Peter's death, though he didn't deserve what he got." He shook a solemn fist at the black sky, and said, "We have given our all for Scotland's freedom, so Scotland shall be free!"

Your parents weren't even churchgoers. I had no words to say as he walked away. There are no suitable words, in any language.

But I waited dutifully, my fingertips growing numb inside my tattered gloves. When a quarter of an hour had passed I set off, ending up in a rundown industrial area that took about twenty minutes to walk to. The place was a boarded-up three-storey building that might once have contained a workshop. I knocked on the door. Had Angus misled me—or led me into a trap? A moment later a miniature shutter set high in the door clicked open, then shut, followed by the opening of the door itself. The same pretty redhead who had answered the door at the McIntoshes' old house stood there. She must be the daughter, Kate, who Gus had mentioned.

"Right, Dad said you'd be here ten minutes ago. Come along now," she said, bundling me inside.

The room we entered first was dark, dusty, and full of broken furniture. The girl picked up a frayed rope which opened a trap door. When I hesitated at the top of the rickety-looking wooden staircase leading down into the basement, she huffed a breath and started down first, gesturing impatiently for me to follow and shut the trap door behind me.

At the bottom was a tidy little room with a fresh coat of white paint on the walls. It was lit by a row of bare electric bulbs in the ceiling, probably battery powered so that the police couldn't track the flow of gas for ordinary gaslights. There was a wooden desk weighed down by a miniature printing press, beside which was a stack of pamphlets apparently ready for distribution. I picked one up idly and replaced it just as quickly. I did not wish to read the blood-curdling threats against the "occupying tyrant" and "collaborating Judases" that made Miss D'Angelo's leaflets look like nursery rhymes.

Kate directed me to stand against a blank wall, aiming a bulky camera at me. "Watch the birdie," she barked in the same tone she might have used to shout, "Open fire!"

Before I'd finished blinking away the afterimage of the flash, she'd already darted into a tiny room that gave off the telltale fumes of developer and fixer. I'd barely sat down when she bustled out, blowing on the completed photograph to dry it, then sat at the work table, unlocked a drawer and casually produced a blank Imperial passport. She pasted the picture in, asked me for my name, address and so forth, and handed me the finished document, stamped with an unlimited tourist visa to British America, less than twenty minutes after I had knocked on the door.

"Thank you," I said over my shoulder as she ushered me up the steps and out through the trap door.

"The only thanks I need," she said drily, "is for you to forget the location of this place, and to carry out your mission against the Empire." She gave me a savage grin. "Which I hope involves lots of dead Frenchmen. Let *their* women and children sit and weep for them for once."

"Yes. Well, goodbye." I vowed never to return to Glasgow again, whether Scotland was free or not.

I hurried to the railway station, just making the last train of the day. Despite the unpleasantness, things had gone much better than I'd had any right to hope for. Which meant only one thing: my luck couldn't hold.

So I wasn't surprised when I stepped off the train and Tom seized me by the collar, his eyes wide and bloodshot, his hair wild and his coat open to the bitter chill. He was so incoherent I made him repeat himself, but as soon as I understood that Teresa had been arrested I bundled him into my carriage and we took off as fast as the old girl would go, a dizzying forty miles an hour down the slick streets.

I turned to cut through the university grounds, the most direct way to the gendarmerie station. Who in the Law Faculty might be willing to represent Teresa? Most were cowards when political crimes were concerned, and it was hard to blame them. *Avocats* who annoyed the Imperial authorities were liable to end up in prison themselves.

As we neared the Library I suddenly applied the brakes. A crowd of students faced the library steps, their faces upturned.

I stopped the carriage and got out. What was happening? Someone shouted over a loudhailer. A young lady?

Tom, taller than me, whispered in my ear. "It is Teresa. The *other* Teresa, I mean. The one who is a student here."

I groaned aloud. Of course, she was haranguing the crowd about the Evil Empire and the corruption of the "Bone-a-farts." The students laughed every time she said it, but I shuddered—the gendarmes would not let that pass. Any minute now they'd descend on the crowd, clubs swinging.

Tom, however, raised his fist. "It is all her fault my Teresa has been arrested. She tricked us into carrying a stack of radical pamphlets to Geoff Watkins. The gendarmes mistook my Teresa for her. So she must help us rescue her."

"And how is she supposed to that? Storm the gendarme station?" I snapped. Tom nodded and began shoving his way through the crowd, oblivious of discontented looks.

"No, Tom! I was only joking!" I said, struggling to keep up with him.

When he reached the library steps a burly fellow scowled, stepped forward, and shoved Tom back. Miss D'Angelo turned, and her eyes widened.

"Teresa! My Teresa has been arrested!" Tom shouted. "The gendarmes took her—"

He didn't finish the sentence. Miss D'Angelo raised the loudhailer and shouted into it, "The filthy pigs are arresting students for exercising our rights! Are we going to take that lying down?"

"No!" the crowd shouted.

"Are we going to just let them lock up *anglais* women and have their way with them?"

"No!" the crowd shouted again.

"They're lying in wait in their den right now, preparing to round us up! Are we going to let them do it without a fight?"

The crowd roared. *Wait a moment. Pigs don't lie around in dens.* But she had done the trick, and the crowd surged from the Library, carrying me and Tom along as they moved across the grounds and onto the river road. I could not have wriggled free even if I had tried.

Miss D'Angelo strode out in front, leading the chant of, "*A bas* with *l'Empire! A bas* with *l'Empire!*" Would there be gunfire as we neared the squat, ugly box of the gendarmerie station?

She's going to get killed. The crowd parted for a moment and a door swung open. *Here it comes.* I ducked my head.

A loud pop was quickly drowned out by the roar of a thousand voices. A scream stopped abruptly. There was a commotion at the front of the crowd, then cheers.

I stared at both Misses D'Angelo hoisted on the shoulders of the crowd, one a battered and bloody version. Ahead came the sounds of fighting, and more gunshots. But they stopped almost as soon as they had started.

Others appeared on the shoulders of the crowd. A notorious local drunk looked none too pleased to have been rescued from his warm and cozy cell. But it was all the same to the happy, cheering crowd, which had begun to sing "Rule Britannia," the most forbidden song. I yelped in surprise at the sound of shattering glass. Intense heat scorched the side of my face. The gendarmerie station was burning.

The Sicilian Miss D'Angelo had climbed down and was pushing her way toward me, a rapturous expression on her face. "Isn't it wonderful, *Dottore* Urquhart? It is the storming of the Bastille all over again! It is *la rivoluzione!*"

"Perhaps it is," I said drily, "but you may remember that it didn't work out well for the French."

"Pah! If I see any would-be Bone-a-fart I will personally kick him in the *coglioni*!"

"Yes, I'm quite sure you will," I said. "Just take care of yourself, please?"

She nodded, beaming, and was swept away by the crowd.

* * * *

It took a while to find Tom and the other Teresa, who was leaning heavily on him. Her face was swollen and she had the beginnings of a black eye, and she was favouring one arm. Tom scowled and hugged Teresa at the same time. He whispered to her and took something from his pocket. He placed tiny, crystalline drops in her mouth and she swallowed. After that, she appeared steadier on her feet. Still, I helped Tom shepherd her back to my office, where she washed and changed clothes. Then we all piled into my carriage and I started down the main road to London.

"Don't you need to pack a bag?" Tom asked from the back seat, where he fussed over Teresa.

I shook my head. "We need to leave Oxford as quickly as possible. The army is probably already on the way. Besides, I have a bag in the boot for when I travel to conferences. How is Teresa doing?"

"She seems to have fallen asleep."

Asleep, or unconscious? She'd managed the stairs to my office, but how could I be sure she hadn't broken anything? I was no doctor, and we didn't dare take her to hospital in case the gendarmes or the military were keeping an eye out for casualties from the growing chaos in Oxford.

"Tom, did Teresa tell you anything about what happened to her in the gendarme station?"

"Not much," he said. "Why?"

"Did she have her British passport with her when she was arrested?"

"What? Oh, no, they must have taken it… No, here it is." He pulled it from her bag.

"Good. Then there's a chance they don't have a record of her real name—or rather, the name she's traveling under, as your wife."

An hour and a half later I parked the carriage at the edge of Thermidor Aerodrome. Teresa woke and confirmed my fears. She had tried to convince her interrogator that her name was Teresa Purnell.

"Well, let's hope he didn't have time to pass that information on before the station was overrun," I said.

"I don't think so," she said. "I hit him pretty hard, then some more cops came and pulled me off him, and then they opened the door and I was rescued."

And the *flics* holding her were probably lynched, along with her interrogator, but I didn't say that. This Teresa seemed gentler than Sicilian Teresa.

I checked my pocketwatch. Two o'clock in the morning. We wouldn't be able to book an airship flight before eight o'clock, so I suggested to Tom and Teresa that they get some sleep while I kept a lookout for *flics* or soldiers. They didn't need to be asked twice, though Tom called out sleepily that I should wake him if I started to get tired myself. In less than a minute they had both fallen asleep, Teresa with her head on Tom's shoulder and Tom leaning against her in turn. They looked like a couple of bedraggled kittens. How could I protect them?

The hours crawled by. I was leaving the Empire illegally and would never be able to return to my post at Oxford. Why wasn't I more concerned? After twenty-five years at Oxford, I should be fonder of the place. I should care more about my colleagues and students. But now, in this moment of truth, I understood that I had been spinning my wheels for years and years. This mad adventure could be just what I needed—I might even obtain an academic position in Britain, if they granted me asylum.

Light grew and I woke the young people. They stretched, and Teresa whimpered as her bruises blossomed. As I had expected, her right eye had swollen so much she could barely open it. But she insisted she was oh-kay, whatever that meant. She shook us off and hobbled toward the main terminal.

Tom smiled as he raced to catch up. "Gloria's tears are really something," he said mysteriously.

There seemed to be more gendarmes and soldiers about than the last time I had been in the aerodrome, when I'd been on my way to Prussia for an academic conference. Had the news of the revolt in Oxford spread? As soon as we queued for tickets the man in front of us complained loudly to his wife.

"Damned *anglais* hooligans!" he said in a Parisian accent as he rattled his copy of *L'Empire*. We'd made the front page of the newspaper's *l'Angleterre* edition, unfortunately. "We ought to give them a whiff of grapeshot, just like the first emperor said!"

"I'm sure we already are, dear," his wife soothed him, glancing around nervously. "Everything will soon be under control, if it isn't already."

"They're so ungrateful, that's what bothers me," her husband said. He carried himself straight and wore the rosette of the Imperial Legions in the lapel of his tan overcoat. "Here we do everything for them, modernising their rainy little island with high-speed railways and the very latest babbages. Not to mention the metric system! If not for us they'd still be using miles and ounces and Reason knows what else."

"Yes dear, I know," his wife said, in the tones of one who has heard it all many times before.

"And what do we get for it! Arson and murder, that's what! We ought to leave them to their miserable climate and their horrible food, that's what I think!"

"Maybe you should—*oof!*" Tom said as Teresa neatly drove her elbow into his middle.

But it was too late. "What was that, you young barbarian?" the Legionnaire barked.

"You must to excuse. My husband, she does not speak so well the French," Teresa said in horribly mangled French.

"Oh, yes I do," Tom said, shaking off her attempt to grab his arm, "and I *said*, it is a *capital* idea for you to return to your own country!"

"Maybe you should return to *yours*, you foreigner!"

The Legionnaire's face grew as red as Tom's. A gendarme strolled our way. In moments we would be headed to the Tower of London and never emerge alive. "I am an Englishman!" Tom roared, his hand clenched. I edged forward, preparing to grab Tom if he threw the first punch.

"Pardon *messieurs*, is there some sort of problem here?" a voice asked mildly.

I spun around. The *flic* stood close. And he was a big fellow, too, tall enough to tower over both the young fool and the old fool. I gazed up at him. Did he have terradraco blood? I glanced at Tom. The colour drained from his face. Was he ill? No, Teresa was twisting his right arm behind his back.

"There is no problem, officer," Tom squeaked.

The Legionnaire also made a conciliatory noise. *His* wife's heel dug into his instep. The *flic* beamed and tipped his kepi.

As he moved away I let my breath out slowly. "Young man, you'd better control your temper," I murmured to Tom.

"Yeah, or I'll pop you one," Teresa said softly, letting go of his arm. "I gotta warn you Tom, and you too, professor, if it looks like they're about to catch us, I'm gonna run. I can't go back to gaol."

Tom and I both nodded. The *flics* might shoot Teresa in the back. Normally even the Imperials wouldn't do that to a woman, but with nationalist riots under way and the dangerous radical who had started them attempting to flee the country, who knew what they might do?

The queue shuffled forward. I rubbed my eyes and yawned, lack of sleep finally catching up with me. The minutes ticked by, and the line shuffled forward again. I pulled out my pocketwatch, gritting my teeth. It was almost half-past nine. At this rate we'd never board a flight today, and I couldn't stand another night in my carriage, waiting on tenterhooks for the gendarmes to arrest us all.

When it was the Legionnaire's turn he of course began an argument with the clerk about some discount he said he was entitled to for his military service. The clerk called in his supervisor while the poor man's wife suggested various compromises. It took them forever to sort it all out.

"I've got a good mind never to come back to this stinking colony," he growled as he stalked off toward the departure lounge, his luggage in tow.

"I am sure he will not be missed," Tom murmured, watching him go.

"Next please!" the clerk snapped.

I stepped forward and smiled. He scowled. He was about my age, a short, pudgy man with a big nose and greying sideburns who shivered in his shabby coat. Yes, it was cold in the aerodrome. Until that moment I'd been too preoccupied to notice.

"I need a ticket to Philadelphia for today, please," I said, pushing our fraudulent passports across the counter.

"Why not ask for three tickets to the moon?" he snapped. "All our airships are overbooked."

Sweat trickled down my back. "Can you please look for something? I'm willing to go on a separate flight from Mr and Mrs Purnell, if need be—they already have return tickets to their home in Philadelphia." As unobtrusively as possible I pushed a 50-franc note across the counter. Napoléon I's Empress Josephine stared disapprovingly up at me.

The clerk sniffed and noisily blew his nose into a ragged handkerchief. "I'll see what I can do," he said, as the money disappeared. "Wait here, please." He walked to his supervisor. They huddled together and once the clerk pointed in our direction.

"I'm giving them ten more seconds," Teresa whispered, "and then I'm getting out of here. I'll walk quickly rather than run."

"Teresa, don't," I began, but she was already counting.

"One, Mississippi. Two, Mississippi. Three, Mississippi…"

Tom swallowed and breathed heavily. Teresa reached nine-Mississippi before the clerk strolled toward us.

"That'll be 1,500 francs, please," he said in a bored voice.

I sighed and emptied most of my savings, which I'd withdrawn from my bank before traveling to Glasgow, onto the counter.

After that, boarding the airship was anticlimactic. A gendarme even shorter and pudgier than the ticket clerk glanced sleepily at our passports, stamped them and waved us through.

Thank you, Kate and whoever had forged Tom and Teresa's passports. I was sleepy, so I headed straight to my cabin.

"Don't you want to watch us take off?" Teresa called.

"No, you young people can enjoy it," I yawned. By the time I woke up, we were already passing over Land's End, the violet Atlantic waters crashing into spume far below us in the fading twilight.

Tom and Teresa were nowhere to be seen, so I sat in the lounge and enjoyed the scenery over a ham and cheese croissant. I saw a great deal of the young couple over the nine days of the ocean crossing. They were so much like Mike and Viv I was filled with joy and regrets.

Enough of this useless nostalgia. *That's no way to be when I'm visiting the New World for the first time. Anyway I should be devoting every scrap of mental energy to rescuing Mike.*

* * * *

Every evening the three of us met in the observation lounge to plan a course of action. It wasn't until our last night aboard, though, that anything useful came of it.

"I still fail to understand how we are to convince Sheriff Watson or this Agent Connery from the R.C. to listen to us," Tom said. He rubbed his temples. There were dark smudges under his eyes.

"Well, they might dismiss you and Teresa as children, but I should think they'll pay attention to an Oxford professor," I said. "My doctorate must be good for something."

"We've been over and over this all week," Teresa said. "We don't know how they'll react, but we'd better have a backup plan in case they do tell us to get lost. But whether they agree to help us or not, the question is, where is Ranger Rogers likely to be holding your father?"

Tom frowned but said nothing. But Teresa's question was an excellent one. "Where does this ranger go when he's not at work?" I asked him.

"Nowhere. I mean, he lives on Assa Teag Island," Tom said.

"Well, it shouldn't be too difficult to work out where he's hidden Mike," I said. "He lives there alone, right?"

"True, but the island is miles and miles long," Tom said, "and there are at least two abandoned villages, one near the lighthouse and one at a place called Green Run. He might be keeping Dad anywhere."

"He might, but wouldn't it make more sense to hold him in or near his own home, where he could keep an eye on him?" Teresa said.

I nodded enthusiastically. What if Rogers had decided to kill Mike rather than go to all the trouble of kidnapping him? After all, how could the ranger know when Assa Teag Ashley would be past her egg-laying years so that it would be safe to let Mike go? I hoped Tom didn't consider that possibility.

"That lighthouse looked abandoned, and he wouldn't invite us into his house," Teresa said.

"True. The lighthouse was decommissioned long before I was born," Tom said, excitement creeping into his voice. "Since Assa Teag has grown so much at its southern end, they built a new lighthouse further south. That old lighthouse would be the perfect place to hide somebody!"

29

"That's the most ridiculous thing I've ever heard!" Sheriff Watson exploded.

I had slipped out of school and hurried to my eavesdropping post in the pantry as soon as Marcia told me that Tom and Teresa had come back to Gingo Teag on the morning ferry, along with a mysterious stranger from the Home Islands.

"*I* think he's a spy who's come to tell the police where the Frenchies are holding your father!" she exclaimed.

"I hope so," I said. "But if he's one of our spies, why would my big brother have to find him and bring him back? That doesn't make any sense."

"You're always ruining a good story, Jodie," Marcia said with a pout. Then she yelped as I grabbed her by the neck.

"Take it back!" I growled. Good thing we were in an isolated corner of the playground. "My name's not Jodie!"

"All right, Jo, all right! I take it back," she gasped, and I let her go. She rubbed her neck and glared at me. "I'd tell on you right now if your dad wasn't being held hostage by the Frenchies!"

"I don't care if you do tell. Just give me enough time to get away."

I sneaked through a hole in the schoolyard fence, ran all the way home, and slipped into the pantry in time to hear the stranger explain why he suspected that Ranger Rogers and not the Frogs had kidnapped Dad. Sheriff Watson got all red in the face and interrupted before he could even say where he thought Dad was being held prisoner.

"I've known Ron since we played rugby together for the Nanticoke Shorebirds," the sheriff said. "He had the right attitude to make it into the big leagues, but he wanted to stay right here in Nanticoke doing what he loves—caring for wildlife on Assa Teag, including Ashley! The idea that he would hurt a scale on her body, much less a hair on Mike's head, makes me so mad I'd like to arrest you right here and now, even if you are a professor and you did just escape from the Empire!"

"Calm down, Paul," Mum said, "no-one is going to arrest anyone."

"Exactly," the sheriff said, "there's no way I'm going to bother Ron on the say-so of some Oxford snail-eater."

Tom, Teresa, and the stranger all began talking at once, until Tom finally shouted, "Do you not care about finding Dad at all?"

"That does it," the sheriff said, standing and hitching his belt. "I've been going easy on you, Thomas Jefferson Purnell, because your father is in trouble and you're under a great deal of stress. But it is my duty to inform you that since you and this young lady have violated the law by traveling to the Home Islands on forged passports—"

Uh-oh. Sometimes grown-ups aren't as stupid as you think. They were probably going to hang my big brother for that, and then Mum would ground him for life! And they hadn't even let me go with them.

Now everyone was shouting, and Mum tugged on his arm as he handcuffed the stranger.

"Get off me, Viv, or I'll run you in, too," he said, swatting her away. "I'm going to call your good friend Agent Connery at the Royal Constabulary and have him interrogate the so-called professor. We'll get to the bottom of this. And you'd better retain Sam Withers since Tom's in a lot of hot water! I really *should* be arresting him too, but this-here foreigner is even more suspicious."

Yes, and sometimes grown-ups *are* as stupid as you expect. Sheriff Watson hustled the stranger, who was the most academic-looking person I'd ever seen, out the door, slamming it behind him. Mum, Tom, and Teresa all stood stock still for a long moment.

Then Mum walked slowly over to the easy chair and sank down in it, holding her head in her hands. "You stole our passports, illegally altered them, and went off to the Home Islands. *Merde,*" she said.

"Mum, I—"

"You may be six inches taller than me, but I ought to give you a beating you would never forget," she said, and sighed. "Only that will not help bring Dad back. It *was* good seeing Ram again, even if he might be deported and guillotined." She turned toward the pantry. "You might as well come out of there, Jo."

I opened the door and slunk out, my eyes on the ground.

"But what about his theory, Mum?" Tom said. "That is the only important thing. Sheriff Watson may not want to investigate his old rugby mate, but do you not think it makes sense?"

"It is the most absurd thing I have ever heard—except that it might be true," she said, burying her head in her hands again. "Ron has always been an odd duck. But that does not make him a kidnapper and a dragon-poisoner. Listen to me! A dragon-poisoner! What in the name of Reason is a dragon-poisoner?"

"So you will not even go see for yourself?" Tom said.

"That is not what I said," Mum said, standing up, her jaw set. "We shall go early tomorrow morning, when Ron will be patrolling further up the beach. We shall take the boat over and anchor right below the lighthouse. If I hear anything from inside, I shall break down the door myself."

I couldn't control myself and started hopping up and down. Of course Mum had to spoil the fun.

"I forbid you even to *think* of trying to sneak over to the island with us, missy! This is serious, dangerous business. Grown-up business!"

"If it's grown-up business, how come you're taking Tommy along?" I asked.

He narrowed his eyes and glared at me.

I stuck out my tongue.

"That is more than enough from you, young lady," Mum snapped.

Teresa said, "Jo, we need you to stay here and throw Sheriff Watson off the scent if he shows up and starts asking questions. It's really important."

That might have worked before, but it wasn't working now. After all, *they'd* gone to the Home Islands, and now they weren't even taking me across the channel to *Assa Teag?* It really wasn't fair.

Even Mum softened. "Fluff, if we don't come back, it is essential that you tell the sheriff. No one can do that except you."

"But what about school? Old nosey parker Mrs Withers will see me at home tomorrow. And I asked you never to call me Fluff, especially in front of strangers!"

"Tomorrow is Saturday," Mum pointed out.

"And I'm not a stranger," Teresa said.

"I didn't mean it like that. Mum! You have to let me go!"

"No, and that is final. Now go up to your room. I have to prepare," she said. "And if you sneak into the pantry again, I shall ground you for two weeks!"

I dragged my feet going up, but as soon as I reached my room and shut the door I could actually hear even better, thanks to an old gas pipe that goes down to the living room.

Mum talked quietly with Tom and Teresa about their plans. They would leave before light and hide the boat behind fallen trees so they'd be able to see when the ranger left home. A click—Mum was unlocking Dad's gun closet.

"I'll load it, Mum. If we are wrong—" Tommy said.

"I trust Ram more than anyone in the world, except your father," she said. "If he says that Ron is guilty, he is probably right. And if that is not so, I am still bound to ensure Ram gets out of gaol and stays in this country. I would not be here if not for him, and neither would you. It will be a frosty day in Hades before I allow that blowhard Paul Watson to mistreat one of my friends!"

It seemed like forever before Mum called me down to supper, which was leftover chicken and potato salad.

I decided on my own plan, and I lay awake all night perfecting it. If they thought they would keep me from helping rescue Dad, they had a surprise coming! After making a show of putting on pyjamas for Mum's benefit, I shut the door and pulled on my warm coat and leggings. Then I opened my toolbox and took out a pair of wire-cutters I'd used for my science fair project last year. They would be strong enough to cut through the cables the watermen used to moor their oyster-dredging boats and the toffs who had money to burn used to anchor their pleasure-boats. Neither type of craft would sail again till spring, and the bayside docks were thick with them.

I hid the cutters under my coat and climbed into bed just before Mum opened the door to see if I was asleep. Satisfied, she closed the door again.

Now I had nothing to do but wait. And wait. And wait. The hours ticked by. I imagined a dozen different ways to rescue Dad, every one of which involved me saving the day. Oh, the things I would do to Ranger Rogers when I caught him! I'd scratch his eyes out! I'd kick him somewhere it really hurt! I'd…

* * * *

I must have dozed off, because I woke up with a start to a grey dawn. I sat up and listened closely, but the house was quiet; Mum, Tommy, and Jo had already left. Just in case I was wrong, I held my boots in my hand so I could tiptoe down the stairs.

I glanced out the window. The *Lady Vivian* was already gone. I put on my boots and eased out the front door, shutting it quietly behind me. Fortunately, nobody was up and about at six-thirty on a midwinter Saturday, and I reached the bayside docks without any trouble.

I carefully looked over the boats. Finally I settled on Mr Withers' speedboat, as payback for all the grief Mrs Withers had given me, hunting me all over town when I needed a break from school. Adults take breaks all the time, don't they?

The wire-cutters worked just fine. I checked the boat's battery level. It was only a quarter charged, which just goes to show that solicitors have no business out on the water. Still, there was more than enough juice to get me to Assa Teag and back ten times over if I wanted.

The main reason I chose the sleek little Royal National was that the motor was very quiet, like a bobcat purring. I powered it away from the dock, the wake spreading out behind me.

It was a cold morning, but the air was still, so I was warm enough in my coat. A heron standing in the water rose and flapped lazily away at my approach, a flash of pale blue against the grey sky.

"Hi, Max!" I whispered softly.

Was Dad's funny old friend actually here, protecting me? When tall dunes appeared to port I was nearing the southwestern tip of Gingo Teag Island. On a map it looks like a fat cigar.

As I turned east and started up the other side of the island, my heart began to pound. To starboard tall loblolly pines grew on the thick waist of Assa Teag Island north of Dragon's Cove. Above them showed the topmost of the lighthouse's fat candy stripes.

I motored into Assa Teag Channel, just about where the Dragonfire Club holds the annual pony swim in the summer. I cut the engine and drifted to a landing on a sandy patch beneath two trees. That should hide the boat from anyone looking from the lighthouse. I hopped out, tied the boat to one of the trees and made my way into the forest, shadowing the trail that led to the lighthouse and thanking God for the thick layer of soft brown pine needles that covered the ground, muffling my footsteps. When the ground began to rise I was getting close. My heartbeat was so loud it sounded like little drummers were sitting in my ears, pounding on my eardrums.

I stumbled into a clearing where a band of five Gingo Teag ponies stood grazing. One whinnied, and their heads turned toward me.

"Hi," I whispered. "Please be good horsies and don't make a noise."

But the biggest one, a chocolate-brown stallion, snorted and took a menacing step in my direction. I backed away and bumped into one of the brown and white piebald mares, which turned and nipped my hand. I bit down on my lip to avoid letting out a yelp. I kept backing out of the clearing. Meanwhile the stallion was leading his mares through the trees and onto the lighthouse trail.

Would that give away the fact that someone was blundering around in the woods? I hoped not, but I pushed my way through the trees to the edge of the trail so I could keep an eye on the ponies and make sure. And I stifled a scream.

It was already full light, so there was no mistaking the figures outlined against the sky. Ranger Rogers was pointing a pistol at Mum, Tom, and Teresa! Dad's shotgun was lying off to the side, and even though she had Teresa's purple scarf wound around it, Mum's right hand was bleeding heavily.

The ranger turned his head at the sound of the approaching horses. He raised the gun and fired. I ducked back into the trees. The ponies naturally panicked and ran down the trail, one of the mares bleeding from her right rear leg.

Mum made a grab for the ranger's gun but he dodged her, holding the pistol directly against her temple. He handed a set of keys to Tom and ordered him and Teresa to go in first. Then he shoved Mum through the door, followed her in and slammed it behind him.

Suddenly my knees gave way and I fell, crying hard. What could I do? Sheriff Watson wouldn't listen to a word against his good buddy Ron. He'd probably arrest me instead for stealing the Withers' stupid boat and throw me in gaol with the professor. How was I supposed to save everybody then?

That's when a voice exploded in my head.

JO? IS THAT YOU?

All was quiet except for the distant rush of the ocean waves and the wind sighing through the tops of the loblolly pines.

I sat up and hugged my knees. Teresa had been right about Ashley's mind-speaking after all, and I could do it too!

Ashley?

TERESA WARNED ME YOU MIGHT HAVE FOLLOWED EVERYBODY OUT HERE. KEEP AWAY, THE RANGER IS ARMED AND DANGEROUS!

I know! He shot that poor mare, and he's poisoning your eggs so they won't hatch, and—

TERESA TOLD ME EVERYTHING. STAND BACK, JO, AND COVER YOUR EYES.

The whole mind-speaking conversation with Ashley had taken less time than it took a black-headed laughing gull to glide by overhead. But I didn't intend to let Ashley order me around and "protect" me as if I was still a baby. If she was going to barbecue Ranger Rogers, I wanted a front-row seat!

Now a new, louder rushing sound drowned out the wind. The treetops bent, and a huge shadow passed over me. I jumped to my feet. Ranger Rogers came out of the lighthouse, locking the door behind him.

He looked up as the shadow fell over him, and his eyes widened. Then he held up Dad's duck-hunting shotgun, aiming it at Ashley.

"In the name of the Order of Saint George, prepare to die, thou foul worm!" he shouted.

I pressed my hands against my ears, but the noise of the explosion still seemed as loud as summer thunder. There was a screech like a cat in pain, but a million times louder. Ashley thrust her huge green head forward, the nozzle of her fire-horn pointing straight at Ranger Rogers.

He threw away the shotgun and ran over a sand dune. Ashley turned her head and flames spouted through the air. There was a high scream of pain. *Drat it, I missed everything!* When the noise stopped, Ashley turned the nozzle of her horn towards the lighthouse door, and again flames shot out in front of her. Her horn melted before my eyes, dropping away in huge chunks. The door burst into a bright blaze and fell open, and I could hear everybody yelling inside.

I ran up the hill.

30

"Are you sure this is the right place?" Tom asked, glancing around.

"I think so," I said.

The pier on the Delaware River was crowded in the bright May sunshine. The dancing water, the silvery airships drifting by overhead, the people laughing as they walked past, talking in an accent that was no longer strange to me, all made me smile. Then I squinted at the entrance to South Street. Was my six-month-old memory of this moment accurate?

"I think we'll be okay here. Professor Urquhart will come from that direction," I said, pointing toward South Street, "and we—our younger selves—will come walking up from the pier. As long as we stay behind this newsstand, they won't be able to see us."

Tom nodded but still frowned as he ran his hands through his sandy blond hair. I reached up and tousled it.

"Stop worrying! Gloria told us this was fine. In fact, she told us we *have* to meet with the professor today."

"I know. But what if we bump into our younger selves by mistake and create a paradox? What if they disappear? What if *we* disappear? What if *all of us* disappear? What if—"

"Shh," I said, taking his face in my hands and kissing him, something I never got tired of doing. In fact, it only gets better as time goes by. "Calm down. Let's buy a paper, it will take your mind off things."

"All right," he said.

I handed the newsagent tuppence—I was quite familiar with their funny money by now. He smiled as he handed me a copy of today's *Philadelphia Bulletin*. Then the newsagent focused on Tom's face and his eyes widened.

"Blimey, ain't you the bloke what—"

"Saved Assa Teag Ashley, yes," he said. "Please do not make a fuss. I am here on official business."

"Oh—oh, yes. Mum's the word," he said, lowering his voice. "Still, I think it's wonderful what you and your father did. This wouldn't have been possible without you."

He tapped his finger on the front page, which announced the hatching of no fewer than six dragonets to Assa Teag Ashley, all sired by Carolina

Joe. It was less dramatic than the headline five months ago, which had announced the arrest of "A REAL NEST OF VIPERS"—Pierre La Wayne, and the other members of the Order of St. George, who had infiltrated the staff of all five Royal Dragon Refuges.

It sucked not getting the recognition the Purnells had, but we had all figured I'd better keep a low profile as an, um, illegal alien. Still, today's news was even more satisfying, and there was a full-color picture in a special supplement inside, which just goes to show how excited everybody was—color printing was expensive in this world. The little dragons were so cute, and unexpectedly pink. Tom's father smiled at the camera as he held one of them. He had become chief ranger at the Assa Teag Royal Dragon Refuge instead of the late Ronald Rogers, but the work at DRRAGON Base continued smoothly enough with his part-time help, and there was talk that "heavier-than-air craft" might be available for civilian use in just a few years. Which would only make them a little over a century late, by the standards of my home world.

"It was hardly just us. We had lots of help from Tom's mother, his sister, and, uh, another person who wishes to remain anonymous," I said, catching Tom's warning look.

The newsagent nodded. I envied him. We'd had four months to prepare for this moment, and still I was terrified. But not as terrified as I'd been when facing something I dreaded even more than an irreversible time paradox that might kill us and destroy the universe.

My mother.

And the fact that Tom had gone with me then and helped me face my fears, gave me the courage to help him face his fears now.

* * * *

It had been bitterly cold with snow flurries drifting out of the dusk when, hand in hand, we walked up to the familiar old rowhouse on Wolf Street that day in mid-January. I was as scared as if I was walking into an actual wolf's lair, but Tom squeezed my hand, and the strength of his grasp gave me the courage to walk up the steps. Mrs. Peruzzo stepped outside with a bag of trash and stared at us.

"Your mom's been looking for you, you know."

Something harsher than the wind stabbed at my guts. "Well, I'm here now," I managed to say.

"Yeah. She had the cops out here and everything."

I tightened my grip on poor Tom's hand until he winced. The windows of our house were dark. "Have you seen my mom today?"

"Let me think. Not since this morning. She's got a longer shift at the Hilton, now that she made manager. But she should be back any minute."

So she doesn't have to work at Dino's Diner anymore. She's wanted that for so long, she worked so hard for it, and I wasn't here to celebrate with her.

"Thanks, Mrs. Peruzzo," I said around the lump in my throat.

"Call me Angie, now." She smiled. "You turned eighteen last week, didn't you? Well, didn't you? I never forget a birthday."

"We missed your birthday?" Tom exclaimed.

"We did have other things on our minds," I said.

"Who's this handsome young man?" Mrs. Peruzzo asked, dropping the trash bag and dusting her hand off on her shirt. She held out her hand.

Tom hesitated, then shook her hand, quickly dropping it—men didn't shake hands with women in his America.

"Tom, Mrs. Peruzzo—Angie Peruzzo. Mrs., uh, Angie, Tom," I said as I fumbled with my keys.

I wanted to get inside as fast as possible, before she started asking awkward questions. My key wouldn't turn. *What if Mom had the locks changed?* But it must have been the cold, the key always sticks in the cold, and a little wiggling got it working.

I walked inside, closely followed by Tom. It was dark, and the familiar furniture looked strange now. I flipped on the light switch and started pacing and chewing on my nails, a nervous habit I thought I'd outgrown the year before. Should I look in my room? What if Mom had thrown out all my things?

"Calm down," Tom said, "I'm sure your mother will be glad to see you."

"You don't know her," I said.

Just then we heard her key in the lock. I turned to Tom and clutched his arm.

"I love you," he whispered.

Mom's head was bowed when she walked in. She was wearing a new coat. *Because she's got a promotion now, right.* But she still talked to herself. Worse than ever, in fact.

"Thought I turned the light off—I *know* I didn't leave it on—must be going crazy—" Then she looked up and froze.

"Hi, Mom," I said, stepping forward.

Gloria could have saved me from this moment. She could have picked me up in her eleven-dimensional arms and nudged me back a couple of weeks. But she only smiled sadly when I pleaded with her to do that.

"I'm sorry, dear. You will have to make your own peace with your mother." So here I was.

Mom just stared. A moment passed, and then another. Nobody moved.

"Th-this is Tom," I said. "Tom, my mother, Celine D'Angelo."

For another long moment, nothing happened. What was Mom thinking? Would she shriek at me? Maybe she was embarrassed to act that way in front of a stranger. She licked her lips. *Can it be that* she's *nervous?*

"I," she said and stopped. "I, I have a missing persons report out on you. The FBI has started a file. I made them do it. I went all the way downtown to their field office." Then she grabbed and squeezed me so hard I could barely breathe.

"I'm sorry!" I gasped.

She broke the embrace and glared at me. "And you. Just. Waltz. In. Here!" *Here it comes.*

But Tom stepped in.

"Ma'am," he said, "Teresa has frequently spoken of you. She told me how you have reared her alone these past two years. She is sad you work so hard and are so tired that you cannot have fun together the way you used to."

Mom went dead white. She sank slowly down into the horrible orange easy chair.

"Who are you," she said hoarsely, "who are you to say..." But her eyes filled with tears.

I was crying, too. "Mom, I'm sorry," I said. "I had to help Tom. He's my friend—no, he's my *boy*friend—and his family was in terrible trouble. I told Heather to let you know. Did she? Nana always used to say nothing is as important as family and the way they help each other out, right?"

Mom opened and closed her mouth, but no sounds came out.

"I'll make up my schoolwork," I said. "I'll go to the police and the FBI myself and explain that it was all a mistake...you don't have to do anything..."

"Ground you," she murmured, "I should ground you... I've barely slept since you've been gone."

"Mom, I'm eighteen now," I said as gently as I could. "I didn't have to come back. I don't have to stay. But I want to."

She looked up, tears streaming down her face. *She's mad at me because there's nothing she can do to me anymore. But I'm still mad about those letters from Dad...*

She wiped away tears with her sleeve and turned to Tom. "You, you'd better be treating my daughter right," she said, waving a finger at him.

"Mom!"

"And you'd better like cooking. Real Italian cooking."

"I do. Of course I do."

"Good. 'Cause Teresa's making us all dinner." She looked at me. "From scratch."

Tom was as pale now, standing under the bright May sun, as Mom had been back then. I squeezed his hand.

"Don't worry," I said, as much to myself as to him, "remember what Gloria said when she sent us here today?"

He shoved his hands in his pockets and scowled. "Yes, but I don't truly understand it. Some ancient Jewish sage, Rabbi Akiba, once said, 'Everything is foreseen, and yet free will is granted.' But that makes no sense!"

"And she said it's a paradox and we don't have to understand it. I don't get it either, but—look, here they come!"

We ducked behind the newsstand and stared at our younger selves walking toward us from the pier. The younger me looked so scruffy! She was talking loud and fast, like I always do when I'm nervous.

"I don't think there is any such thing as real time," Younger Me was saying as she and Younger Tom advanced on us. "This is just as real as the time we left, isn't it? I mean, I *hope* so," she said, linking her arm with his. He smiled. "It's like relativity," she continued. "Miss Chen explained in class last year…"

"God, couldn't I have dressed any better for our first date?" I moaned. "Just look at that horrible patchwork skirt! I actually thought I looked cool! Can you believe it?"

Tom patted my arm. "It's all right," he said, "just look at that food stain on my school blazer."

"Shh! Here comes the professor."

Now that we knew him we could see that he was actually quite upset, though he was pretending to be calm as he asked our younger selves to meet him in his Franklin University office the next morning, "if you don't have school, that is!"

We waited impatiently while he handed them his card and they walked away toward South Street, looking confused. I wished I could run after them and tell them everything was going to be all right. That when Tom's father was kidnapped a few weeks in their future, five months in our past, he would be rescued unharmed and would even end up famous. That they would discover that they had more courage than they thought, and that they could depend on each other, then and always.

But it was more important that we catch up to the professor and find out what "*our friends* are up to." As soon as our younger selves disappeared into the crowd on South Street we ran after the professor.

"One thing has always puzzled me about this moment," Tom said as we hurried along.

"Yes, what's that?" I asked, puffing to keep up with him.

"What did the professor mean that we saved his life? Wasn't it the other way round?"

"Maybe he didn't mean it quite the way you think," I said. "Wasn't he wearing a wedding ring when we first saw him?"

Tom frowned. "Maybe…there he is! And you are right, he is wearing a ring. Professor!"

"Tom? Teresa?" he said, turning around. He took off his glasses and frowned at us. "Why did you change your clothes? And how did you do it so fast?"

I giggled. "Never mind that right now, Ram," I said, taking him by the arm. "Please explain what you mean about *our friends*. Now, not to-morrow morning." I glanced up at the sky, where dark gray clouds were beginning to boil. "And let's go inside. It looks like it's going to rain."

About the Author

Martin Berman-Gorvine is the author (as Martin Gidron) of *The Severed Wing* (Livingston Press, 2002), which received the 2002 Sidewise Award for Alternate History (Long Form) at the International Science Fiction Convention in Toronto in 2003, the novel *36* (Livingston Press, 2012), and *Seven Against Mars* (Wildside Press, 2013). His short story "Palestina," set in an alternate history in which Israel lost its war of independence, was published in *Interzone* magazine's May/June 2006 issue, and his short story "The Tallis" appeared in *Jewish Currents* magazine, May 2002. He is a professional journalist, currently serving as a reporter for Bloomberg BNA's *Human Resources Report*. His website is www.martinbermangorvine.com, and he can be found sharing blog space with the characters from *Seven Against Mars* at http://martianperspective.blogspot.com. He lives in the suburbs of Washington, D.C. with his wife, two orange tabby cats, two other cats of unknown color that are always hiding, and a sort of Muppet dog.

www.ingramcontent.com/pod-product-compliance
Lightning Source LLC
Chambersburg PA
CBHW02075250626
47155CB00003B/1079